KU-764-457

Simply Love

9899900337686

ALSO BY MARY BALOGH
FROM CLIPPER LARGE PRINT

Simply Unforgettable

Simply Love

Mary Balogh

W F HOWES LTD

This large print edition published in 2009 by
W F Howes Ltd
Unit 4, Rearsby Business Park, Gaddesby Lane,
Rearsby, Leicester LE7 4YH

1 3 5 7 9 10 8 6 4 2

First published in the United Kingdom in 2006
by Piatkus Books

Copyright © Mary Balogh, 2006

The right of Mary Balogh to be identified as
the author of this work has been asserted by her
in accordance with the Copyright, Designs and
Patents Act, 1988.

All rights reserved

A CIP catalogue record for this book is available
from the British Library

ISBN 978 1 40744 1 672

Typeset by Palimpsest Book Production Limited,
Grangemouth, Stirlingshire
Printed and bound in Great Britain
by MPG Books Ltd, Bodmin, Cornwall

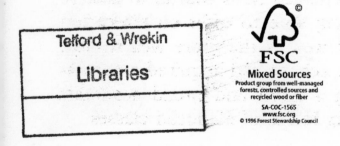

Telford & Wrekin

Libraries

FSC
Mixed Sources
Product group from well-managed
forests, controlled sources and
recycled wood or fiber
SA-COC-1565
www.fsc.org
© 1996 Forest Stewardship Council

CHAPTER 1

The crocodile of schoolgirls neatly uniformed in dark blue that was making its way along Great Pulteney Street in Bath at the spanking pace set by Miss Susanna Osbourne, one of its teachers, was proceeding from Miss Martin's School for Girls on the corner of nearby Daniel and Sutton streets in the direction of the Pulteney Bridge and the city itself on the other side of the river.

The two lines consisted of only twelve girls, the others having gone home just the day before with parents or guardians or servants for the summer holiday. The twelve were Miss Martin's prized charity girls, supported at the school partly by the fees of the others and partly by generous donations from an anonymous benefactor. This benefactor had kept the school afloat when it would have been forced to close its doors several years ago for lack of funds and had enabled Miss Martin to achieve her dream of being able to offer an education to the indigent as well as the more well heeled. Over the years the school had acquired a reputation for providing a good and broad academic education to young ladies of all social classes.

The charity girls had nowhere else to go during the holidays, and so two or more of the resident teachers were forced to remain in order to care for them and entertain them until school resumed.

This summer all three resident teachers had remained – Miss Martin herself, Susanna Osbourne, and Anne Jewell.

Miss Martin and Miss Jewell strode along at the back of the line of girls. Not that it normally took three teachers to accompany one group of twelve on an outing, since the pupils at the school were very well disciplined – at least, they were once they had been there for a week or two. But it was the first day of the summer holiday, and they were on their way to Sally Lunn's tearoom for the famous buns served there and for tea, a much anticipated annual treat that the paying pupils never enjoyed.

Miss Martin and Miss Osbourne were going to Sally Lunn's with the girls. Miss Jewell was not, but since her destination lay along their route, she walked with them. Her son, David, was sandwiched between two of the girls, and chattered away merrily to them though they were both several years older than he.

'Why you would give up a chance to take tea in the cramped confines of Sally Lunn's with twelve noisy, giggly schoolgirls in order to take it in the refined atmosphere of an elegant, spacious drawing room with the rich and titled, I do not know, Anne,' Miss Martin said dryly.

Anne laughed.

'I was specifically invited for today,' she said, 'but you would not put off the visit to Sally Lunn's until tomorrow. It was very unsporting of you, Claudia.'

'Very *practical* of me,' Miss Martin retorted. 'I would have been strung up from the nearest tree by my thumbs if I had suggested any such postponement. So would you and Susanna. But really, Anne, taking tea with Lady Potford is one thing. She has been kind enough to you in the past. But to take tea with *that woman*!'

By *that woman* she meant the Marchioness of Hallmere, the former Lady Freyja Bedwyn, sister of the Duke of Bewcastle. Miss Martin had once been governess to Lady Freyja, who had frightened away a whole string of governesses before her. Miss Martin had left too, but more in outrage than in fright. She had left in the middle of the day, on foot, carrying all her worldly possessions with her, having refused either severance pay or a letter of recommendation or transportation from the Duke of Bewcastle. She had figuratively thumbed her nose at the lot of them.

Anne had been invited to take tea with Lady Potford on Great Pulteney Street because Lady Potford's grandson, Joshua Moore, the Marquess of Hallmere, was in town staying with her – as were his wife and children.

'I have been invited because of Joshua,' Anne said.

'You know how good he has always been to me and David, Claudia.'

He had been her friend at a time when the whole world had turned against her – or so it had seemed. He had even provided her with some financial support for several years when she was close to being destitute, giving rise to the very distressing and quite erroneous rumor that he must be David's father. To say that he had been *good* to her was markedly to understate the case.

Susanna had started the girls singing a song in rounds, and they sang out lustily, heedless of any attention they might draw from passersby. Miss Martin, severe looking and ramrod straight in posture, did not blink an eye.

'And if I had suspected for *one moment*,' she said, 'when you applied for the position of mathematics and geography teacher here four years ago, Anne, that *that woman* had suggested this school to you, I would not have hired you in a million years. She came to the school a few months before that, snooping around with her offensive, supercilious air, noting every worn spot on the carpet in the visitors' parlor, I do not doubt, and asking if I needed anything. The nerve of it! I sent her packing in a hurry, I do not mind telling you.'

Anne half smiled. She had heard the story a dozen times before, and all of Miss Martin's resident teachers knew of her undying antipathy toward the aristocracy, particularly toward those unfortunate enough to bear the title of duke, and

4

most particularly to the one who bore the title Duke of Bewcastle. But Lady Hallmere came in a very close second on her blacklist.

'She has her good points,' Anne said.

Claudia Martin made a sound that resembled a snort.

'The least said on that point the better,' she said. 'But lest you misunderstand, Anne, I am not one whit sorry that I *did* hire you, and so I suppose it was just as well that at the time I did not understand the connection between Lydmere in Cornwall, where you came from, the Marquess of Hallmere, who lived at nearby Penhallow, and Lady Freyja Bedwyn. *Miss Osbourne.*'

Her voice rose above all other sounds as the girls paused in their rounds, and Susanna turned a bright, laughing face and halted the line.

'Lady Potford's, I believe,' Miss Martin said, indicating the house next to which they had stopped. 'I would rather you than me, Anne, but have fun.'

David detached himself from his position in the line to join Anne, Susanna grinned at her, and the crocodile continued on its way toward Sally Lunn's beyond the abbey on the other side of the river.

'Good-bye, David,' a few of the girls called, bolder than they would normally have been when out in public – the holiday spirit prevailed. 'Good-bye, Miss Jewell. Wish you were coming too.'

Claudia Martin rolled her eyes and struck off after her cherished girls.

★   ★   ★

As Miss Martin had just indicated, it was not the first time Anne had called upon Lady Potford at her home on Great Pulteney Street. She had called here – with some trepidation – with a letter of introduction four years ago when she first came to teach at Miss Martin's school and she had been invited to return several times since.

But today was a special occasion, and looking down at nine-year-old David after she had rapped the knocker against the door, Anne could see the light of excited anticipation in his eyes. The Marquess of Hallmere was his favorite person in the world even though they did not often see each other. Joshua had been invariably kind to him, though, when they *had* met – twice when Anne and David had been invited to spend a week of a school holiday at Penhallow, the marquess's country seat in Cornwall, and twice when the marquess had been in Bath and had called at the school to take David out in his curricle. And he never forgot to send gifts for birthdays and Christmas.

Anne smiled down at her son as they waited for the butler to open the door. He was growing up fast, she thought ruefully. He was no longer an infant.

He behaved rather like one, though, when they stepped inside and could see that the marquess was coming down the stairs to meet them, grinning cheerfully. David dashed toward him, all childish eagerness and voluble chatter, and was swept off his feet and spun about in a circle while he laughed joyfully.

Anne, looking on, felt an almost painful constriction about the heart. She had poured out a mother's love on her son for nine years, but of course she had never been able to provide him with a father's love too.

'Lad,' the marquess said, setting David back down on his feet, 'you must have a few bricks in the sole of each shoe. You weigh a ton. Or maybe it is just that you are growing up. Let me see now. You must be . . . twelve?'

'No!' David chuckled gleefully.

'Never tell me you are thirteen?'

'No! I am *nine*!'

'Nine? Only nine? I am speechless with amazement.' The marquess ruffled David's hair with one hand and turned his smile on Anne.

'Joshua,' she said, 'how good it is to see you.'

He was a tall, well-formed man, with blond hair, a handsome, good-natured face, and blue eyes that almost constantly smiled. Anne had always loved him with feelings that had occasionally bordered on the romantic, though she had never allowed them to spill over into passion. As plain Joshua Moore he had also been her friend when she was a governess at his aunt and uncle's house and after she had been dismissed. His friendship had been of infinitely more worth to her than any unrequited passion might have been.

Besides, she had loved another man when she

first became acquainted with Joshua Moore. She had even had an understanding with that man and considered herself betrothed to him.

'Anne.' He took both her hands in his and squeezed them tightly. 'You are in remarkably good looks. The Bath air must suit you.'

'It does,' she assured him. 'How is Lady Hallmere? And how are the children?'

'Freyja is in the drawing room,' he said. 'You will see her in a moment. Daniel and Emily are with their nurse upstairs. You must see them before you leave. Daniel has declared at least two dozen times in the last hour that he simply cannot wait another moment for David to come.' He looked at David with an apologetic grin. 'A three-year-old will not be much of a playmate for you, lad, but if you can find it in your heart to entertain him for a short while, or to allow him to entertain you, you will make him the happiest child alive.'

'I would love to play with him, sir,' David said.

'Good lad.' Joshua ruffled his hair again. 'But come and pay your respects in the drawing room first. It is only very young children who are whisked off straight to the nursery and you certainly do not fall into that category, do you?'

'No, sir,' David said as Joshua offered Anne his arm and winked at her.

Lady Potford received them graciously in the drawing room, and Lady Hallmere got to her feet to nod in acknowledgment of David's bow and to look assessingly at Anne.

8

'You look well, Miss Jewell,' she said.

'Thank you, Lady Hallmere,' Anne said, curtsying to her.

She had always found the marchioness rather intimidating, with her small stature and strange, rather harsh, rather handsome features. She had disliked her on first acquaintance and considered her quite unsuited to the kindhearted, easygoing Joshua. But then she had discovered that her former pupil, Lady Prudence Moore, Joshua's mentally handicapped cousin, adored Lady Freyja, who had been unexpectedly kind to her. Prue had always been a good judge of character. And then Lady Freyja, recognizing that Anne was living only a half-existence as an unwed mother and would-be teacher in the small fishing village of Lydmere, had appeared on her doorstep one morning and offered her a position at Miss Martin's school, of which she was the anonymous benefactor.

If Claudia Martin ever discovered *that* truth, there would be trouble! Anne had, of course, been sworn to secrecy.

She had grown to respect, like, and even admire Lady Hallmere – and her marriage to Joshua appeared to be a love match.

For several minutes David was the focus of attention as he answered questions, seated beside Joshua and gazing almost worshipfully up at his hero. Then, just before the tea tray was brought in, he was sent up to the nursery, where he was promised fairy cakes and lemonade.

'We have just come from Lindsey Hall,' Joshua explained to Anne as the tea was being poured, 'and a grand family celebration for the christening of Bewcastle's son and heir.'

'I trust he is a healthy child,' Anne said politely, 'and that the duchess has recovered her health.'

'Both.' Joshua grinned. 'I do believe the new Marquess of Lindsey is going to be worthy of the Bedwyn name. He has a powerful set of lungs and has no hesitation at all in using them to get whatever he wishes.'

'And now,' Lady Hallmere added, 'we are all on our way to Wales for a month. Bewcastle has an estate there and was planning a brief visit. But the duchess insisted upon accompanying him, and then we all decided to go too since it was far too soon to disperse and go our separate ways.'

'A holiday by the sea is a pleasant prospect,' Joshua said with a grin, 'despite the fact that *we* live within a stone's throw of it in Cornwall. But the Bedwyns are not often all together, and all our children were in such transports of delight at having one another with whom to play and quarrel at Lindsey Hall that it seemed almost cruel to deprive them of one another's company for a month or so longer.'

How lovely it must be, Anne thought wistfully, to belong to a large, close-knit, boisterous family. How lovely for the children.

'School has finished for the year, Miss Jewell?' Lady Potford asked.

'Most of the girls went home yesterday, ma'am,' Anne told her.

'And will you be going home too?' Lady Potford asked.

'No, ma'am,' Anne said. 'I will remain at the school. Miss Martin takes in charity pupils as well as paying ones, and they must be cared for through the holidays.'

Of course, there was no need for Claudia, Susanna, and Anne all to remain. But none of them had anywhere else to go unless their close friend Frances Marshall, Countess of Edgecombe, a former teacher at the school, arrived home from the Continent, where she had gone with the earl on a singing tour, and invited one of them to Barclay Court in Somersetshire, as she often did whenever she was at home during a school holiday.

'You still have not been home, then, Anne?' Joshua asked.

'No,' she said.

Not since the year before David was born – more than ten years ago now. It was a long time. She had been only nineteen then, her sister Sarah, seventeen. Matthew, their brother, now a clergyman, a mere twenty-year-old, had still been up at Oxford. Henry Arnold had just turned twenty at that time too – she had been home for his birthday. They had spoken of his coming-of-age birthday the following year, and she had felt no premonition at all of the fact that she would not be there for that occasion – or ever see him again, in fact.

'We have a request to make of you, Anne,' Joshua said.

'Oh?' Anne looked from him to Lady Hallmere and back again.

'I am increasingly aware,' Joshua said with a sigh, 'that David is my blood relative, Anne, my cousin.'

'No!' Anne stiffened. 'He is my son.'

'And he would have had my title too,' Joshua continued, 'and everything that came along with it, if Albert had married you.'

Anne shot to her feet, slopping some of her tea over into the saucer before setting it down on a table beside her chair.

'David is *my son*,' she said.

'Of course he is,' Lady Hallmere said, sounding haughty and even somewhat bored, though her eyes regarded Anne keenly. 'It occurred to Joshua as we left Lindsey Hall that your son might enjoy a summer in the company of other children, though most of them admittedly are considerably younger than he. There will be Davy, though, Aidan and Eve's adopted son, who is now eleven. It is rather unfortunate that he and your son have the same name, but I daresay everyone will contrive to know them apart – and it might actually be fun for each of them to ignore unwelcome orders and claim afterward that they thought the command was for the other. The duchess's nephew Alexander will also be there, and he is ten.'

'We would really like to take the lad with us, Anne,' Joshua said. 'What do you say?'

Anne bit her lip and sat down again.

'It is always one of my greatest concerns,' she said, 'that he is growing up at a girls' school with women teachers except for the art and dancing masters. He is a general favorite and is made much of by everyone – I could not be more fortunate in that respect. But he has very little contact with men and almost none at all with boys.'

'Yes,' Joshua said, 'I realize that. I still intend to send him to school when he is older, with your permission, of course, but in the meantime he ought to have some contact with other children. Daniel and Emily are much younger than he, but they *are* his second cousins. And therefore all the other Bedwyn children are loosely related to him too. I will not press the issue because I know it distresses you, but it is the truth nevertheless. Will you let him come?'

An unreasonable sense of panic balled in the pit of Anne's stomach. She had never been separated from David for longer than a few hours at a time. He was *hers*. Though he was only nine, she knew she would lose him in the not too distant future. How could she deny him a proper schooling with boys of his own age, after all? But must it start even now? Must she give him up for a whole month or longer now, this summer?

But how could she say no? If the question were put to David, she knew very well that she would see that brightness of excited anticipation in his eyes as he looked to her for permission.

Her hands, she realized as she spread them across her lap, were actually shaking. For the first time in the more than ten years that she had known him, she resented Joshua. She almost hated him, in fact – especially his insistence that David was his blood relative and therefore partly his responsibility.

David was *not* his relative.

He was *her son*.

'Miss Jewell,' the marchioness said, 'a child of nine is too young to be separated from his mother for a whole month. And though I can speak at present only as the mother of a three- and one-year-old, I am even more convinced that no mother is ready to be separated from her child when he is only nine. Of course you must come to Wales too.'

'You are quite right, Freyja,' Lady Potford said. 'Is your presence at the school for the summer quite essential, Miss Jewell?'

'No, ma'am,' Anne said. 'Miss Martin and Miss Osbourne will both be remaining there too.'

'Then it is settled,' Joshua said cheerfully. 'You and David will both come, Anne, and Daniel will be so excited that we may well have to tie him down. *Will* you come?'

'But how can I?' she asked, aghast. Inviting her,

14

she was well aware, had been an afterthought. 'It is the Duke of Bewcastle's home.'

'Oh, pooh,' Lady Hallmere said with a dismissive gesture of one hand. 'It is a Bedwyn home, and I am a Bedwyn. It is also a very large home. You must certainly come.'

The Duke of Bewcastle, Anne reflected, was reputed to be one of the coldest and most toplofty aristocrats in the country. All the Bedwyns had a reputation for being impossibly high in the instep. She was the daughter of a gentleman of very little social significance beyond the neighborhood in which he lived. She was also a teacher, an ex-governess. All of which paled beside the fact that she was also *the unmarried mother of an illegitimate son.*

How could she possibly . . .

'We will not take no for an answer,' Lady Hallmere said imperiously, looking along the length of her rather prominent nose at Anne. 'And so you might as well resign yourself to returning to your school after tea to begin packing your bags.'

The house in Wales was a large one, the marchioness had said. There were many Bedwyns, and they were all now married with children. It would surely be easy enough, then, to remain aloof from them. She could spend most of her time making herself useful with the children. And in the meantime, David would have the freedom of a country house and estate close to the sea, and – more important – he would have other children to play with, some of them boys of his own age. He would have Joshua, whom he adored, as an adult male role model.

She could not possibly deny him all that. But equally, she could not possibly let him go alone.

'Very well,' she said. 'We will come. Thank you.'

'Splendid!' Joshua said, beaming at her and rubbing his hands together.

As Anne walked back to the school a short while later, though, she was not at all sure she agreed. But it was too late to change her mind now. Joshua had already told David and Daniel while Anne was acquainting herself with his young daughter in the nursery, and her son was now skipping along at her side like a much younger child and prattling in a loud, excited voice that drew more than one glance from passersby.

'And we are to go boating and swimming and rock climbing,' he was saying. 'And we will build sand forts and play cricket and climb trees and play pirates. Davy is going to be there – do you remember him, Mama, from years ago, before we came to Bath? And there is to be a boy called Alexander. And some girls – I remember Becky. Do you? And the little ones will need someone to play with them, and I will enjoy doing that. I like Daniel – he follows me around as if I were a great hero. Is he really my cousin?'

'No,' Anne said quickly. 'But to him you *are* a

hero, David. You are a big boy. You are all of nine years old.'

'It is all going to be *such* fun,' he said as they turned the corner from Sutton Street onto Daniel Street and knocked at the school doors. 'Let *me* tell, Mama.'

And he proceeded to do just that to the elderly porter, who exclaimed in amazement in all the right places.

'Yes,' Anne said, meeting his eyes over her son's head. 'We are going to Wales for the summer, Mr Keeble.'

David was already on his way upstairs to tell Matron the glad tidings.

'You are doing *what*?' Claudia Martin asked an hour later after the crocodile had returned to the school and resolved itself into a group of chattering girls, who all declared as they passed Anne on the stairs that she had missed a treat and that the Sally Lunn buns were so huge that they were sure they would not be able to eat another *thing* until morning.

Claudia's question was rhetorical, of course, since she was not by any means deaf and the only other occupant of her private sitting room was Susanna, who was sprawled in a chair beside the fireplace recovering from the long walk in the summer heat. She was fanning her face with the straw bonnet she had just removed from her head.

Claudia, in contrast with the younger teacher,

looked as cool as if she had spent the whole afternoon in this very room. She looked neat too, her brown hair drawn into a severe knot at the back of her neck.

'I am going to Wales for a month, if I can be spared, Claudia,' Anne repeated. 'It is said to be a beautiful country. And it will be good for David to enjoy the sea air and meet children both older and younger than he, and boys as well as girls.'

'And those children are *Bedwyns*?' Claudia spoke the name as though she referred to some particularly odious vermin. 'And your host is to be the *Duke of Bewcastle*?'

'I will probably not even set eyes upon him,' Anne said. 'And I will have little or nothing to do with the Bedwyns. Apparently there are a number of children. I will spend my time in the nursery and the schoolroom amusing them.'

'Doubtless,' Claudia said tartly, 'they will have nurses and governesses and tutors enough to fill a mansion.'

'Then one more will make no difference,' Anne said. 'I could hardly say no, Claudia. Joshua has always been very good to us, and David loves him.'

'I pity the man from my heart,' Miss Martin said, resuming her seat on the other side of the hearth from Susanna. 'It must be a severe trail to him to be married to *that woman*.'

'And to have the Duke of Bewcastle for a brother-in-law,' Susanna said, smiling at Anne, her

18

eyes dancing with merriment. She even winked when Claudia was not looking. 'It is a great shame that he is married. I would have come with you and wooed him. It is still my primary goal in life to marry a duke.'

Claudia snorted – and then chuckled.

'Between the two of you,' she said, 'you will have me plucking gray hairs from my head every night until I am bald before the age of forty.'

'I do envy you, Anne,' Susanna said, setting down her bonnet and sitting up straighter in her chair. 'The idea of a month by the sea in Wales is very appealing, is it not? If you do not want to take David yourself, *I* will take him. He and I get along famously.'

Her eyes were still twinkling, but Anne could see some wistfulness in their depths. Susanna was twenty-two years old and exquisitely lovely, with her small stature and auburn hair and green eyes. She had come to the school at the age of twelve as a charity girl, after failing to find employment in London as a lady's maid by pretending to be older. Six years later she had stayed at the school after Miss Martin offered her a position on her staff, and she had accomplished the transition from pupil to teacher remarkably well. Anne did not know much about her life before the age of twelve, but she did know that Susanna was all alone in the world. She had never had any beaux even though she turned male heads whenever she stepped out on the street. Sunny-natured though she was, there was always an air of melancholy about her that only a close friend would sense.

'Are you quite, quite sure, Anne,' Claudia asked, 'that you would not rather stay here for the summer? But no, of course you would not. And you are quite right. David *does* need the companionship of other children, especially boys, and this is a very good opportunity for him. Go then with my blessing – not that you need it – and try to steer as clear of adult Bedwyns as you would the plague.'

'I solemnly swear,' Anne said, raising her right hand. 'Though it is just as likely to be the other way around.'

CHAPTER 2

It was not that he felt intimidated, but Sydnam Butler was nevertheless moving out of Glandwr House into the thatched, whitewashed cottage that lay in a small clearing among the trees not far from the sea cliffs on one side and the park gates and driveway on the other.

As steward of the estate for the past five years, Sydnam had lived in his own spacious apartments in the main house, and he had always continued to live there even when the owner, the Duke of Bewcastle, was in residence. Bewcastle had always come alone and had never stayed for longer than a few weeks at a time. He had always kept much to himself while he was there, though he had visited and entertained neighbors as courtesy dictated. He had spent part of his days with his steward, since catching up with estate business had been the main reason for such visits, and he had usually invited Sydnam to dine when there was no other company.

Those visits had been totally unthreatening, though Bewcastle could be a strict taskmaster. Since Sydnam was a conscientious steward and took as

21

much pride in running Bewcastle's Welsh estate as he would have done were it his own, there had never been any cause for unpleasantness.

But this coming visit was going to be altogether different from what he was accustomed to. This time Bewcastle was bringing his wife with him. Sydnam had never met the Duchess of Bewcastle. He had heard from his brother Kit, Viscount Ravensberg, who lived on the estate adjoining Lindsey Hall, that she was a jolly good sort, who had been known to coax laughter even from such a perennial iceberg as Bewcastle. And he had heard from his sister-in-law Lauren, the viscountess, that the duchess loved everyone and everyone returned the compliment, including – to the incredulity of all who had witnessed the phenomenon – Bewcastle himself. Lauren had added that the duke was, in fact, in a fair way to doting on her.

Sydnam was somewhat shy with strangers, especially when they were to be sharing a roof with him. And no sooner had he grown accustomed to the idea that the duchess was accompanying Bewcastle on this particular visit than he received another brief letter from his grace's secretary to the effect that all the other Bedwyns were coming too, with their spouses and children, to spend a month or so by the sea.

Sydnam had grown up with the Bedwyns. They had all been playmates together, despite a broad range in their ages – the boisterous Bedwyn boys, the fierce Freyja, who had always refused to be treated as a girl, and young Morgan, who though the youngest of them all and female to boot had usually found a way to be included in the frolics; and the Butlers, Kit and Sydnam and their late eldest brother, Jerome. All except Wulfric, now Bewcastle, in fact.

Sydnam was not intimidated by the prospect of their coming to Glandwr, then. He was only a little overwhelmed by it. They were all married now. He had met some of their spouses – Lady Aidan, Lady Rannulf, the Marquess of Hallmere – and he had found them all amiable enough. And they all had children now. Perhaps if there *were* some small feeling of intimidation, that was its cause. They were very young children who would very possibly look at him with fear and not understand.

And even apart from all else there was the fact that the house, large as it was, would be unceasingly busy with so many people coming and going and making noise.

Sydnam was not a recluse. As Bewcastle's steward he had to see all sorts of people on business. There were also neighbors who liked to consult him on farming issues and other matters to do with the land and the community in which they all lived together. And he had a few personal friends – the Welsh minister and the schoolmaster in particular. His acquaintances were almost exclusively male, though. There had been one or

23

two women during the past five years who had indicated a willingness to pursue a relationship with him – it was no secret, he supposed, that he was a son of the Earl of Redfield and independently wealthy even though he worked for a living. But he had given them no encouragement. He had always been very well aware that it was his social status and his wealth that had encouraged them to overlook a physical revulsion that none of them had been quite able to hide.

He had been content to live a quiet, semireclusive life since coming here. He liked this part of southwest Wales, which was in many ways anglicized but in which one nevertheless heard lilting accents in the English language and often the Welsh language itself being spoken, and where one sensed a love of sea and mountain and heard a love of music and was aware of a deep spirituality that denoted a culture both ancient and richly developed.

He wanted to live out the rest of his life here. There was a house and property – Tŷ Gwyn, White House in English, though in fact it was a manor built of gray stone – that were separate from Glandwr though they adjoined it and were owned by Bewcastle, having been purchased by a former duke. Tŷ Gwyn was unentailed. It was Sydnam's dream and his hope that he could persuade Bewcastle to sell it to him. He would then own his own home and land, though he would be able to continue as Glandwr's steward if Bewcastle so wished.

Having to face the bustle of a large gathering at

Glandwr was just too much for him when he was accustomed to the vast, empty, quiet house. And so he was moving out and into the cottage, at least until the house was empty again.

He resented the expected intrusion, if the truth were known, even though he knew that he had no right to object to a man's coming to his own home with his own wife and his brothers and sisters – and anyone else he chose to invite for that matter.

He did not look forward to the summer.

He would stay out of the way as much as he was able. He would try at least to remain out of sight of the children. He did not want to frighten them. The worst feeling in the world was to see fear, revulsion, horror, and panic on the faces of children and to know that it was his own appearance that had caused it.

One month, Bewcastle's secretary had written. Thirty-one days, if that statement was to be taken literally. It seemed like an eternity.

But he would survive it.

He had survived a great deal worse. There had been days – and nights – when he had wished he had not done so. Survived, that was.

But he had.

And in more recent years he had been glad that he had.

Anne had insisted upon traveling the long distance to the Duke of Bewcastle's estate in Wales in the marquess's second carriage with the children and their nurse, despite the fact that at each stop she was urged to join Joshua and Lady Hallmere in theirs. She preferred to think of herself as a servant rather than a guest – and, good heavens, the duke and duchess did not even know she was coming!

It was a thought that sometimes brought her close to panic. They would quite possibly have strong objections even if she did hide in the nursery for the whole month.

She busied herself with amusing the children, since the nurse, though willing, suffered from motion sickness. Anne had David help Daniel count cows, or sometimes sheep, beyond the windows while she took young Emily on her knee and played clapping and singing games with her. Emily had a low, merry chuckle that she loved to hear.

The rolling hills of South Wales and the lush green countryside with its patchwork arrangement of fields framed by hedgerows and the waters of the Bristol Channel occasionally visible to her left reminded her that she was already far from home, and several times she wished that she had not come after all but had let David come alone with Joshua.

But it was too late by then to change her mind.

They arrived late in the afternoon of the third day, turning off the coast road with its scenery that reminded Anne of Cornwall to pass between two large open gates and proceed along a driveway that wound between shrubs and trees and eventually rolling lawns to either side. There was a fleeting glimpse of a pretty thatched cottage among the trees just inside the gate, and Anne thought wistfully that she could be quite happy to hide out there for the month, well away from the main house.

'Oh, look, Mama.' David, who had been seated quietly beside her while both Daniel and Emily slept on the seat opposite, Emily in the nurse's arms, suddenly plucked at her sleeve and pointed ahead. The side of his face was pressed against the glass.

Anne tipped her head sideways and looked. The house had come into view, and the sight of it did nothing to settle the butterflies that were dancing in her stomach. Glandwr was indeed a vast mansion of gray brick in the Palladian style. It was both impressive and beautiful. And yet, she thought, this was not even the duke's principal seat. He spent only a week or two of each year here, Joshua had said.

How could anyone be *that* wealthy?

'I can hardly *wait*,' David said, his eyes huge, his cheeks flushed. 'Will the other children be here already?'

He felt none of Anne's misgivings, of course. He felt only excitement over the prospect of having other children – other boys – to play with for a whole month.

Fortunately their actual arrival occurred in a flurry of cheerful confusion as the three carriages drew up on the graveled terrace before the main doors and disgorged their passengers and luggage while at the same time a vast number of people spilled out of the house to greet them. Among them Anne recognized the tall, dark figure of Lord Aidan Bedwyn with his military bearing and the dark, lovely Lady Morgan Bedwyn, whose married name she could not recall. She had met them in Cornwall four years ago.

David was swept forward by a newly awakened, bright-cheeked Daniel to be caught up in all the noise and bustle of the greetings – one would have thought that none of them had seen one another for a decade instead of a week or so. Anne abandoned him and hurried inside through a side entrance with the nurse.

She had no wish whatsoever to be mistaken for a guest.

She was not to remain unnoticed, though, she soon discovered. The housekeeper came looking for her after she had been in the nursery for a while, seeing David settled in the large room he was to share with Davy and Alexander and watching him glow with excitement as he met all the children and was absorbed into their midst as if he had been one of them all his life.

He was in safe hands, Anne realized as she followed the housekeeper down to the floor below and into a sizable bedchamber with comfortable furnishings and pretty floral curtains and bed hangings and a view of the sea in the distance.

It was unmistakably a guest chamber rather than a servant's room, she saw with some dismay. She ought to have clarified her exact status here with Joshua and Lady Hallmere before their arrival. She ought to have made it clear to them that she wanted to be classed with the servants, or at least with the nurses and governesses – if there were any of the latter. But then she had assumed that it did not need to be said.

'I hope I have not put you to a great deal of trouble,' she said with an apologetic smile, 'arriving unexpectedly like this.'

'I was delighted, mum, when Mr Butler said the duke and duchess were coming with a large party,' the housekeeper told her with a pronounced Welsh accent. 'We don't see company often enough here. Mr Butler hired extra help and I had every room in the house prepared just in case. So it's no trouble at all. I'm Mrs Parry, mum.'

'Thank you, Mrs Parry,' Anne said. 'What a lovely view.'

'It is that,' the housekeeper agreed, 'though the view from the back rooms is just as grand. You will want to tidy up and maybe rest a while, mum. I'll send a maid up to unpack your things for you.'

'There really is no need,' Anne assured her hastily. Heavens, she was not *really* a guest. She was certainly not entitled to the services of a maid. 'But the idea of a rest sounds very inviting.'

'The roads hereabouts aren't all they ought to be, are they?' Mrs Parry said. 'Though there are enough toll gates to pay for repairs, the good Lord knows. You are probably all bounced to pieces. I'll leave you alone, then, mum. But if you should want to go down to the drawing room later, just pull on the bell rope here and someone will come to show you the way. I'll have a maid come up before dinner to help you dress and tell you the way to the dining room. Will there be anything else?'

'Nothing.' Anne smiled at her again. 'Thank you.'

Go down to the drawing room? Take dinner in the dining room?

What had Joshua *said* about her? He could not possibly be expecting her to mingle with the Bedwyn family – and to make her curtsy to the Duke and Duchess of Bewcastle. *Could he?* But one never knew with Joshua. He had some peculiar notions about her – and about David.

She unpacked her modest trunk and put everything away – she even found that there was a dressing room attached to her bedchamber. She lay down on the bed when she was finished, more because she did not know what else to do than because she was weary.

She would cheerfully cower right here in this room for the next month given half a chance, she thought. But – sadly – it was too late to wish yet again that she had remained in Bath.

She fell asleep while she was in the middle of worrying.

When she awoke an indeterminate amount of time later, she jumped hastily off the bed and washed her hands and face. If the promised maid should arrive, she would perhaps not be able to avoid going down to dinner. She could not *possibly* do that. She was ravenously hungry, she realized, not having eaten since luncheon at a wayside inn, but being hungry and alone seemed preferable to having to dine with the duke and his family.

Good heavens, did Joshua really expect that she would be *welcomed* into their midst? As a social equal?

She slipped on her outdoor shoes and wrapped a cloak about herself in case the sea air was chilly. She could not avoid mealtimes for a whole month, of course, but perhaps by tomorrow she would feel sufficiently rested and in command of herself to suggest to the housekeeper that other arrangements be made for her accommodation and meals.

She slipped out down the back stairs and through the side door by which she had entered the house earlier. She hurried down the driveway, not sure where she was going exactly, but not really caring as long as it was far enough away to be out of sight of the house. Just past the thatched cottage, before she had to make the decision whether to leave the park entirely or turn back, she noticed a well-worn path to her right that must lead to the sea, which she had been able to see from the window of her bedchamber.

She turned and walked along it and soon found

that she was indeed on top of high cliffs with the sea below and coarse grass to either side of the path and some gorse bushes and other wildflowers.

She was reminded again of Cornwall. Below the cliffs there was a wide, golden beach.

She left the path and first stood and then sat in a sheltered hollow from which she could gaze down at the sea, which was calm and almost translucent in the light of early evening though there were ripples of waves close to the shore, a few of them breaking into foam before meeting the beach. The beach itself stretched in a wide golden arc. Just to her left the land curved outward toward the sea and then fell away into huge, jagged rocks to form an abrupt end to the beach. To the right the sands stretched for a few miles before being cut off by a craggy, grass-topped tongue of land that thrust out into the sea like a humpbacked dragon with lifted head roaring defiance to the deep.

She still missed Cornwall, Anne realized. She had loved it even though there had been much pain to endure during her time there.

There was something about the sea that had always called to her spirit. Somehow it reminded her of her littleness in the grand scheme of things, and yet strangely that was a soothing rather than a belittling thought. It made her feel a part of something vast, her own little worries and concerns of no great moment after all. When she was close to the sea, she could believe that all was well – and somehow always would be.

She could have lived contentedly in Cornwall for the rest of her life if only . . .

Well, if only.

She would not have lived there all her life anyway. She had been going to marry Henry Arnold, and he lived in Gloucestershire, where she had grown up.

She sat where she was for a long time until she realized that the evening was now well advanced. She was suddenly glad of her cloak. The day had been warm, but dusk was approaching, and the breeze blowing off the sea was fresh and slightly moist. It smelled and tasted salty.

She got to her feet, scrambled back up to the cliff path, and strolled onward, her face lifted to the breeze, alternating her gaze between the beauty of the gradually darkening sky above and the corresponding loveliness of the sea below, which seemed to be absorbing the light from the sky so that it turned silver even as the gray overhead deepened – one of the universe's little mysteries.

If she were a painter, she thought, pausing again in order to look about with half-closed eyes, she would capture with her brush just this effect of light before dark. But she had never been much of an artist. Somewhere between her brain and the end of her arm, she had always said, her artistic vision died. Besides, a canvas would not be able to capture the salt smell of the air or the light touch of the breeze or the sharp cry of the seagulls that clung to the cliff face and occasionally wheeled overhead.

It was as she walked onward that she became aware that she was not the only person out taking the evening air. There was a man standing out on a slight promontory ahead of her. He was gazing out to sea, unaware of her presence.

Anne stood quite still, undecided whether to turn back in the hope that he would not see her at all or to hurry past him with a brief greeting and a hope not to be detained.

She did not believe she had seen him before. He was not either Lord Aidan Bedwyn or Lord Alleyne. But he was probably one of the other Bedwyns or their spouses. This was, after all, the duke's land, though it was possible he allowed strangers to wander here beyond the cultivated bounds of the park.

It was still only dusk. There was light by which to see the man. And as she looked Anne found it difficult either to retreat or to advance. She stood and stared instead.

He was not dressed for evening. He wore breeches and top boots, a tight-fitting coat and waistcoat, and a white shirt and cravat. He was hatless. He was a tall man, with broad shoulders and slender waist and hips and powerfully muscled legs. His dark, short hair was ruffled by the breeze.

But it was his face, seen in profile, that held Anne transfixed. With its finely chiseled features it was an extraordinarily handsome face. The word *beautiful* came to mind, inappropriate as it seemed to describe a man. He might have been a poet – or a god.

He might well be, she thought, the most beautiful man she had ever set eyes upon.

She felt a craving to see him full face, but he was obviously still quite unaware of her presence. He looked as if he were in a world of his own, one that held him quite motionless, the gathering gray of the evening sky sharpening his silhouette as she gazed at him.

Something stirred inside her, something that had lain dormant in her for years and years – and something that must *remain* dormant. Good heavens, he was a total stranger, and if her guess was correct he was someone's husband. He was certainly not someone about whom to weave romantic fantasies.

She could not simply retreat, she decided. He would probably see her and think her behavior peculiar, even discourteous. She could only continue on her way and hope that a cheerful *good evening* would take her past him without the necessity of introductions or the embarrassment of having to walk back to the house with him, making labored conversation.

Was he perhaps Lady Morgan's husband? Or Lord Rannulf Bedwyn? Or the Duke of Bewcastle himself? Oh, please, she thought, *please* do not be the duke. And yet he was said to be a handsome man.

She wished then that she had decided to go back. But it was too late to do that. As she approached closer to the man, keeping to the footpath that would pass behind the promontory on which he stood, he became aware of her and turned rather sharply toward her.

She stopped short, not more than twenty feet from him.

And she stood transfixed again – but with horror this time. The empty right sleeve of his coat was pinned against his side. But it was the right side of his face that caused the horror. Perhaps it was a trick of the evening light, but it seemed to her that there was nothing there, though afterward she did recall seeing a black eye patch.

He was a man with half a face, the extraordinarily beautiful left side all the more grotesque because there was no right side to balance it. He was beauty and beast all rolled into one. And all of a sudden his height and those powerful thighs and broad shoulders seemed menacing rather than enticing. And equally suddenly the beauty of the gathering darkness and the peaceful solitude of the scene were filled with danger and the threat of an unknown evil.

She thought he took one step toward her. She did not wait to see if he would take another. She turned and ran, leaving the path and the cliff top behind her, half stumbling over the uneven ground, tugging at her cloak as it snagged against gorse bushes, and feeling the sharp sting of their scratches on her legs. Her stockings would be torn to ribbons, a part of her mind told her.

The trees surrounding the inner park were dark and threatening as she crashed through them, making all sorts of loud noises to reveal where she was. The lawn when she reached it looked dauntingly wide and very open, but she had no alternative but to dash across it and hope that at least she would be within screaming distance of the house before he caught up with her.

But her first panic was receding, and when she glanced quickly and fearfully over her shoulder, she could see that she was alone, that he had not followed her. And with that realization came a return of some rationality.

And deep shame.

Was she a child to believe in monsters?

He was merely a man who must have suffered some fearful accident. He had been out to take the air, as she had. He had been minding his own business, enjoying his own solitude, gazing quietly at the view, perhaps as affected by its loveliness as she had been. He had not said or done anything that was remotely threatening except to take that one step toward her. Probably all he had intended was to bid her a good evening and go on his way.

She felt quite mortified then.

She had run from him because he was maimed. She had judged him a monster purely on the strength of his outward appearance. And yet she had a reputation for tenderness toward the weak and handicapped. When she became a governess, she had deliberately taken a position with a child who was not normal according to the definition of normality that society had concocted. She had loved Prue Moore dearly. She still did. And she was forever instilling into the girls at school and into David her conviction that every human being was a precious soul worthy of respect and courtesy and love.

Yet she had just fled in panic because the man whose left profile was godlike had turned out to be horribly maimed on the right side. He had no right arm. What had she expected he would do to her?

Hunger and shame made her feel somewhat light-headed. But she closed her eyes, drew in deep lungfuls of sea air, and then opened her eyes and deliberately returned the way she had just come.

Darkness was definitely falling now, and she was aware that she ought not to be wandering thus in a strange place. But she had to go back and make amends if she could.

She came to the path she had been following. And there, she thought as she looked about to get her bearings, was surely the promontory. She looked to left and right and decided that yes, that was certainly the place where he had been standing.

But he was no longer there.

She could not see him anywhere.

She hung her head and stood where she was for some time. She might have said good evening to him and nodded genially. He probably would have replied in kind. And she might then have walked onward, content with her behavior, and mourned whatever it was that had destroyed his beauty.

But she had recoiled from him, run away in fright and revulsion. How had he felt? Was this how other people treated him too? Poor man. At least all her hurts were inner ones. People – especially men who had looked on her with admiration and interest – sometimes shrank from her when they knew her for what she was, an unwed mother, but at least she could walk along a street, or along a cliff path without causing anyone to turn in horror and run.

How *could* she have done it? How could she? And now she had been suitably punished for her cowardice in running away from the house. She had been discourteous – worse! – to a fellow human being who had in no way offended or hurt her.

Perhaps, she thought as she made her way back toward the house again, he was a stranger passing through and had just wandered by chance onto the duke's land. Perhaps she would never see him again.

She despised herself for hoping that was so.

It was suitable punishment, she thought as she drew near to the house and her stomach rumbled with emptiness, that she must go hungry to bed.

She could not get the maimed man out of her mind all night. She kept waking and thinking of him.

Poor man. What must it be like to carry one's pain and one's deformities like that, for all to see? Ah, the loneliness of it!

Poor man.

But such beauty! Such physical perfection to have been so cruelly destroyed!

Sydnam watched her go. For a moment he considered going after her, but he would only increase her panic by doing that.

Besides, he did not feel at all kindly disposed toward her.

Who the devil *was* she? Lady Alleyne Bedwyn perhaps? She was the only one of the Bedwyn wives he had not met. But what had she been doing out here alone? Why was Alleyne not with her? And had no one warned her about the monster who was Bewcastle's steward?

He had been in another world. Or rather, he had been in this world, but he had been deeply immersed in the final, breathtaking moments of a dying day, with the sun just dropped behind the western horizon but the night not yet quite descended. It was a scene of grays and silvers and majesty. His right hand had itched to grasp his paintbrush more tightly so that he could reproduce the scene both as he saw it and as he felt it, but he had resisted the urge to flex the fingers

40

of that hand, knowing that as soon as he did so he would have to admit to himself, yet again, that it was a phantom hand he carried at his side, that both it and his right arm were no longer there just as his right eye was no longer there. And there was no paintbrush. He would have had to admit to himself that his vision of the scene was distorted, the depth and the perspective as well as the breadth of vision no longer feeding accurate information to his artist's soul.

But he had still not come to the moment of that admission. He had still been transported by beauty. He had still been immersed in the illusion of happiness.

And then something – a flutter at the corner of his eye, a footfall, perhaps – had brought aware-ness crashing back and he had sensed that he was no longer alone.

And when he had turned, there she was.

Or perhaps the crash back to awareness had come a moment after he turned to look.

For that moment before it happened the woman standing on the path had seemed a part of the beauty of the evening. She had looked tall and willowy slender, her cloak flapping in the breeze and revealing a dress of lighter color beneath. She had not been wearing a bonnet. Her hair was fair, perhaps even blond, her face oval and blue-eyed and lovely, though truth to tell he had seen it one-eyed from twenty feet away in the dusk and could not be sure he had observed accurately,

41

especially as far as the color of her eyes was concerned.

She had looked like beauty personified. For one moment he had thought . . .

Ah, what was it he had thought?

That she had walked out of the night into his dreams?

It was embarrassing even to consider that that was perhaps what he had thought before he had come jolting back to reality.

But certainly he had taken a step toward her without speaking a word. And she had stood there, apparently waiting for him.

And then he had seen the horror in her eyes. And then she had turned and fled in panic.

What had he expected? That she would smile and open her arms to him?

He gazed after her and was again Sydnam Butler, grotesquely ugly, with his right eye gone and the purple scars of the old burns down the side of his face, paralyzing most of the nerves there, and all along his armless side to his knee.

He was Sydnam Butler, who would never paint again, and for whom no woman would ever walk beautiful out of the night.

But he had left self-pity behind long ago, and resented moments such as this when his defenses had been lowered and it crept back in like a persistent and unwelcome guest to torment him. He knew that it would take him days to recover his equilibrium, to remind himself that he was now

42

Sydnam Butler, the best and most efficient steward of the several Bewcastle employed to run his various estates – and that was the duke's assessment, not his own.

He was Sydnam Butler, who had learned to live alone.

Without a paintbrush in his nonexistent right hand.

Without a woman for his bed or his heart.

He did not linger on the promontory. The magic was gone. The silver had gone from the sea to be replaced by a heaving gray, soon to be black. The sky no longer held even the memory of sunset. The breeze had turned chilly. It was time to go home.

He headed off along the path, in the direction from which the woman had come. After a few steps he realized that he was limping again and made a determined effort not to.

He was more glad than ever that he had moved out of the house and into the cottage. He liked it there. He might even stay after Bewcastle and all the others had returned home. A cottage, with a cook, a housekeeper, and a valet, was all a single man needed for his comfort.

Belatedly it struck him that there had been nothing grand about either the woman's cloak or the dress beneath it, and her hair had not been dressed elaborately. She must be just one of the servants who had come with the visitors. She *must* be. If she were indeed Lady Alleyne, she would

43

be at dinner now or in the drawing room with the rest of the family.

It was a relief to realize that she was only a servant. There was less of a chance that he would see her again. Whenever she had any free time from now on, he did not doubt that she would stay far away from the cliffs and the beach, where she might encounter the monster of Glandwr again.

He hoped he would never see her again, never have to look into that lovely face and see the revulsion there.

For an unguarded moment he had yearned toward her with his whole body and soul.

He thought resentfully that she would probably haunt his dreams for several nights to come.

If only he knew exactly how long Bewcastle intended to stay, he thought as he let himself in to the cottage and closed the door gratefully behind him, he could begin counting down the days, like a child waiting for some longed-for treat.

CHAPTER 3

'She simply disappeared off the face of the earth,' Joshua explained. 'She was not in her room, she was not in the nursery, and she certainly was not in either the drawing room or the dining room.'

'I daresay,' Gervase, Earl of Rosthorn, Morgan's husband, said as he cut into his bacon, 'she is intimidated by us – or by all you Bedwyns anyway,' he added with a chuckle.

'Oh, but she need not be,' Eve, Lady Aidan Bedwyn, said. 'We are really quite ordinary people. But you may be right, Gervase. I can remember a time when *I* was intimidated.'

'So can I,' Judith, Lady Rannulf, added fervently.

'And now she is taking breakfast in the nursery?' Christine, Duchess of Bewcastle, grimaced. 'Oh, I do feel ashamed for having let it happen. I ought to have made far more of an effort yesterday to find her and welcome her to our home. We both should have, Wulfric. I'll go up there immediately.'

'Perhaps,' Lord Aidan Bedwyn suggested, 'she should be given time to finish her breakfast first, Christine. You are the *duchess*, you must remember, and the sight of you might take away her appetite.'

Most of those gathered about the table chose to find that remark worthy of laughter. The duke grasped the handle of his quizzing glass and half raised it to his eye, but he lowered it again when he saw that his duchess, far from being offended, was laughing too.

'It was remiss of Freyja and Joshua to lose one of our guests yesterday,' he said. 'I would encourage you to find Miss Jewell, Christine, and invite her to dine with us this evening.' He indicated to a footman with the mere lifting of one finger that his coffee cup needed replenishing.

'And you ought to explain, Christine,' Lord Rannulf said with a broad grin, 'that an invitation from Wulf is the equivalent of an imperial summons. Make it clear that the poor woman really has no choice at all.'

'And speaking of empty chairs at the dinner table last night,' Lord Alleyne said, 'whatever happened to Syd? I have been looking forward to seeing him again but have not yet so much as set eyes on him.'

'I think, Alleyne,' the duchess said apologetically, 'he must be afraid of me.'

That pronouncement provoked another burst of merriment from those gathered about the breakfast table and a haughty lift of the eyebrows from the duke.

'He behaved most properly when we arrived,'

the duchess explained. 'He was out on the terrace waiting to greet us. But I have not seen him since, and last night, well after dinnertime, he sent an apology for not coming. He had apparently just arrived home and found our invitation.'

'A bouncer if ever I heard one,' Alleyne said.

'I suppose,' Rachel, Lady Alleyne, commented, 'it would not be the most comfortable thing in the world to dine out in company when one has only one arm – and that the left arm.'

'If that was his reason for not coming,' Freyja said, frowning, 'then he needs a good talking to. Syd was always the quiet one among us, but he was never a coward.'

'As witness the way in which he acquired his wounds,' Aidan said dryly.

'I can remember watching him learn to ride again after he had recovered his health,' Rannulf said. 'On the morning I was there at Alvesley he must have mounted thirty times and fallen off twenty-nine before finding a secure seat. But he would not allow either a groom or me within ten feet of him. And *that* was only learning to *mount*.'

'Oh, the poor gentleman,' Rachel said. 'I remember my lessons when Alleyne insisted that I learn to ride – and I had two arms. I was convinced every bone in my body would be broken before I was finished, though I never did actually fall off.'

'I enjoyed catching you too much, Rache,' her husband said, waggling his eyebrows at her.

'Never call Sydnam *poor* in his hearing, Rachel,' Freyja advised. 'Do not even *think* it.'

'Wulfric,' the duchess said, leaning eagerly across the table in his direction, 'you will be seeing Mr Butler this morning on estate business, will you not? Do invite him to dinner again. He really must not think of himself as a servant even if he is your steward. You told me that he took the position only because he felt he must do something useful with his life.'

'Your wish is, as ever, my command, my love,' the duke said. 'He will be invited. Or rather, if Rannulf is to be believed, he will be issued a ducal summons.'

'And so we will have two reluctant guests at table tonight,' Rannulf said with a grin. 'Perhaps they should be seated side by side, Christine. They can commiserate with each other.'

'You will be putting ideas into the ladies' heads, Ralf,' Gervase said with a theatrical grimace. 'You will be having them matchmaking again.'

Aidan groaned.

'The last time we tried it, though,' Alleyne added, 'we were remarkably successful. If we had not been, Christine would not now be at the table with us. Neither would she be the Duchess of Bewcastle.'

The duchess laughed.

The duke set down his coffee cup and raised his quizzing glass again.

'The knock on the head that once robbed you

of memory for a few months appears to have left you with a tendency toward occasional delusions, Alleyne,' he said. 'The Duchess of Bewcastle is at the table here because I wooed her and won her.'

He viewed his spouse severely along the length of the table through his glass while his family indulged in another outburst of merriment and his duchess smiled tenderly back at him.

'I really must go up now to disturb poor Miss Jewell's appetite,' she said, getting to her feet. 'But I hope only for a moment. You are quite right, Eve. We are really just ordinary people. And she has every right to be here with us. Her son's father was Joshua's cousin.'

'A fact you would be wise not to mention in her hearing, Christine,' Joshua warned her. 'Albert was never her favorite person. Or mine for that matter.'

'And with very good reason,' Eve said. 'I will come up with you, Christine, if I may. I met Miss Jewell when we went to Cornwall the year Freyja was betrothed to Joshua.'

'So did I,' Morgan said, pushing back her chair with her knees. 'I remember rather liking her. I'll come too.'

'The poor woman,' Aidan observed. 'I'll wager she has been hoping to hide away in the nursery for the whole month.'

When a maid arrived to help her dress for dinner, Anne greeted her with some embarrassment, not

49

knowing quite what to do with her. She had never had the services of a personal maid, and she had already donned her best green silk.

'I'll do your hair, mum, if I may,' the girl offered, and Anne sat obediently on a stool before the dressing table mirror.

She had spent a not entirely unpleasant day, all of it indoors, since there was a drizzling rain outside. She had helped organize games for the children, though she had not by any means been the only one doing so. In the course of the day she had met most of the members of the Bedwyn family except for the duke himself. They all had children and most of them had turned up in the nursery at some point in the day and stayed to play – or to be played with.

They had all treated her with courtesy, though she had stayed as far away from them as she was able.

But she had not been able to avoid taking dinner with the family this evening. The duchess had issued a personal invitation and it really had been quite impossible to refuse.

'You got lovely hair, mum,' the maid said as she brushed it out after removing all the pins.

It was honey-colored, thick and slightly wavy when it was down. Her crowning glory, Henry Arnold had once called it – not very originally – with admiration and something more shining in his eyes. And later someone else had called it the same thing while twining his fingers in it . . . She had hacked most of it off with small embroidery scissors the day she had realized beyond all doubt that she was with child. It had not been cut since except for an occasional trimming of the ends.

She looked different with her hair down out of its usual neat, prim knot. She knew that and usually avoided using a mirror while combing it and putting it up. With her hair down she looked . . . voluptuous. Was that the right word? She thought it probably was, though it was a word she hated. She hated her shining fair hair, her oval face with its large blue eyes and straight nose and high cheekbones and soft, generous lips. She hated her full breasts, her small waist, her shapely hips, her long, slim legs.

She had once loved to be called beautiful, and she had been called it often. But her beauty had become a curse to her.

'There, mum,' the girl said at last, stepping back to admire her handiwork in the mirror, having curled and coiled and twisted and braided and teased Anne's hair into a wonderfully artistic creation. 'You are lovely enough to attract a lord. A pity all the ones at the house here are spoken for. But there is Mr Butler, and he is the son of a lord even if he is only a mister himself.'

'If Mr Butler falls passionately in love with me on sight this evening,' Anne said, 'and offers me his hand and his heart and his fortune before the night is out, then I will have you to thank, Glenys.'

They both laughed.

51

'And who is Mr Butler?' Anne asked.

'He is the steward here,' Glenys said. 'He is . . . Well, never mind. But I am not even sure he will be here this evening. I may have done all this work for nothing.' She sighed aloud. 'But no matter. I can do it again another time. And there are bound to be outside visitors on other evenings, Mrs Parry says. There always are when the duke comes. Perhaps there will even be parties this time, with the duchess and all the others being here too. I will do something *very* special with your hair if there is a party.'

'And this is not special?' Anne asked, indicating her coiffure with a laugh to hide her unease. Dressed thus, it emphasized her features and the long arch of her neck.

'You wait and see,' Glenys said saucily. 'You had better go down now, mum. I have taken a bit longer than I ought. Mrs Parry will be mad with me if you are late, and won't let me come here again.'

Anne felt very conspicuous as she descended the stairs to the drawing room, though she guessed that she would still look remarkably plain in comparison with the finery the other ladies were bound to be wearing. She also felt very reluctant to keep on putting one foot ahead of the other as she walked. But what choice did she have?

Perhaps after this evening she could fade away into the shadows.

She looked about anxiously for Joshua when she

arrived in the open doorway, but it was the duchess herself who came hurrying toward her.

The Duchess of Bewcastle had been a surprise. She had dark, short, curly hair and was extremely pretty, but her beauty came more from her bright vitality than from any particular physical attribute, Anne had decided. She smiled frequently, there seemed to be a permanent sparkle in her eyes, and there was nothing at all in her manner or bearing to proclaim the great elevation of her rank. She was a great favorite in the nursery.

When she had arrived there soon after breakfast with Lady Aidan and Lady Rosthorn, both of whom Anne had met several years before in Cornwall, she had gone out of her way to make Anne feel at home, drawing her up from her curtsy, linking an arm through hers, and leading her away into the darkened room where her young baby slept in his crib, his two little hands curled into fists on either side of his head as if he fully intended swinging them as soon as he awoke. She had even somehow worked into the conversation the fact that she was the daughter of a country gentleman who had been forced to supplement his income by teaching at the village school and that she herself had been teaching part-time at that same school when she had met the duke at a house party she had really not wanted to attend.

'It can be an abomination, Miss Jewell,' she had added as if she were really saying nothing of any great significance, 'to find oneself stuck in a country manor surrounded by strangers who might possibly think themselves superior and wishing that one were anywhere else on earth but right there. I tried at first to remain aloof from it all, observing satirically from a shadowed corner. But Wulfric found me there and provoked me, the horrid man, and I emerged from that corner in order to preserve my very self-respect.' She had laughed lightly.

Wulfric, Anne gathered, must be the Duke of Bewcastle.

And she had, she had also realized, just been challenged into emerging from her own shadowed corner, the nursery, in order to preserve her self-respect.

But the duchess, she thought, had never borne an illegitimate son.

Now the duchess linked an arm through Anne's again.

'I will make sure that you have been presented to everyone, Miss Jewell,' she said. 'And here is Wulfric first.'

Even if everyone in the room had still been a stranger, she would immediately have known the identity of the man who was coming toward her, Anne was convinced. Tall, dark, and austerely handsome, he was also the consummate aristocrat – aloof and dignified, with a powerful presence. And here she was, an ex-governess, an unwed mother, an uninvited guest in his home – and about to dine at his table.

She would have turned and fled if the duchess had not had an arm linked through her own, she believed.

Or perhaps not. She did have some pride.

'Wulfric,' the duchess said, 'here is Miss Jewell at last. This is my husband, the Duke of Bewcastle, Miss Jewell.'

Anne curtsied. She half expected that the next moment she would be banished into outer darkness.

'Your grace,' she murmured.

He inclined his head to her and she noticed his long fingers close about the handle of a jeweled quizzing glass, though he did not raise it. It was somehow a terrifying gesture.

'Miss Jewell,' he said. 'Her grace and I were sadly remiss yesterday in not welcoming you personally to Glandwr. You will, perhaps, be good enough to forgive us. I trust you and your son have been made comfortable and will enjoy your stay here.'

They were gracious words, but his strange silver eyes did not smile.

'She has been busy in the nursery all day, Wulfric, breaking up fights and organizing games,' the duchess said, smiling brightly at him as if he were the warmest of mortals.

'I see no bruises, ma'am,' his grace said with perhaps the merest glimmering of humor. 'But perhaps our nephews and nieces were merely warming up today for worse to come tomorrow. And perhaps it is as well for your health that our son is still but an infant in the cradle. We have great hopes of his keeping alive the Bedwyn reputation for hellery in the years to come.'

The duchess laughed.

And yes, Anne decided, there was definitely humor in his words. And she liked the way he had referred to his child as *our* son rather than as *my* son, as many men in his position would have done.

And then she was whisked away by the duchess to meet those to whom she had not yet been introduced – Mrs Pritchard, Lady Aidan's elderly Welsh aunt; Lord and Lady Rannulf Bedwyn and the Earl of Rosthorn, who had visited the nursery but had come while she was in David's room playing word games with him and some of the older children; Baron Weston, Lady Alleyne's uncle; Mrs and Miss Thompson, the duchess's mother and eldest sister; and her middle sister and brother-in-law, the Reverend and Mrs Lofter, Alexander's parents.

Anne tried to memorize faces and names – though she hoped not to be in a position to use them for the next few weeks.

'Ah,' the duchess said, her arm still linked through Anne's, 'and here comes Mr Butler at last.'

The steward, who was supposed to fall violently in love with her elaborate coiffure and propose marriage to her before the night was out, Anne thought as she turned and looked toward the doorway, feeling the first flickering of amusement she had felt since leaving her room.

For a moment she was again arrested by the

56

extraordinary good looks and manly physique of the man standing there, fully visible this time in the early evening sunshine that streamed through the west-facing windows. And again it was his left profile at which she gazed.

But even as a jolt of recognition half robbed her of breath, he was obscured from sight as Lord Alleyne, tall, dark, and handsome himself, and Lord Rannulf, even taller and fair and ruggedly good-looking, converged on him and slapped him on the back and greeted him heartily.

'Syd, old chap,' she heard Lord Rannulf say, 'where the devil have you been hiding? But Wulf put the fear of God in you this morning, did he?'

So he was not a stranger, Anne thought. She *was* fated to meet him again. He was Mr Butler, the steward at Glandwr.

She felt slightly sick to the stomach. The little appetite she had had as she made her way downstairs to the drawing room fled.

How she *wished* she had not behaved so badly last evening – or that she had been able to find him afterward to apologize.

And this on top of everything else.

If she could have crept back up to her room without his seeing her, she would have done so. But he was standing almost in the doorway. Besides, the duchess still had an arm linked through hers. And besides again, she had behaved cravenly and even cruelly last evening. Now she had a chance – perhaps! – to make amends.

Though she would surely be the very last person he would wish to encounter again today.

Sydnam had walked up to the main house despite the drizzle. He would a million times rather be at home in his cozy cottage, he reflected as he let himself in through the front door, handed his wet cloak and hat to a footman, and climbed the stairs to the drawing room. But Bewcastle had issued the invitation in person this morning, and when Bewcastle invited he was really commanding – especially, Sydnam gathered, when he invoked the name of his wife.

'The duchess was disappointed when you did not come to dine last evening,' he had said while pulling one of the estate books toward him across the desk in the library, where he always did business while at Glandwr. 'I have a curious aversion to seeing her grace disappointed, Sydnam, though of course it was unavoidable last evening since you did not receive your invitation until well after the dinner hour. There will not be that problem this evening.'

Bewcastle had recognized a lie when he heard one, of course. Not that it had been an outright lie. Sydnam had not actually read the invitation before going outside to walk, but he *had* seen it and guessed what it was and deliberately avoided opening it until it was too late.

'I will apologize in person to her grace this evening,' he had said while Bewcastle turned pages as if he were not even listening.

58

And so here he was to eat humble pie before dining. He amused himself grimly with the mental picture of all the Bedwyns and their spouses being forced to sit at table with a patch over one eye and their right arms bound behind their backs. But he must not be vicious, even in his thoughts. The invitation was a kind one. And being human, with all the contrariness to which human nature was prone, he supposed that if they were here for a month and never once extended an invitation to him to join them, he would be hurt and offended.

He grinned ruefully at the admission.

He must be somewhat late, he thought as he approached the drawing room doors. Or if he was not late – and he knew he was not – he nevertheless was last to arrive. A grand entrance was all he needed. But even as he stood in the doorway looking about for Bewcastle or the duchess, Rannulf and Alleyne bore down on him, one from either side, and suddenly he felt that the ordeal would not be so bad after all. Many of the people here were old friends of his, and none of the others would bear him any ill will. It was not as if he were a houseguest to be in their sight every moment of every day, after all. And none of the children would be here.

'I have been cowering inside a cave down on the beach,' he said in answer to Rannulf's question, 'as you might have discovered for yourself if you had come down there to look, Ralf. But a little rain kept you indoors, did it? Or is it the steep cliff path that deterred you?'

Alleyne clamped a hand on his right shoulder, a gesture that endeared him to Sydnam since most people avoided his right side whenever they were able.

'How are you, Syd?' he asked. 'It is a veritable age since I saw you last. We have brought a stack of messages from home, some from Lauren, a dozen or more from your mother, one or two from Kit, one from your father – but I cannot for the life of me recall a single one of them. Can you, Ralf?'

'Something about wearing warm woolens in the damp weather, at a wager,' Ralf said with a grin. 'Of course I do not remember. The ladies will, though. You had better come and meet the people you do not already know, Syd. Ah, here comes Christine. Have you met our formidable duchess?'

'He has,' the duchess said, smiling warmly at him. 'I am so glad you were able to come this evening, Mr Butler.'

She gave him her left hand and he bowed over it.

'I must apologize most humbly, your grace,' he said, 'for last evening. I was from home and did not read your invitation until – until it was too late.'

The sudden pause had been occasioned by the glance he had stolen at the lady through whose arm the duchess's right hand was drawn.

He recognized her instantly.

He had certainly not been mistaken about one thing, he thought. She was quite breathtakingly beautiful, with hair the color of warm honey and blue eyes made smoky by long lashes, and regular, perfect features. And now that she was no longer wearing a cloak, it was obvious that she had a figure to do justice to the face.

So his first guess had been correct, he thought. She *was* one of the Bedwyn wives.

He felt a curious, quite unreasonable bitterness.

'No apology is necessary,' the duchess assured him. 'May I make you known to Miss Jewell, a particular friend of Freyja and Joshua's? Mr Butler is Wulfric's steward at Glandwr,' she explained for the lady's benefit.

Sydnam bowed and she curtsied. *Miss Jewell.* Her name suited her well. And she was *not* one of the wives. But he felt no kindness toward her.

He remembered suddenly that he had dreamed of her last night. She had stood on that path waiting for him, and he had walked close enough to touch her cheek – with the fingertips of his right hand. And he had looked into her lovely blue eyes – with both his own. He had asked her please not to pinch him as it was important never to wake up, and she had told him that they needed to wake up without delay so that they could go searching for his arm, which had fallen over the cliff, before the tide came in and washed it away. It had been one of those strange, bizarre dreams that sometimes have one hovering between reality and fantasy, dreaming but knowing that one dreams.

'Miss Jewell,' he said now.

'Mr Butler,' she murmured in return.

The duchess took him about the room then, without Miss Jewell's company, and introduced him to the people he did not know.

He still disliked meeting strangers, though he was long past the stage of trying to keep the right side of his body out of sight. His ugliness had been hard to accept. He had been accustomed to seeing nothing but admiration in the eyes of others – and even adoration in some female eyes. Not that he had taken a great deal of advantage of the latter. He had still been very young when everything changed. And he had never been conceited about his good looks. He had taken them for granted – until they were destroyed forever.

Everyone here had known about him in advance, he realized as he made his way to the dining room a short while later with Miss Eleanor Thompson, the duchess's sister, on his arm. None of them had openly flinched.

But *she* had not known – Miss Jewell, that was. She had run from him last night as if he were the devil himself. He found himself resenting her incredible beauty even though he recognized that it was somewhat childish to do so. Some people just had an easy path through life.

62

He turned his head to note that Morgan was seated on his blind side and set himself to making conversation with her as well as with Miss Thompson. At least, he thought, the kitchen staff here knew him and understood that they must not place anything before him that could not be cut one-handed, preferably with the edge of a fork.

Miss Jewell, he could see, was smiling warmly at Baron Weston beside her and saying something to him that brought an answering smile to his face. She was charming him, enslaving him.

No, he would *not* dislike her, he decided. Or resent her. Or envy Weston or Alleyne on her other side.

Good Lord, he was not a man normally given to petty jealousies.

Or to spite. Or resentment.

He picked up his soup spoon with his left hand and tackled the first course.

CHAPTER 4

The evening turned out to be slightly less of an ordeal than Anne had anticipated. Not all the guests were aristocrats or the offspring of aristocrats.

Mrs Pritchard, near whom Anne sat at the dining table, had once earned her living down a Welsh coal mine, and her niece, Lady Aidan Bedwyn, had been brought up as a lady only because her father had made his fortune in coal and then set up as a gentleman on an English estate he had purchased. Lady Rannulf Bedwyn, Anne discovered in the drawing room later, was the daughter of a country clergyman – and the granddaughter of a London actress, she mentioned as something of which she seemed proud. The duchess herself was of the lower gentry class, as she had freely admitted during the morning. Her brother-in-law was a clergyman in a small country parish. Her mother and sister lived together in a cottage in the same parish.

Yet here they all were, as fully accepted by the Bedwyns as if they had all been born with the bluest blood.

It was true, of course, that no one else here at

Glandwr had an illegitimate child, but no one treated Anne as if she were a pariah – or as if she had no business being among present company. Indeed, Lady Aidan asked her particularly about her son and laughed when Anne told her how he had been spoiled by teachers and girls alike at Miss Martin's school.

'Though for his sake I must send him to a boys' school when he is a little older,' Anne said. 'It will be hard – for me if not for him.'

'It will,' Lady Aidan agreed. 'We will be sending Davy to school next year when he is twelve, and already I am feeling bereft.'

They exchanged a smile, just two concerned mothers commiserating with each other.

'That poor man,' Mrs Pritchard said softly in her musical Welsh accent as the gentlemen joined the ladies. 'It is a good thing he is not of the working classes. He would never have found employment after the wars were over. He would have become a beggar and starved as so many of those soldiers did.'

'Oh, I am not so sure of that, Aunt Mari,' Lady Aidan said. 'There is a thread of steel in him despite his quiet manners. I believe he would have overcome any adversity, even poverty.'

They were talking, Anne realized, of Mr Butler, about whom she had been feeling horribly guilty all evening and whom she had consequently avoided even looking at – though she had been aware of him almost every moment.

'What happened to him?' she asked.

'War,' Lady Aidan said. 'He followed his brother, Viscount Ravensberg, to the Peninsula against everyone's wishes but his own. His brother brought him home not long after, more dead than alive. But he recovered, and eventually he offered his services to Wulfric and came here. That all happened before I met Aidan, who was still a cavalry colonel in the Peninsula at the time, the superior officer of my brother, who never came home. How *glad* I am that the wars are over at last.'

It was some time later when Anne noticed that Mr Butler was seated alone in a far corner of the room after all the groups had just rearranged themselves with the setting up of some card tables. She herself was with Miss Thompson and the Earl and Countess of Rosthorn, all of whom had declined a place at the tables. But Anne stood and excused herself before she could lose her courage. She could not allow the whole evening to go by without speaking to Mr Butler, though she doubted he would have any wish to speak with her.

He looked up sharply when he saw her approach and then got to his feet.

'Miss Jewell,' he said.

Something in his manner and voice told her that indeed he would have preferred to remain alone, that he did not like her – but she could hardly blame him for that, could she?

66

She looked into his face and quite deliberately adjusted her focus so that she looked at both sides. He wore a black patch over his right eye – or perhaps over where his right eye had been. The rest of that side of his face was covered from brow to jaw and on down his neck with purplish burn marks. His empty right sleeve was pinned to the side of his evening coat.

He was, she noticed, half a head taller than she – and she had not been mistaken about his broad chest and shoulders. He was clearly not a man who had wallowed in his disabilities.

'I went back last night,' she said, 'a few minutes after I ran away. But you had gone.'

He looked back at her in silence for a few moments.

'I am sorry,' he said abruptly then, 'that I frightened you. I did not intend to do so.'

Courteous words, courteously spoken. Yet she could still feel his dislike, his reluctance to speak with her.

'No, you misunderstand,' she said. '*I* am sorry. It is what I went back to say. I truly am. Sorry.'

What else could she say? She could only make matters worse by trying to offer an explanation for her behavior.

Again there was a silence between them long enough to be uncomfortable. She almost turned and walked away. She had said what she had felt compelled to say. There was nothing else.

'Going back was a courageous thing to do,' he

said. 'It was getting dark and the cliff top is a lonely, dangerous place to be at night. And I was a stranger to you. Thank you for returning even though I had already gone home.'

She had, she supposed, been forgiven. She did not know if he still disliked her, but that did not really matter. She smiled and nodded and would again have turned away.

'Will you have a seat, Miss Jewell?' He indicated the chair close to the one he had been occupying.

She had hesitated too long, she thought, and courtesy had compelled him to offer to prolong their encounter. She would rather have moved off somewhere else. She did not like being close to him. Ashamed as she was to admit it, she did not like having to look at him.

And how difficult it was to look at him as if he were any normal man, not to focus only on the left side of his face, not to look away lest he think she was staring. Did some people who knew about her find it equally difficult to look at her, to treat her as if she were a normal woman? But she knew very well that there were such people.

She sat straight-backed on the edge of the chair and folded her hands in her lap.

'You are a brother of Viscount Ravensberg, Mr Butler?' she said politely, her mind having turned blank to all the many possibilities of interesting conversational topics.

'I am,' he answered.

And there was nowhere else to go with the topic.

68

She did not even know who Viscount Ravensberg was. But he took pity on her.

'And son of the Earl of Redfield of Alvesley Park in Hampshire,' he told her. 'The estate adjoins that of Lindsey Hall, Bewcastle's principal seat. My brothers and I grew up with the Bedwyns. They were all hellions – but then so were we.'

'Brothers?' She raised her eyebrows.

'Jerome, the eldest, died of a chill taken while rescuing farm laborers and their families from flooded homes,' he said. 'Kit and I are the only two remaining.'

There must have been much nerve damage to the right side of his face, she thought. It was immobile, and his mouth was rather lopsided as he talked.

'It must have been hard to lose a brother,' she said.

'Yes.'

She did not usually have undue difficulty making conversation, but everything she had said during the past minute or two was markedly stupid. Her mind, meanwhile, chattered incessantly with questions she knew she could not ask.

What happened out there in the Peninsula?
In which battle did it happen?
Did you sometimes wish you had died?
Do you sometimes still wish it?

He must have been extraordinarily, *impossibly* handsome once upon a time.

'What an utterly foolish thing to say,' she said.

'As if you could possibly reply that no, it was not hard at all.'

His one dark eye met hers with a hard, bleak look for a moment as if he were about to make a sharp retort. Then it twinkled, and surprisingly they both laughed. The left side of his mouth lifted higher than the right in a lopsided grin that was curiously attractive.

'Miss Jewell,' he said, 'shall we agree, for both our sakes, to pretend that last evening did not happen, that we have met here for the first time this evening?'

'Oh.' She relaxed back a little farther on her chair. 'I should like that.'

His left hand was resting on his thigh. It was a long-fingered artist's hand, she thought. She hoped she was wrong about that last point – or that he was left-handed. She looked up into his face.

'I have been feeling horribly intimidated all evening,' she was surprised to hear herself admit.

'Have you?' he asked her. 'Why?'

She wished she had not said it. But he was waiting for her reply.

'Joshua – Lord Hallmere – offered to bring my son here for the summer so that he would have other children to play with,' she explained. 'But he is only nine years old, and I have never been separated from him. And so, when I hesitated, the marchioness invited me too and I accepted because I did not want to disappoint my son. But I did not expect to be treated as a *guest*.'

From his short silence, she realized that she had just told him volumes about herself. And perhaps now it was *his* turn to run from her or to show some unmistakable sign of revulsion.

'I teach and live at a girls' school in Bath,' she said. 'I like it extremely well, and David has always been happy there. But he is getting older. I suppose I ought to have let him come with Joshua – David worships him.'

'Children do need other children,' he said. 'They also need a father figure, especially perhaps if they are boys. But most of all, Miss Jewell, they need a mother. I daresay you did the right thing in coming here with him.'

'Oh.' She drew unexpected comfort from his words. 'That is very obliging of you.'

'I hope,' he said, 'Bewcastle has not intimidated you. But if he has, you may be consoled to know that he intimidates almost everyone. He was removed abruptly from a wild childhood when his father knew he was dying, and he was carefully, even ruthlessly trained to take over all the vast responsibilities of the dukedom, which he inherited when he was only seventeen or eighteen. He learned his lessons consummately well – too well, some would say. But he is not unfeeling. He has been remarkably good to me.'

'I met him for the first time this evening,' Anne told him. 'He was very gracious, though I must confess I was ready to sink through the floor with fear.'

They both laughed again.

'The duchess is exceedingly amiable,' she said.

'According to Lauren, my sister-in-law,' he told her, 'it was a love match. It was the sensation of last year. No one would have predicted that Bewcastle would marry for love. But perhaps he did.'

The tea tray was being brought in, and two of the card games were coming to an end.

'I must be going home,' Mr Butler said. 'I am pleased to have made your acquaintance, Miss Jewell.'

She set both hands on the arms of her chair and got to her feet. She noticed that he got up a little more slowly from his low chair, and it occurred to her that being without one arm and one eye must shift the natural balance of the body that she took so very much for granted. How long had it taken him to adjust to the change? Had he ever adjusted completely?

'I shall go and convey my thanks to the duchess,' he said, holding out his hand to her. 'Good night.'

'Good night, Mr Butler.'

She held out her own hand and he shook it before releasing it and turning away.

Anne was left biting her lip. She should, of course, have given him her *left* hand as she remembered the duchess had done earlier. Their handshake had been horribly awkward – as if they had been holding hands and swinging them. It had felt almost intimate. Embarrassingly so.

He was bowing to the Duchess of Bewcastle, who smiled warmly at him and set one hand on his arm while she leaned a little toward him to say something. Lord Rannulf came up behind him and slapped a hand on his right shoulder. The two men left the room together.

Where did he live? Anne wondered.

Would she see him again?

But it would not matter too much if she did. She had got past the awkwardness of what had happened last night. She was vastly relieved about that. It would be easier to meet him next time.

But how tragic for him to have lost a limb and an eye and to have had his looks so marred.

Was he lonely? she wondered.

Did he have friends?

Outcasts were frequently both lonely and friendless. Her mind touched upon her years in the Cornish village of Lydmere, living on the very fringes of local society.

She had never ceased to give thanks for the fact that she finally had found friends at the school in Bath and that three of those friends – Claudia herself, Susanna, and Frances – had come to be as close as sisters to her. It was so much more than she had ever expected – or felt she deserved – after those long, lean years.

She hoped Mr Butler had some close friends.

'Come and have tea, Anne,' Joshua said, appearing suddenly at her side. 'I hope you are enjoying your stay here.'

'Oh.' She smiled at him. 'I am, yes, thank you, Joshua.'

But most of all, Miss Jewell, they need a mother. I daresay you did the right thing in coming here with him.

The remembered words that Mr Butler had spoken warmed and comforted her. She *had* done the right thing. David had been animated and happy all day long with the other children. But he had hugged her when she went to say good night to him before dressing for dinner.

'Thank you, Mama,' he had said, 'for bringing me here. I am so glad we came.'

We, not *I*.

She would suffer the discomfort and embarrassment of the month here only to see David happy – for though he was well loved at the school by staff and girls alike, *he* had no close friends.

And no father.

Sydnam was busy for most of the next day. It was never hard to find things to do. But now, in addition to his usual routine, there was Bewcastle to accompany on a morning inspection of the home farm and calls at a few of the tenant farms. The duke might spend very little time on his Welsh estate, but he knew all there was to know about it, since he conscientiously studied each monthly report that Sydnam sent him. And whenever he did visit, he spent only a little time poring over the books and a great deal of time riding and tramping about the land observing and talking with the people.

But Bewcastle was now also a husband, and it intrigued Sydnam to find that he returned home at noon because the duchess had arranged a picnic on the beach for everyone during the afternoon. The old Bewcastle would not have dreamed of participating in such frolics.

The Duchess of Bewcastle seemed like a very ordinary person to Sydnam. She was pretty without being beautiful, trim and smart without being elegant, courteous and amiable without being overrefined or in any way domineering. She was vivacious and filled with laughter. And she was the daughter of a country schoolmaster. She was, in fact, the very antithesis of the woman one would have expected Wulfric to choose for a bride – which fact left Sydnam wondering about the strange power she seemed to wield over him. Good Lord, he had even noticed Bewcastle *smiling* at her once last evening.

She made Sydnam feel lonely. Not that he fancied her himself. But it must be wonderful beyond belief, he thought, to have someone to go home to after work, someone for whom to cut the workday short on occasion, even for something as seemingly unimportant as a picnic on the beach. It must be wonderful to have someone to draw one's smiles.

And there was a baby in Bewcastle's nursery.

He avoided the beach and the cliff top above it

and the lawns leading to it all afternoon. He was not, after all, a member of the house party, and besides, he did not want to frighten any of the children. He kept himself busy on the home farm, being reluctant to spend a sunny, warm day indoors when it so often rained along the coast of South Wales.

Late in the afternoon, though, when he was riding back to the cottage, he could see that a noisy game of cricket was in progress on the lawn before the main house and that there appeared to be a vast number of people of all sizes involved. The picnic on the beach was obviously over.

It would be safe to go there himself.

He loved the beach. He loved the cliff tops too, but the perspective was different. From the cliff top one was aware of the wildness of nature, the potential cruelty of it, the panoramic beauty of it, with the land above and the sea stretched beneath and spreading to a far horizon, beyond which lay the coast of Cornwall and beyond that the coast of France and the Atlantic Ocean.

But on the beach he was aware only of the golden sands stretching in a great arc before him and behind him and to either side of him, land in its most elemental form, land worn away by the power of the ocean. And there too he was aware of the vastness and power of the deep, of the great, elemental mystery of this origin of all life.

It was on the beach that he could feel most strongly the paintbrush clasped in his right hand

and see the vision that would never be captured on any real canvas. It was on the beach that sometimes the vision was enough.

He was halfway down the steep but quite wide path that led along a fault line from the top of the cliffs to the beach when he realized that not everyone had returned to the house. Someone remained. She was walking along the shiny wet sand over which the ebb tide had just receded, parallel to the water, her skirt caught up in one hand while the other held what must be her shoes.

He sighed aloud and almost turned back. He felt unreasonably resentful. He had come to think of this park and this beach as his own, he realized. But they were not his. They were Bewcastle's, and Miss Jewell was Bewcastle's guest here.

It was Miss Jewell down there on the sands.

There was room for both of them, he supposed. The beach was vast enough, and the tide was going out and making it larger by the minute.

He continued his descent.

She had a son. Yet she was *Miss* Jewell. She taught at a girls' school and had her son there with her. The Marquess of Hallmere and Freyja knew her and had invited her here. No, correction – Hallmere had wanted to bring her son here, and then Freyja had invited the mother to come too.

It seemed strange to him that either one of them would want her here, since she had not mentioned any connection with Hallmere that would explain his interest in her son. It seemed stranger that Bewcastle would countenance such an intrusion into his family circle – an unwed woman with a bastard son. And she herself had not expected to be received as a guest but presumably as a servant. Intrigued as he was, though, he recognized that her presence here at Glandwr was none of his business.

He wished, even so, that Freyja had not invited her. He wished she were not here at Glandwr. He had been pleasantly surprised when she apologized to him last evening. He had found her company congenial during their short conversation. But he had dreamed about her again last night. She had been the one standing on the promontory this time, and he was the one on the path. She had been wearing something loose and diaphanous that blew against her shapely form in the breeze, and her long honey-colored hair had been loose and blowing back from her head. But when he had approached her this time and reached out to touch her, she had looked suddenly horrified and had turned to run – right off the edge of the cliff while he tried to grab her with an arm that was not there. But somehow in the dream he had become the faller. He had woken up with a jolt just before he landed on the rocks below the cliff.

He had no wish to be dreaming such idiotic dreams. He had enough problems with the usual nightmares.

He reached the bottom of the path, clambered over the loose rocks and pebbles at the base of the cliff, and then stood on the sand looking at Miss Jewell as she walked, unaware of his presence. She had lifted her face to the breeze and was moving her head slowly from side to side. He could see now that she held her bonnet as well as her shoes in one of her hands.

It was strange how he could see her differently now than just twenty-four hours ago. Then he had thought of her as a superbly beautiful woman who could not possibly have known troubles in her life and must therefore be without either depth of character or compassion. Without knowing anything about her except that she had fled from him that first evening, he had disliked her.

But last evening she had deliberately sought him out to beg his pardon. And then she had mentioned her child and her feeling of intimidation as Bewcastle's guest. Her beauty, he had realized, did not give her an immunity to feelings of insecurity. But then he supposed that unwed mothers did not have easy lives. In her own way she had quite possibly gone through hell and back just as he had, the only real difference being that his hell was visible to the beholder whereas hers was not.

He moved, intending to turn and walk in the opposite direction from the one she took. But something must have caught at the edge of her vision, and she turned her head to look at him and then stopped walking.

It would have been churlish to make off in another direction. And of course, he did not really want to even though he did not wish to walk with her either. He made his way reluctantly across the beach toward her.

She was wearing a pale blue high-waisted dress, whose hem she held above her ankles on one side. Her hair was dressed more simply than it had been last evening. Somehow she looked more beautiful. She looked quite achingly lovely, in fact. She looked strangely as if this were her proper milieu, as if she belonged here.

'Mr Butler,' she said as soon as he was within earshot. 'Everyone went back to the house quite awhile ago. I stayed to enjoy the quiet after all the noise and turmoil.'

'I am sorry to have disturbed you, then,' he said.

'Oh, you need not be,' she said. 'I daresay *I* am disturbing *you*.'

'Did everyone enjoy the picnic?' he asked her, stopping at the edge of the wet sand a short distance from her.

'I believe so.' For a moment she looked bleak, but then she smiled and her eyes sparkled with such merriment that he was suddenly dazzled by her. 'The duchess went paddling in the waves with a few of the children, but somehow she lost her balance and fell right in. And then the duke waded out to rescue her, Hessian boots and all, and got himself almost as wet as she. The other adults thought it all a huge joke, and the children screeched with glee.

The duchess was laughing helplessly too even though her teeth were chattering. It was all quite extraordinary.'

'That would have been something to behold,' he said. 'Bewcastle wading into the sea with his boots on. Did he laugh too?'

'Oh, no,' she said. 'And yet there was a certain gleam in his eyes that might possibly have been inner laughter.'

They grinned merrily at each other. To add to all her other perfections, she had white, even teeth.

'I should go back to the house,' she said, her smile fading, 'and leave you here in peace.'

It was what he wanted, surely. It was what he had come in search of. He certainly had not come here looking for her. And yet . . .

'Shall we stroll together for a while?' he suggested.

He realized suddenly what it was he had most admired about her last evening – and she was doing it again today. She was looking directly into his face. Most people, he had observed, either did not look quite at him at all or else focused their eyes on his left ear or his left shoulder. With most people he felt the urge to turn his head slightly to the side so that they would not have to be repulsed quite so badly. He did not feel that urge with her, though she *had* run from him at first.

She might be repulsed by him, he thought – and how could she *not* be? – but she was displaying unusual courtesy in her dealings with him. He was grateful to her.

'Yes.' Her gaze dropped to his top boots and she smiled again. 'Shall I come onto the dry sand?'

But he walked deliberately onto the wet sand and fell into step beside her.

They strolled in silence for a while. He watched the sun sparkle off the water and felt the light breeze against his left cheek. He breathed in the salt warmth of the air and had the feeling that had assaulted him more and more of late – the feeling of home. He had come here to this particular corner of Wales five years ago because Kit's return home from the wars and marriage to Lauren had made it impossible for him to remain at Alvesley, a mere younger son clinging to his family because he was too broken to step out into the world on his own account. He had come here as Bewcastle's steward and had concentrated all his energies upon doing the job twice as well as a two-armed man might have done it. He had felt like an alien, though. And he had been treated for some time as something of an outcast. He had known that people found it hard to be in company with him, to look at him.

But he had persevered. And sometime during the past year or two he had come to understand that a force beyond himself had had a hand in bringing him here – in bringing him home. Fate, perhaps.

He had not yet broached the subject of Tŷ Gwyn with Bewcastle. But he would. He must. He needed his own home here.

82

His awareness of the woman beside him was almost a pleasant thing. She had not been forced to walk beside him. She might easily have said no.

'Do you ever feel lonely?' she asked him suddenly and abruptly. And then, as he turned his head to look down at her in some surprise, *she* looked at *him* in apparent dismay. 'I am so sorry. Sometimes I think aloud.'

Because he was maimed and ugly and lived in what she must see as a remote corner of civilization? His first reaction was anger. She really was no different from anyone else after all. Why had he imagined that perhaps she was?

'Do *you*?' He threw the question back at her.

She looked away from him again. She had dropped the hem of her dress, he noticed. She held her shoes and her bonnet with both hands behind her back.

'I live at a girls' school,' she said. 'I scarcely have a minute to myself. I have my son to fill every spare moment while he is awake. And I have dear friends among the teachers, particularly Miss Martin herself and Susanna Osbourne, who is also resident at the school. I correspond frequently with another friend who used to teach there. She is now the Countess of Edgecombe. How could I be lonely?'

'But are you?' he asked her.

He knew suddenly that she was, that she had asked her question, not out of morbid curiosity, but out of her own loneliness. Perhaps she had recognized in him a kindred spirit. And perhaps he had recognized the same in her. He *knew* she was lonely, incredible as it seemed. How could such a beautiful woman be lonely? But she was an unwed mother.

'I am not even sure what loneliness is,' she said. 'If it is not literally being solitary, is it the fear of solitude, of being alone with oneself? I feel no such fear. I *like* being alone.'

'What *do* you fear, then?' he asked her.

She glanced briefly at him and smiled, a fragile expression that spoke for itself even before she found words.

'Never finding myself again,' she said after a minute or two of silence, during which he thought that perhaps she would not answer at all.

'Have you lost yourself, then?' he asked softly.

'I am not sure,' she said. 'I have tried to be the best mother I can possibly be. I have tried somehow to be both mother and father to David. If he grows up to be happy and productive, *I* will be happy too. But what will I discover about myself when he leaves me as he inevitably must, first to go to school and then to live his own adult life? Will I discover an empty black hole that is seventeen or eighteen years wide and deep? And what on *earth* am I talking about? I have never said these things to anyone else. I have not even allowed myself to *think* them.'

'Sometimes,' he said, 'it is easier to confide in a sympathetic stranger than in a friend or relative.'

'Is that what you are?' She glanced at him again and he noticed that her face had caught the sun and would be unfashionably bronzed for a while.

'A sympathetic stranger?' he said. 'Yes. And have you noticed that people will admit to almost any vice or shortcoming before they will admit to loneliness? It is as if there were something rather shameful in the condition.'

'I *am* lonely,' she said quickly and rather breathlessly. 'Terribly lonely. And yes, it does seem shameful. It also seems ungrateful. I have my son.'

'Who is busy forging his own life in company with other children,' he said.

'A dreadful thing just happened,' she said in a rush. 'It is why I was walking here alone. Everyone was leaving the beach, and without thinking I held out my hand to take David's – I sometimes forget he is no longer an infant. He said, "Oh, Mama!" and dashed off to walk with Joshua, who ruffled his hair and set a hand on his shoulder and talked to him even though his own son was riding on his shoulders. Neither of them meant to be cruel – Joshua had not even seen what had happened. It was ridiculous of me to feel hurt. There were any number of other children and other adults to whom I might have attached myself for the walk back to the house. But I felt very alone and very frightened. How can I compete for my son's affections with other children and men who are willing to give him their attention? And why would I want to? I am *glad* for him. And I hate my own pettiness.'

Ah, yes, Sydnam thought, he had been very wrong about her. Her beauty counted for nothing in the life that had been mapped out for her and that was slowly and inexorably changing as her son grew older. He wondered briefly about the man who had fathered her child. What had happened to him? Why had she not married him? More to the point, perhaps, why had he not married her?

'*No one*,' he said decisively, 'can or ever will be able to compete with you, Miss Jewell. You are the boy's mother. He relies upon you for love and comfort and support and security and approval. And in some ways he always will. No one could ever replace my own mother in my heart for the things I look for from her. But a mother-son relationship is not a coequal one, is it? He is lonely with only you just as you are lonely with only him.'

'But I have my friends,' she protested.

'I do too,' he told her. 'I have been here for five years and have made friends, some of them quite close, on whom I can call at any time and with whom I can talk comfortably on any subject under the sun. I have a family in Hampshire – mother, father, brother, sister-in-law – who love me dearly and would do anything in the world for me.'

She had not mentioned family of her own, he noticed – except her son.

'But you are lonely?'

'But I *am* lonely,' he admitted, turning his head

so that he could see the sun shining on the cliff face, making it more silver than gray, and on the deep blue sky above.

He did not believe he had ever said those words aloud before – even to himself. But they were, of course, starkly true.

'Thank you,' she said unexpectedly. She drew breath as if to say something else, but she did not speak.

Thank you? And yet he felt a certain gratitude to her too. She had asked if he was lonely and then admitted her own loneliness and given him a glimpse into the insecurities of her life. She had bound them in the common human experience of pain and uncertainty, as if there were nothing peculiar and pathetic about his own.

So many people saw him as an object of pity that it had always taken more than usual fortitude not to pity himself – and he had not always been successful, especially at the beginning. He did not pity himself in his loneliness. It was just a fact of his life to which he had adjusted – if one ever adjusted to loneliness.

'I had better go back,' she said. 'After I have been away from David for an hour or two, my heart yearns for him – and what a foolish way of expressing myself. Thank you for walking with me, Mr Butler. This has been a pleasant half hour.'

'Perhaps,' he said, 'if your son is well occupied with the other children and you feel somewhat uncomfortable with being a houseguest here, you would care to walk with me again some other time, Miss Jewell. Perhaps . . . Well, never mind.' He felt suddenly, horribly embarrassed.

'I would,' she said quickly.

'Would you?' He stopped and turned to look at her, deliberately presenting her with a full-face view of himself. 'Tomorrow, perhaps? At the same time? Do you know where I live? The cottage?'

'The pretty thatched one close to the gates?' she asked him.

'Yes,' he said. 'Will you walk that way tomorrow?'

'Yes,' she said.

They looked at each other, and he noticed her teeth sinking into her lower lip.

'Tomorrow, then,' she said, and turned and hurried away barefoot across the sand in the direction of the cliff path.

He watched her go.

. . . *after I have been away from David for an hour or two, my heart yearns for him.*

She had apologized for the sentimentality of the words, spoken of her son. But they echoed in his mind and for a moment he indulged in a waking fantasy without even the excuse of sleep.

What if those words had been spoken of him, Sydnam Butler, instead of David?

. . . *my heart yearns for him.*

CHAPTER 5

The Reverend Charles Lofter and his wife drove into the nearby village the next morning to pay their respects to the vicar. They took Mrs Thompson and their children with them, including ten-year-old Alexander. The Duchess of Bewcastle went calling upon some neighbors with Lord and Lady Aidan, who had met them during a previous visit to Wales. Davy and Becky went too, though both her grace's baby and Lady Aidan's two-year-old daughter, Hannah, remained in the nursery.

Both groups invited David Jewell to accompany them, but he chose to remain behind. Anne found him in the nursery, playing good-naturedly with several of the younger children, who were squabbling fiercely over which of them was to ride on his back next.

'It is Laura's turn,' he was telling Daniel, 'and then Miranda's.'

One of Lord Alleyne's young twins climbed triumphantly on and David crawled across the floor with her, bucking and neighing a couple of times as he went and causing her to squeal and giggle and grasp him more tightly about the neck while Lord Rannulf's Miranda and the other children jumped up and down in anticipation of their next turn.

Ten minutes later he announced that the horse needed its oats and came toward Anne, his hair tousled, his face flushed, his eyes sparkling and happy.

'They wanted me to stay,' he explained, 'and so I did.'

'That was good of you,' she said, pushing back an errant lock of hair from his forehead. Almost immediately it fell back into place again, as it always did. She realized how much it meant to her son, who had always been very much the youngest of all the pupils at the school in Bath, to be the older hero to the little children.

'I am going to play cricket with everyone again this afternoon,' he said. 'Cousin Joshua is teaching me to bowl.'

Cousin Joshua? For a moment Anne felt angry. She had never wanted to acknowledge that relationship between the Marquess of Hallmere and her son, much as she was fond of Joshua and much as she appreciated all he had done for her and continued to do. But she curbed her first instinct, which was to instruct her son rather sharply to call Joshua *Lord Hallmere*. Calling him *Cousin Joshua* had clearly not been David's idea.

'And are you good at it?' Anne asked.

'Not yet,' he admitted. 'But the duchess told me

I had promise after she had hit a four off me, and I shattered the wickets when Lord Rannulf was up at bat, though I think he let me do it.'

'And so,' she said, smiling at him and stooping to pick up Jules Ashford, the toddler son of the Earl of Rosthorn, who was pulling insistently at David's leg, 'you are going to learn how to bowl him out even when he is not letting you, are you?' She held the young child suspended above her head until he giggled, and then lowered him far enough to rub noses with him.

'Mama,' David said, a renewed element of eagerness in his voice. 'Lady Rosthorn is going painting this morning, and she has said I may go with her. She has an easel and paints I can use. May I go? *Please?* And will you come to watch?'

'That is remarkably kind of her,' Anne said, while the child in her arms bounced and giggled and otherwise indicated that he wanted to be lifted into the air again. Anne obliged him and laughed up at him.

David had always loved to draw and paint, and she had always thought him good at it. Mr Upton, art master at Miss Martin's school, insisted that he had real talent that should be nurtured.

'You have made a friend for life, Miss Jewell,' the Earl of Rosthorn said from behind her. 'But he will exhaust you given half a chance. Come here, *mon fils.*'

Jules was already reaching for him.

The countess had come into the nursery with her husband.

'Has your mama given you permission to come and paint, David?' she asked.

'I hope,' Anne said, 'he will be no trouble to you.'

'None whatsoever,' the countess assured her, stooping to pick up her three-year-old, who had come skipping across the nursery to meet her. 'I am delighted to discover a dedicated artist in a young boy. And you, Jacques, my sweetheart, are to go outside with Papa and Jules and Aunt Judith's William to look at the sheep, perhaps even to ride one if Papa can catch one. Will that be fun?'

'Watching me chase after the sheep doubtless will be,' the earl said ruefully.

'You will come with David and me, Miss Jewell?' the countess asked. 'I am going to paint the sea. I persist in believing that one day I will capture the very essence of it, though I have been told that doing so is as impossible as it would be to hold a cupful of it in my bare hand.'

'But you have not been told that by me, *chérie*,' the earl said. 'I have seen you do it with a river – capture the essence of it, that is.'

It was a lovely, sunny morning, and Anne enjoyed herself even though she chose not to paint. The countess set up her easel on the very promontory where Mr Butler had been standing three evenings ago. It seemed a rather bleak setting to Anne, who would have chosen somewhere more picturesque, but the countess explained her choice before sitting down on the coarse grass, clasping her arms about her knees, and withdrawing into a silent world of her own.

'My poor governess used to despair of me,' she said. 'She would find the prettiest parts of the park at Lindsey Hall and instruct me to paint the flowers and the trees and the birds. And then she would hover over me as I painted and disapprove of everything I did while telling me exactly how I ought to be doing it. But painting has nothing to do with prettiness, Miss Jewell, or with following the rules. At least to me it does not. It has to do with getting inside what I see with my eyes to the reality within.'

'To see things as they see themselves,' David said unexpectedly.

'Ah.' The countess laughed. 'You *do* understand, David. Have I chosen a place you would not have chosen for yourself? Have I been very selfish?'

'No, ma'am,' David assured her. 'I can paint anywhere.'

Anne sat basking in the sunshine for what she was sure must have been a couple of hours while her two companions worked in silence.

She was to go walking with Mr Butler again this afternoon, she thought. But this time they had a deliberate assignation. He had asked her and she had agreed. It was surprising that either had happened. She had had the distinct impression just two evenings ago that he did not really like her, though admittedly that was before they had

93

sat and talked with each other for a while. And he was someone with whom she was not physically comfortable even though they had strolled on the beach with each other. It was *not* easy to look at him.

And yet what a conversation they had had! She could hardly believe she had spoken so openly to him about things she usually avoided admitting even to herself.

She rarely thought of herself as lonely.

She was twenty-nine years old. Ten years ago – a little longer than ten actually – she had looked forward to a life of conventional happiness with the man of her choice. She had still believed in happily-ever-after at that time. But then there had been David – and what had preceded David – and her planned future had been in tatters.

For nine years – almost ten – David had been her all in all. He was her present. But he was not her future – she was well aware of that. Was the future so important to her, then, even though it did not really exist except in the imagination? Ought not the present to be enough?

But it was not so much the future that she needed, she realized, as *hope*.

It was her lack of hope that made her lonely and occasionally brought her to the edge of what felt frighteningly like despair.

Would she live out her life at Claudia Martin's school? She loved teaching there. She really did. And she was very fond of all the girls, especially the charity pupils, and of Claudia and Susanna, and the other teachers too to a slightly lesser degree. There was nothing at all bleak about the prospect of spending the rest of her life there.

Except that there was.

Now Mr Butler had invited her to walk with him, and absurdly such a little thing felt like something rather momentous. He, a gentleman, the son of an *earl*, had invited *her* to walk out with him simply because he wished to spend more time with her. There could be no other reason. And she had agreed because *she* wished to spend more time with him.

It was as simple as that.

His looks did not really matter. This was no courtship, after all.

And truth to tell, she felt grateful – even honored – that he had even asked. In ten years no other man had asked her to go walking with him.

David was the first to finish painting. He cleaned his brushes and looked up at Anne.

'Do you want to come and see, Mama?' he asked her.

He had chosen to paint a single rock. It jutted out from the edge of the promontory, Anne could see, and would eventually break away altogether and fall to the beach below. But it still clung to the headland at a slight angle, and plants still grew in its cracks, connecting it to the land. David had painted it in such a way that Anne was made aware of details she had not noticed until now even though she had been sitting idle and with open eyes for a couple of hours. And he had used a multitude of colors to depict what to her unpracticed eye had seemed simply pale gray and green. Many an adult would have been proud to produce such a painting. *She* would have.

'Oh, David,' she said, squeezing his shoulders, 'Mr Upton really is right about you, is he not?'

'But it is so *flat*, Mama,' he protested.

The countess was smiling at them over the top of her easel.

'Miss Jewell,' she said, 'you have been remarkably patient. Your son and I have not been scintillating company, have we? May I see your painting, David?'

She came and looked at it after he had nodded.

'Ah,' she said after staring at it for a whole minute in silence. 'You *do* have an artist's eye. Would you care to see mine?'

David dashed around to her easel and Anne followed.

'Oh, I say!' David said.

They both stood for several silent moments looking at her work.

She had painted the sea, sparkling in the sunshine and reflecting the blue of the sky and the few fluffy clouds that floated across it. But it was not a *pretty* picture, Anne thought. It was not merely a reproduction of the visual reality. It was hard to put into words what it *was*. It somehow took the viewer under the water and up to the

96

sky. Or perhaps it was not even that. It was more as if one were being drawn *into* the water and *into* the sky.

What had David said? *To see things as they see themselves*. How had he known to say that?

'Oh, do look who is coming,' Lady Rosthorn said suddenly, smiling warmly and raising one hand to wave. 'Sydnam, well met.'

Anne turned her head sharply to look, and sure enough Mr Butler was walking along the cliff path, dressed as he had been when she first saw him, with the addition of a hat. He doffed it even as she looked.

David collided hard with her side and shrank half behind her.

'Mama,' he whispered. It was half whimper.

'Good morning, Morgan, Miss Jewell,' he called, staying on the path. 'Is it not a lovely one? I am taking a shortcut back from one of the farms.'

'And we have been painting, as you can see,' Lady Rosthorn told him. 'Do you want to come and point out all the faults in my poor offering?'

It seemed to Anne that he hesitated for a few moments, but then he came. His eye met hers briefly, and she felt an absurd quickening of the pulse, as if they shared a secret. She was to meet him later. They were to go walking alone together.

How foolish to feel as if there *were* some sort of courtship proceeding. And how . . . horrifying.

'When did I ever criticize anything you painted,

97

Morgan?' he asked, coming to stand before her easel while David pulled Anne out of the way. 'I would not so presume.'

'You never did,' she admitted. 'You were always kind and always encouraging. But I was always nervous when you of all people came to take a look.'

'This,' he said after standing in silence for what seemed like a long time, his head bent toward the painting, 'is very good indeed, Morgan. You have grown immensely as an artist since I last saw any of your work.'

Lady Rosthorn smiled and moved closer to him, her head tilted to one side as she looked at the painting.

'Now I can see that perhaps it *does* have some merit,' she said, laughing. 'But I brought out a fellow artist with me this morning. Have you met David Jewell, Miss Jewell's son? David, this is Mr Butler, the duke's steward here and a very dear childhood friend of mine.'

'David,' Mr Butler said, turning to look at him.

'Sir.' David bobbed his head and pressed harder against Anne. 'My painting is no good. I cannot see things that big.' He indicated Lady Rosthorn's painting with one sweep of the hand.

'And I cannot see things that little,' the countess said, nodding in the direction of his own painting. 'But big and little both exist, David, and they both show us the soul of God. I remember you telling me that once, Sydnam, when I was about your

98

age and I was convinced that I could never paint as well as you.'

Ah, Anne thought with an uncomfortable lurching of the stomach as she stared at his back and remembered her impression that his long fingers looked artistic. He really had been a painter, then?

'May I see your painting, David?' Mr Butler asked, and they all moved around to look at it, David still pressed as close to Anne as he could get.

'It is too flat,' David said.

But Mr Butler was examining it in silence as he had done with Lady Rosthorn's.

'Someone has taught you,' he said, 'to use a great variety of colors to produce the one the untutored eye thinks it sees when it looks at any object.'

'Mr Upton,' David said. 'The art master at Mama's school.'

'You have learned the lesson well for one so young,' Mr Butler said. 'If you were to paint this same rock at a different time of day or in different weather, the colors would be different, would they not?'

'And it would look different too,' David said. 'Light is a funny thing. Light is not just light. Mr Upton told me that too. Did you know, sir, that light is like the rainbow all the time – all those colors, even though we cannot see them?'

'Remarkable, is it not?' Mr Butler said. 'It makes us realize that there are all sorts of things – millions of things – around us all the time that we are not aware of because there are limits to our senses. Does that make sense to you?'

'Yes, sir,' David said. 'Sight, touch, smell, sound, and taste – five of them.' He counted them off on the fingers of one hand. 'But maybe there are hundreds more that we do not have. Miss Martin told me that once.'

Mr Butler pointed at the place on the painting where the rock was joined to the rest of the promontory, held there, it seemed, by clumps of grass.

'I like this,' he said. 'That rock is going to fall soon and begin a new phase of its existence down on the beach, but at the moment it is clinging bravely to its life up here, and the life up here is holding on to it as long as it can. How clever of you to notice that. I do not believe I would have. Indeed, I have stood here many times and not noticed.'

What Anne noticed was that David had moved from her side to stand closer to the easel – and Mr Butler.

'I can see the slope of the rock, with a hint of the depths below and the land above,' Mr Butler said. 'The perspective is really quite good. What did you mean when you said your painting was flat?'

'It . . .' For a few moments it seemed as if David could not find the words to explain what he meant. He pointed at the painting and made beckoning gestures with his fingers. 'It just *stays* there. It is *flat.*'

Mr Butler turned to look at him, and Anne was

struck again by his breathtaking good looks – and his kindness in giving time and attention to a child.

'Have you ever painted with oils, David?' he asked.

David shook his head.

'There aren't any at the school,' he said. 'Mr Upton says that only watercolors are suitable for ladies. I am the only boy there.'

'Watercolors are fine for gentlemen too,' Mr Butler said. 'And oils are fine for ladies. Some artists use one or the other. Some use both in different circumstances. But there are some artists who *need* to paint with oils. I believe you may be one of them. Oil paints help to create texture. They help the artist bring the painting off the canvas. They also help one paint with passion, if you are old enough to understand what that means. Perhaps your mama can have a talk with Mr Upton when you return to school to see if there is any chance he can teach you to paint with oils. However, this watercolor is very, very good. Thank you for letting me see it.'

David turned toward Anne, his face beaming.

'Do you think Mr Upton will, Mama?' he asked.

'We will have to talk with him,' she said, smiling down at him and pushing the lock of hair off his forehead again before glancing up to see Mr Butler looking steadily at her.

He took his leave then. He bade them all a good morning, put his hat back on, and touched his hand to the brim.

'Oh, Syd,' Lady Rosthorn said as he made his

way back to the path, 'I *do* wish you could come and paint with us someday.'

He looked back.

'I don't think, Morg,' he said, his tone light, 'Wulfric would be too delighted if I so misused the time for which he is paying me.'

For a few moments as she watched him walk away, Anne wondered what he had done to hurt himself. He was limping. But even as she thought it he adjusted his stride and walked normally.

'Mr Butler,' David said excitedly when he was only just out of earshot, 'is the monster.'

'David!' Anne cried.

The countess set a hand on his shoulder.

'The monster?' she said.

'That is what Alexander calls him,' David told her. 'He says he is monstrously ugly and lies in wait for children on stormy nights to eat out their liver.'

'David,' Anne said sharply. 'Mr Butler is the Duke of Bewcastle's steward. He was a brave soldier in the wars against Napoléon Bonaparte that you have learned of in your history lessons, and he was horribly wounded while fighting. He is a man to be admired, not someone to be turned into a monster.'

'I am only saying what Alexander said,' David protested. 'It was stupid and I will tell him so.'

'I grew up at Lindsey Hall, David,' the countess said as she washed her brushes and tidied up her painting things. 'My brothers and sister and I used to play with the Butler boys from the neighboring

102

estate. I was very much the youngest in my family, and they were usually impatient with me and would have left me behind if they could when they went to play. Kit Butler was my hero because he would usually take me up on his shoulders so that I could keep up with them all. But it was Sydnam who was always most kind to me and most willing to talk to me and listen to me as if I were a real person. He was the one who encouraged me to paint as I wished to paint. When he was brought home from the wars deathly ill and dreadfully maimed, I felt as if a little part of me had died. I thought he would never be the same again, and indeed I was right. He made himself into a new person and came here. Those who did not know him before and those who do not take the time to get to know him now will perhaps always look at him and see a monster. But you and I are artists. We know that the real meaning of things lies deep down and that the real meaning of things is always beautiful because it is simply love.'

'He knows about painting,' David said. 'I wish *he* could show me how to use oil paints. But he cannot, can he? He doesn't have his arm.'

'No, he does not,' the countess said sadly. 'And, oh, dear, we must have been here far too long. Here come Gervase and Joshua to drag us home.'

. . . *the real meaning of things is always beautiful because it is simply love.*

Could that possibly be right? Anne wondered. Was it true?

103

'Well, *chérie*,' the earl called as he came within earshot, 'did you do it this time?' He stepped up to the countess's easel and set one hand on her shoulder.

'Not quite.' She laughed ruefully. 'But I will never stop trying, Gervase.'

She tipped her head sideways and touched her cheek to his hand.

It was a brief gesture and quite unostentatious. But it smote Anne with its suggestion of a close marital relationship.

Joshua meanwhile was complimenting David on his painting and squeezing the back of his neck affectionately.

He walked beside Anne on the way back to the house, carrying David's easel and painting while the boy ran on ahead through the trees and then across the lawn, his arms stretched to the sides, pretending to be a kite in the breeze.

'He says you are going to make him into a formidable bowler at cricket,' she said.

Joshua laughed. 'He will be tolerably competent if he works hard at it,' he said. 'Are you going to join in the game this afternoon, Anne, or are you going to play coward as you did yesterday and hide out on the beach again?'

'I have promised to go walking,' she said.

'Have you, by Jove?' he said. 'With another truant? It cannot be allowed. Give me her name and I will set to work on her.'

'I am going walking with Mr Butler,' she said.

104

'The duke's steward.' Her cheeks felt hot. She hoped it would not be obvious that she was blushing. And why *was* she blushing?

'Indeed?' He looked down at her and kept looking as they walked on in silence.

'Joshua,' she said at last, 'I am merely going for a walk with him. I met him on the beach yesterday and we strolled together for a while. He asked if I wished to do it again today.'

He was smiling at her.

'I wondered why you stayed down on the beach,' he said. 'You had a clandestine tryst there, did you?'

'Nonsense!' She laughed. But she sobered almost immediately. 'I wish you would not encourage David to call you *Cousin Joshua*.'

'You would prefer *sir* or *my lord*, then?' he asked her. 'He *is* my cousin.'

'He is *not*,' she protested.

'Anne,' he said, 'Albert was a black-hearted villain. I am glad for your sake and David's and Prue's that he is dead. But he was my first cousin, and David is his son. I am David's relative, not just any man who has taken an interest in him. Prue and Constance and Chastity are his *aunts* and are very ready to acknowledge the fact. And he needs all the relatives he can get. He has none on your side, has he – none you will allow him to know anyway.'

'Because *they* do not wish to know *him*,' she cried.

105

He sighed. 'I have upset you,' he said. 'I am sorry. I truly am. Freyja assures me that she knows exactly how you must feel and has advised me to respect your wish to raise David alone. But let the child call me Cousin, Anne. All the other children here have someone to call Papa – or Uncle, in Davy's case, since Aidan and Eve have always actively encouraged him to remember his own dead father.'

She might have argued further even though she recognized the sense of what he said – and his kindness in accepting an illegitimate child as a relative. It was just that she could not *bear* to acknowledge that relationship herself. But the Countess of Rosthorn turned her head at that moment to make some remark to them, and they proceeded the rest of the way as a group of four.

CHAPTER 6

Anne watched the cricket game for a few minutes before slipping away to walk down the driveway in the direction of the thatched cottage she had noticed on the day of her arrival. She was not after all, she was relieved to notice, the only one not playing. The duchess was playing a circle game with the infants a little distance away, and the duke was watching her, looking his usual severe self, though he had their son in his arms, wrapped warmly in a blanket. No one seemed particularly to notice Anne's leaving. She hoped Joshua would not draw attention to it.

The very idea of the Bedwyns all knowing where she was going and drawing quite the wrong conclusions was horrifying. This was not a romantic tryst. But surely they would think she was trying to take advantage of a lonely, wounded man.

She turned off the driveway and approached the cottage in some trepidation. Were there servants there? What would they think of a strange woman knocking on the door and asking for Mr Butler?

But she was saved from having to find out. Even before she reached the low stone wall and wooden gate that enclosed a pretty flower garden surrounding the whitewashed cottage, the door opened and he stepped outside.

Anne stopped on the path.

'I wondered if you would come,' he called, coming toward her, opening the gate, and closing it behind him. 'It was presumptuous of me to ask you when you are a guest at the house. And this morning you were with your son and Morgan. Perhaps—'

'I wanted to come,' she said.

'And I wanted you to come.' He smiled uncertainly at her.

She felt suddenly shy with him, as if this were indeed a romantic tryst. How foolishly pathetic they would look to any observer, she thought, hoping no servant was peering through a window. They must look as awkward as any boy and girl half their age.

'Have you seen the valley?' he asked her.

She shook her head. 'Only the park about the house and the cliffs and the beach.'

'It is not the very best time of year to see it,' he said, indicating that they should return to the driveway and cross it to the other side. 'In spring the wild daffodils and bluebells carpeting the ground in the woods make the whole scene magical, and in autumn there is a multicolored roof above one's head and a multicolored carpet beneath one's feet. But it is always lovely, even in winter. Now all is green, but if you have an artist's eye, you will understand that there are so many shades of green that summer trees and grass are a complete and sumptuous feast for the senses without any accompaniment of flowers.'

She could soon see that there was indeed a valley – they walked through a copse of widely spaced trees and shrubs until the land fell away at their feet to reveal a thick forest of trees growing below them.

They scrambled down a long, steep slope, clumps of coarse grass and firm soil and exposed tree roots enabling them to find safe footholds, until they reached the bottom, where a wide, shallow stream gurgled and meandered its way toward the sea. The sea itself was not visible from where they stood, but Anne could smell it. She could also smell the trees and feel the warmth of the summer air, though the branches above her head provided a welcome shade from the bright glare of the sun.

There was an instant feeling of seclusion and peace down here, as if they had come miles from where they had been mere minutes before. The leaves of the trees rustled softly about her.

'It is beautiful,' she said, her hand against the bark of a tree, her head tipped back. She could hear a single seagull calling overhead.

'Wales is a beautiful country,' he told her. 'It is quite different from England here even though most of the landowners in this part are English. There are ancient Celtic history and mysticism and peace and music to be discovered here, Miss Jewell – riches untold. Until you have heard a Welsh man or woman play the harp or until you have heard Welsh voices sing – preferably together in a choir – you cannot claim to know what music can do for the soul. Tudor Rhys, the Welsh minister at the chapel here, is teaching me the language, but it is a long, slow process. It is a complex tongue.'

'I can see,' she said, 'that you have fallen in love with Wales, Mr Butler.'

'I hope to spend the rest of my life here,' he said, 'though not necessarily right here at Glandwr. A man needs a place of his own, a sense of his own belonging. His own home.'

She felt an unexpected wave of longing and pressed her hand hard against the rough bark of the tree.

'And do you have such a place in mind?' she asked him.

'I do.'

She thought for a moment that he would say more, but he did not do so. He turned away so that she could see only the perfect, handsome side of his body. It was too private a subject for him, she thought. She was, after all, just a stranger. But she was envious.

A man needs a place of his own, a sense of his own belonging. His own home.

Yes. A woman needed those things too.

'If we walk along beside the stream,' he said, 'we

will pass beneath the bridge by which you must have approached Glandwr when you came here, and come out onto a small beach that is connected to the larger one at low tide. Would you like to see it?'

'Yes,' she said, and fell into step beside him. 'Oh, I remember the bridge now and the impression I had that it spanned a lovely wooded valley, but I had forgotten. Now here I am in the valley itself.'

For a minute or two their silence was companionable and she was content to let it stretch between them. But she was the one who broke it eventually.

'It was good of you,' she said, 'to spend some time with David this morning. Your comments on his painting meant a great deal to him.'

'For a nine-year-old,' he said, 'he has a remarkable vision and considerable skills. He deserves to be encouraged. But I do not need to tell that to you of all people.'

'You were a painter yourself?' she asked.

She realized even before he answered that it was a question she ought not to have asked – there was a certain stiffening in his manner. But it was too late to recall her words. He took some time to answer.

'I was but am not,' he said then rather curtly. 'I was born right-handed, Miss Jewell.'

The silence resumed, but it was no longer as comfortable as it had been before. Clearly she had intruded too far into his private world – into his

111

private *pain*, she supposed, if the Countess of Rosthorn had spoken truly of his artistic talent. He was right-handed, but no longer had his right hand. He could no longer paint.

He stopped walking suddenly and set his back against a tree. She stopped too, close to the bank of the stream, and looked rather warily up at him. He was gazing off over her head to the opposite slope.

'I am sorry,' she said. 'I ought not to have asked that last question. Please forgive me.'

His gaze lowered to rest on her. 'That is part of the trouble. Miss Jewell,' he said. 'There are so many topics people – especially my loved ones – are afraid to broach with me that nothing is safe except the weather and politics. And even with politics people feel the need to steer clear of some events, like anything to do with the recent wars. Everyone is afraid of hurting me and as a consequence I have become touchy. Because parts of my body have been permanently broken, I must be seen forever, it seems, as a fragile flower.'

'But you are not?' she asked him.

He smiled ruefully.

'Are *you*?' he asked in return. 'Because you have an illegitimate child?'

People did not usually state that fact quite so bluntly in her hearing.

'I asked first.' She stooped to pick up some loose pebbles and lifted one hand high to drop them one at a time with a plop into the water.

'I have learned,' he said, 'that humans can be

remarkably resilient creatures, Miss Jewell. I thought my life was over. When I realized it was not, I *wished* it were for a long time. And I could have gone on wishing it and feeling sorry for myself and drawing the pity of others, and so lived miserably ever after. I chose not to live that way. I took my life in a totally new direction, and have been rather successful at it. I have avoided having anything to do with painting and painters until this morning. It was painful to accept Morgan's invitation to view her painting – excruciatingly so. Even the smell of the paints . . . Well, I survived it, and even felt rather proud of myself as I walked home. I brought all the account books up to date when I got there and wrote a few letters that needed writing. Life goes on, you see.'

'And are you happy most of the time?' she asked him. But he had admitted to being lonely.

'Happy? *Most* of the time? Happiness is always a fleeting thing,' he said. 'It never rests upon anyone as a permanent state, though many of us persist in believing in the foolish idea that if this would just happen or that we would be happy for the rest of our lives. I know moments of happiness just as most other people do. Perhaps I have learned to find it in ways that would pass some people by. I feel the summer heat here at this moment and see the trees and the water and hear that invisible gull overhead. I feel the novelty of having company when I usually come here alone. And this moment brings me happiness.'

113

She felt an unexpected rush of tears to her eyes and turned her head away. He was happy to be here with her. A stranger – a man – was happy to be with *her*.

'Your turn,' he said.

'Oh, I am not fragile,' she said. 'My life changed when David was born, and it is sometimes tempting to think that it was a dreadful change. But he brought a love into my life that was and is so intense that I know myself to be one of the most blessed of mortals. And then, like you, I turned my life in a new direction, with some help, and made a meaningful life for myself at Miss Martin's school. You are right, Mr Butler. We adjust our lives to circumstances and take happiness where it is to be found, even if only in fleeting moments. It is either that or miss our chance to welcome grace into our lives. This *is* a happy moment. I will remember it.'

'*To welcome grace into our lives,*' he said softly. 'And I will remember that phrase. I like it.'

She rubbed her hands together to rid them of the particles of soil she had picked up with the pebbles and lifted her head to smile up at him.

'Did you love his father?' he asked.

She felt an almost physical shock at the words. She closed her eyes and felt slightly dizzy. Now he had intruded upon her private world – her private pain. Perhaps it was a fair exchange.

'No,' she said. 'No, I did not. I hated him. God help me, I hated him.'

'Where is he?' he asked.

'Dead.'

She had never ever been able to feel one moment's sorrow over that fact – or one pang of guilt over the fact that she may have been in some small way to blame.

'Shall we continue on our way?' he suggested, pushing away from the tree.

'Yes.'

It was a relief to walk again, and she could see the bridge and the end of the valley ahead and the grassy dunes that separated it from the beach.

They admired the three stone arches that supported the bridge as they passed beneath it and a few minutes later waded over the grassy sand dunes to the harder, more level sand of the small beach, which was enclosed by cliffs that drew the eye ahead to the blue, foam-flecked sea and upward to the paler blue of the sky. The stream had separated into many strands around the dunes and flowed in little runnels down the beach to the sea.

Yesterday, Anne thought, they had admitted their loneliness to each other. Today they had denied their fragility. Yesterday they had spoken the truth. Today, she suspected, they had both lied.

They were both fragile. He would never again paint. She would never have a husband and home and more children of her own.

'One cannot dwell upon what is forever lost,' he

said as if his thoughts had been following a parallel path to hers. 'I cannot grow back my eye and my arm just as you cannot get back your innocence or your reputation in the eyes of society. I have gained something that *was* possible for me, though. I have made myself into the best steward in all of Britain. Have you made yourself into the best teacher?'

He turned to look at her and she could see that his lips were drawn up into that strangely attractive, lopsided grin again.

'In Britain?' She set one hand over her heart and looked at him in mock horror. 'I would disdain to set my goals so low, Mr Butler. I have made myself into the *world's* best teacher.'

They both laughed at the silly joke – and she felt a sudden, totally startling sexual awareness of him.

She turned and ran lightly down the beach, stopping only when her feet threatened to sink into the wet sand left behind by the receding tide. She was seriously discomposed by her feelings. She usually had far better control over them. And to have such feelings for *him* – for Mr Butler! She still found it hard to look directly at him.

He had come after her, she realized. She turned her head to smile at him.

'Listen!' she said.

'Some people do not even hear it,' he said after a few silent moments. 'The elemental roar of the sea can easily be mistaken for silence.'

They stood side by side listening intently.

But after a while it seemed to Anne that it was her heartbeat she heard.

Or his.

And she was terribly aware that she was alive. Not just living and breathing, but . . . *alive*.

Sydnam found her company both exhilarating and disturbing.

She asked some very direct questions, ones that his family and close friends carefully avoided, and ones that even in his thoughts he skirted around whenever possible. But he had asked her some rather personal questions too. He supposed that those who knew her avoided asking about the father of her child.

She had hated the man.

Had she been raped, then? Or did she hate him because he had refused to marry her after impregnating her?

She was beautiful beyond belief, especially when she smiled or was lost in the loveliness of her surroundings. Yet she was with *him*. He had asked her to come walking and she had said yes. When he was with her he almost forgot what she had to look at when she looked at him. With her he felt . . . undamaged.

Looking at her, it was hard to realize that in her own way she was as damaged and as vulnerable as he. He turned his head and watched the waves break into foam at the edge of the beach and

117

then get sucked back by the force of the ebbing tide.

Was he vulnerable, then? He had spent the past six or seven years making very sure that he was strong in every way possible. But in some ways he knew very well that he had not fully succeeded and never would. He had admitted to loneliness, had he not? Despite fulfilling work and several good friends, he was essentially lonely. Just as she was. And one reason why he liked living here was that he met very few strangers. Looking as he did, it was impossible not to cringe from the look in the eyes of strangers when they saw him for the first time.

While he was enjoying feasting his eyes on a lovely woman, she must look at least occasionally at monstrous ugliness. He had never been conceited about his good looks, but . . . Well.

'When the tide is fully out,' he told her before he could be consumed by the dreaded self-pity, pointing to their right, 'it is possible to walk around the end of those jutting rocks to the main beach. But as the tide is now, this area is cut off and secluded.'

'All this reminds me very much of Cornwall,' she said. 'Every mile of the coastline reveals a new and quite different splendor. If we were to climb up on those rocks, would we be able to see the other beach?'

'Yes, but they are high and rather rugged,' he warned.

She laughed.

'That sounds like a challenge,' she said, and strode toward them.

He always enjoyed clambering over the rocks, sometimes with the sea on three sides of him while he gazed at the panoramic view or searched the pools the high tides had left behind for shellfish and other marine life. He liked to challenge himself, climbing out where the absence of one arm and eye and the presence of a somewhat weak knee made progress difficult, even hazardous.

Some things were now impossible to him. But they had to be undeniably impossible, and not just improbable, before he would give up on them.

Painting was one impossibility.

Rock climbing was not.

'Oh, look!' she said when they were up on the rocks, well above the level of the small beach but not yet high enough to see over the top. She had noticed a cluster of seashells in a small sandy indentation at her feet and was stooping to examine and pick up a few of them. She set one on her palm and held it out for him to see. 'Could anything possibly be more exquisite?'

'I cannot think of anything,' he admitted.

'Is not nature a marvel?' she said, sitting down on a flat-topped rock and arranging the shells on her knee.

'Always,' he agreed, 'even when its effects are catastrophic to the humans who have tried to control or defy it. It is the quintessentially perfect

119

artist and can also produce something as fragile and exquisite as these.'

He seated himself on a rock close to hers and looked down at the beach with the valley above it. Why would anyone choose to live inland when they could live close to the sea?

They sat in silence for a while, the sun warm on their heads, the breeze cool on their faces. How lovely it was, he thought, to have a companion here with him. And it struck him that though he had friends in the neighborhood, he never went walking or even riding with any of them. Whenever he came here, he was always alone – until now.

But in the future he would always remember that she had been here with him. He would remember her as she was at this moment, the brim of her bonnet fluttering slightly in the breeze, her posture graceful but relaxed, her long, slim fingers touching one of the shells almost reverently, the rocks behind one of her shoulders, the sea beyond the other, one shade darker than her dress – the same dress she had worn yesterday.

She lifted her head and met his gaze.

'How did it happen?' she asked him.

The question could have referred to any number of things. But he knew exactly what she was asking.

'I was an officer,' he said, 'in the Peninsula Wars.'

'Yes,' she said. 'I knew that.'

He looked away from her.

'It was torture,' he said. 'I was on a special mission

with my brother and we were trapped in the mountains by a French scouting party. There was the possibility that one of us could escape with the important papers we carried if the other acted as a decoy and courted certain capture. Kit was experienced while I was decidedly not. *And* he was my superior officer. I volunteered to be the decoy so that he would not have the painful duty of ordering me to do so. We were not in uniform.'

And that fact had made all the difference, of course. If he had been wearing a uniform, he would have been treated with courtesy and honor as a British officer by his captors.

One of her fingers was smoothing over the shell she had held up for his inspection.

'They wanted information about Kit and his mission,' he told her, 'and they set out methodically over the next week or so to get it from me. They started with my right eye and worked their way down. Kit and a group of Spanish partisans rescued me when they had reached my knee.'

'They were still torturing you,' she said. It was not a question. 'You had not given them the information they needed, then?'

'No,' he said.

Her fingers curled about all the shells and held them enclosed in a white-knuckled fist on her knee.

'You are incredibly brave,' she said.

Her praise warmed him. He had been expecting her to say something like – *oh, you poor man.* It was

121

the usual reaction. It had been his family's reaction. Kit had spent years tormenting himself and blaming himself.

'More stubborn than brave,' he said. 'I was the youngest of three brothers, the quiet, sensitive one among two vigorous, boisterous siblings. I wanted to prove something when I insisted that my father buy my commission. Sometimes we get more than we wish for, Miss Jewell. I was indeed given the chance to prove something and I did – but at rather a high cost.'

'They must be proud of you,' she said. 'Your family.'

'Yes,' he agreed.

'But you did not stay with them?' she asked him.

'Families are wonderful institutions,' he said. 'I value mine more than I can possibly say. But each of us has an individual life to live, our own path to tread, our own destiny to forge. You can imagine, if you will, how my family wished to shelter and protect me and do my living for me so that I would never again know fear or pain or abandonment. Eventually I had to step clear of them – or I might have fallen into the temptation of allowing them to do just that.'

She opened her hand to reveal the shells again, and he reached over to take them from her and set them carefully in a pocket of his coat.

'Do you have a family?' he asked her.

'Yes,' she said.

'Ah, then you know what I mean,' he said.

'I have not seen any of them for more than ten years,' she told him.

Had she not said her son was nine years old? There was clearly a connection.

'They rejected you?' he asked her.

'No,' she said. 'They forgave me.'

There was a silence between them while a pair of gulls cried loudly overhead and then landed on the rocks not far away and pecked at something they found there.

'*Forgave?*' he asked softly.

'I was with child,' she said, 'but I was unmarried. I was a fallen woman, Mr Butler. And an embarrassment, at the very least.' She was clasping her raised knees now and gazing off at the horizon.

To her family? Their own embarrassment meant more to them than she did?

'But they must have wanted you to come home if they had forgiven you,' he said. 'Surely?'

'They have never once mentioned David in any of the letters they have written,' she said. 'Presumably they understand that if ever I were to go home he would go with me. They have never extended an invitation.'

'And you have not thought of going anyway?' he asked. 'Perhaps one does not need an invitation to go home. Perhaps they would be pleased if you took the initiative.'

'I have no wish to go there,' she said. 'It is no longer home. That is just a habit of language. Miss Martin's school is home.'

No. A workplace, no matter how pleasant, could never be home. Glandwr was not his. He doubted the school was hers. Like him, she had no home of her own. But at least he had hopes of acquiring one and the wherewithal to do so.

'What happened?' He almost reached across to set his hand on her arm, but he stopped himself just in time. She certainly would not appreciate his touch.

'I was governess to Lady Prudence Moore at Penhallow in Cornwall,' she said. 'She was the sweetest, sunniest-natured young child anyone could hope to meet – living in the body of a growing girl. Her brother was doing his best to – to *interfere* with her, and I knew there was no point in appealing to the marquess, her father, who lived in a world of his own, or to her mother, who doted on her son and hated her daughter for being simple-minded. Her sisters were powerless though they loved her. And Joshua – the present marquess, her cousin – was living in the village some distance away and came only once a week to visit Prue. I lured Albert away from her. I wanted desperately to save her. I thought I could deal with him myself. But I could not.'

For a few moments she rested her forehead against her knees and stopped talking – though really she did not need to say any more.

'David was the result,' she said, lifting her head. 'I wish . . . oh, I *wish* he had not come of such ugliness.'

Again he wanted to touch her but did not.

'I will say what you said to me,' he said. 'You are incredibly brave.'

'Just foolish,' she said. 'Just one of numerous women who believe they can reason with such men and change them. Some women even marry them believing that. I was saved from that fate at least.'

And yet, Sydnam realized, if the bounder had married her, her son would now be Marquess of Hallmere, and she would be the widowed marchioness, someone of considerable social significance and wealth.

'But the child was saved,' he said. 'Lady Prudence Moore, I mean.'

She smiled rather wanly out to sea. 'She married a fisherman a few years ago,' she said, 'and has two sturdy sons. She writes me sometimes, helped by her sister. She writes with impeccable correctness in a large, childish hand. And if there is a type of happiness that is prolonged, Mr Butler, then she is living it.'

'Because of you,' he said.

She got abruptly to her feet and brushed sand off her skirt. He got up too, but his preoccupation with her painful story had made him careless. His right knee gave out from under him and he had to twist sharply in order to use his left arm to save himself from falling. It was an awkward, undignified moment that embarrassed him. And even as he straightened up he was aware of the hand she had stretched out to steady him – though she had not actually touched him.

They gazed into each other's eyes, uncomfortably close together.

'Clumsy of me,' he said.

She lowered her hand to her side.

'When I decided to climb up here,' she said, 'I did not think . . .' Her teeth sank into her lower lip.

'I am glad you did not,' he said quickly. 'We are both maimed, Miss Jewell. But we both know the importance of refusing to live as cripples.'

She did something then that took him so much by surprise that he stood rooted to the spot, high on the rocks that divided the beaches, one foot slightly above the level of the other. She lifted her hand again and set her fingertips against his left cheek.

'We have both learned to see to the very heart of pain, Mr Butler,' she said. 'And so we have both changed – for the better, I believe. We are not cripples. We are survivors.'

She seemed to realize then what she had done, and even in the shade provided by the brim of her bonnet he could see her flush as she removed her hand hastily and rather jerkily.

'Has there been any man since – since Moore?' he asked her.

She shook her head quickly.

'No,' she said. And then after a brief pause, 'Has there been any woman since your . . . I cannot call it an accident, can I?'

126

'No,' he said. 'None.'

Awareness of their long, lonely celibacy pulsed between them, though neither of them put it into words. How could they? They were still virtually strangers to each other – and a man and a woman.

The embarrassment of their shared awareness of such an intimate thing took her suddenly and she turned and scrambled upward again until she stood on the crest of the rocks and looked over to the other side, one hand shading her eyes. He stood where he was for a few moments before going after her.

It was impossible to hide from himself the knowledge that there had been some revulsion in her hasty withdrawal of her hand from his cheek.

He must not even begin to think that because she was as lonely – and as sexually deprived – as he they could therefore . . .

He could never subject any woman to that.

And perhaps she was too damaged to have anything to offer another man.

He climbed up after her and stood beside her, not too close.

'It is awe-inspiring,' she said, gazing along the length of the main beach on which they had strolled the day before. And yet he sensed that she spoke the words that seemed appropriate to the view rather than ones that were deep-felt.

'It is,' he agreed. He had always wished he had two eyes with which to see it. But one was better than none.

The tide was almost fully out. Already it would be possible to walk about the end of the outcropping of rock on which they stood. They could have avoided the climb if they had waited.

'We can go down to the beach or back the way we came,' he said, 'or we can climb to our right and get back up onto the cliff top that way. It is not a difficult climb. The choice is yours.'

When she looked at him this time, her eyes focused somewhere on a level with his chin rather than into his eye.

'It must be getting late,' she said, her voice cheerful – and impersonal. 'I suppose we ought to go back by the quickest route. I have been totally unaware of passing time. I have enjoyed this afternoon very much, Mr Butler. Thank you.'

Something irretrievable had gone from an afternoon that had seemed magical to him in many ways.

They had come too close to each other in the sharing of their stories. For a moment perhaps they had both mistaken a friendly sympathy for a physical closeness – until she had touched him and realized the impossibility of it all. And until she had touched him and he had realized how very wounded she was, how impossible it was for him to take her on emotionally even if he had been offered the chance.

He turned without another word and led the way to the cliff top and then along the footpath to the main driveway just below the cottage. They did very little talking on the way.

'I'll walk up to the house with you,' he said when they drew level with the cottage.

'Oh, there is no need,' she assured him. 'You would have to walk all the way back again.'

They stopped and looked politely and cheerfully at each other, like two strangers who had talked for a while but had nothing left to say and were eager to exchange goodbyes and go their separate ways.

And really, that was all they were – strangers.

'Thank you for coming,' he said. 'I have enjoyed the afternoon. I hope you enjoy the rest of your month here. I will not say goodbye. I daresay we will see each other again before you return to Bath.'

'Yes.' She smiled at his chin. 'I suppose we will. Thank you for showing me places I have not seen before.'

And then she turned rather abruptly and strode off up the driveway in the direction of the house.

Sydnam stood looking after her, feeling an unwelcome dejection. She was merely a guest at the house, someone who had touched his life briefly and was now gone again. His life would not change because of his five brief encounters with her – and perhaps as many more before she returned to Bath.

But he ought not, perhaps, to have walked with her yesterday or invited her to walk with him today. He would not do it again. He did not want to go doing anything stupid, like falling in love with her.

He shook his head as if to clear it of such thoughts as she disappeared from view around a bend without looking back. He turned his steps in the direction of the cottage.

He set his hand in his pocket, remembering that her shells were still there. His fingers curled about them.

CHAPTER 7

More than a week passed before Anne saw Sydnam Butler again – except for a brief glimpse one afternoon when she was returning to the house after a stroll outdoors with David. He was standing on the terrace some distance beyond the front doors, in conversation with the Duke of Bewcastle. His grace inclined his head in their direction and Mr Butler, on whose blind side they had been approaching, swiveled right about to see them and also made them a little bow before turning back to his conversation.

She also heard that Lord Alleyne, Lord Rannulf, and Lady Hallmere had gone riding with him one afternoon, and was amazed to learn that he could ride. But she ought not to have been surprised, she admitted to herself. He was a man who fought his disabilities in almost every way imaginable – except his disability to paint. She wondered if there was any possibility that he could fight that battle too and win. But probably not. Some things were simply impossible.

It was not an unpleasant week despite the fact

that she was not allowed to remain in the nursery area as a sort of governess but was drawn into the very thick of the daily activities with everyone else, adults and children alike. They all spent a great deal of time out of doors – walking, playing cricket and other ball games, swimming, boating, building sandcastles on the beach, climbing trees, playing hide-and-seek among them, climbing the lower reaches of the cliffs, having picnics.

The Earl of Rosthorn explained to her one day that most of their lives were necessarily busy through much of the year – he and Joshua and the duke, for example, were members of the House of Lords – and kept them from their children and even their spouses for long hours at a time. When they did have free time, then, as they did now in the summer, they spent it together as families and played hard.

David was happier than Anne had ever seen him. And she was surprised to discover that he could be as boisterous and demanding and mischievous as any of the others. Indeed, if the trio of Davy, Alexander, and David had a leader, it was usually David. Becky, Davy's sister, adored him. So did all the younger children, with whom he always had the patience to play. He adored Joshua – and Lord Rannulf and Lord Alleyne and all the other gentlemen too, to an only slightly lesser degree. He was in awe of the Duke of Bewcastle, it was true, but Anne spied him one day practicing lifting an imaginary quizzing glass to his eye while examining his aloof, haughty expression in the looking glass in his room, and it was perfectly obvious whom he was trying to imitate.

For his sake she wished the holiday need never end.

On her own account Anne was content to let the month run its course. Lady Aidan and Mrs Pritchard, her aunt, became Anne's particular friends, as did the duchess, who as a former teacher herself liked to talk to Anne about school. And Miss Thompson, the duchess's bookish sister, also drew Anne into lengthy discussions of books and educational theory and proved herself to be both an intelligent and an interesting – even humorous – conversationalist. Indeed, there was no one who was *not* amiable to her. Even the duke engaged her in conversation for a full half hour one evening after discovering that she had read a book he had just finished.

But contrarily she felt her aloneness far more acutely here at Glandwr than she had ever felt it at Claudia's school in Bath. For one thing she felt like an impostor, even though everyone here must know exactly who and what she was. For another, all the other younger people had partners, with the exception of Miss Thompson, who seemed content in her spinsterhood. One night, when Anne was standing at her bedchamber window, brushing her hair and gazing out onto the moonlit garden and the sea beyond, she became aware of a couple strolling across the lawn away from the house in the direction of the cliffs, his arm about her shoulders, hers about his waist, and realized with something of a shock that they were the duke and duchess.

The stabbing of envy she felt was quite involuntary and quite acute. And her aloneness was exposed for what it was at that moment – raw loneliness for a man in her life.

She thought briefly of Mr Butler, but she dismissed the memory of him. She had liked him, and she thought he had liked her. But she had touched him up there on the rocks between the beaches without at all knowing she was about to do so. She had felt the instant stiffening of his body and seen the look of shock on his face – and she had felt an answering shock and incipient panic in herself when she saw her fingertips resting against his cheek and felt the warmth of his sun-heated skin.

But for one mindless moment before that she had felt a yearning so intense that it had been like a stabbing of near-pain down through her body, setting her throat to aching and her breasts to tightening and her womb to throbbing and her inner thighs to pulsing with raw sensitivity. She had recognized her feelings for the sexual desire they were, of course.

And only one short moment later part of her had recoiled. The other side of his face, so close to where her fingers had rested, was purplish and nerveless. He had no eye. He had no arm. Who knew what other disfigurements lay beneath his clothing?

She dismissed him from her mind – but even so she found herself thinking occasionally about how he had acquired those dreadful wounds. It happend at night, sometimes keeping her awake, sometimes weaving its ways into her dreams.

Finally, though, they did meet once more. The duke and duchess had invited guests from the neighborhood to dine one evening, and when Anne went down to the drawing room, clad again in her best green silk, her hair elaborately piled and curled by an enthusiastic Glenys, one of the first people she saw on the far side of the room, in conversation with Lord and Lady Aidan, was Mr Butler.

Her heart leapt with a gladness that seemed quite in excess of the circumstances. The last time they met he had recoiled from her – and she from him.

Mrs Pritchard invited Anne to sit down beside her, and Anne was glad to do so, since she had not met any of the neighbors and was extremely nervous about doing so. She would have avoided coming down this evening altogether if the duchess had not pointedly invited her.

Introductions were not to be avoided, of course, after the guests began arriving. There were a few English landowners with their wives and older children, a couple of the duke's tenants with their wives, the vicar and his wife and son and daughter, and the Welsh minister and the village school-master, both of whom spoke English with such pronounced Welsh accents that Anne had to listen carefully in order to understand them. Though she had had some practice – Mrs Pritchard spoke with almost as thick an accent.

And then dinner was announced – and it was Mr Butler who had been appointed to lead Anne in and to seat her at his left side.

She smiled uncertainly at him as she took his offered arm, and he smiled back at her.

She felt curiously like crying – and curiously like laughing with joy.

She *had* missed him. She had told him more of her inner self than she had told even Claudia or Susanna or Frances. He had confided some of his deepest self in her. But he had been content to let more than a week go by without making any attempt to see her again.

What had she expected?

That he would *court* her?

He had said during their walk together that humans can be remarkably resilient creatures. Anne saw the truth of that statement as she observed the way he used his fork in his left hand to cut his food and convey it to his mouth with deft movements that bordered on elegance and the way in which he turned his head without any apparent awkwardness to look at Lady Hallmere on his blind side while he conversed with her.

He spoke with Lady Hallmere through much of

the meal – but perhaps only because Anne had given her attention to Mr Jones, the village school-master, almost as soon as he sat beside her. He was interested to know that she too was a teacher. Most teachers in Wales, he explained to her, were male.

She felt strangely self-conscious with Mr Butler – perhaps because their conversations with each other had bordered upon intimacy. How many near-strangers admitted to each other that they were lonely, that there had been no one of the opposite sex in their lives for years and years?

Inevitably, though, as good manners dictated, Lady Hallmere turned toward one of the English landowners on her other side and Mr Jones turned toward Mrs Lofter on his.

'Miss Jewell,' Mr Butler asked politely, 'are you and your son enjoying your stay at Glandwr?'

'Enormously,' she said. 'Thank you.'

'And has he done more painting?'

'Yes,' she said. 'Twice, both times with Lady Rosthorn.'

'I am delighted to hear it,' he said. 'Did you know there is to be entertainment this evening?'

'Yes,' she said. 'Lady Rannulf is going to act. Apparently she is very good at it. And Joshua and Lady Hallmere are going to sing a duet even though Lady Hallmere was *very* belligerent when everyone was trying to persuade her. It was only when Joshua commented that no one was going to be allowed to bully his wife when he was there to protect her that she bristled with indignation at *him* and agreed to do it. She did not see the winks he exchanged with her brothers.'

Mr Butler laughed and she joined him.

'It has always amazed me,' he said, lowering his voice, 'that Hallmere seems to know just how to handle Freyja. She was always a hellion and a spitfire. There is to be another duet too tonight. Huw Llwyd is to sing while his wife accompanies him on the harp.'

Mr and Mrs Llwyd were the duke's tenants, a youngish couple.

'They are good?' Anne asked.

He set his spoon down in his empty dish and tapped two fingers over his heart.

'Their music comes in through the ears,' he said, 'but it lodges here. You will know what I mean when you have heard them.'

'I look forward to doing so, then,' she said.

'What you ought to hear,' he said, 'is the congregation of the Welsh chapel singing hymns on a Sunday morning. They come close to raising the roof off the building, though not with indiscriminate noise. They sing in four-part harmony without ever coming together during the week to rehearse. It is quite extraordinary.'

'It must be indeed,' Anne said with feeling.

'I would like to take you there next Sunday,' he said. 'If you can bear the prospect of not understanding a word of the service, that is. It is all in Welsh. But the *music*!'

Anne had gone to church the previous Sunday, as she did almost every week. But she had gone to the English church with the Bedwyn family. She had sat in the special padded pews set aside for them at the front of the church. Many of the other pews, she had noticed, were empty.

'I should like to go,' she said.

'Would you?' He looked up from the plate of fruit and cheese a footman had set before him and focused full on her. 'Will you walk by the cottage on Sunday morning, then, and we will go together?'

'Yes,' she said. 'Thank you.'

And suddenly she felt breathless, as if they had made some sort of secret assignation. She had agreed to go to *church* with him, that was all. But what would everyone think of her? And why should it matter what anyone thought? She *wanted* to go.

And he was looking at her, she thought, as if *he* wanted it too.

Lady Hallmere claimed his attention again at that moment and soon Mr Jones turned back to Anne, and they conversed for a few minutes before the duchess got to her feet and invited the ladies to follow her to the drawing room while the gentlemen remained behind to enjoy their port.

More than half an hour passed before the gentlemen joined the ladies. Anne felt almost annoyed with herself when she realized that her eyes had gone immediately in search of Mr Butler among them. It was no big thing, after all, that he had invited her to attend the Welsh church with him on Sunday so that she might hear Welsh singing for herself.

Except that it was.

She felt stupidly like a girl again, being singled out for a gentleman's attention. It *was* stupid. She was twenty-nine years old and this was nothing remotely connected to courtship. But until less than two weeks ago she had not stepped out with a man, even in simple friendship, since Henry Arnold. And that was a whole lifetime ago.

She had offered to sit behind the tea tray, pouring tea, and the duchess had accepted her offer. But she was not so busy that she could not observe the way people gathered into conversational groups – the wealthier English landowners with the Bedwyns, Mrs Llwyd with Mrs Pritchard and Mrs Thompson, the vicar and his wife with Baron Weston and Miss Thompson, Mr Llwyd, Mr Jones, Mr Rhys – the Welsh minister – with Mr Butler and the Duke of Bewcastle. The duchess moved from group to group, drawing smiles wherever she went.

Mr Butler was deep in conversation and did not once glance Anne's way – she was on his blind side. But later, after she had got to her feet and brushed her hands over her skirt during the bustle of the removal of the tea tray, she found that he was standing beside her.

'Shall we sit together, Miss Jewell?' he suggested. 'Unless you have other plans, that is.'

140

'No.' She smiled at him. 'Thank you.'

And so she had all the pleasure of observing and listening to the entertainment in company with a gentleman who was not also someone else's husband. It felt absurdly exhilarating.

Joshua and Lady Hallmere sang a few English folk songs first, with Joshua accompanying them on the pianoforte. They were surprisingly good, though Lady Hallmere began with a disclaimer.

'I have absolutely insisted that we be the opening act,' she explained to the audience. 'I have a strong suspicion that the others are going to be vastly superior – I *know* Judith will be – and I have no wish to be forced to follow them.'

Joshua, at the pianoforte, grinned while the audience laughed.

One could not help liking Lady Hallmere, Anne thought, for all her prickly ways.

'Just sing, Free, and put us out of our misery,' Lord Alleyne called out.

Mrs Llwyd – a small, dark-haired, very Celtic-looking lady – played next on her large, beautifully carved harp, and Anne soon found herself blinking away unshed tears and feeling as if she had been transported into another world and another culture, so beautiful was the music she produced.

'It always seems to me,' Mr Butler said softly, leaning toward Anne during the short pause between pieces, 'that the harp somehow captures the very soul of Wales.'

'Yes,' she said. 'Oh, yes, you must be right.'

And then Mr Llwyd got to his feet and sang to his wife's accompaniment in a light, pleasant tenor voice to which Anne could have listened all night though he sang in Welsh and she did not understand a single word.

She felt rather sorry for Lady Rannulf, who was to conclude the entertainment. Lady Hallmere was the wise one in having insisted upon going first.

Lady Rannulf was extremely beautiful, with a full, voluptuous figure and glorious red hair. But the idea of her acting alone, without any supporting characters, somehow embarrassed Anne even though she had been told that the lady was a good actress.

'I hope,' Mr Butler said, 'she does Lady Macbeth. I have seen her do it before, and she is quite extraordinary.'

She played Desdemona first, her hair down, her elegant green evening gown somehow transforming itself into a nightgown purely through the power of suggestion as Desdemona waited in bewilderment and misplaced trust for Othello to come to her in her bedchamber and then pleaded her case with him and begged for her very life.

It truly was extraordinary, Anne agreed, how she gave the impression that her maid and, later, Othello were there in her bedchamber with her and yet carried the scene alone. It was more than extraordinary how she lost all resemblance to the

Lady Rannulf Anne had known for almost two weeks and became the innocent, loving, loyal, frightened, but dignified wife of Othello.

The return to reality when the scene was over was disorienting for a moment.

And then, at the special request of the Duke of Bewcastle, Lady Rannulf did indeed play the part of Lady Macbeth, also with hair loose and dress become nightgown – also a night scene. But there the resemblance between the two scenes and characters – and even the actress herself – ended. She became the powerful, ruthless, mad, tormented Lady Macbeth, sleepwalking and trying desperately to wash away the blood of her guilt. Anne found herself sitting forward on her chair, her eyes fixed on the lady's hands, as if she really expected to see the blood of King Duncan dripping from them.

She was, she realized as she applauded enthusiastically with everyone else, in the presence of greatness.

Mr Butler was looking expectantly at her.

'Well?' he said.

'I have not been so well entertained for a long time,' she told him.

He laughed. 'I thought perhaps you would admit that you have *never* been so well entertained,' he said.

'I have a friend,' she explained, 'who has become all the rage throughout Europe. She has the most glorious soprano voice I have ever heard.

She taught at Miss Martin's school until just two years ago.'

'And she is?' he asked.

'The Countess of Edgecombe,' she said. 'She was Frances Allard before she married Viscount Sinclair, now the earl.'

'Ah,' he said, 'you mentioned her before, and I believe I had heard of her before that. But I have never had the pleasure of listening to her sing.'

'If you ever *do* have the chance,' she said, 'you must not miss it.'

'I will not.' He smiled again while all about them family and guests were getting to their feet and conversing and laughing, the formal entertainment at an end.

'There is to be dancing,' he said. 'It is my cue, I believe, to return home.'

'Oh,' she said before she could stop herself, 'please do not leave yet.'

The carpet was being rolled up from the drawing room floor and the French windows at one end of it thrown back, since the room had grown stuffy. Mrs Lofter was taking her place at the pianoforte, having offered earlier in the day to play. It had been the duchess's idea that some informal country dancing would be a more pleasant way of ending the evening than playing cards would be, though a couple of tables were being set up for the older people.

Anne felt instantly embarrassed. What if he had

been waiting for some excuse to get away from the gathering – and from her?

'Must I sit and watch you dance, then?' he asked, smiling at her. 'I would be envious of your partners, Miss Jewell.'

It was the first thing he had said to her that was remotely flirtatious.

'But I have no wish to dance,' she said, not quite truthfully. 'We will sit and talk, if you wish. Unless, that is, you have your heart set upon returning home.'

'What I do have my heart set upon,' he said, 'is drawing some cool night air into my lungs. Would you care to step outside, Miss Jewell, to see how brightly the moon shines tonight?'

How foolish they had been, she thought, getting to her feet, to have wasted more than a week of days during which they might have met occasionally and walked and conversed together. But at least there was this evening – and there would be Sunday morning to look forward to.

'Yes, I would,' she said. 'May I run and fetch a shawl?'

A few minutes later they stepped out through the French windows while the card players settled into a game and two lines of dancers were forming amid a great deal of noise and merriment. No one would have noticed them leave, Anne thought.

'Ah,' Mr Butler said, standing still and looking upward. 'I thought it would be a bright night. There is not a cloud in the sky, and see – the moon is almost at the full.'

145

'With a million stars to supplement its light,' she said. 'Why is it we are not constantly awed by the size and majesty of the universe?'

'Habit,' he said. 'We are accustomed to it. I suppose if we had been blind from birth – in *both* eyes – and could suddenly see, we would be so overwhelmed by a night like this that we would either gaze upward at it until dawn or else cling to the earth, afraid that we were about to fall off. Or perhaps we would simply assume that we were at the center of it all and the lords of all we beheld.'

The air was deliciously cool after the heat of the day. Anne let her shawl fall to her elbows and drew in a deep breath of the slightly salt air.

'What a good idea of yours,' she said, 'to step out here.'

'If you want a night view that will truly awe you,' he said, 'you should climb to the top of the hill over there. Have you been up it in the daytime?'

The hill to which he pointed was part of the park, but it was also part of the cliff-top scenery, a rise of land that was covered with gorse bushes and wildflowers and grass. None of the walks and games had ever taken Anne actually to it, but she had often admired it and thought she must go there alone or with David one day before they left.

'No,' she said, 'but I can believe there is a lovely view from up there.'

He looked down at her evening slippers. 'Is it too far to go now?'

It struck her suddenly that perhaps it was too far for a single lady to go with a single gentleman at night, but she dismissed the thought. She was twenty-nine years old and an independent woman. She was no delicate young girl to be hedged about by propriety and chaperones.

'It is not,' she said.

They walked slowly, talking as they went. It had not occurred to either of them to bring a lantern, but it would have been quite superfluous anyway. It was one of those nights that are almost as bright as day. The hill was higher and steeper than it looked. By the time they had scrambled to the top Anne was breathless, and the soles of her feet were smarting from having stepped on a few jagged stones with only her thin evening slippers for protection. But she knew immediately that the climb had been worth the effort and the pain.

'Oh, look!' she said as she did just that herself.

But Mr Butler was looking at her, the breeze, which was stronger up here, ruffling his hair.

'I knew you would be impressed,' he said.

Even at this time of night she could see that there was land visible for miles about, slumbering peacefully under a summer sky. But it was the sea that drew her attention. It stretched below them in a huge arc, faintly silver in the light from above, one wide band of moonlight stretched across it from horizon to shore. The long outcropping of land to the right jutted into the middle of the moonbeam, looking very black in contrast, and more than ever like a roaring dragon. From this high up the sea beyond it was visible too.

'One cannot help but admire that dragon,' she said, pointing. 'It is roaring defiance to the whole ocean, not at all intimidated by the sheer size and power of it.'

'We could all learn a lesson from it,' he said, laughing. 'Can there be a lovelier view anywhere?'

'I doubt it,' she said fervently. 'I am very glad you brought me here.'

'I would suggest sitting for a while,' he said, 'but you are wearing a pretty gown. Perhaps you would sit on my coat.'

'My shawl will do,' she said, taking it from about her elbows and opening it out. 'You see? It is big enough for both of us.' She turned and spread it on the rough grass at their feet and sat down on one side of it.

After a moment he joined her there.

'I come here sometimes,' he said, 'when I just want to sit and meditate. I come here even in the winter when it is cold and blustery. That is one thing about wild, natural beauty. It is never the same and yet it is always lovely and soothing to the soul.'

They sat in companionable silence for a while. Then he asked her about the school, and she told him about her friends there and about the rest of the staff, about the girls and their lessons and other activities. She talked for a long time, prompted by his questions and his obvious interest in her answers, and she realized anew how very fortunate she was to have found employment that felt more like a happy way of life than work.

'And what about you?' she asked him. 'Is being steward here something that really interests you?'

He described his duties to her and told her about the home farm and laborers, about the tenant farms, about some of the villagers, about his particular friends there.

'The trouble with being steward to an absentee landlord,' he said, 'is that one comes almost to believe that one is the owner. I have grown very attached to Glandwr and the countryside and people hereabouts. I hope never to leave. But I have told you that before.'

Finally they lapsed into silence again. And Anne, though she still gazed in wonder at the sea, realized that the loveliest view of all was above her head. But it made her dizzy to tip back her head to look up.

She lay back on the shawl, crossing her hands beneath her head.

'Ah,' she said, 'that is better. I wonder just how many stars we can see.'

'If you wish to count them,' he said, chuckling as he turned his head to look down at her, 'please do not let me stop you.'

'And there must be as many more that we cannot see,' she said. 'How far does the universe stretch, would you say?'

'Forever,' he said.

'My mind cannot grasp forever,' she told him. 'There must surely be an end somewhere. But the big question is – what is beyond the end?'

He lay down beside her, still chuckling.

'I suppose,' he said, 'there are astronomers and philosophers and theologians who will not cease seeking the answers and perhaps one day they will succeed. I share your curiosity. But sometimes I just marvel.'

'Yes.' Her eyes roamed across the sky. 'We were meant to seek. But we were also meant simply to accept and enjoy. You are right. I can see the Big Dipper. It is the only thing I can identify by name, alas. But it does not matter, does it?'

'It does not matter,' he agreed.

They turned their heads to smile at each other and then both gazed upward again, glorying in the wonder of it all.

And yet . . .

And yet there was suddenly another dimension to the awareness Anne felt. They were close enough that she could feel his body heat along her right side. They were a man and a woman lying together on a deserted hilltop at night, almost but not quite touching. They had talked and talked together. They had laughed together.

They were friends, she thought.

But it was not friendship that added a certain spice to the heightened sensual awareness that star-gazing had brought. It was something far more carnal. She felt his masculinity and secretly reveled in it though she had no wish whatsoever to act upon it – or to have him do so.

Or perhaps she did.

She was just terribly afraid – afraid of him, afraid of herself.

She did not explore either her thoughts or her feelings in any depth, though. She simply enjoyed the moment, knowing that when she was back at school, deep into the routine of the autumn term, she would remember this night and relive every moment, every sensation, and perhaps even shed a few very private tears for what might have been in her life if only . . .

But how could she ever wish to change anything from her past, even the ugliest thing of all? Without it there would not be David.

'Miss Jewell,' Mr Butler said softly at last, 'it has just occurred to me that we must have been out here for a long time. Perhaps the dancing is over and the neighbors gone home. Country people do not usually keep late hours. I hope I have not compromised you in any way.'

'Of course you have not.' But she sat up, checked her hair, and got to her feet while he got to his. 'Nobody even noticed us leave, and no one will notice our return. And even if anyone does, it does not matter, does it? We are merely two friends out taking the air together.'

'Friends.' He looked at her and smiled as she shook out her shawl and draped it about her shoulders.

'I am glad we are. I wondered after the last time we walked together.'

They were standing very close to each other, she realized. She felt an almost overwhelming urge to reach out her hand and touch his cheek again. But he was making no move to touch her in any way. She wondered if he wished to – and if she really wished to touch him.

She did not touch him. And she was glad he did not touch her. For if she did, or if he did, it would surely be more than just a simple touch this time. She would not be able to bear being kissed by him. She wanted it and cringed from it.

And the idea that she might cringe gave her pause. Cringe because of his appearance? Or because the last man to touch her had been . . . ?

She turned away.

'I'll race you to the bottom,' she said, and took off running and slipping and sliding and shrieking and laughing – and hurting her feet – until she arrived at the bottom of the hill all in one piece a few moments after him.

He was grinning his lopsided grin as she fell into step beside him, breathless and still laughing.

The dancing was just ending as they entered the drawing room through the French windows. There was a bustle of activity as all the outside guests found one another and their belongings and took their leave of the duke and duchess and the house-guests and one another.

It was an opportune time for their return, Anne

thought. No one would have even noticed that she and Mr Butler were gone.

'I must go too, Miss Jewell,' Mr Butler said, making her a half-bow. 'You still wish to join me on Sunday morning?'

'Oh, yes,' she said. 'I shall look forward to it.'

She watched him as he took his leave of the duchess and realized that right now at this moment she felt buoyantly happy.

Like her son, she thought, she needed male companionship as well as female. It had been so lacking in her life. She would miss him when . . . But no, she would not think of that.

Today was Thursday. There were three days to go to Sunday – she actually counted them off on her fingers.

In three more days she would see him again.

CHAPTER 8

'To a service that will be all in Welsh so that she will not understand a single word?' Morgan, Lady Rosthorn, said, staring at Joshua. Then her face lit up with mischief and delight. 'How very promising, to be sure.'

'Promising?' Lord Aidan said, his brows coming together in a frown. 'A church service? I will go to my grave, Morgan, without a glimmering of an understanding of the female mind.'

'He has invited her to go to *church* with him?' Lord Alleyne rolled his eyes. 'A bold and risqué move indeed. I did not know Syd had it in him to be such a devil of a fellow.'

'Perhaps,' Lord Rannulf said, grinning, 'they need a chaperone. Any offers? Josh, you are the one who claims a relationship with the lady.'

'But I am also the one who has been entrusted with the task of taking her son to church with everyone else,' the marquess said. 'I cannot be in two places at the same time, Ralf.'

Judith clucked her tongue.

'Putting them together at dinner on Thursday

154

evening certainly was an inspired move, Christine,' she said. 'It worked just as we thought it might.'

'Though Free almost ruined all by talking Syd's ear off,' Lord Rannulf said. 'I almost gave myself the migraines with all the nodding and winking I did in her direction.'

'Oh, nonsense, Ralf, you did no such thing!' Freyja retorted. 'Of course I talked to him. One cannot be *too* obvious about these things. If Syd had suspected even for a single moment that we were busy matchmaking for him, he would have run a hundred miles without stopping, and who could blame him?'

'Not me, Free,' Lord Alleyne assured her.

'And I believe Miss Jewell would run *two* hundred, Freyja,' the duchess said. 'Indeed, she would be spending this whole month hiding in a dark corner if we gave her half a chance, would she not? Did you notice how she slipped away from the breakfast table a few minutes ago instead of lingering like the rest of us? I like her exceedingly well. And I do agree that she and Mr Butler might well suit if they are just given a fair chance to become acquainted.'

'*Fair* being the operative word, Christine,' Lord Aidan said. 'Why it should be thought that merely because Sydnam and Miss Jewell are both lonely souls they must therefore belong together escapes my understanding.'

'Perhaps because you do not possess a romantic bone in your body, Aidan,' Lord Rannulf said with a chuckle.

'But do you not agree, Aidan,' Rachel, Lady Alleyne, asked him, 'that they ought to be given a chance to see if they belong together? And it was they who made the first move, after all, by walking on the beach together and then planning another walk the next day. And it was you, Rannulf, who pointed out to us on Thursday evening that they had been outside together for an hour and a half. Though, of course, we had *all* noticed.'

'All of which would seem to prove,' Lord Aidan said, 'that they are quite capable of conducting their own grand romance if they so choose. Just as Eve and I did.'

'But with a little help from Wulfric, you must confess, Aidan,' his wife added.

'Wulfric as matchmaker,' Gervase said. 'Good Lord! The mind boggles.'

His grace did not seem amused at having his name dragged into such a conversation. He raised one eloquent eyebrow as he set down his coffee cup.

'It would seem to me,' he said, 'that my steward and one of my guests ought to be allowed to walk out on a warm summer evening and attend church in company with each other – even a *Welsh* church – without arousing such fevered speculation in the bosoms of my family that my very digestion has been threatened. Christine, has word been sent to the nursery that the children are to be brought down in ten minutes' time?'

'It has indeed, Wulfric,' she said, smiling warmly at him along the length of the breakfast table. Her eyes twinkled. 'And those children are to include David Jewell so that his mama and Mr Butler may walk to and from the Welsh chapel *alone* together.'

His grace touched the handle of his quizzing glass, but his fingers did not quite curl about it. Indeed, an observant spectator might even have sworn that his lips twitched as he gazed back at his wife.

Precisely fifteen minutes later the last of the cavalcade of carriages moved away from the front doors of Glandwr, taking the Bedwyn family and all their children and guests – including David Jewell – to the morning service at the English church in the village.

Anne Jewell watched them leave from the window of her bedchamber, happy in the belief that her absence had gone quite unnoticed by everyone except Joshua and David.

Sydnam stood at the window of the sitting room in his cottage, watching the driveway. A number of carriages had passed down some time earlier – the service at the church was an hour earlier than the one at the Welsh chapel – but he had not seen Miss Jewell in any of them. She must intend to keep her appointment with him, then. For some reason he had half expected her to send an excuse – perhaps because he had looked forward to this so much.

It had looked earlier on as if it were going to rain, and the sky was still cloudy. But he thought the fine weather would hold after all.

He was tired. He was accustomed to the old nightmares, but they were never easy to bear, and pulling himself out of them after he had awoken was always akin to a nightmare in itself. The servants, including his valet, knew not to disturb him on such nights even if they heard him cry out or scream, as he sometimes did. In latter years he had been very thankful to be away from his family, whose concern and insistence upon bearing him company on such occasions was not so easily deterred. During the day after one of his nightmares he was always tired and listless, and usually depressed too. But the old, familiar enemy did not have quite the power it used to have. He had pulled himself determinedly free of it this morning.

He just wished last night had not been one of the nights. He wanted to be fully alert this morning. It might be the last opportunity he would have to be alone with her.

He wondered if she realized how close he had come to kissing her up on the hill a few nights ago. It was a night he would long remember. Her beauty and his attraction to her had proved almost irresistible. Thank heaven he *had* resisted.

They were not a couple who could fall into any easy flirtation or romance.

When he saw her coming down the driveway, tall and graceful and lovely in a cream-colored muslin dress with a straw bonnet tied with brown ribbons, he felt his spirits rise after all. It was such a rare thing to have female companionship, and he genuinely enjoyed hers. He donned his hat, let himself out of the cottage, and went to meet her beyond the cottage gate.

'I hope,' he said, looking up at the sky after greeting her, 'we are not going to be rained upon. But the clouds do not look as threatening as they did earlier.'

She looked up too.

'I did not even bring an umbrella,' she said. 'I am determined to be optimistic even if I ruin a bonnet in the process.'

And indeed she looked happy, as if she really were glad she had agreed to accompany him to the chapel. How foolish they had been to miss longer than a week of an acquaintance that seemed to give them both pleasure. He had thought of her a great deal during that week, he realized – and she was to be here for only a month in total.

Now that he was outdoors he felt less tired.

'The others all drove to church,' he said. 'I saw the carriages pass. What excuse did you give for not going with them?'

'None,' she said. 'I spoke privately with Joshua to ask if David could go to church with him. I told him why I would not be going myself, but I daresay he will not tell the others. Why would anyone else be interested to know where I am anyway?'

Ralf had brought her into the conversation while a few of them had been out riding last week – and had asked Sydnam's opinion of her looks in such a contrived, offhand manner that it could only have been deliberate. Then the other night Sydnam had caught Alleyne's eye as he stepped back into the drawing room with her, and there had been amused speculation there. And then he had intercepted Morgan's glance, and she had smiled fondly at him. The Bedwyns might be very much more interested than Miss Jewell realized – but he would not alarm her by saying so. Bedwyns be damned – the women he chose to be friendly with were none of their business.

'The duchess has arranged for us all to go for a drive this afternoon,' she said. 'I must not be too late back.'

'And I am planning to go over to Tŷ Gwyn later on if it does not rain,' he told her.

'Tea what?' she asked.

'Tŷ Gwyn,' he repeated. 'Two Welsh words meaning *white house*, though in fact it is not white at all, but a sizable gray stone manor set in its own park. I believe the old house was indeed white, but it was pulled down and rebuilt a century or more ago. It belongs to the Duke of Bewcastle at present, but I have hopes of purchasing it from him and making it my own.'

He had finally broached the subject with Bewcastle two days ago. The duke had not said yes. Neither had he said no. He had merely stared at Sydnam, his silver eyes slightly narrowed, his fingers seeking out the handle of his quizzing glass.

'Doubtless,' he had said at last, 'you have marshaled all sorts of irrefutable reasons why I should comply with this request, Sydnam. I will hear them all before I leave Glandwr, but not today. Today the duchess awaits my presence in the drawing room for tea.'

That had been that. But he had not said no.

'You spoke of it,' Miss Jewell said, 'when we went walking in the valley, though you did not name it. *Tŷ Gwyn.* I like the name both in its Welsh form and in translation. It sounds cheerful.'

'Perhaps,' he said, 'you would like to go over there with me one day before you leave here?'

As soon as the words were out, he regretted them. Tŷ Gwyn, he hoped, was going to be his future home. It was where he would belong, where he would set down roots, where he would be as happy as it was possible to be for the rest of his life. He was not sure it was at all wise to take Miss Jewell there, to have memories of her there – though *why* not he did not know.

But the words were out.

'I would like to show it to you,' he said. 'I always make sure that the park is kept tidy and that the house is kept clean, though it is almost a year since the last tenants left.'

'Then I would like to go,' she said. 'Thank you. I shall look forward to it.'

They did not speak much after that, but after

161

stepping through the park gates and turning left along the narrow road with its hedgerows on either side and over the stone bridge that spanned the valley, they were soon in the village. It was small and picturesque, its gray stone houses, some thatched, some roofed with gray slate, set back a little way from the road at various angles, a green privet hedge all about the perimeter of each garden, flower beds and grass in front, long lines of vegetables growing at the back. The church was tall with a narrow spire, the chapel more squat and solid-looking a short distance farther along the road.

He did not always attend the chapel. Although he was taking Welsh lessons from Tudor Rhys, the minister, and could both understand and speak a few sentences and read a great deal more, he was quickly lost when people around him started to speak at normal conversational speed, and the lengthy sermons went right over his head. But he did come sometimes. He loved the sound of the language and the fervor of the minister and congregation. It was the music that drew him most, though.

He no longer felt self-conscious with the villagers, who had grown accustomed to his appearance long ago. But he felt self-conscious this morning as he arrived at the chapel with Miss Jewell and was aware of the hush that fell over the congregation and then the renewed whisperings and head noddings. And one glance at her told him that she was feeling equally embarrassed.

But it was a morning service that he knew he would long remember. Perhaps he always would, in fact. Though the villagers and country people were accustomed to him, most of them nevertheless kept their distance from him, perhaps more out of respect than revulsion. He always had the pew to himself – except today.

Today he had a beautiful woman seated beside him for all of an hour and a half and it was just as well no one could read his thoughts. During the long sermon he entertained all sorts of fantasies about her relationship to him.

Most of all, though, he would remember the way she blushed and smiled when Tudor Rhys suddenly switched to English in order to introduce her to his congregation and welcome her. And the way she stood enthralled during every hymn while a hundred or more Welsh men and women around them opened their throats and sang praises in perfect, unrehearsed harmony.

Yes, he thought as they left the chapel after shaking hands with the minister and nodding and smiling at the people grouped outside in the street, gossiping and exchanging news, he would always remember this morning.

He might as well take her to Tŷ Gwyn one day within the next two weeks and have that to remember too after she had returned to Bath.

He had no idea if he would remember with pain or pleasure – or even indifference. Time would answer that question, he supposed.

'Mr Butler,' she said as they walked back and paused for a few minutes on the bridge to gaze down into the valley. 'I can understand why you have fallen in love with Wales. It is more than just a different country, is it not? It is like a different world. I am so glad I came here.'

'I am glad too,' he said.

And then he felt foolish and even a little alarmed because she did not respond and neither of them moved, and his words seemed to hang in the air before them until they had walked on and turned between the park gates again and he thought of something else to say.

He was not even sure he *was* glad she had come. His celibacy and womanless state had become bearable to him over the years because there had been no one to remind him of all he had missed since he had been made untouchable.

But then Anne Jewell had arrived at Glandwr and in his life, and as fate would have it she was not only gloriously beautiful, but also chose to be his friend. He must never forget, though, how she had reacted to him at first sight and how she had shrunk from him after inadvertently touching his cheek on the rocks between the two beaches. Or how she had turned and run down the hill a few evenings ago just when he had been about to give in to the temptation to kiss her.

She was his *friend* – nothing more than that.

He was, he believed, going to have to fight certain demons all over again after she had left.

He was going to miss her – and try his very best to forget her.

After the Sunday morning on which Anne Jewell and Sydnam Butler went to church together and he walked all the way back to the main house with her before returning alone to his cottage, they met almost every day.

Anne had enjoyed that outing more than she could possibly have expected. It was strange, really, in light of the fact that the Welsh service had been quite unintelligible to her. Though that was not strictly true. It had somehow spoken to her heart, bypassing the intellect – not just the music but all of it. And there had been something undeniably seductive about being accompanied by a man, about walking to church with him, sitting beside him on the pew, walking home with him.

Sometimes over the next week and a half she met him by chance – out on the cliffs, for example, when she went walking there one evening after tucking David into bed. More often, though, it was by design, usually in the afternoon when his work was finished and David was busy with the other children about some activity or other.

He took her to see the village school, with Mr Jones attending them, and since the children were on holiday, they sat, the three of them, at the narrow wooden desks in the single square classroom and conversed for longer than an hour – or, to be more accurate, Anne and Mr Butler listened while the schoolmaster spoke eloquently of Wales and Welsh history and education. He taught in both English and Welsh, Anne was interested to discover, since he had pupils with both languages. And his pupils almost invariably became bilingual after a few weeks.

Mr Butler took her to call upon Mr and Mrs Llwyd, since she had spoken wistfully of the lovely harp music she had heard, and Mrs Llwyd spent half an hour or longer with her, showing her the instrument, demonstrating various tones and chords, and playing for her while Mr Butler talked with Mr Llwyd about farming. Mrs Llwyd insisted that they take tea before they left, and they were joined by the two sons of the house, aged eleven and twelve. Both boys wished that David had come too after Anne had mentioned him. And both boys attended the village school.

Anne went walking with Sydnam Butler along country lanes or sat by the stream in the valley with him or strolled on the beach. Once they went for a long walk to the distant outcropping of land that they both spoke of as the Dragon.

'Some people hereabouts have even told me that it is the original Welsh dragon, petrified by a sea deity,' he told her with a laugh. 'It is an attractive legend, but I believe they are merely trying to see how gullible an Englishman can be.'

They took a picnic tea with them on that day and sat eating wafer-thin slices of bread and butter with cheese followed by currant cakes and drinking lukewarm lemonade far out from the mainland, the water on three sides of them sparkling in the sunshine.

'I feel as if I am on a ship,' she said, 'sailing . . . oh, somewhere exotic, somewhere wonderful.'

'A journey to forever,' he said. 'An enticing, perfect forever.'

'No, not forever,' she told him. 'There is much I would miss if I could not come back. And I could not go without David.'

'You are quite right,' he said. 'Not forever, then. Just for a long, long afternoon.'

'Agreed,' she said, stretching out on the grass and gazing up at the blue sky as she had gazed at the stars a week earlier. 'A long afternoon. Wake me when it is time to go home.'

But he tickled her nose with a long piece of grass only moments after she had closed her eyes, and they both laughed, their faces not very far apart. She closed her eyes again only so that they would not feel the tension and be compelled to move away from each other in order to cover it up.

There was a certain guilty pleasure to be taken from the tension. And yet she could not bear the thought of his actually touching her – and she still did not know if it was his appearance from which she shrank or her own memories of intimacy. Perhaps it was a little – or a lot – of each.

It did not rain once during those days. There was scarcely even a cloud in the sky.

They talked about anything and everything, it

seemed to Anne. He was as comfortable to be with as any of the closest of her friends – except that he was a man.

It felt so *good* to have a man friend. She no longer even minded being seen with him – and inevitably the Bedwyns and the other guests at the house did see them together. Why should she mind, after all? There was nothing between them that needed to be hidden, and no one – not even Joshua – ever teased her about her friendship with Glandwr's steward.

Even David saw them together one afternoon. He was playing out on the lawn with the other children when Anne and Mr Butler were coming from the hill and left the group to come dashing toward them.

'Mama,' he cried, 'I cut my finger on tree bark, see? But Lady Aidan took me up to the nursery and cleaned it and bandaged it for me, and it really does not hurt very much at all except that it is harder to catch the ball. How do you do, sir? I went painting again this morning, but I can't wait to get Mr Upton to teach me to paint with oils. Oh, there is Jacques calling – I must go.'

And off he went without waiting for any response. Anne looked at Mr Butler and found him smiling at her.

'When I was a boy,' he said, 'I do not believe I had even that much time to spare for adults. I feel honored.'

'He is very happy here,' she told him. 'I am

afraid he is going to be dreadfully dejected when we return to Bath.'

'Except,' he said, 'that he will have the challenge of Mr Upton to tackle when he gets there.'

It felt good to have a friend to whom she could talk about anything, but from whom she could also withhold certain things about which she did not want to speak without provoking either undue curiosity or resentment. On one occasion, for example, when he had asked about her family again, she talked instead about Frances and how she had furnished a room especially for her or Susanna or Claudia at Barclay Court in Somersetshire and kept it for their visits whenever a school holiday coincided with her being at home. Mr Butler had made no comment on the change of subject. He too had silent places where she would not tread. She knew that his artistic talent was a painful subject with him, and she did not quiz him on it again.

It came as something of a surprise when one day she worked out dates and realized that the final week of the holiday in Wales had already begun. She had expected her stay here to seem endless, yet now she could not believe it was already almost over. She felt rather sad for David's sake, but she felt equally sorry for herself. Most of all she felt sad at the imminent end of a friendship that was only just blossoming but was giving her such pleasure.

And it *would* end. It was hardly likely that they

would meet again or that they would exchange letters after she had gone. By this time next month, she thought, they would only half remember each other. By this time next year they would think of each other only fleetingly, if at all.

She thought he had forgotten about his offer to take her to see Tŷ Gwyn, the house and property he hoped to purchase from the Duke of Bewcastle. But he mentioned it again when there were only three days left before her departure. He had been at Glandwr for dinner, and they were sitting slightly apart from everyone else in the drawing room afterward, the two of them, as they had done on other occasions too. No one had ever remarked upon their partiality for each other's company or made them feel either unsociable or self-conscious.

But then she supposed that she was unimportant enough that no one particularly noticed her anyway – though everyone had been unfailingly kind and amiable toward her. And Mr Butler was only the steward. Why should anyone single them out for notice?

'Will you come there the day after tomorrow?' he asked. 'Unfortunately, I need to be busy all day tomorrow, but the day after I will be free. I thought we could take a picnic tea over to Tŷ Gwyn, and at the same time I can see that the work I assigned after my last visit has been done.'

An excursion had been arranged for the day after tomorrow – they were all to go on a lengthy outing

170

to Pembroke Castle. The older children were very excited at the prospect of climbing up onto the battlements and descending to the dungeons. Anne had been looking forward to going too. But she knew that her presence was not strictly necessary. Although all the adults gave special attention on occasion to their own children, all of them also parented all the children equally on most occasions with the result that David had a number of substitute fathers – and a number of substitute mothers too.

And it was not as if she had neglected him. Quite the contrary. Despite her frequent outings with Mr Butler, she had actually spent far more time with David – or at least with the large group of adults and children that included him – than she ever did during the school term.

She really wanted to see Tŷ Gwyn. It was the place that Mr Butler hoped would be his own one day. It was where he would perhaps live out the rest of his life.

She wanted to see it. She wanted to be able to picture him there when she remembered him.

She also wanted to spend one more afternoon with him before leaving. It would be the last one.

It was a rather depressing thought.

'I would love to come,' she said. 'I will have a word with David to be sure that he does not mind my not going to Pembroke Castle with him, and I will ask Joshua if he minds watching David for me. But I do not believe either of them *will* mind.'

'I will have a gig outside the door here at one o'clock, then,' he said, 'if I do not hear otherwise from you.'

A gig. It would be the first time they had ventured anywhere they could not reach on foot. She wondered if a groom would drive them. Three of them would be very crowded on the seat of a gig.

But she looked forward very much to the outing even though going would mean giving up seeing the castle. She even found it difficult to get to sleep after she went to bed – like a child with a promised treat, she thought, rather disgusted with herself. Though it was not all excitement that kept her awake.

It would be their *last* afternoon together.

She hoped the fine weather would hold for one more day.

CHAPTER 9

The fine weather did hold.

When the carriages left for Pembroke Castle in the middle of the morning, the sun was beaming down from a clear blue sky. When Mr Butler arrived on foot later and a gig appeared on the terrace from the direction of the stables at almost the same moment – Anne had been watching from the window of her bedchamber – there was still not a cloud in the sky.

She tied the ribbons of her straw bonnet beneath her chin and half ran down the stairs without waiting to be summoned. She felt like a girl again.

Mr Butler was standing in the middle of the hall, looking up at her, a smile on his face. It was strange, she thought, how quickly she had become accustomed to his looks – to the empty right sleeve, the purple, nerveless right side of his face, the eye patch.

'It looks as if we are going to have a lovely afternoon for a drive,' he said.

There was a groom standing at the horse's head, Anne saw when they stepped outside, but he

173

pulled his forelock respectfully to them both and stayed where he was as Mr Butler handed her up to the seat on the left side of the vehicle and then took the seat beside her. The groom handed him the ribbons and stepped back, and they were on their way.

Mr Butler was going to drive them himself, then? She ought to have expected it. She knew he was up to most challenges – including riding a horse.

'You will be quite safe,' he assured her as if he had read her thoughts. 'I have had a great deal of practice at doing this. It is amazing what can be done one-handed. I have even driven a *team* of horses on occasion, though admittedly that was somewhat hair-raising.'

His left hand, which she had noticed first for being long-fingered and artistic and then for being deft and skilled as it wielded a fork, was also very strong, as well as the arm that went with it, she realized as he turned the horse onto the driveway without any apparent effort and later, after they had stopped at his cottage for a servant to load a picnic basket onto the back of the gig, drove through the gates and across the bridge and made the sharp turn off the main road onto the narrower road through the village and beyond.

'Are you able to write with your left hand?' she asked him.

'I can produce something that looks like a cross between a spider's web and the tracks of chicken feet,' he said. 'But remarkably, it seems to be

174

decipherable to other people. I am also now able to produce more than one three-letter word in a minute, though only if my tongue is tucked into my cheek at just the right angle.'

She laughed as he chuckled. It seemed strange now to remember that she had seen him at first as a tragic, broken figure of a man, and he *had* admitted to loneliness. But he was certainly not a man sunk into self-pity or defeat. He was able to laugh at all sorts of absurdities, and even at himself, the sign of a man with considerable inner strength.

'Can you not hold a paintbrush in your left hand, then?' she asked.

She regretted the words as soon as they were out of her mouth. Although they had been deliberate and she really wanted to know if he had tried – if he had taken on that challenge as he had others and had simply been defeated by it – she also realized that she had crossed an invisible line they had set between them early in their acquaintance. There was no outer sign that his mood had changed, but there was a tense quality to the short silence that ensued that had not been there before.

'No,' he said after a while. 'My brushes are always in my right hand, Miss Jewell.'

Present tense. She did not know what he meant. But she would not ask. She had already intruded too far.

They negotiated another sharp bend beyond the village, and the road became so narrow that the hedgerows brushed against the wheels on both sides.

'What if we were to meet another vehicle?' she asked.

'One of us would have to back up,' he said. 'It would be more productive than sitting and glowering at each other. One becomes an expert at backing up in this part of the world.'

Green crops waved in the breeze beyond the hedgerows to their right. Sheep grazed on the more stony land to their left. And always in the distance there were the ever-present cliffs and the sea. And there was the warm salt air to breathe.

'You must be very proud of your son,' he said. 'He is a lovely child.'

She looked at him in surprise and gratitude.

'Ralf and Alleyne and Freyja were telling me a few days ago how eager to please and to learn he is,' he explained, 'and how ready to play with all the younger children. There is rather a crowd of them, is there not?'

'He is always a good boy,' she said. 'The teachers and girls at the school are all fond of him. At first, when he was younger, I thought the school a wonderful environment for him. But he cannot stay there indefinitely. I have become more than ever aware of that this month. I dread the thought of letting Joshua find a boys' school for him, though. Oh, Mr Butler, it is very much harder to be a parent than I could possibly have expected.'

'Is it?' He looked across at her before turning

the gig off the narrow road and onto a rutted path between two fields.

'I find myself wanting to mold him and control him,' she said, 'because I know what is best for him and because I know what sort of person I wish him to be. I have tried, for example, to persuade him to think of painting merely as an interesting pastime. He is going to have to earn his *living* when he grows up. But I have been surprised to discover that he is a unique individual quite separate from myself and very different from me – and with a will of his own. Why should that be a shock? I have always known with my intellect that it is true of all people. But some lessons have to be learned with the heart too before we really understand them. It is so easy to be a parent before we have children of our own.'

He laughed softly. 'You make me believe, Miss Jewell,' he said, 'that perhaps it is fortunate I will never have children of my own.'

'Oh,' she said, turning sharply toward him, 'please do not misunderstand me. David is the most precious being in my life.'

And she felt immediately guilty because she had been enjoying a day without him. She had scarcely spared him a thought, in fact. Was he enjoying the castle? Was he taking unnecessary risks on the stairs or battlements? Was Joshua keeping a careful enough eye on him? Was he behaving well?

Mr Butler turned his head to smile at her.

Why would he never have children of his own?

Because he intended never to marry? Because he could not? Had the torture included . . .

But her attention was suddenly distracted. He had drawn the gig to a halt, and Anne saw that ahead of them the land fell away into what looked like a large, shallow bowl. It was ringed about with trees, except here where the track gave way to a wider, graveled driveway beyond a wooden, five-bar gate with a rustic stile beside it and a footpath. Ahead of them wide grassy meadows stretched to either side of the driveway, woolly sheep grazing on them, some taking shelter from the sun beneath the shade of a few old oaks and elms.

There must be a ha-ha close to the bottom of the slope opposite, Anne thought. Above it she could see close-cropped lawns and flower beds and what looked like a rose arbor. But it was the house, also on the far slope, that drew most of her attention. It was of gray stone, and architecturally it was not particularly beautiful. It was three stories high and square and solid, with long windows on the bottom two floors and square windows at the top. The walls were more than half covered with ivy. It was framed by trees.

It was neither house nor mansion. It was small in comparison with Glandwr just a few miles away. *Manor* was the right word for it. The hollow in which house and park were nestled gave an impression of seclusion and intimacy if not quite of smallness.

The sea was on the other side of the road they had turned off, maybe a mile or two away.

Mr Butler had made no move to get down to open the gate, Anne realized. He was looking at her.

'What do you think?' he asked.

'I think,' she said, her eyes drinking in the house, the trees, the flower garden, the sheep-dotted meadow, the whole circle of the park, 'you will be happy here, Mr Butler. How could you not be?'

How could *anyone* not be happy here? Suddenly she was consumed by such envy and such a yearning that it seemed there was a definite physical pain about her heart.

'A retired naval captain and his wife were living here on a ten-year lease when I came to Glandwr,' he said. 'When they left last year, I made very little effort to find new tenants. I believe it is the only instance of neglect I have been guilty of in my duties as Bewcastle's steward.'

'Will he sell it to you?' she asked.

'He has not said no,' he told her. 'But he has not said yes either. He will give me an answer before he leaves here, though.'

It struck her suddenly that he must be a very wealthy man if he was able to make an offer for such a property. There was a huge distance between them socially. It was a good thing she did not have designs on him.

But she was very glad they had become friends.

'Will you hold the ribbons while I open the gate?' he asked.

'Let me do it.' She did not wait for his answer but jumped out of the gig, opened the gate, and swung it back on its hinges. She stood on the bottom bar and rode part of the way, looking up as she did so to laugh at Mr Butler in the gig. She was very aware suddenly of the rural beauty of her surroundings, the green grass, the blue sky, birds singing, insects whirring, a very slight breeze. She could smell vegetation and animals and the sea. She could feel the heat of the sun.

It was one of those vivid, blessed moments, she realized, that burn themselves into the memory and are there forever.

He was gazing back at her, unsmiling. It was impossible to know what he was thinking. Perhaps she had offended him by opening the gate herself. Perhaps he thought she believed him incapable of doing it for himself.

'I could not resist,' she said. 'Will you wait a moment longer while I climb over the stile?'

'When the gate is open?' He grinned his lopsided smile at her.

'Stiles were made to be climbed over,' she said. 'I have never been able to resist one.'

He gestured toward it, making her a mocking little half-bow from his seat as he did so.

But by the time she had climbed up the two stone steps and swung both legs over the wooden bar and sat on it in order to turn and smile down at him, he had got out of the gig and looped the ribbons loosely over the top bar of the gate, and was striding toward her in order to offer her his hand to help her descend.

'Now if I just had two arms,' he said, 'I could play the complete gallant and lift you down.'

'But then,' she said, placing her right hand in his left and holding up her skirt with the other, 'I would miss the chance of descending like a queen, Mr Butler.'

She became a very undignified queen, though, when the bottom step wobbled precariously under her weight and she came rushing down to the ground and stopped only just in time to prevent herself from colliding headlong with him. She laughed and looked up into his face – only a few inches away from her own.

Déjà vu struck hard, like a fist to her lower abdomen. It was like the scene up on the rocks between two beaches all over again.

His left eye looked very dark, very intense, his unsmiling mouth very beautiful. She could feel his breath against her face. She could feel his heat along the full length of her body. For one dizzying, mad moment she swayed a little closer to him. She half closed her eyes.

And then she pulled sharply away and laughed again, removing her hand from his as she did so.

'Thank you, sir,' she said lightly. 'I would doubtless have come to grief if you had not been holding on to me. I suspect my pride and my dignity would have been hurt more than any other part of me, but pride and dignity must also be preserved.'

'I must have that step seen to,' he said.

They were seated side by side in the gig a few moments later and proceeding down into the shallow bowl that held the house and park of Tŷ Gwyn.

She had almost touched him again, Anne thought – not just his hand, but *him*. She had almost *kissed* him – and he had known it. He was seated rigidly beside her now, aware that she had shrunk from him. But he would have misunderstood the reason.

It was not him. Not really.

It was her.

She was terrified of physical intimacy.

But perhaps he was as relieved as she that she had turned away. She was not a virgin. She had been raped. She had a child. All of those facts might well make him feel a revulsion quite equal to anything she could feel about him.

But she did not believe he felt revulsion.

She looked about the meadow and ahead to the house and gardens and tried to feel simply happy again.

There were no servants resident at Tŷ Gwyn. Sydnam did see to it, though, that the garden was regularly tended and the house aired and cleaned. As the Duke of Bewcastle's steward he would have done so even if he had had no personal interest in the property. But perhaps he would not have come so often in person to see that the work had been done.

He drove the gig into the stable block, unhitched the horse, and gave it oats and water while Miss Jewell looked on – he had declined her help. He left the picnic basket where it was – they could decide later where they wanted to take it.

He felt curiously reluctant to take her into the house. Or perhaps it was just the opposite. He badly wanted to show it to her, but he wanted the time to be right. When they first arrived, he was still feeling somewhat discomposed after the incident at the stile, when he had almost kissed her. What a horrible faux pas that would have been. Even as it was he had felt her withdrawal and had been powerfully reminded of how foolish it would be to allow himself to fall in love with her.

Sometimes, because they had grown to be friends, because he was generally so comfortable in her presence, he forgot that there could never be anything *but* friendship between him and any woman.

For the present he did not want to be alone inside any building with Miss Anne Jewell, who looked more than usually appealing today in her sprigged-muslin high-waisted dress and her floppy-brimmed straw bonnet, both trimmed with blue ribbons, though he had seen both before on a number of occasions. And she was looking bronzed and healthy from her weeks at Glandwr, though she might be less than delighted if he remarked upon the fact – ladies generally did not like to have bronzed complexions. He did not believe he would ever forget the sight of her, standing on the bottom bar of the gate as it swung open and looking up to laugh at him, like a carefree girl.

It had torn at his heart.

He took her walking about the park, along the rustic trail through the trees, across the open meadow, avoiding sheep and sheep droppings, admiring the daisies and buttercups and clover that were absent from the more carefully cropped lawns above the ha-ha, across the lawns themselves, first to the back of the house, where rows of vegetables grew even though the house was empty, and then to the front and the colorful flower beds, in which he was pleased to observe that there were no weeds, and the rose arbor.

He was glad to sit down there – his right knee was aching after walking almost nonstop for more than an hour. The air here was heavy with the perfumes of dozens of roses that grew in beds and trailed over trellises. He could hear the low droning of bees.

She did not sit down, though. He would not have seated himself if he had realized it, but he did not get up again. He sat and watched her as she bent over the rose beds to take a closer look at some of the more exquisite blooms, to touch them lightly, to smell them.

She looked contented and relaxed, he thought. She looked as if she belonged here as he belonged . . .

He did not know how he would be able to support the disappointment if Bewcastle should refuse to sell to him. He did not believe he would be able to remain in this part of the world. It was an alarming thought, since there was no other part of the world he wanted to be.

But if he *did* ever live here, if he ever sat here again on another hot, drowsy summer afternoon, he would be alone.

There would be no woman beautiful among the flowers.

'You may cut some roses if you wish,' he said, 'and take them back to Glandwr with you. I can fetch a knife from the house.'

'They would wilt,' she said, turning toward him. 'I would rather leave them here in their natural setting to live out the natural span of their lives. But thank you.'

He stood as she approached him and then sat again after she had seated herself. But he should have moved over, he thought belatedly. She was seated on his blind side. He was not usually so clumsy.

'When I was forced to leave my employment as Lady Prudence Moore's governess,' she said, 'I moved into a small cottage in the village of Lydmere. I eked out a living by giving private lessons, though I was also forced to accept the financial support Joshua offered me. I had my few pupils and my young son to keep me occupied almost every moment of every day. But I was still

185

very aware of my aloneness. When I shut the cottage door behind any pupil who happened to come, there were just David and me. I sometimes found it . . . hard.'

'It was a good thing for you, then,' he said, 'that you were eventually offered employment at a boarding school.'

'Yes,' she said, 'it was the best thing that had happened to me in a long while. Do you like living alone?'

'I am never quite alone,' he told her. 'There are always servants. I almost always have friendly relations with them, especially my valet.'

He could not see her unless he turned his head right about. He felt at a distinct disadvantage.

'Will you like living alone here?' she asked him. 'Will it bring you the happiness you crave?'

Just an hour ago, when they had stopped in the gig at the top of the hill, she had assured him that he could be happy here. During the past hour they had walked with a spring in their step and talked and laughed and sometimes been comfortably silent with each other. They had been warmed by sunlight and summer. When had melancholy descended upon them both?

He had been trying all afternoon not to think about the fact that this was her last day at Glandwr – that tomorrow she would be gone, that everyone would be leaving before another week had passed. At first he had counted days in his eagerness to have them gone again. Now he was counting days unwillingly and for a different reason. But for Miss Anne Jewell he had just run out of numbers. He thought ruefully of all the wasted days when he had not seen her. But even if he had been with her every moment of every day, this would still be the last one.

'My life will be what I make it,' he told her. 'That is true for all of us all the time. We cannot know what the future will bring or how the events of the future will make us feel. We cannot even plan and feel any certainty that our most carefully contrived plans will be put into effect. Could I have predicted what happened to me in the Peninsula? Could you have predicted what happened to you in Cornwall? But those things happened to us nevertheless. And they changed our plans and our dreams so radically that we both might have been excused for giving up, for never planning or dreaming again, for never living again. That too is a choice we all have to make. Will I be happy here? I will do my very best to be – *if*, that is, Bewcastle is willing to sell to me.'

'What *were* your dreams?' she asked him.

He turned his head then until he could see her. She was sitting slightly sideways on the seat, facing toward him, and she was gazing at him with large eyes made smoky by her long lashes and the shade of her bonnet brim. She was apparently gazing quite deliberately at his bad side. He could have suggested that they change places, but he would not do so. It would be safer thus. He would be constantly reminded that she had shrunk from him up there at the stile – yes, that was exactly what she had done – and that he must not allow his feelings for her to stray beyond friendship.

'They were reasonably humble ones,' he said. 'I wanted to paint. I wanted a home of my own and a wife and children. No, let me be perfectly honest, since you have asked. I wanted to be a *great* painter. I wanted to be displayed at the Royal Academy. But there were choices, you see – there are always choices. I also wanted other people to see that I was as brave and as manly as my brothers. And so I talked my father into purchasing a commission for me. And the more my family protested that it was not the life for me, the more stubbornly I insisted that it was. Now I must live with the consequences of the choice I made. And I will not call it the wrong choice. That would be foolish and pointless. That choice led me to everything that has happened since, including this very moment, and the choices I make today or tomorrow or next week will lead me to the next and the next present moments in my life. It is all a journey, Miss Jewell. I have come to understand that that is what life is all about – a journey and the courage and energy always to take the next step and the next without judgment about what was right and what was wrong.'

'Were you as wise before your injuries?' she asked him.

'Of course not,' he said. 'And if I am alive ten,

twenty years from now, the words I have just spoken will seem foolish to me or at least shallow. Wisdom comes from experience, and so far I have had only twenty-eight years of it.'

'One fewer than me,' she said. 'You are younger than I.'

'What were your dreams?' he asked her.

'Marriage to someone for whom I could feel an affection,' she said. 'Children. A modest home of my own in the country. I did achieve at least a part of my dream. I have David.'

'And did you have a potential husband picked out?' he asked her.

'Yes.'

He would not ask the next question. The answer was all too obvious. The man, whoever he was, had abandoned her after discovering that she was with child by someone else.

Was he someone from Cornwall?

'But you are right,' she told him. 'We have to continue with the journey of life. The alternative is too terrible to contemplate.'

He was uncomfortable with the silence that ensued. He could tell that she had not moved. She must still be sitting sideways beside him, then. He could simply have got up, of course. He still had not taken her inside the house. But some stubborn part of himself kept him where he was. Let her look her fill. It was not as if she had not seen him before.

'It is not a pretty sight, is it?' he said abruptly

at last – and then could have bitten his tongue out. What could she possibly say in response to such self-pitying words except to rush into uttering foolish lies to console him?

'No,' she said. 'It is not.'

The words amused more than they hurt him. He turned his head about again and smiled at her.

'But it is part of who you are to those who know you now,' she said. 'That cannot be avoided, can it, unless you become a hermit or wear a mask. I daresay that for you it is a terrible thing to be blind on the one side, to have no arm, to be unable to do many things you once did without thought. And it must be a terrible thing to look in a mirror and remember how you once looked and will never look again. You were extraordinarily handsome, were you not? You still are. But those who see you now – especially, I suppose, those who did not know you before – soon become accustomed to seeing you as you are. The right side of your face is not pretty, as you say. But it is not ugly either. Not really. It ought to be, perhaps, but it is not. It is part of you, and you are a man worth knowing.'

He laughed, his face still turned toward her. Truth to tell, though, he was deeply touched. She was not, he sensed, speaking just to console him.

'Thank you, Miss Jewell,' he said. 'In all the years since this happened, I have never found anyone, even my family – *especially* my family – willing to speak so frankly about my looks.'

She got to her feet suddenly and went to stand by one of the trellises over which roses grew. She bent her head to smell one particularly perfect red bloom.

'I am sorry,' she said, 'for what happened earlier.'

A number of things had happened earlier. He knew to what she referred, though.

'It was my fault,' he said. 'I ought not even to have thought of kissing you.'

But he had *not* thought about it. That was the whole trouble. If he had, he would not have come so close to doing it. He would have released her hand as soon as she regained her balance and moved away from her.

She turned her head to look at him.

'But it was I,' she said, 'who almost kissed *you*.'

Her cheeks suddenly flamed.

Ah. He had not realized that. But she had stopped herself – and now felt that she owed him an apology. He looked down and brushed a speck of dirt from his breeches.

Once, three weeks or so ago, she had set her fingertips against his cheek – and then removed them as if she had scalded her hand.

Today she had almost kissed him – and then moved jerkily away.

He was aware suddenly that she was standing in front of him. He looked up at her, prepared to smile and suggest that they go and look at the house. But her eyes were huge and deep, giving him the curious impression that he could see right

191

through to her soul. And she set her fingertips again just where they had been that other time.

'You are not ugly, Mr Butler,' she said. 'You are not. Truly you are not.'

And she bent her head and set her lips against the left side of his mouth. They trembled quite noticeably, and he felt her breath being released in awkward little jerks against his cheek. But she did not give him just a token little peck of a kiss to prove that she had the courage to do it. She kept her lips where they were long enough for him to taste her, to want her with a yearning so intense that he gripped the arm of the seat almost hard enough to put a dent in the wood.

When she lifted her head, she looked down at him again in that peculiar way she had of focusing on both sides of his face. Her eyes were swimming with tears, he noticed.

'You are *not* ugly,' she said again almost fiercely, as if, perhaps, to convince herself.

'Thank you.' He forced himself to smile, even to chuckle. 'Thank you, Miss Jewell. You are very kind.'

He understood fully what it must have cost her to touch him thus. But she was a woman of some compassion. It was not her fault that he felt bleaker than he had felt in a long, long while.

She had tasted of sunshine and woman and dreams.

'May I show you the house?' he asked her, getting to his feet.

'Yes, please,' she said. 'I have been looking forward to it all day.'

And then he did something terribly distressing that he had not done for a long time. He offered her his right arm to take.

Except that nothing happened.

It was not there.

She fell into step beside him, not even knowing he had made the gesture.

For a fraction of a moment he had forgotten that he was only half a man.

CHAPTER 10

S he was terribly aware of him as they entered the cool, silent house and he showed her each of the rooms upstairs and down. She was aware of him as a man, as a sexual being for whom her own woman's body ached.

She was half terrified by the feeling, half fascinated by it.

She had been very careful as she kissed him not to touch his right side. But she had been very conscious of that right side, afraid that she would reach out and touch him after all – rather as people who are afraid of heights are terrified that they will jump from a tower or cliff.

Yet it was not his right side she most feared.

She had also been very aware as she kissed him of his masculinity, of the intimacy that had lain just a heartbeat away, though his lips had not moved against hers, and his hand had not touched her.

It was his masculinity she most feared.

Or, rather, her own damaged femininity.

'It is a lovely house,' she said after a while. 'I can understand why you are so attached to it.

The rooms are square and high-ceilinged and almost stately, are they not? And the windows fill them with light.'

The back windows looked out on the vegetable garden and the wooded slope, while those in front faced onto the flower garden and the rest of the park. The house was enclosed by beauty. And yet all the splendor of the sea and the coast lay just a mile or so away.

'I fell in love with it the first time I came here to visit,' he said. 'There are some places like that, though there is not always a rational explanation of why they grab the heart when other places, equally lovely or even more so, do not. I am very fond of Glandwr and of the cottage where I now live, but they do not cry out *home* to me.'

No place had ever done that to Anne, though she had grown up happily in her parents' home in Gloucestershire and had felt as if her cottage at Lydmere was a blessed sanctuary. And she loved Claudia's school, where she now lived. But it was not *home*. Again she envied Mr Butler that he had Tŷ Gwyn and hoped the Duke of Bewcastle would agree to sell it to him. Tŷ Gwyn was a place where a person could set down roots that would last for generations. It was a place where one could be happy, where one could raise children, where one could . . .

But Mr Butler would live here alone.

And she would never live here. There was no point in weaving dreams about it.

'The house feels blessedly cool,' he said when they had seen every room and were standing in the tiled hallway again. 'Shall we eat our picnic tea in here? Or would you prefer to sit out on the lawn?'

'In here,' she said. 'Let me fetch the basket.'

'We will take one handle each,' he said.

She ought to have opted for the lawn, she thought ten minutes later as they set out their little feast on the small table in the morning room. It was true that they had become overheated by the sun. But outdoors there were more sounds from nature to distract one's attention and more to look at and less awareness that they were a man and woman together and that there was something going on between them that both of them were aware of and uncomfortable with.

Something that made the air about them taut with tension.

His cook had made little meat pasties for them and cucumber sandwiches and an apple tart. She had included generous slices of cheese and the inevitable lemonade. Anne arranged it all on the table with the dishes that were also in the basket. She poured their drinks.

They ate in near silence, and when they did talk, it was on the sort of inconsequential topics that strangers would have chosen. They must have spent ten whole minutes discussing how long they expected the hot, sunny spell to continue.

'I heard one member of the chapel congregation

remark to someone else after the service last Sunday,' he said, his eye twinkling, 'that we are bound to suffer for all this sunshine and heat with terrible weather later on. The eternal pessimist, I would say.'

She had been there with him again.

'But they were all speaking Welsh,' she said.

He looked arrested for a moment.

'And so they were,' he said. 'Perhaps I understand more of the language than I realized. Goodness, soon I will be a full-fledged Welshman. Before long I will be playing the harp. But no.' He glanced down at his empty sleeve. 'Perhaps not that.'

They both laughed, and some of the tension dissipated.

Finally she talked about the house.

'If it becomes yours,' she asked, 'will you keep everything as it is?'

It was fully furnished.

'For a while, yes,' he said, sitting back as she cleared up the remains of their picnic and put everything away in the basket before crossing the room to stand looking out the front window. 'I fell in love with it as it is, and it would be foolish to change everything merely because I could. I would make changes gradually as I became convinced that I wanted something different. The prevailing browns in the hall can be gloomy on a gray winter's day, for example. They might be the first to go.'

She watched the sheep grazing in the meadow and felt the pain of a nameless longing tighten her chest. The longing to see the hall as it would be, perhaps? And the certain knowledge that she never would.

'What would you change if it were yours?' he asked.

'Nothing much,' she said. 'It has been well and tastefully furnished. But perhaps I would replace the reds in this room with primrose yellows. It is a morning room with windows facing both south and east. It is the room in which one ought to be able to start the day in a sunny mood – even a stormy day in January.'

'Perhaps,' he said, chuckling, 'I will change the predominant colors in here to primrose. *If* the house is ever mine, that is.'

He had come up to stand just behind her right shoulder, she realized. She turned her head and smiled at him, only to find that he was closer than she had thought. She swallowed and turned back to the window. But there was no cliff to climb and no hill to run down this time to break the tension.

'You must be looking forward to getting back to Bath,' he said.

'Yes.'

There was a silence that pulsed with discomfort.

'You must be looking forward to getting your quiet life at Glandwr back,' she said.

'Yes.'

There was another silence in which even breathing was uncomfortable because it was audible.

She turned determinedly to face him. She thought he might take a step back since she could not do so without going through the window, but he stayed where he was.

'I want you to know,' she said, 'that you are *not* ugly. I know you must sometimes see people flinch when they first set eyes on you. I actually ran away from you. But it is because people instantly understand that you have endured something unspeakably painful and will never be quite free of it. When people see you for a second and third and thirty-third time, they no longer really notice. You are *you*, and the person shines through the appearance.'

She felt horribly self-conscious then and wished he would step back or turn away.

'I wish,' he said, 'we did not live in a society that is so ready to judge others on one single fact concerning their life. I wish you were not judged on the fact that, through no fault of your own, you are an unwed mother. I wish you were not lonely.'

'Oh, I am not,' she protested, feeling the heat rise to her cheeks. 'I have friends. I have my son. I have—'

'Too late,' he said. 'You admitted to me weeks ago that you are lonely.'

Just as he had admitted to her that he was. She drew a slow breath.

'For ten years,' he said, 'there has been no man in your life – merely because one scoundrel forced himself on you and destroyed your dreams before he died. It is an empty feeling, is it not – knowing oneself untouchable but wanting to be touched?'

It was even worse, she thought, to be afraid to be touched. But she would not say it aloud. And perhaps there was a way to get past her fears. Perhaps there was.

She blinked her eyes and swallowed against the telltale gurgle in her throat.

'You are not untouchable,' she said.

'Neither are you.'

'I will . . . remember you after I have left here,' she said.

'And I you.'

She swallowed again. He gazed steadily at her. She shut her eyes tightly suddenly and mustered all her rash courage.

'I do not want to be lonely any longer,' she said almost in a whisper. 'I do not want *you* to be lonely.'

She kept her eyes shut until he answered, his voice as low as her own.

'I cannot comfort you, Anne,' he said. 'You can look at me without revulsion, perhaps, but . . . what we are talking of is intimacy. I cannot inflict myself on you for that.'

She opened her eyes and looked at him. How could she know if he was right? How could she know what it would be like to be touched by any man – but especially by him?

She raised her hand to touch the right side of

his face, but instead she laid it flat against his shoulder – and even then she wondered what disfigurements lay beneath his clothing. But there was something in her more powerful than the physical reluctance to touch him – or the reluctance to be touched.

Life, she realized, so often became a determined, relentless avoidance of pain – of one's own, of other people's. But sometimes pain had to be acknowledged and even touched so that one could move into it and through it and past it. Or else be destroyed by it.

'I am someone to arouse revulsion too,' she said. 'I have been raped. I have borne another man's child without ever having been married to him. I am not a virtuous woman. I have *seen* men cringe from me when they discover the truth.'

'Anne,' he said. She saw his eye brighten with unshed tears. 'Oh, Anne, no. But the same consequences might happen again, you know. Though I would, of course, marry you. Imagine if you will what a dreadful fate that would be for you.'

'Don't,' she said. 'Don't belittle yourself in that way.'

'You cannot pretend,' he said, 'that you would wish to be bound to me for life.'

She had not been talking or even thinking of marriage. Or – foolishly – of being got with child again. She did not want to think of either. By this time next week she would be back in Bath with David, resuming her old life and duties at the school though it was still vacation time. Mr Butler would remain here alone – everyone else would have left too.

He would be all alone.

And so would she – surrounded by people, by friends.

But there was today. There was *now*.

'I just do not want to be lonely any longer,' she said again. 'I do not want you to be. I want the memory of this lovely afternoon and of this whole month to be complete.'

'Anne,' he said. 'Anne.'

Only now did she realize that he was calling her by her given name. It warmed her heart to hear him say it.

And then he lifted his hand and set his palm against her cheek, his fingers pushing up into her hair. She leaned into his hand and closed her eyes again.

'Forgive me,' she said. 'Please forgive me. Here I stand trying to seduce you and proving that I am indeed what many people call me.'

He demonstrated then what she had observed earlier, that his left arm was as strong as both were with many other men. He circled her waist with it and drew her hard against him, making a sound very much like a growl as he did so. She stood pressed against him, her face against his left shoulder.

'There is no seduction here,' he said, his voice low against her ear. 'Not on either side. Good

God, Anne, you must know that I want you every bit as much as you can possibly want me. And I do not wish to be lonely any longer either. Let us take away each other's loneliness, then, at least for this afternoon so that it may be made perfect.'

She wrapped her arms about his waist.

Perfect.

. . . so that it may be made perfect.

Please, God. Please, God.

The master bedchamber had green brocaded walls with gilded friezes below the high ceiling. Heavy burgundy velvet curtains hung on either side of the long window from frieze to floor. The great four-poster, canopied bed was hung with burgundy-and-green-striped draperies. A matching spread lay over the bed. A Persian carpet covered most of the floor. Paintings of horses in heavy gilded frames hung on the walls.

It was not a pretty room, but it had struck Anne earlier that it had character, that it was indeed a *master* bedchamber. It was where Mr Butler would surely sleep if he purchased Tŷ Gwyn, she had thought.

The window looked out over the meadow to the trees on the slope opposite. Looking out through it as she stepped into the room now, Anne could see the five-bar wooden gate and the stile in the distance.

The stile – where this had all started.

She shivered slightly. But she was not allowing

her thoughts to speak too loudly to her. She did know, though, that she had wanted – and dreaded – this almost from the beginning of their acquaintance. Perhaps from the moment when they had admitted their loneliness to each other.

It was a mutual loneliness that impelled them now. It was not a bad motive, surely, for what they were about to do. There was compassion in sharing and alleviating another's loneliness. There was a certain tenderness in it.

She felt an overwhelming tenderness for Sydnam Butler, who had demonstrated almost incredible courage and suffered so much yet had pieced his life back together with determination and dignity though he had believed himself untouchable ever since.

Now she would touch him and prove that he was mistaken about himself. And he would touch her and she would feel again like a desirable woman. Perhaps.

Please, God.

She turned as she heard him close the door and looked uncertainly at him. But her resolve had not weakened in the distance from morning room to bedchamber. She *did* want him with a knee-weakening desire.

'Please,' he said, smiling at her and closing the distance between them, 'may I be the one to take down your hair? You could do it ten times faster with your two hands, I daresay, but may I do it?'

She smiled and stood still while his fingers

fumbled awkwardly with the pins that held her hair up. She looked deliberately into his face as his hand worked. She did not even know, she realized, what lay behind the black eye patch. But she was struck again by the extraordinary beauty of the left side of his face. He was twenty-eight years old – one year younger than she. He could never have been a rake, she thought, even if *this* had not happened to him. He was a serious, gentle, affectionate man. He would have been married by now to some woman with a beauty and social rank to match his own. He would have had children. He would have had a family to bring with him to Tŷ Gwyn.

But no – he would never even have come to Wales if he had not also gone to the Peninsula against the advice of everyone who knew and loved him.

She would never have met him.

And if she had not been raped, she would be married to Henry Arnold now and living in Gloucestershire. She would not be standing here in the master bedchamber at Tŷ Gwyn, having her hair taken down by a one-armed man who had become strangely precious to her.

How strange were the ways of fate.

But she was mentally prattling, she thought, when her hair came cascading down over her shoulders and he reached behind him to set her hairpins down on a table without taking his eye off her.

Her thoughts came crashing to a halt then, and she felt horribly, horribly vulnerable – not because she did not believe in her own beauty but precisely because she did. Beauty could blind the beholder to all else, even the personhood of the one who possessed it. And she could see in his eye that he found her beautiful.

I am Anne, she wanted to cry out to him. *Please do not forget that I am Anne.*

Please, please, please do not call my hair my crowning glory.

He leaned forward and kissed her mouth with closed lips. Desire shot through her like a lightning bolt, almost causing her knees to buckle. And with it came the return of thought.

All was going to be well. Surely it was.

'Anne,' he murmured so softly that she almost missed it.

And then he turned away and shrugged out of his coat and sat down on the side of the bed to pull off his Hessian boots. It was a hard thing to do one-handed – she could see that. His valet must, of course, do it for him at home. She did not know if she should offer to help, but she did not do so, and he managed. She guessed that he managed most tasks that a two-armed person would find impossible to do one-handed.

His right shirtsleeve was pinned to his side just as his coat sleeve was.

She waited tensely.

But when he got to his feet again, he drew back

the bedcovers and turned to reach out his arm to her, and she realized that he did not intend to remove any more of his clothes.

'Anne,' he said, 'will you take off your dress yourself? It would take me too long.'

He watched her until she stood before him in just her shift and her stockings. She sat on the bed to take off the latter, but he kneeled before her and removed them one at a time himself.

'Ah,' he said, sitting back on his heels and gazing up at her when the task was complete, 'you are incredibly beautiful, Anne. I am sorry. I am so very sorry—'

'No.' She leaned forward and set her hands on his shoulders, and her hair fell forward to frame both their faces. 'Please don't be. Please, please do not. I would never have met you if you were not like this. I would not be here with you now. And I would not be here if I were not as I am. I *want* to be here with you. And if you say you are sorry, then I must say it too. I do not want either of us to be sorry for anything this afternoon.'

'Anne,' he said, 'I am not very experienced. And I have had no experience at all since . . . this.'

It was somehow reassuring to know that he felt his own insecurities and anxieties just as she felt hers. Perhaps that was why she had found the courage to come this far.

'I am not very experienced either.' She smiled at him.

He closed the gap between their mouths and

kissed her. And this time he deepened the kiss, parting his lips, passing his tongue over her lips until she opened her mouth and his tongue came warm inside and she wrapped both arms about his neck and pushed her fingers up into his hair, making a sound of appreciation deep in her throat as she did so.

Or perhaps it was he who made the sound.

'Lie down,' he whispered against her mouth as he raised his head. 'Will you remove your shift? But only if you feel comfortable doing so.'

She crossed her arms and pulled it off over her head before lying down and moving over so that he could lie beside her. And strangely she did not feel uncomfortable though he stood looking down at her for several moments. He had called her beautiful and he desired her. But he had also called her by name, and she knew somehow from the look in his eye, though there was desire there, that it was *her* he saw, not just her voluptuous beauty. Beneath his gaze she could feel simply herself.

And this at least was new. She had never been naked with a man before.

She throbbed with wanting him.

He lay on his right side facing her, and his hand moved over her, warm, sensitive – and trembling. She turned toward him, smiled at him, and caressed him through his clothing with her own hand – and on his left side.

He was all warm, hard-muscled masculinity.

She could feel the muscles in his arm and shoulder and rippling along his back. She could feel the muscles in his buttock when she rested her hand there while her eyes drifted closed and she licked her lips. He was doing exquisite things with his thumb and forefinger at the nipple of one breast and then the other.

Curiously, the presence of his clothing against her own bare skin excited her as much as nakedness would have done. Perhaps more.

Desire pooled hot and sharp between her thighs. And she moved closer to him, pressing her breasts to his shirt while his hand moved lower, slid between her legs, and found that aching spot and caressed it.

He set his mouth to hers and his tongue came inside again and circled her own slowly before moving to the roof of her mouth.

'Turn onto your back for me,' he whispered against her mouth.

He was, she realized then, unbuttoning his pantaloons at the waist and opening the front flap.

She almost forgot his disabilities as he rolled on top of her and his legs pressed between her own, spreading them wide until she twined them about his powerful thighs encased in the warm fabric of his pantaloons. His weight was heavy on her. She felt him position himself against the sensitive opening to her desire and her womb and spread both hands over his buttocks as he slid his hand beneath her.

He came into her with one slow, hard, deep thrust.

And memory flooded every inch of her body.

She did not fight him. She did not call out or try to push him away. Her mind was sharply at work with a different message from the one her body was sending her. Her mind told her that he was Sydnam Butler, that he was filling her with himself because it was something they both wanted, that until the very moment of entry she had been filled with wonder and pleasure and the desire for more.

Her body was rigid with tension, she realized, and his was heavy on her. He was deep inside her – and holding still.

'Anne,' he said. 'Anne?'

'Sydnam.' She had never spoken his given name aloud before, even to herself. But it saved her now, the knowledge that that was who he was. 'Sydnam, it is all right. It is all right. Don't stop.'

She moved her hands up his sides until she became suddenly, horribly aware that there was no arm on the right side.

But at the same moment he moved in her, withdrawing to the brink of her, pressing in again, smooth and hard against the slickness of her inner passage.

It was all terribly, terribly carnal, terrifyingly intimate.

Body and mind waged a war – and both won, both lost. She knew he was Sydnam, she recognized the beauty of what he did with her, she still desperately wanted it, she relaxed and opened to him.

And yet physically, sexually, she felt nothing. Not horror. Not pleasure. Only the mental satisfaction that this was happening to her again and that perhaps the memory of it would replace the memory of the other time.

His left hand took her right, twined fingers with hers, and lifted their joined hands over her head as he worked in her for several minutes until finally he sighed against the side of her face and she felt liquid heat at her core.

His fingers relaxed about her own.

She felt like weeping then. It had been beautiful, yet somehow she had missed the beauty. It had been intimate, yet she had hidden away from it in some deep, secret part of herself. She might have shared something deeper than their joined bodies with him, but she felt very separate from him.

He rolled awkwardly off her almost immediately and sat up on the side of the bed facing away from her without looking at her. He buttoned the flap of his pantaloons and got to his feet to cross to the window, where he stood looking out.

He was indeed beautiful, she thought, looking at his broad shoulders, his narrow waist and firm buttocks, his long, well-muscled legs. And he had just been inside her body. He had made love to her.

And he knew that it had not been good for her.

She knew what reason he would give himself for that.

She opened her mouth to assure him that it had not been so very bad, and that his disfigurements had had nothing to do with her lack of complete pleasure.

But how could she say that aloud? What reassurance would there be in such words?

And how could she tell him the truth – that the shadow of another man had come between them at the moment of their joining, that for that moment she had felt such a revulsion that she had almost fought him in maniacal panic?

How could she tell him that for a moment he had become Albert Moore to her?

What *could* she say to him?

She said nothing. She had *not* fought him after all or said or done anything that had shown open revulsion. And she *had* told him beforehand that she was inexperienced.

Perhaps for him their lovemaking had demonstrated no more than that fact.

But she had so wanted the afternoon to be perfect.

She had so wanted . . .

Ah, dear God, she had so *wanted*.

CHAPTER 11

Sydnam stood at the bedchamber window looking out. It was still only late afternoon. Probably no more than half an hour had passed since they had come up here.

He did not know if Anne Jewell was sleeping on the bed behind him. He would not look to see. But he doubted it.

He felt sexually satiated, and that ought to have been a wonderful feeling after such a long celibacy. Instead, he felt a terrible sense of failure. Not that his sexual techniques were so lacking, he supposed, especially to a woman of no real experience. No, it was something else that had caused her to withdraw as soon as they reached the point of real intimacy.

Had he expected that she would find him beautiful, that she would find it beautiful?

Had he not realized from the moment she kissed him in the rose arbor that she had steeled herself to show him compassion, to assure him that in her eyes he was a normal man? Had he not realized too that her offer of herself had come out of her terrible loneliness? She ought to have been married years ago to a man of her own choosing, but circumstances beyond her control had made her virtually unmarriageable.

Perhaps, he thought, they had both got what they deserved from this ill-advised ending to their afternoon together – and to their acquaintance. Loneliness was not a good enough reason for what they had done together – not when each of them was lonely for commitment and permanency. Yet it was impossible for them to find such things together.

That had just been made painfully obvious.

He wished the matter had not been put to the test.

Too late he realized that sex did not take away loneliness. It probably made it far worse. The next few days would reveal the truth of that to him, he suspected.

He did not want to turn his head to look at her. He would, he thought, find that Anne Jewell, his friend and confidante, the woman with whom he supposed he had allowed himself to fall in love during the past few weeks, was gone, to be replaced by a stranger with whom he would feel uncomfortable because they had been intimate together when there was after all no real intimacy between them.

And tomorrow she *would* be gone – literally. When he next returned here, he would come to this room and stand just here and try to pretend that he could turn around and find her asleep on the bed.

Or perhaps not. Perhaps he would stand here and wish he could forget that she had ever been to Tŷ Gwyn with him.

He turned. She was lying with the covers drawn up under her arms, those arms and her shoulders bare, her glorious honey-colored hair in a shining tangle about her head and shoulders and over the pillow. Her crowning glory, he thought, though he did not say so aloud. It was too much of a cliché. And the time for such words was past anyway.

She was looking steadily at him, her expression unfathomable. She was probably hoping he had not noticed that their mating had not been good for her.

He smiled and said what he had not known he was going to say though it was what he realized must be said – later even if not now.

'If you wish, Anne,' he said, 'we will marry.'

It was not much of a proposal. He realized that as he spoke the words. But how could he ask her any other way? How could he lay an obligation upon her by speaking of emotions that would doubtless embarrass and even dismay her? He certainly did not want her pity.

'I am well able to support you,' he added, 'and your son. I think it might be a good idea. Don't you?'

It struck him that it was possibly the worst idea in the world.

She gazed at him for a long time before answering.

215

'I think,' she said then, 'that friendship and need and some mutual attraction have been justification enough for what we have just done together. But they are not a good enough justification for marriage.'

'Are they not?' He felt a terrible sorrow – and an enormous sense of relief. 'Not even friendship? Is it not desirable that a man and his wife like each other and find it easy to talk with each other? And laugh with each other?'

'Yes,' she said. 'But there ought to be very much more than just that.'

Love? It was such an overused, underdefined word. What *did* it mean? But he did not think she was talking about love. There should be a physical attraction between husband and wife – that was what she meant. Or at the very least, there should be no actual revulsion.

It would not be possible for her to marry him, to share a bed with him for the rest of their lives. But he had always known that it would not be possible for any woman.

Had she said yes to his tentative marriage proposal, then he would have pressed forward with wedding plans. Had she even looked as if she *wanted* to say yes, he might have assured her that his feelings were engaged, that he was not merely making an honorable offer because he had bedded her. He might then have proceeded to a proper marriage offer.

But she had neither said yes nor wavered.

And part of him was relieved. Since coming to Glandwr he had retreated into a deeply private life, and on the whole he had been happy with that life.

He smiled at her again.

'I will say no more on the subject, then,' he said. 'But you must promise, please, Anne, to let me know without delay if you find after your return to Bath that you are with child. And you must promise to allow me to marry you if you are.'

She gazed silently at him.

'Promise?' he said.

She nodded.

Perhaps he ought to have asked differently, he thought belatedly as he stooped to pick up his coat and tuck it beneath his arm while he picked up his boots. Perhaps he ought to have thrown his heart into his proposal and trusted her to make her own decision without pity. But it was too late now. He had asked, and she had refused.

Yes, sex *did* make loneliness worse. He already felt his own like a raw pain.

'I'll leave you some privacy to dress,' he said, crossing the room toward the door, taking his own clothes with him – and then of course having to set down the boots until he had opened the door. 'I'll see you downstairs.'

'Thank you,' she said.

The gig bounced along the lane and turned onto the narrow road that would take them back through the village to the gates of Glandwr. The sky was still cloudless, the late afternoon sun still hot.

Anne could feel the unexpectedly pleasant aftermath of love in her body – the slight languor, the sensitivity in her breasts, the leftover ache between her thighs, the near-soreness inside. She tried to concentrate her mind only on the beauty of what had happened. It had been undeniably beautiful – it *had*.

It ought to have been the perfect end to the perfect day – and the perfect holiday.

A bend in the road sent her swaying sideways, and her arm pressed against Sydnam's. She looked up at him as she set some distance between them again. She gazed at the left side of his face, which was impossibly handsome, though truth to tell she no longer found the right side ugly. As she had told him earlier, it was simply part of him.

'I hope the weather remains good for your journey,' he said.

'Yes.' They were back to talking about the weather, were they?

By this time tomorrow she would be far away from Glandwr.

Panic grabbed at her stomach.

She did not look away from him. She knew that in the days to come, until memory started to recede, as it inevitably would, she would desperately try to remember him as he looked at this moment – and that she would just as desperately try to assure herself that what had happened between them had *felt* as beautiful as her mind told her it had been.

But above all else they were friends, she thought, and friendship was a very dear thing.

She ought not to have offered herself to Sydnam this afternoon. It had been a terrible mistake. Loneliness and compassion and even sexual need had not been enough. And she still could not bring herself to try to explain to him. That, she believed, could only make matters worse. Besides, neither of them had said anything about its not having been quite perfect. Perhaps for him it had been.

She had refused his marriage proposal, she reminded herself. She had refused a man whom she liked and respected and admired and a man moreover who was able to support her in comfort – she, who had thought no man would ever again offer her marriage. Why had she said no?

If you wish, Anne, we will marry.

Kind words, kindly and dutifully spoken – because they had lain together.

He did not wish to marry her.

And she could not marry him even if he did – or any man. She was still too deeply wounded by the past. Any approach to intimacy sent her scurrying into her mind, where she was safe from her emotions.

She could not impose a frigid iceberg of a body on Sydnam, who deserved so much more.

Friendship would not be sufficient to offer. Only love might be – but she did not know what love was, not sexual, marital love, at least. She closed her eyes for a moment and remembered what Lady Rosthorn had said one morning out on the cliffs.

. . . the real meaning of things lies deep down and the real meaning of things is always beautiful because it is simply love.

But she did not trust love. Love had let her down at every turn – in the persons of her mother, Henry Arnold, her father, her sister. And her love for her pupil, Prue Moore, had led to disaster. Love had caused her nothing but pain. She was afraid to love Sydnam or to be loved by him. It was as well that there was no real question of love between them.

'Anne,' Sydnam said softly, restoring her wandering mind to the present, 'perhaps by tomorrow morning you will have different thoughts. Shall I ask you again before you leave?'

'No,' she said. And looking ahead, she could see the village approaching. 'It has been a lovely afternoon, Sydnam, has it not? Let us just remember it and be grateful for it.'

Bottle it up, cage it up, hide it away with all its imperfections and lost possibilities.

'It has been pleasant,' he agreed.

But you must promise, please, Anne, to let me know without delay if you find after your return to Bath that you are with child. And you must promise to allow me to marry you if you are.

She smiled as they entered the village and he

220

greeted an elderly villager who was sitting on an old chair outside the door of his cottage, smoking a pipe.

'You spoke in Welsh,' she said as they drove on.

'I did.' He turned his head to grin at her. 'I wished him a good afternoon – *prynhawn da* – and asked how he did and how his daughter and son-in-law did. Are you impressed?'

'Vastly,' she said.

They laughed.

It struck her then that she would miss more than just him. She would miss this place. She would miss Wales. It did not surprise her at all that it had become home to him, that he intended to spend the rest of his life here.

She envied him.

Perhaps if . . .

No. No, she would not even think of that.

But ah, she *would* miss him. And how she wished suddenly that they could go back to Tŷ Gwyn and set right what had gone wrong there. But there was only the future left – almost none of it that they would share. And that little bit would be an agony. She wished she could click her fingers and find herself two weeks farther on in her life, the pain of tomorrow's departure well in the past.

She turned her head to gaze at his profile again, to imprint it upon her memory.

Sydnam drove the gig straight back to the stables. The others had not yet returned from their excursion, a groom told them.

221

And so instead of walking the short distance to the house and taking their leave of each other within the next few minutes, they strolled away from the house, and their steps took them without conscious volition in the direction of the hill they had climbed the night of the country dancing. They climbed it again now and stood on the top, looking out over the sea, which was a deep blue in the late afternoon light, while the land was bathed in the golden glow of a sun that was beginning to sink in the direction of the western horizon.

They were standing a couple of feet apart, two friendly strangers who just happened to have lain together an hour or so ago.

It had been a mistake, but they had no more time together in which to regret it.

He heard her swallow. He heard the gurgle in her throat. And he knew that though she had cringed from the intimacy of sex with him, she liked him, she would find leaving him difficult. She was his *friend* – it was gift enough.

'I will miss you,' he said.

'Yes.' Her voice, though steady, was higher pitched than usual. 'I did not want to come, you know. It seemed horribly presumptuous to come only on an invitation from Lady Hallmere. As the carriage approached Glandwr, I would have done anything in the world to be going back to Bath. But now I find it hard to leave.'

She did not have to leave. She could stay here

with him for the rest of her life. But he did not say so aloud. He knew the impossibility of it. And she had made her decision back at Tŷ Gwyn. She had said no.

'Perhaps,' he said, 'you will come back another year.'

'Perhaps,' she agreed.

But they both knew she would not. They both knew that once she left tomorrow they would never see each other again.

And if it was true that they were just friends, that it was merely loneliness that had brought and held them together, it would not matter that they would never see each other again. Not really. They would quickly forget and resume the normal course of their lives.

But he knew he would not forget.

Losing Anne Jewell was going to be one of the most excruciatingly painful experiences of his life.

He reached for her hand, and her fingers curled about his and clung tightly.

'I have enjoyed knowing you, Anne Jewell,' he said.

'And I you, Sydnam Butler.'

He turned his head to look at her and they both smiled.

Perhaps there was a possibility . . . Perhaps if she were given time to . . .

But she pulled her hand abruptly away from his even as he opened his mouth to speak and pointed in the direction of the house and driveway.

'Here they come,' she cried. 'I must be there when David arrives. I have been away from him all day. Oh, I do hope he has come to no harm.'

A line of carriages was making its way up the driveway.

'Go,' he said. 'You can be there on the terrace waiting for him by the time he arrives.'

She turned her head to look at him.

'Go,' he said. 'I'll take the shortcut back to the cottage.'

She hesitated for only a moment, an instant's indecision in her face, and then she turned and ran down the hill as she had the other night, when he had run beside and a little ahead of her to reach the bottom before her.

He looked after her now and wondered if he was sorry or glad that he had been prevented from speaking, from begging her to reconsider.

He rather thought he was glad.

Or would be by next week.

Or next year.

Or the next lifetime.

Anne was very close to tears by the time she reached the terrace just as the first of the carriages rolled to a stop before the doors. She was desperate to see her son, to hear his voice, to hold him in her arms. And yet she was aware too that she had just left Sydnam behind, without any sort of good-bye, that in all probability she would never see him again.

But she hated good-byes. She *hated* them. It was better this way.

David came tumbling out of the second carriage as soon as he spied her standing there and came dashing toward her, his legs pumping, his eyes sparkling, his mouth in motion, the volume of his treble voice almost deafening. She caught him up in a tight hug, laughing, and kissed the top of his head.

'You should have *been* there, Mama . . . Cousin Joshua . . . and you should have *seen* me . . . Davy . . . and then we . . . Lord Aidan . . . it was such *fun* . . . Cousin Joshua . . . Becky and Marianne were scared of the winding stairs, but I helped them up and Lady Aidan said I was a perfect gentleman and . . . Alexander . . . Cousin Joshua and Daniel . . . the little ones . . . I *wish* you had been there, Mama, to see . . .'

Anne laughed again as they made their way up to the nursery. She had missed most of the details of his day, but it did not seem to matter.

'It would seem, then,' she said, 'that you had a good time.'

'I had the *best* time,' he said. 'But I wish you could have seen the castle, Mama. You would have loved it.'

'I am quite sure I would have,' she said.

'Did you enjoy the place Mr Butler took you?' he asked her.

'Tŷ Gwyn?' she said. 'Very much.'

'But you really ought to have come with us,' he

said. 'You would have had much more fun. Cousin Joshua . . .' And he was off again.

It was wonderful to see him happy and animated, his face bronzed from the sun.

But the day out had tired him. When Anne went looking for him after returning to her room to wash and change for the evening, she found him in his room alone, sitting on his bed in his nightshirt with his knees drawn up and his arms wrapped around them. He was looking listless and anything but happy.

'Tired?' she asked, bending over him to push back a lock of his hair and kiss his forehead.

'We are going home tomorrow,' he said.

At the foot of his bed, his trunk was almost completely packed.

She felt weak-kneed at the thought and sat down on the side of the bed.

'Yes,' she said. 'It is time. We have been here a whole month.'

'I do not see,' he said, sounding aggrieved, 'why everyone has to go home when we are all having such a jolly time.'

'But the trouble with jolly times,' she said, 'is that they would lose their jolliness if they went on forever and become merely tedious.'

'No, they would not,' he protested.

And perhaps he was right. Who had first mouthed that piece of dubious wisdom anyway?

'Everyone else's mama went today except you,' he said, the words coming rather jerkily from his mouth.

It was unlike David to be petulant. Anne was smitten with dismay – and guilt.

'I asked you if you minded my not going,' she said, 'and you said no. I would have come if—'

'And everyone else's papa went too,' he said. 'Except Davy's, who is dead. But he has his Uncle Aidan, who is as good as a papa because Davy lives with him and they do things together. They go riding and fishing and swimming and other things.'

'Oh, David,' she said.

'And Daniel lives with Cousin Joshua,' he continued. 'Cousin Joshua is his *papa*. He takes him into the village where we used to live and out in a fishing boat. And he lets him ride on his shoulders and pull his hair and do all sorts of things.'

'David—'

'I did *so* have a papa once, didn't I?' he asked. 'You said no, but Davy says everyone *has* to have a papa even if he is dead. Is my papa dead?'

Anne closed her eyes briefly. Why did all of life's crises seem to come along when one felt least ready to deal with them? She was still feeling raw from a goodbye that had not quite been said. But this was of greater importance. She tried to focus her mind.

It was true that every time David had asked her in the past why he did not have a father she had told him that he was special and had only a mama, who loved him twice as much as any other mama loved her child. It had been a foolish answer even for a young child, and she had always known that she must do better eventually.

She just wished it had not happened tonight of all nights.

'Yes, David,' she said. 'He is dead. He drowned. He was swimming at night and he drowned. I am so sorry.'

She braced herself for the question about his father's identity that was surely going to come next. But it seemed there was a more important question to ask first.

'Did he love me?' he asked, his eyes like two large bruises in his pale face. 'Did he do things with me?'

'Oh, my sweetheart,' she said, setting the backs of her fingers against his cheek, 'he would have loved you more than anyone else in the world. But he died before you were born.'

'How could he have been my papa, then?' he asked her, frowning.

'He had . . . *given* you to me before he died,' she said, 'and I kept you safe until you were born. I will explain to you one day when you are a little older. But right now you are having a hard time keeping your eyes open and tomorrow is going to be a busy day. Wriggle under the sheets now and I'll tell you a story and tuck you in and kiss you good night.'

Ten minutes later he looked up at her with sleepy eyes – and then smiled with pure mischief.

'I am glad you did not come to the castle,' he said. 'Now I get to tell Mr Keeble and Matron and Miss Martin all about it myself.'

She laughed softly. 'And about cricket and boating and playing pirates and painting,' she said. 'I promise to let you tell it all. It will be good to see everyone again, will it not?'

'Mmm,' he said.

And just like that, in the way of children, he was asleep.

Anne sat beside him until Davy and Alexander came tiptoeing in a while later.

One day soon David was going to think of the questions he had not asked tonight, and she was going to have to give him answers. She was going to have to tell him about Albert Moore. His father.

She shivered.

Glenys, sniffling just as if they had been mistress and maid for years, had insisted upon doing her packing for her. There was nothing to do now, then, except go downstairs to the drawing room to be sociable for an hour or two. And sociable she must be. No one must suspect that the visit to Tŷ Gwyn had been anything more than a pleasant afternoon's outing.

But just so many hours ago – she counted them off on her fingers – she had lain with Sydnam Butler and it had been good. She *knew* it had been good. Perhaps if it could just have happened again her body would have known that as well as her mind.

She ached with a sudden longing to have it happen again.

Was she quite, quite mad to have refused his offer of marriage?

But how could she have said yes? What did she have to offer him?

And what did he have to offer her but a dutiful willingness to take the consequences of what they had done?

If you wish, Anne, we will marry.

CHAPTER 12

'This really must be one of the loveliest places on earth,' the Duchess of Bewcastle said with a contented sigh, tipping her head sideways to rest on her husband's shoulder. 'You were quite right about that, Wulfric. The sight of the moon on the water like this makes me almost weep with awe.'

'It is to be hoped, my love,' his grace said dryly, 'that you will resist the urge. I have already got my boots wet this month, not to mention my unmentionables. I was hoping to save my neck-cloth from a similar fate.'

She laughed and he tightened his arm about her shoulders.

They were walking along the beach close to the water's edge as they sometimes did late at night after James had been fed and everyone else had retired and they might be assured of some private time for themselves.

'Nevertheless, I will be quite happy to return to Lindsey Hall,' she said.

'Will you?' he asked.

'It is home,' she said with a sigh. 'I will be glad to go home.'

'Will you?' he said again, and he paused for a few moments in order to kiss her with unhurried thoroughness.

'Will you sell the white house to Mr Butler?' she asked him as they walked on.

'It is not really a white house, my love,' he said. 'I ought to have taken you over there and shown it to you.'

'But that is what its name means in Welsh,' she said. '*Will* you sell it?'

'My grandfather bought it as a young man,' he told her. 'Apparently the rumor was soon making the rounds of fashionable drawing rooms that he was housing his mistress there, but it turned out – though not before my grandmother had blackened both eyes of the man who was foolish enough to drop a malicious word of warning in her ear – that it was her particular friend, a severely battered wife, who had taken sanctuary there. My grandfather killed the husband when challenged to a duel over the matter – an incident that was quite efficiently hushed up, by the way, as such matters usually were in those days. He was a colorful man, my grandfather – and my grandmother no less so. The Bedwyn men, of course, never ever employ mistresses after they are married.'

The duchess laughed softly. 'I daresay,' she said, 'they gave it up as a hazardous practice after a few of them acquired wives like your grandmother.'

The duke uttered one of his rare barks of laughter.

'I suppose I will sell Tŷ Gwyn to Sydnam,' he said after they had strolled in silence for a few minutes. 'In fact, I undoubtedly will, since I know it will be passing into very good hands. But I am not expected to give in too easily on such matters, you know. I will tell him before we leave here.'

'I have been so very disappointed,' she said, 'that nothing seems to have developed between him and Miss Jewell after all our efforts. I was convinced that they were made for each other. We all were.'

'I shudder,' he said, 'at the realization that a whole generation of Bedwyns and their spouses have descended to the ignoble sport of match-making. It is enough to make me seriously wonder where I went wrong with them. They even appear to hold the extraordinary conviction that they had a hand in bringing us together, Christine.'

'He needs someone,' she said as if she had not heard him, 'and so does she. And whenever I have seen them together, they have always looked right. Has it struck you, Wulfric, that she might have been the Marchioness of Hallmere if Joshua's cousin had married her, and that Joshua might have been plain Mr Moore?'

'I do not imagine,' he said dryly, 'that Freyja would have liked being plain Mrs Moore.'

'And I like them both exceedingly,' she added, clearly still talking about Anne and Sydnam.

'I daresay,' he said, 'logic seems to point to the conclusion that therefore they must belong together, Christine. But if such logic always prevailed, what in heaven's name are you and I doing together?'

'I had high hopes,' she said, 'after he took her to see the white house this afternoon while we were all at Pembroke Castle that we would arrive home to find that he had offered for her and there would be a betrothal to celebrate. I even had tentative plans for persuading everyone to stay another day or two for a grand celebratory party. But instead Miss Jewell had hardly a word to say this evening about Tŷ Gwyn but merely wanted to know everything about Pembroke. And she scarcely stopped smiling all evening. Did you notice? But of course, I ought to have realized it before now – that was the problem, was it not? Why would she have been *smiling* if she had not been secretly nursing a broken heart? Perhaps he simply did not have the courage to make her an offer. I suppose he thinks he is unbearably ugly, foolish man. I wish now I had invited him for the evening, but I did not know when we would be back. Wulfric, do you think—'

'Christine,' his grace said sternly, stopping altogether and swinging her around to face him before gazing down at her with eyes that matched the moonlight, 'I did *not* bring you out here in order to discuss the sad state of Sydnam Butler's love life – or that of Miss Jewell.'

'I do beg your pardon,' she said with a sigh. But then she smiled up at him and set her hands on his shoulders, not noticeably chastened by the reproof. 'Why *did* you bring me out here?'

This time his kiss was not so much thorough as it was ruthless.

Her grace said no more about Anne Jewell and Sydnam Butler.

The long spell of hot, dry weather appeared to have broken at last. The clouds hung low and gray overhead and rain was drizzling down as Sydnam made his way on foot up the driveway toward the main house. The weather seemed appropriate to the occasion.

There was no real need for him to go there since Bewcastle and the duchess were staying for two days longer, and in fact it was only the Hallmeres and the Rosthorns who were leaving today. But it seemed the courteous thing to do to pay his parting respects to Freyja and Morgan.

Not that he was *that* adept at self-deception, of course.

Anne Jewell was leaving today too, and his heart felt literally heavy within him. He dared not think yet about what his life was going to be like without her.

He ought perhaps to have stayed away this morning. They had effectively said good-bye yesterday, though the return of the carriages from Pembroke Castle had prevented the actual words from being spoken. It probably would be as well to leave them unspoken.

But though he had been up since dawn and had paced his cottage and made a new decision every few minutes, he had known from the start that he would come.

Good-byes, painful as they were, needed to be said.

The end needed to be written beneath every story.

And so he was on his way to Glandwr.

Halfway up the driveway he realized that he was limping and immediately strode more firmly onward.

He could see that several carriages were already drawn up on the terrace. He pulled the brim of his hat lower in order to shield his face from some of the fine rain.

It seemed to Sydnam as he came around the carriages and glanced toward the open front doors of the house that all the Bedwyns must be gathered in the hall with their spouses and children and other guests. There was a great deal of noise and bustle going on in there.

He stayed outside on the terrace, and finally Hallmere and Rosthorn stepped outside and shook his hand and helped their children's nurses lift their children inside the carriages before they could get too wet. Then Freyja came out between Alleyne and Rannulf, and she shook Sydnam's hand too and informed him in her usual forthright manner – and without explaining herself – that she had never before taken him for a fool.

Hallmere handed her into the carriage while Ralf grinned at Sydnam and Alleyne waggled his eyebrows.

Then Morgan came out, hugged her brothers, saw that Sydnam was standing with them, and hugged him too despite the fact that his clothes were considerably wetter than theirs.

'Sydnam,' she said, gazing up into his face, and he could have sworn that there were tears in her eyes. 'Oh, my dear Sydnam. I *so* want you to be happy.'

'Morgan,' he protested, 'I *am* happy.'

'We are missing Anne,' Hallmere said.

'Mrs Pritchard is weeping over her,' Rannulf explained with a grin. 'And Judith and Christine are still awaiting their turn.'

'Come, *chérie*,' Rosthorn said to Morgan, 'and get in out of the rain.'

'We had *all* better get in out of the rain,' Rannulf said, and almost simultaneously he and Alleyne headed back into the house and Hallmere and Rosthorn followed their spouses into the carriages.

Sydnam was left abruptly alone on the terrace – alone with Anne Jewell, who was just hurrying out, head down, her son's hand in hers. Aidan, who was accompanying them, was hauled back inside by someone's hand on his arm.

Ah, Sydnam thought – the Bedwyns were being tactful, were they?

Her head came up when she was no farther than a foot or two away from him, and she looked at him, startled.

237

It seemed to him that she was pale, though perhaps it was only the absence of sunlight that gave the impression.

'I came to take my leave of everyone,' he said.

Her son smiled up at him, though he looked as if he had been crying.

'I am going to ask Mr Upton about those oil paints,' he said.

Sydnam smiled back at him.

'David,' Anne said, without taking her eyes off Sydnam, 'make your bow to Mr Butler if you please, and then climb inside the carriage where you will be dry.'

'Good-bye, David,' Sydnam said, 'and thank you for letting me see one of your paintings.'

'Good-bye, sir.' The boy bobbed his head in a quick gesture of respect and half dived into the carriage out of the rain.

And so they were left alone together for the last time, he and Anne Jewell – with people beyond the open door into the house on one side and people inside the row of carriages on the other side. The setting could hardly have been more public.

But he ignored everything except the woman standing before him.

Anne. Whom he liked exceedingly well. Whom perhaps he loved.

No – whom he *did* love.

She was leaving. He would never see her again even though his body felt its knowledge of hers like a dull ache.

And his heart? Well, it felt now rather as if it had acquired lead weights to drag it downward.

'You will remember your promise?' he asked, offering her his hand.

'Yes.'

She was looking at his chin. But she set her left hand in his. He bent his head over it and raised it to his lips for a few moments. He was terribly aware then that they had an audience – which quite possibly had assiduously turned its collective attention elsewhere since undoubtedly it had collectively arranged for this final, brief tête-à-tête.

She looked up into his face as he raised his head and released her hand, and he could see the drizzle beaded on her cheeks and eyelashes. A frown creased her brow.

'Good-bye,' she said, her voice little more than a whisper.

'Good-bye.' Somehow he smiled at her.

She turned and scrambled up the steps into the carriage with the children before he could offer to assist her, and her attention was taken by Freyja's young daughter, who opened her arms to be picked up.

The coachman put up the steps and slammed the door shut before climbing to his perch, and the carriage rocked into motion and turned almost immediately to follow Hallmere's down the driveway.

She did not look out.

Sydnam was scarcely aware that several other people had stepped out of the house to wave.

He felt lonelier than he ever remembered feeling.

Just this time yesterday he had been looking with satisfaction at the sunshine and anticipating a whole afternoon alone with her at Tŷ Gwyn.

Just yesterday.

Now she was gone.

A hand came to rest on his right shoulder, and he looked up into Bewcastle's austere, impassive face.

'We will withdraw to the library, Sydnam, since you happen to be here,' he said, 'and discuss what is to become of Tŷ Gwyn.'

Anne was exhausted with play by the time she arrived in Bath. The nurse's motion sickness was worse than ever on the return journey, and Anne vigorously kept the children amused so that they would not grow petulant with the tedium of long hours spent in the carriage.

When they stopped for meals and for the night, she was determinedly cheerful as she conversed with Joshua and Lady Hallmere. She would not for one moment have them believe that she was in low spirits, though in fact they were as low as they could possibly be.

How foolish of her to have believed that she could lie with a man and then simply forget about it.

How foolish to have believed that they could

take away each other's loneliness for an hour and remember simply with gratitude.

And how foolish to have hoped she could lie with Sydnam Butler and taken pleasure from the experience just as if she were a normal woman.

Memory was like a raw wound that each passing mile only aggravated.

She had *known* him. She had been known *by* him. And yet her body had somehow remained aloof from the wonder of it.

She had been terribly afraid that he would not come to say good-bye.

She had been terribly afraid that he would.

And then when he *had* come, when she had looked for the very last time into his handsome, damaged face, there had been only pain.

And the terrible temptation to tell him that she had changed her mind.

She had not.

They had gravitated toward each other during the past month and spent time with each other – ah, yes, and lain together – because they were both lonely.

But that explanation was wearing very thin.

Surely it was not just the knowledge that she was alone again, without a man in her life again, that caused the sharp pain in her throat and chest that would not go away?

She supposed she had fallen ever so slightly in love with Sydnam Butler. Or perhaps a whole lot in love with him.

She had fallen in love with an impossibility.

The carriages stopped outside Lady Potford's house on Great Pulteney Street, since Joshua and his family were to stay there for a couple of nights before returning to Cornwall. The one carriage was to continue on its way to Daniel Street with the baggage, but Anne and David chose to walk the rest of the way in order to stretch their legs. Joshua insisted upon accompanying them. He offered Anne his arm. David walked close to his other side.

'Anne,' he said, 'it was a pleasant month, was it not?'

'Very pleasant indeed,' she assured him. 'Thank you so much for thinking to invite us, Joshua.'

'And yet here you both are,' he said, 'Friday-faced on a Tuesday.'

'I am not—' Anne protested.

'I wish we could have stayed forever and ever,' David cried passionately. He had come very close to shedding tears again a short while ago as he said goodbye to Daniel and Emily and shook hands with Lady Hallmere.

'Yes, it would have been desirable,' Joshua agreed. 'But all good things end, lad. If they did not, there would be no new good things to look forward to. If Miss Martin can spare you, perhaps you will both come to Penhallow for Christmas. That will give us all something new to look forward to.'

David, Anne suddenly noticed, was actually

holding Joshua's hand, something he normally considered quite beneath his nine-year-old dignity.

'Anne,' Joshua said, turning to her as they made their way up Sutton Street toward the school. 'I am sorry Sydnam Butler does not live closer to Bath. Yours was a friendship we all watched with interest.'

She was very glad she had not realized that at the time.

'It was *just* a friendship,' she assured him.

'Was it?' He looked into her face.

But they had rounded the corner onto Daniel Street, and Claudia and Susanna, alerted by the arrival of the carriage with their bags, were out on the doorstep watching for them. Anne was swallowed up in hugs and greetings and laughter. And just as she drew free and looked beyond them to the doorway, she saw another lady standing there, looking tall and dark and slender and elegant and exquisitely fashionable – and smiling joyfully.

'Frances!' Anne exclaimed, and stepped into her open arms.

'Lucius and I are just back from the Continent,' Frances, the Countess of Edgecombe, told her, 'and came to Bath on our way home to see if one of you would like to spend the final two weeks of the holiday with us at Barclay Court. Susanna is going to come. Anne, how *delighted* I am that you have arrived home just in time for me to see you. I never stop missing you. And just *look* how bronzed you are!'

Frances had found love in a snowstorm when her carriage ran into a snowbank, driven there by the reckless driving of the earl and his coachman as they overtook it. It had been hate at first sight – and love ever after. For some time after Frances's wedding the three remaining friends had looked at life with more hope, though they had not admitted as much to one another.

'I would have *hated* missing you,' Anne said. 'Oh, Frances, just look at *you*.'

But she turned back to the doorway before going inside and could see that David was right up in Joshua's arms out on the pavement, his arms wrapped tightly about Joshua's neck, his face buried against his shoulder. Joshua had one hand spread over the back of the boy's head and was kissing the side of it.

Anne's eyes were blinded by tears and she blinked them away.

Why did everything wonderful have to be left behind? she wondered. Why was life so heavily punctuated with good-byes?

Joshua set David down, cupped his face with both hands, kissed his forehead, and turned to Anne.

'You have done a fine, fine job with him, Anne,' he said, reaching out his right hand. 'He is a great lad. I'll write from Penhallow.'

She set her hand in his as David darted past her into the school, not pausing to greet any of the ladies or even Keeble, one of his favorite people.

'Thank you again,' she said.

'Anne,' he said, lowering his voice and tightening his grip on her hand, 'you *are* doing a fine job, but that lad needs a family. And there is one waiting to acknowledge him in Cornwall – Prue and Ben, Constance and Jim Saunders, Freyja and me. And Chastity and Meecham too, though they don't live there. David has aunts and uncles and cousins even if he *was* born out of wedlock. You must at least think about telling him something of his lineage. Will you?'

'I can look after my own son, Joshua,' she said stiffly, withdrawing her hand. 'But I do thank you for being so kind to him.'

'I'll write,' he said, shaking his head, clearly in frustration. 'Good-bye, Anne.'

'Good-bye,' she said, and watched him until he had turned the corner and gone out of sight.

But there were different kinds of good-byes, she thought. This one was not heart-wrenching for her, though it clearly was for David. She would see Joshua again – perhaps as soon as Christmas.

She would never see Sydnam again.

Not ever.

Susanna linked an arm through hers and she stepped inside the school with her friends.

She was back home and it was good to be here.

But never was an awfully long time.

CHAPTER 13

By the time Anne got David to bed that night she seemed finally to have convinced him that Christmas was not so very far away. He had been partly consoled too by the interest Matron and several of the girls had shown in his holiday. He had regaled them with tales of where he had been and what he had done.

'Mama,' he admitted after she had told another episode of an ongoing bedtime story and tucked him in for the night, 'it *is* good to be back. I like having my little room all to myself.'

Yes. It was good to be back. And there would be much to do in the coming days. Susanna was going to Barclay Court with Frances and the Earl of Edgecombe, and so there would be only Anne and Claudia to amuse the girls. And there were classes for the coming year to prepare. There were letters to write – of thanks to the Duchess of Bewcastle, of simple friendship to Lady Aidan and her aunt, to Lady Rosthorn, and to Miss Thompson and the other Bedwyn wives.

It was good to be back.

Tired as she was after the long journey and the

teeming emotions with which she had left Glandwr, Anne sat up late in Claudia's sitting room, the quartet of friends complete again with her return and Frances's visit. Frances was staying the night at the school despite the fact that the earl had taken rooms at the Royal York Hotel. He had come to dinner but had then left, telling the ladies that he realized his presence would be decidedly de trop for the rest of the night, besides which he needed his beauty rest but realized they would all sit up talking for at least half the night.

Anne liked him. They all did, and they all rejoiced in Frances's happily-ever-after.

They talked about Frances's travels and singing successes on the Continent, about Anne's month in Wales – minus all reference to Sydnam Butler – about the school holiday in Bath, and about numerous other topics. They had always been able to talk to one another about anything and everything. It had always seemed to Anne that they were far more like sisters than mere friends. They still missed Frances's constant presence among them, even though she had been gone for two years.

It *did* feel good to be back.

Anne hugged Susanna and Frances the following morning when the earl came for them in his carriage and waved them on their way from the pavement, Claudia at her side. And then they smiled at each other and went back inside the school to organize the girls for their planned walk and picnic in nearby Sydney Gardens.

247

Two weeks passed with busy holiday-time activities, including walks and picnics and games in the meadow beyond the school and treasure hunts within the school itself. Sometimes Anne sat with the girls, in the common room or in their dormitory, talking with them, listening to them, trying to give them some sense of family, some realization that there were adults who cared about them. But inevitably the new school year approached. There were to be a number of new girls. Indeed, the total number of both boarders and day pupils was to increase, since the school was prospering. Lila Walton, a promising senior pupil from last year, had stayed on in order to become a junior teacher – just as Susanna had done four years before. Anne spent several hours with her, helping her to prepare.

And finally Susanna returned, relaxed and bronzed and full of energy and stories of her holiday at Barclay Court.

Claudia was engaged to dine that evening with the parents of one of the new day pupils. Anne and Susanna sat up alone together in Anne's room after everyone else had retired for the night, Susanna seated on the bed, her arms clasped about her raised knees, Anne on the chair beside her small desk.

'I hated to lose Frances when she left here two years ago to marry the earl,' Susanna said with a sigh. 'But, oh, Anne, she made the right decision. I am so very envious. The earl is very charming.

And he is terribly proud of her. He does not at all resent having to travel such long distances so that she can sing. Indeed, I believe he revels in her fame.'

'And he is as much in love with her as he always was when he pursued her so relentlessly,' Anne said. 'That was obvious when he dined here with us.'

Susanna sighed again. 'Was it not like a fairy tale, their romance?' she said. 'He would *not* let her go, would he, even though he was *Viscount Sinclair* and heir to the earldom and Frances was a lowly teacher at our school. But she was *so* beautiful. She is even more so now. Marriage and travel and a singing career obviously agree very well with her.'

They were quiet for a moment, both glad of Frances's happiness, both rather melancholy for their own sakes.

'And what of you?' Anne asked. 'Did you really have a lovely time? Did you meet anyone interesting?'

'Like a duke to sweep me off my feet and bear me off to his castle as his bride?' Susanna laughed. 'No, not quite, alas. But Frances and Lord Edgecombe were very obliging, Anne, and made sure there was some entertainment for me to attend almost every day, even though I am sure they would have been just as happy to relax and be quiet together after being away for so long. I met some amiable and interesting people, most of whom I knew from before, of course.'

'But no one special?' Anne asked.

'No,' Susanna said. 'Not really.'

Anne raised her eyebrows.

'Only one gentleman,' Susanna admitted, 'who made his intentions very clear, and they were not honorable ones. It was the old story, Anne. Yet he was very handsome and very amiable. Never mind. And you? You told us a great deal about your Welsh holiday the evening before I left, but nothing that was very personal. Did *you* meet anyone interesting?'

'The Bedwyns,' Anne said, smiling, 'are all quite fascinating, Susanna – and that is actually an understatement. The Duke of Bewcastle is every bit as formidable as he is reputed to be. He has cold silver eyes and long fingers that are forever curling about the handle of his quizzing glass. He is quite terrifying. And yet he was unfailingly courteous to me. The duchess is a delight and not at all high in the instep, and it is quite clear that he adores her though he is never ever demonstrative in public. He also adores their son, who is a cross, demanding little baby – except when his father is holding him. And he holds him rather often. He is a strange, mysterious, fascinating man.'

Susanna rested her chin on her knees.

'All this talk of married dukes is depressing me,' she said, her eyes nevertheless twinkling. 'Was there no one who was *unmarried*?'

'No dukes.' Anne smiled too, but she had a sudden, unbidden memory of sitting on the stile at Tŷ Gwyn, smiling down at Sydnam Butler and setting her hand in his before descending. And of the perfect summer day that had surrounded them.

Susanna was looking very directly at her.

'Oh, Anne,' she said. *'Who?'*

'No one really,' Anne said quickly, shifting position on the chair. But she felt instantly contrite. 'Oh, what a dreadful thing to say of another human being. He very definitely is *someone*. He is the duke's steward at Glandwr. He was alone and I was alone, and so it was natural enough that occasionally we walked out together or sat together on evenings when he was invited to dine. That is all.'

She willed herself not to blush.

'All,' Susanna repeated, still gazing steadily at her. 'And was he tall, dark, and handsome, Anne?'

'Yes,' Anne said. 'All three.'

Susanna continued to gaze.

'We were merely friends,' Anne said.

'Were you?' Susanna spoke softly.

'We were.' Anne could not quite bring herself to smile. And she could no longer sit still. She got to her feet and crossed to the window. She pulled back one curtain and looked out onto the blackness of the meadow. 'We were very . . . dear friends.'

'But he did not make an offer,' Susanna said. 'Anne, I am so sorry.'

There was a lengthy silence, during which Anne did not contradict her friend.

'Do you think,' Susanna asked as last, 'life would be easier, Anne, if one had parents and family to take one about, to make sure one met suitable people, to arrange for one to meet eligible suitors? Would it be easier than living at a girls' school as one of the teachers?'

'I am not sure,' Anne said, closing the curtains again, 'that life is ever easy. Very often girls and women make disastrous marriages even while surrounded by family to help guide their choice or make it for them. I think given the choice between a bad marriage and life here, I would choose being here. In fact, I am certain I would.'

She set her forehead against the curtain for a moment before turning back into the room.

'It was *so* ungrateful of me,' Susanna said, 'even to ask that question. Good fortune was smiling on me when I was sent here to school, and I was blessed beyond belief when Claudia offered me a position on the staff. And I have such very good friends here. What more could I ask of life?'

'Ah, but we are women as well as teachers, Susanna,' Anne said, sitting down again. 'We have needs that nature has given us for the very preservation of our species.'

Needs that could sometimes be horribly damaged but not destroyed.

Susanna stared at her for several silent moments.

'And sometimes,' she said, 'they are very hard to ignore. I was *very* tempted this summer, Anne. To be a man's mistress. Part of me is still not

252

convinced that I made the right choice. And will I be able to make the same choice next time? And the next?'

'I don't know.' Anne smiled ruefully at her.

'What poor, sad spinsters we are,' Susanna said, laughing and pulling herself off the bed. She brushed out the creases from her skirt. 'I am for my lonely bed. The journey has tired me out. Good night, Anne.'

Three days later all the boarders returned to school from their holiday and greeted one another – and their teachers – with boisterous good cheer and noisy chatter, and all the new girls arrived with stiff apprehension on their faces, especially the two charity girls who came alone, without even the comfort of parents, sent by Mr Hatchard, Miss Martin's London agent. The fees of one of them were being paid by Lady Hallmere – though Claudia did not know her identity, of course.

Anne took the two under her wing and noted almost immediately that one of them was going to need extra lessons in elocution, since her Cockney accent made the English language on her lips virtually unintelligible and that the other was going to have to be coaxed firmly and patiently – and with large doses of love – out of her unfortunate manner of belligerent bravado.

The following morning, the day pupils arrived and classes began.

For the next month life was busy. Anne fulfilled

all her teaching duties and gave special care to the new charity girls. She spent most of her free time with David – who was excited at the promise Mr Upton had made to introduce oil paints to his art classes after Christmas. She wrote and received several letters from the Bedwyn ladies and Joshua. She helped David reply to the letters Davy and Becky and Joshua had written to him.

Indeed, life seemed remarkably normal considering the fact that it was becoming increasingly obvious to Anne that there was nothing normal about hers at all. She had missed her courses before school started and had desperately tried to convince herself that it was merely because of the upsets in her life during the previous month. She had continued to hope even when she started to feel slightly nauseated after rising in the mornings – as she had done ten years ago.

But of course – had she expected a miracle? – she missed her courses for a second time at the end of September and thought about what Sydnam Butler had once said about choices. She had chosen a month and a half ago to lie with him because she had wanted him and he had wanted her and it was their last day together. And that choice had forever changed her life.

It was a terrifying thought.

But there was nothing she could do now to change that choice or avoid its repercussions. She could only move onward with her life.

She waited for a chilly Saturday morning after

Susanna had taken most of the girls outside for games in the meadow and David had gone with them. Then she knocked on the door of Claudia Martin's office and let herself in when she was summoned.

'May I disturb you?' she asked. She and Susanna and Lila had sat in Claudia's private sitting room just the evening before, drinking tea and chatting on a wide variety of topics, and Anne might have remained when the other two retired for the night. But she had known that she needed a more formal setting for what she had to say.

Claudia looked up from her desk.

'The last of the stragglers has just paid the school fees,' she said. 'I do believe we are going to do well financially again this year, Anne. Within two or three years I hope to be able to inform Mr Hatchard that we no longer need the assistance of our benefactor.'

She set down her quill pen and gestured to a chair on the other side of her desk for Anne to sit down.

'You handled Agnes Ryde's tantrum very well at breakfast, Anne,' she said. 'You calmed a potentially explosive situation. You have a great gift with difficult girls.'

'She is still a little bewildered by her new environment, that is all,' Anne said. 'When she is afraid, her experience of life has taught her that she must fight, with her tongue even if not with her fists. But she has an affectionate heart and a sharp mind, Claudia. I hope both will be nurtured while she is here. But I am quite sure they will be. This is a very good school. Any girl who is privileged to attend can only leave the better for having been here.'

Claudia cocked her head to one side and leaned back in her chair. She was silent for a moment.

'What is it, Anne?' she asked. 'There is something I have been unable to put my finger on for quite a while now. You are as diligent and cheerful and patient as you have ever been. But there is some . . . hmm. There is some loss of serenity, if that is the right word. It has been of concern to me. Are you unwell? Shall I summon Mr Blake?'

Mr Blake was the physician who came to the school whenever one of the boarders was indisposed.

'I am going to be leaving here, Claudia,' Anne said abruptly, and somehow it seemed as if she were standing behind herself, listening to the words, appalled, as if someone else had spoken them. They were finally out. And they were true and irrevocable.

Claudia looked keenly at her but did not make any comment.

'I believe,' Anne said, closing her eyes briefly, 'I am going to be married.'

She had planned and rehearsed this for a whole week, ever since last Saturday morning, when she had walked into the center of Bath to post her letter to Glandwr. But so far she had said none of the words she had practiced. And she had not smiled or looked bright and happy, as she had planned to do.

'Married?'

She realized that Claudia had spoken the single word.

'I met him in Wales during the summer,' Anne explained. 'He asked me to marry him then, and I have decided that I will say yes. I have written to him.'

'My felicitations.' Claudia was looking at her rather sternly, her back ramrod straight. 'Might I be permitted to know his name?'

Anne sighed and slumped a little in her chair.

'I cannot do this,' she said, 'as if you were simply a headmistress, my employer, and I a teacher. Or as if this were something I have been secretly considering for almost two months and have only now made a decision upon. I owe you better than this. I am so very sorry, Claudia. I told you everything about my month in Wales except the most significant part. He is Sydnam Butler, youngest son of the Earl of Redfield, and the Duke of Bewcastle's steward at Glandwr.'

'Sydnam Butler,' Claudia said, 'of Alvesley Park not far from Lindsey Hall? I remember him. He was an extraordinarily handsome boy.'

'I am with child by him,' Anne said bluntly.

Claudia stared at her, and Anne saw her jaw clench hard.

'Rape?' she asked.

'No!' Anne's eyes widened. 'Oh, no, Claudia. Nothing like that. No. I was a willing participant. He offered me marriage but I declined. I did promise, though, that I would let him know if I were with child, and allow him to marry me. I sent a letter off to him a week ago.'

There was a short silence.

'But you do not wish to marry him?' Claudia asked.

'No. Not really.'

But she had missed him far more than she could have predicted. Even before she had begun to suspect the truth with the absence of her monthly courses and the morning nausea, he had dominated her waking thoughts and haunted her dreams. And she had wondered – every day since her return to Bath she had wondered – if her answer would have been different if she had not taken sudden fright – and if he had asked differently.

If you wish, Anne, we will marry.

Such dutiful, kind, *dispassionate* words.

Now they were going to be forced into marrying. She must accept his dutiful willingness to put everything right, and he must accept that she had kept her promise but that he might never have a wife who could offer him physical warmth.

Part of her longed for him. Part of her was terrified. And all of her hated the circumstances that would propel them into matrimony. *He* would hate the circumstances.

'Then you must not do so, Anne.' Claudia set

both hands on the desk and leaned forward, her voice and face firm. 'He is the son of an earl and of wealth and privilege, and he is far too handsome for his own good – or yours. He is an associate of the Duke of Bewcastle. You will be *miserable*.'

'And what is the alternative, Claudia?' Anne asked. 'To remain here at the school? You know that will be impossible.'

She watched the fierce light die out of Claudia's eyes.

A number of parents had asked questions and expressed concern years ago when Miss Martin employed an unwed mother as a teacher – and when that teacher had had the effrontery to bring her bastard son with her. One girl had even been withdrawn from the school in protest.

'Besides,' Anne said, 'I had no choice with David, Claudia, and life has been difficult for him as a result and will continue to be. I will not do that with another child when this time I *do* have a choice.'

'He *will* marry you?' Claudia asked.

'Yes,' Anne said.

With her heart she was quite, quite sure that he would. He would be here any day now. There was, though, an almost panicked doubt in her head. What if he did not come?

'Oh, Anne,' Claudia said. She slumped in her chair and sighed. 'My dear, how could you have been so . . . *foolish*?'

What she had done had, of course, been very

foolish indeed. But there was really no point in regretting it. It had happened.

'I ought to have told you sooner,' she said, 'instead of waiting until I was absolutely sure – and even longer than that while I allowed time for my letter to reach him in Wales. You will need to replace me soon. Lila has been doing little more than apprentice work during the past month, but she shows great promise, Claudia. Like Susanna, she seems able to win the respect of girls who were her fellow pupils just a few months ago, and she is very popular with the new girls. Besides which, she is really quite brilliant in mathematics and earned top marks in geography every year I taught her. If you choose to promote her, I do not believe she will let you down.'

Claudia stared broodingly at her for several moments before pushing abruptly to her feet and rounding the desk and snatching Anne up into her arms.

'Anne,' she said. 'Anne, I ought to shake the life out of you. But . . . Oh, my dear, tell me how I may help you. Is there even the smallest chance that you can feel an affection for Mr Butler?'

Anne relaxed gratefully into the embrace. She had been so afraid that she would lose her friendships at the school – and it was of the very disciplined Claudia Martin that she had been most afraid. A woman who had twice been got with child outside wedlock could not demand the sympathy of her friends as a right.

'I would not have . . . done what I did with him if I had not felt a very deep affection for him,' she said. 'There was no seduction involved, Claudia, and certainly no rape. Please, you must believe that. There was affection on both sides.'

'But you refused his marriage offer.' Claudia stood back, but she still held Anne's arms. 'Are you simply daft, or am I missing something?'

'Marrying him seemed the wrong thing to do at the time,' Anne said, 'for both of us and for reasons that might be difficult to put into words. But now there is to be a third person, and a marriage between us is the only right thing to do.'

Claudia sighed again.

'Sit down,' she said, pulling on the bell rope that hung beside the desk. 'I will have a pot of tea brought in. All matters can be seen more clearly – and more calmly – over a cup of tea. If my ears do not deceive me, I believe the girls are returning from their games – ah, look, it is raining outside. That would explain it. I'll invite Susanna to join us if I may. We *are* a little like sisters, are we not? I still miss Frances quite dreadfully. And *how* I will miss you, Anne, my dear.'

She gave instructions to the maid who answered the bell.

'There is actually a fourth person involved in all this, Anne, is there not?' she said while they waited for Susanna to join them. 'Will Mr Butler be a good father for David? I will forgive him a multitude of sins if the answer is yes.'

261

It was a question that worried Anne more than any other. David desperately wanted a father. But his idea of a desirable father figure was the physically perfect and athletic Joshua or Lord Alleyne or Lord Aidan. However, David had met Sydnam and recognized in him a fellow artist. He did not appear to hold him in any particular aversion.

But how would he feel about Sydnam as a father? As her husband?

'He will be kind to David,' she said.

Of that, at least, she was quite sure.

CHAPTER 14

There had been heavy rains for several weeks, making travel on the main roads slow and hazardous, even impossible at times. Sydnam had been watching with some impatience for the arrival of a letter from the Duke of Bewcastle and his solicitors, the final formality to be gone through before he could call Tŷ Gwyn officially his own.

He was delighted when it finally arrived and opened it before he looked at the rest of the mail, though he could see that there was a letter from his mother at the top of the pile.

He stood in the middle of his office looking down at the official papers and tried to feel the expected euphoria over knowing that his dream had finally come true. He was a landowner in his own right. He owned a home and land in Wales, a country he had come to love deeply. He now belonged. He *fully* belonged. He must call on Tudor Rhys later so that they could celebrate together.

But euphoria was difficult to conjure these days. He was having the hall and the morning room of Tŷ Gwyn redecorated, since the sale had been all but final for longer than a month. But he had not been there to supervise or check on the work. He had not been there at all for almost two months. Not since . . .

Well, not since *then*, in fact.

He could not bring himself to go. He would have to pass through the gate – and drive past the stile. He would have to walk past the rose arbor. He would have to step inside the empty house – empty of all except workmen.

And memories.

He had not yet faced the absurd possibility that he would never actually take up residence in Tŷ Gwyn but would remain indefinitely in the cottage near Glandwr, using the excuse that he was comfortable there and closer to his work.

He picked up the letter from his mother and flicked through the rest of the post. It all related to business – except for one slim letter written in an elegant hand that looked feminine. It was not Lauren's writing. He set down his mother's letter unopened, picked it up, and saw immediately that it had come from Bath.

He stared at it for a few moments while his mouth grew dry. He had stopped looking for it weeks ago and had now been taken quite unawares. Though he did not know what the contents were, of course – or even for certain who the writer was.

But who else would be writing to him from Bath?

And what else would she write about?

He broke the seal with his thumb and opened out the single sheet of paper.

His eye went to the signature first.

Ah. He had not been mistaken.

He read the words she had written, and his mind deciphered them – individually and in small phrases. Their full meaning would not seem to crash through to his heart.

She was with child. She had promised to inform him of that fact. She sent him her kind regards. All expressed in brief, formal sentences.

She was with child.

His child.

His and Anne's.

She was with child, but she was unwed.

Finally full awareness dawned.

She was unwed.

He must go to her. There must not be a moment's delay. His life had suddenly become of infinite and precarious value. Only it stood between Anne Jewell and terrible ruin – between *their child* and terrible ruin. He must not delay.

He folded the letter and put it into his pocket before hurrying from the room and dashing up to his bedchamber and ringing the bell for his valet. Poor Anne – there was no time to lose.

But, of course, as he realized even before his valet arrived on the scene, surprised to be summoned in the middle of an afternoon, going to her rescue was not such a simple thing as donning his riding boots and coat, mounting the closest available horse, and galloping off in the direction of England and Bath.

The letter, he could see as soon as he took it from his pocket and spread it out on his bed to read again, was dated well over a week ago. It had taken twice as long to arrive as it normally would. Of course – the roads! He had known they were virtually impassable. And they would still be bad. Heavy showers were still pouring down on them almost every day. Anyway, he was not his own master. He was Bewcastle's steward, with responsibilities and duties to perform. He was going to have to complete a few urgent tasks before he could go anywhere, and he was going to have to make arrangements with the man who usually stood in for him when he had to leave Glandwr for any length of time.

'We will be leaving for England within the next couple of days,' he told his valet when he *had* intended to say that they would be leaving within the hour. 'Have my bags all ready to go, will you, Armstead, so that we may leave as soon as possible?'

But by the time two days had passed and he was ready to go at last, Sydnam had realized that he could not even go straight to Bath and to Anne's rescue. He had to go to London first.

The weather had not improved during those two days. The muddy, slippery roads, their potholes often filled with water that made them look like village ponds, slowed his journey to London quite considerably. And even when he was finally there, he discovered that the wheels of officialdom moved with agonizing slowness.

Three weeks had gone by since Anne had posted her letter before Sydnam, feeling decidedly nervous, presented himself at Miss Martin's school on Daniel Street in the middle of one afternoon.

An elderly porter opened the door, half recoiled at the sight of him and looked as if he were about to close it again, then appeared to notice that the visitor was dressed like a gentleman, and finally stood squarely in the doorway, squinting at him with undisguised suspicion and hostility, and asked what he could do for him.

'I wish to speak with Miss Jewell,' Sydnam said. 'I believe she is expecting me.'

'She is teaching,' the porter told him, 'and is not to be disturbed.'

'Then I will wait until she has finished teaching.' Sydnam told him firmly. 'Inform her that Sydnam Butler wishes to speak with her.'

The porter pursed his lips, looked as if he would dearly like to shut the door in the visitor's face, gentleman or no gentleman, then turned without a word and led the way to a visitors' parlor on the left side of the hall, his boot heels squeaking the whole way. Sydnam was admitted to the room and shut firmly inside. He almost expected to hear a key turning in the lock.

He stood in the middle of the room, noting both its neat refinement and its slight shabbiness and listening to the distant sounds of girls chanting something in unison, an occasional burst of laughter, and someone playing rather ploddingly on a pianoforte.

He had no idea when classes ended for the day. And it might well be that the elderly porter would forget that he was here or deliberately neglect to tell Anne Jewell that she had a visitor.

At some point he might have to sally forth in search of her.

But the door opened again after he had been there for fifteen minutes or so, and a lady stepped inside. She looked vaguely familiar, and Sydnam assumed she was the famous – or infamous – Miss Martin herself. He had met her no more than a time or two while she was Freyja's governess, but the story of how she had left Lindsey Hall, figuratively thumbing her nose at Bewcastle, was legend. His father had met her marching down a country road, carrying her heavy portmanteau, and had stopped his carriage and persuaded her to accept a ride to the nearest stagecoach stop.

She was a handsome woman in a straight-backed, tight-lipped sort of way.

Sydnam bowed to her while she stood looking at him, her hands clasped at her waist. To do her justice, she controlled her reactions well at the sight of him. Or perhaps Anne had warned her what to expect.

'Miss Martin?' he said. 'Sydnam Butler, ma'am. I have come to speak with Miss Jewell.'

'She will be here in a moment,' she said. 'I have sent Keeble to inform her that you are here. Miss Walton will conduct the rest of her mathematics lesson.'

'Thank you, ma'am.' Sydnam inclined his head again.

'If your tardiness in coming here is indicative of your eagerness to do your duty, Mr Butler,' she surprised him by saying, her posture unchanged, her face stern, 'I beg to inform you that Miss Jewell has friends who are willing and able to offer her shelter and support for as long as she needs them. Women do have some modicum of power when they stick together, you know.'

He could begin to understand why the woman had not crumbled before Bewcastle.

'I thank you, ma'am,' he said. 'But I also am willing and able – and *eager* – to secure Miss Jewell's comfort and security and happiness.'

They gazed at each other, taking each other's measure.

He could not dislike the woman. It pleased him to know that Anne had such a friend. Obviously Miss Martin knew the truth, but far from tossing Anne out of the school in moral outrage, she was prepared to offer her a home and support if need be.

'I suppose,' she said, 'you must be worth

something if you have been able to perform the function of steward to the satisfaction of the Duke of Bewcastle despite your obvious disabilities.'

Sydnam almost smiled as she looked him over frankly and critically from head to foot, particularly down his right side. He did *not* smile, though. He felt that somehow they were engaged in a battle of wills, though over what he was not sure. The only thing he *was* sure of was that he was not going to lose.

The door opened behind Miss Martin before either of them could speak again.

Anne Jewell.

She looked pale and rather unwell, Sydnam thought. She seemed to have lost weight. She was also even more beautiful than he remembered.

There had been a time, for a week or two after she left, when he had tried and tried and failed to recall her face. And then there had come the time when he would have been happy to forget both it and her. Remembering had been painful and deeply depressing. And his solitude, which he had so resented giving up when she came to Glandwr with the Bedwyns, had turned to undeniable, gnawing loneliness after they had all left.

And deep unhappiness.

Her eyes met his across the room, and he bowed formally to her as if she were not standing there with his child in her womb.

The truth of it smote him and made him slightly dizzy.

'Ah, here is Miss Jewell now,' Miss Martin said briskly and unnecessarily.

'Thank you, Claudia,' Anne said without taking her eyes off him.

A suitable name for the headmistress of the school, Sydnam thought – *Claudia*. A strong, uncompromising name. She bent one more severe look upon him, a softer look upon her fellow teacher, and left the room without further ado.

He and Anne Jewell were alone together.

And so good-bye had not been good-bye after all, he thought.

He was painfully glad to see her.

And painfully aware of the reason.

She was pregnant with his child.

'You must have thought,' he said, 'that I was not coming.'

'Yes,' she said. 'I did.'

She was standing to one side of the door, half a room away from him. Three weeks must have seemed an endless time to her, he supposed. She was unmarried and with child – for the second time.

He hated to think that that fact somehow put him on a level with Albert Moore.

'The rain delayed both your letter and my journey to London,' he explained. 'I am so sorry, Anne. But you must have known that you could trust me.'

'I thought I could,' she said. 'But you did not come.'

271

'I would never let you down,' he said. 'And I would never abandon my own child.'

The thought had hammered in his brain all the way to London and back to Bath. He had fathered a child.

He was going to be a father.

She sighed and her posture relaxed. He could see that his explanation had convinced her and that she had forgiven him.

'Sydnam,' she said, 'I am really sorry—'

'No!' He held up his hand and walked closer to her. 'You must never say that, Anne. Nor must I. If you are sorry you had to call on me like this, and if I am sorry that I made it necessary for you to do so, then we must also be sorry for what we did that afternoon at Tŷ Gwyn. Yet we both agreed at the time that it was what we wanted. And if we are sorry, then we are also sorry that there is to be a child. We say that it is unwanted and that there is something *wrong* about it. There can only be everything in the world *right* about any child. And this one is *yours* and *mine* and must be welcomed gladly by both of us. Please do not say you are sorry.'

She stared mutely at him for a few moments, and he was reminded of the blueness of her eyes and the smoky quality her long lashes gave them. 'London?' she said then. 'You have been to *London*?'

'To procure a special license,' he explained. 'We must marry without delay, Anne. You must have the protection of my name.'

Her teeth sank into her lower lip.

'If you really wish to have the banns called,' he said, 'so that our families will have time to gather for our wedding, then I will respect your wishes. But even this three-week delay has made me very uneasy. Only my life stands between you and something unspeakable – despite Miss Martin's determination to care for you if I will not.'

'I have no family,' she said.

'We will wed tomorrow morning, then,' he told her. 'I will make the arrangements.'

He remembered something suddenly as she gazed back at him, even her lips pale. He remembered a very inadequate offer of marriage he had made just after bedding her – just after impregnating her, as it had turned out.

If you wish, Anne, we will marry.

Was she never to hear anything better from him? Was she now to be rushed into marriage because it was necessary and forever feel cheated of some of the trappings of courtship?

'Anne.' He took her left hand in his and lowered himself onto his right knee – so that he would be able to use the stronger left leg to help him rise again. 'Anne, my dear, will you do me the great honor of being my wife?'

He brought her hand to his lips, but not before seeing her eyes grow huge with unshed tears. She bent over him, and he felt her free hand light against the top of his head.

'I will,' she said. 'I will always do my best to

bring you comfort and companionship, Sydnam, and I will be the best mother I can possibly be to your child – to *our* child.'

He got to his feet and drew her against him. She turned her head and rested it against his left shoulder, her hands nestled between them, spread over his chest.

He wished then that he had two arms to wrap about her, to hold her close, to enclose her in the safety of his protection. And he wished he had two eyes to see her with. And he wished . . .

But he was alive. He had learned to cope with the changed conditions of his life. And now he was to have a wife and companion. There would be a child for the nursery at Tŷ Gwyn soon after they moved in there. He could begin to think of his life in terms of the plural – *my wife and daughter, or son, and me*. He had somehow been thinking of the child as female. He was going to have a daughter. Or a son.

He must not dwell upon the fact that he had no right arm and no right eye – that he could never offer Anne a whole man. He must not think of how she had cringed from him when he entered her body. He must not fear the loss of his deepest privacy.

He must give what he could – the protection of his name, his friendship, loyalty, kindness, and affection. And perhaps in time . . .

She lifted her head and gazed into his face.

'It will be all right,' he told her. 'Everything will be all right.'

'Yes.'

Her lips curved into a smile, and he knew she was having similar thoughts to his – that this ought not to be happening but was, and all they could do was make the best of it.

Their prospects were not utterly bleak. They liked each other – he *knew* she liked him. He was in love with her. Perhaps he even *loved* her.

They had the rest of their lifetimes to work on the sort of warm marital relationship he had always dreamed of.

'Anne,' he said, 'what about your son? Does he know?'

She shook her head.

'Until you came,' she said, 'I did not know what I would tell him.'

'I will support him and care for him and educate him and love him as if he were my own,' he assured her. 'I will give him my name if you wish, Anne, and if he wishes it. But will he accept me?'

'I do not know what he will feel,' she said. 'He longs for a father figure in his life. But . . .' She bit her lip again.

But his longing was for a whole and perfect man, like Hallmere or Rosthorn or any of the Bedwyn men.

'Shall we summon him now,' he asked her, 'and tell him together? Or would you rather talk to him alone first?'

She drew a deep breath and released it slowly.

'I'll go and fetch him,' she said. 'Tomorrow his

life will change drastically. He needs to know as soon as possible, and he needs to meet you face-to-face.'

His heart plummeted as soon as she left the room. *Tomorrow his life will change.* All three of their lives would change tomorrow. And they would be changed irrevocably and forever. It was not just he and Anne who were involved in all this. There would be a new child, whom he already loved with a fierce, almost painful tenderness. And there would be the boy, David Jewell, whom he had pledged to love though he did not know how easy it would be or if the boy would willingly reciprocate that love.

And who could blame him if he did not? What child would choose a one-eyed, one-armed father whom most children and even some adults feared as a monster?

Choices.

He and Anne Jewell had chosen to make love together during that afternoon at Tŷ Gwyn, and their lives – and David's – had been forever changed.

Only time would tell if they had been changed for the better or the worse. Not that it would matter. They could only continue to walk the path of their lives to the very end, and for now at least their paths had converged.

It was Saturday again, the sun was shining, and it was a relatively warm day for October. But though the boarders at Miss Martin's school and a few of the day pupils too were out in the meadow playing games as usual, it was Lila Walton who was supervising them rather than Susanna Osbourne.

Susanna was in Anne Jewell's room, laughing as she attempted to thread a string of seed pearls through her friend's hair, which she had just succeeded in pinning up into a more elegant style than usual.

'There,' she said, standing back at last to view the results of her handiwork. 'Now you look fit to be a bride.'

Anne was wearing her best green silk.

Claudia was standing silently just inside the door, her hands clasped at her waist.

'Anne,' she said, meeting her friend's eyes in the mirror, 'are you quite, quite sure?'

It was a foolish question, of course. When one was with child and the father was due to arrive in five minutes' time to marry one, it really did not matter if one was sure or not.

'I am,' she said.

'He was so very, very handsome,' Claudia said with a sigh.

'He still is.' Anne smiled into the mirror.

'You told me,' Susanna said, 'that he was tall, dark, and handsome, Anne. You did not say anything about his war wounds.'

'Because they do not matter,' Anne said. 'I also told you that he and I were friends, Susanna. We were. We are.'

'I am looking forward to meeting him,' Susanna said.

But Claudia turned at that moment and opened the door upon which Keeble was about to knock.

'They are downstairs,' he announced as if he had come to tell them that the devil and his chief assistant had just stepped into the school. Although a man himself, Mr Keeble always carefully guarded his domain against the wicked male world beyond its doors. He looked across the room to Anne, who was getting to her feet. 'You look good enough to eat, Miss Jewell.'

'Thank you, Mr Keeble.' She smiled at him, though her heart felt as if it were lodged somewhere in the soles of her slippers.

Sydnam had arrived with the clergyman who was to marry them. The wedding was going to be solemnized in Claudia's private sitting room, the visitors' parlor having been rejected as too gloomy.

It was her wedding day – her *wedding day* – yet she felt nothing but a heavy heart. She was fond of him, and he was fond of her, but they had not intended to marry, and it seemed somehow worse to be marrying Sydnam than someone of whom she was not fond at all – foolish thought.

She should be able to offer him everything, but she did not believe she had anything but her fondness to give.

And he should be able to offer *her* everything. But he had never spoken of love. He had twice offered marriage, yesterday in a touchingly romantic way,

278

but both times it had been from duty rather than inclination. It would have to be enough, though. He was a gentle, kindly man. He would take his responsibilities seriously.

Ah, but a bride should feel very differently on her wedding day, she thought wistfully.

'I'll go up and fetch David,' she said.

'Let me go,' Susanna offered.

'No.' Anne shook her head. 'But thank you, Susanna. And thank you, Claudia. For everything.'

Keeble had disappeared, though his squeaky boots could still be heard descending the stairs.

She hugged them both quickly and climbed the stairs to the small room next to Matron's that had always been David's. He was sitting on the edge of his bed, wearing his best clothes, his hair carefully combed.

'It is time to go down,' Anne said.

He looked up at her and got to his feet.

'I wish,' he said, 'my papa had not died. I *wish* he had not. He would have played cricket with me like Cousin Joshua and taught me to ride like Lord Aidan did with Davy and he would have climbed trees with me like Lord Alleyne and taken me boating like Lord Rannulf. He would have winked at me and called me funny names in French like Lord Rosthorn. He would have held me when I was a baby like the Duke of Bewcastle with James. He would have kept you away from . . . from *him*, and he would have loved us both.'

It was not a loud diatribe. He spoke quietly but distinctly. Anne quelled her anger and concentrated upon listening to him.

'David,' she said, as she had said half a dozen times yesterday, 'I am not going to love you one iota the less after this morning than I have loved you all your life. The only difference will be that I will not have to teach here and will therefore have more time to spend with you.'

'But you are going to have a *baby*,' he said.

'Yes.' She smiled at him. 'And that means you are going to have a brother or a sister. Someone to look up to you and see you as a great hero of an elder brother – as Hannah does with Davy. The baby will be someone else to love you and someone else for you to love. I will still love you as well as I do now. I will not have to divide my love in half between you and the baby. My love will double instead.'

'But *he* will love the baby,' he said.

'Because he will be the baby's papa,' she said. 'He will be yours too if you wish. He said so to me and then he said so to you. He also said that he will just be your friend if you would prefer that. He is not your enemy, David. He is a good and honorable man. Lord Alleyne and Lord Aidan and the others told you a great deal about him, did they not? He is their friend. They like and admire him. And he was kind about your painting, and you liked him when he praised you and suggested you try painting with oils. Will you try to like him now too?'

'I don't know,' he was honest enough to say. 'I don't see why you need anyone else but me, Mama – especially *him*. Alexander thought he was a monster. And I don't know why you want another baby. Am I not enough for you?'

She stooped down and wrapped her arms around his slender little body, feeling his pain and bewilderment, recognizing his fear of losing all that had given his days shape and anchor through his short life. He had always had her undivided attention and love. And he had always been a cheerful, good-natured child. It hurt to see him petulant – and to know that she was the cause.

'Life changes, David,' she said. 'As you grow older you will learn that. It *always* changes, as it did when we came here from Cornwall. But one thing will always remain the same in your life. I absolutely promise you that. I will always love you with all my heart.'

'We had better go down,' he said, 'or we will be late.'

'Yes.' She straightened up and smiled down at him again. 'You look remarkably handsome today.'

'Mama,' he said as he walked beside her down the stairs, 'I will be polite. I will not make a *scene*. And I will try my very best to like him – he *was* kind about my painting. But don't ever try to make me call him *Papa* because I won't. I have a papa of my own, but he is dead.'

'I will be very happy,' she said, 'if you call him *Mr Butler*.'

And that would be her name too, she thought, feeling suddenly weak in the knees. In just a short while she was going to be Mrs Sydnam Butler.

There was no point now, though, in feeling sudden uncertainty or panic. She was carrying their child in her womb.

She was a bride on her way to her own wedding. Her groom was waiting for her. Part of her yearned toward him – she had missed him so very much. In a moment she would actually *see* him.

Despite herself she felt buoyed by a sudden excitement.

Keeble opened the door to Claudia's sitting room for them with as much gloom in his manner as if he were ushering them in to their own funeral.

CHAPTER 15

S ydnam had felt terribly alone all morning though he had brought his valet with him from Wales. He still felt it after he had taken up the clergyman in his carriage. He rarely missed his family despite the fact that he was deeply fond of them all and wrote regularly to his mother and father and to Kit and Lauren. But today he missed them all with a raw intensity.

And he kept remembering Kit and Lauren's wedding, both of them surrounded by their families and friends, the church packed with people, the bride and groom driving away afterward in their decorated carriage, the wedding breakfast after that, the toasts, the laughter and the happiness.

If the truth were told, he admitted with some disgust at himself as he arrived at Miss Martin's school, he was feeling rather sorry for himself. It was his wedding day, and there was no one to make a fuss over him.

He and the clergyman were taken upstairs instead of being shown into the rather gloomy visitors' parlor again, as Sydnam had expected. The elderly porter with the creaky boots opened the door into what appeared to be a private sitting room, which was cheerfully, even elegantly furnished. It was also unoccupied. In the meadow beyond the window he could see a crowd of girls engaged in some sort of vigorous game.

The clergyman launched into a pompous monologue on the dangers educating young ladies posed for the future of society, and Sydnam waited nervously for the arrival of his bride.

They were not kept waiting very long. The door opened and Anne came into the room with her son and Miss Martin and another young woman who he assumed was Miss Osbourne.

But he had eyes only for Anne.

She was wearing a green silk evening gown he had seen more than once before. Her hair was prettily styled, and it was threaded through with pearls, as if she were about to attend a ball. Instead, she was attending her own wedding.

As her eyes met his, he wished desperately that he could be whole for her, that he could have courted her properly, that this wedding were a joyful celebration involving their family and friends. But at least it *was* a wedding, and that was all that mattered at the moment.

As for their marriage and the rest of their future – well, that would be up to them. The future always held hope.

He smiled at her, and she looked back at him with huge eyes and half smiled as she came toward him.

It seemed to him during that moment, while everyone else stepped into position around them, that he had never encountered any woman more lovely than Anne Jewell. Or more desirable. Or more lovable. And she was his bride.

'Dearly beloved,' the clergyman began in a formal, sonorous tone as if he were addressing a congregation of hundreds.

And suddenly it did not matter to Sydnam that this was not the wedding he had dreamed of. He was being joined in holy matrimony with Anne because they had been lonely and so had taken consolation in each other's arms at Tŷ Gwyn and conceived a child. But the cause did not matter.

He was being married to Anne and suddenly it seemed to him that it was all he had ever desired of life.

He felt a wave of such tenderness for her that he had to blink away tears.

And when she looked at him and promised to love, honor, and obey him as long as they both should live, it seemed to him that her eyes regarded him with yearning and tenderness and . . . hope.

A cathedral and a thousand guests could not have made his wedding more real to him.

And then, as suddenly as it had begun, the brief nuptial service was over and the clergyman was declaring that they were man and wife together.

Anne was his *wife*.

She was safe. So was their child.

He took her left hand in his and raised it to his lips. He felt the smoothness of her new gold ring, which he had bought the afternoon before.

'Anne. My dearest,' he murmured.

'Sydnam.' She smiled at him again.

But weddings, he discovered, even very small weddings, did not allow the newly married couple much time to be alone together. Anne stooped to hug her son, and the clergyman shook hands with Sydnam before Miss Martin did so, her hand clasping his firmly, her eyes regarding him very directly.

'I will expect you to look after her, Mr Butler,' she said. 'She is as precious to me as a sister. And I will expect you to look after David.'

And then she hugged Anne while the other young lady turned to him and reached out her left hand.

'I am Susanna Osbourne, Mr Butler,' she said. 'Anne told nothing but the truth when she described you as tall, dark, and handsome. I wish you every happiness in the world.'

Her green eyes twinkled with mischief. She was a small, auburn-haired, very pretty young lady.

'Did she really say that?' He chuckled and was absurdly pleased. 'What a bouncer.'

And then he found himself face-to-face with David Jewell, who was staring gravely up at him with unblinking eyes. Sydnam had hoped the boy would accept his mother's marriage, but he had shown no enthusiasm for it yesterday. Quite the contrary, in fact. It had seemed to Sydnam after David had been brought down to the visitors' parlor that he had shrunk from the prospect with some horror. And when mention had been made of the new baby that would soon be part of their family, the boy's eyes had looked first bewildered and then wounded – and then blank.

'David,' Sydnam said now, 'I will always do my best to care for your mother and to make you happy. You are my stepson now. You may call me *Papa* or *Father* if you wish.' He held out his hand. 'But only if you wish.'

David set his own limply in it. 'Thank you, sir,' he said with no hostility or defiance – or any other detectable emotion – in his voice.

Ah. Only in fairy tales, Sydnam supposed, did a man and his bride rush off from their wedding into an eternal happily-ever-after.

'Anne, Mr Butler,' Miss Martin said, taking charge, 'I have taken it upon myself to arrange a small reception for you, with Susanna's help. I have invited a few people to join us for wine and cake. I hope you do not mind.'

And so a whole hour passed before Sydnam could finally leave the school with his new wife and her son. He was introduced to the other teachers, including Mr Huckerby, the dancing instructor, Mr Upton, the art master, Mademoiselle Pierre, the French and music teacher, and Miss Walton, the junior assistant. He accepted their good wishes and congratulations and acknowledged the toast

287

that was drunk to his health and Anne's and felt incongruously lonely for a newly married man. There was no one of his own among the small gathering – except his wife and stepson.

But finally they were on the pavement outside the school, Anne having changed her clothes, Miss Martin and Miss Osbourne with them. Both ladies shook hands with him again and hugged Anne and David. Miss Osbourne shed a few tears over them both, though she was smiling with bright tenderness. Miss Martin shed no tears but gazed sternly at Anne with what Sydnam recognized as desperate affection.

Sydnam handed his wife into the waiting carriage and took the seat across from hers after David had scrambled in beside her. Her cheeks were flushed, her hands clasped in her lap – until she leaned forward as the carriage lurched into motion and waved a final farewell to her friends.

'They love you,' he said.

She turned her eyes on him, and he saw in them an awareness that she had just entered irrevocably upon a new phase of her life.

'Yes,' she said. 'I will miss them.'

It was not just a school and a teaching position from which he was taking her, he realized. It was a home and a family. Anne was as dear as a sister, the rather formidable Miss Martin had said yesterday. Why was it that a woman, when she married, had to give up everything in order to accompany her husband wherever he chose to take her? The unfairness of it had never struck him before. What right did he have to feel all alone today, to somewhat resent the fact that she had had two friends – as well as a son – with her at their wedding and a few more friends at the small reception? Now she was leaving all except David behind.

'Where are we going?' she asked as the carriage turned from Sydney Place onto Great Pulteney Street.

She looked surprised, and he realized that she must have expected that they would set out without delay on the journey to Wales. He had not spoken to her yesterday about any plans beyond their wedding. He had not thought to consult her. He had always made his own decisions about the course his life was to take – hence his brief sojourn in the Peninsula. He had every right to continue in the same way, of course – he was, after all, the husband in this new marriage of theirs. But he would prefer to adjust his ways if he could.

'I have taken a suite of rooms at the Royal York Hotel,' he said. 'I thought we would stay here for one night.'

He met her eyes across the narrow gap between their seats and noticed the slight flush of color in her cheeks. He felt an answering shortness of breath and tightening of the groin. It would be their wedding night. The reality of the morning's events had still not quite struck home, he realized.

'I want to take you shopping this afternoon,' he

289

told her. He shifted his gaze to David. 'Both of you.'

The boy's eyes widened with interest though he said nothing. He was sitting very close to Anne.

'I have found a shop on Milsom Street that sells oil paints,' Sydnam said. 'I thought we would purchase some, David, since you seem ready to use them. And if we are to buy the paints, then we must buy everything else you will need at Tŷ Gwyn in order to use them to advantage – canvases and palettes and brushes, for example.'

David's eyes had grown round, giving him for the moment the look of his mother.

'But I do not know how to paint in oils, sir,' he said.

'I will find someone to teach you after we return to Tŷ Gwyn,' Sydnam promised.

Mrs Llwyd, he knew, liked to paint, though he did not know if she painted in oils. Perhaps if she did, she would be willing to give David some lessons. If not, there must be someone else.

'The purchase of paints will be an extraordinarily generous gift,' Anne said. 'But will you not be able to give David some instruction yourself?'

'No!' he said far more sharply than he intended.

She sat farther back in her seat and compressed her lips.

'What is Tŷ Gwyn?' David asked.

'It is your new home,' Sydnam told him. 'The words mean *white house* in the Welsh language. It is not white, though an older version of the house was, or so I have been told. It is larger than a house, though not nearly as large as Glandwr. It is close to it, though, and not far from the sea. There are neighbors, several of them with children. I daresay a few of them are close to you in age and will be delighted to be your friends and playmates. I think you will get along famously with the Llwyd brothers. They go to the village school, and you will be able to go there too if you wish and if your mama wishes it. I hope you will be happy in your new life.'

David gazed back at him and pressed the side of his face against Anne's shoulder. He looked as if he were considering the prospects and not finding them altogether unpleasing. Sydnam looked into Anne's face. The wheels of the carriage were rumbling over the Pulteney Bridge.

'Tŷ Gwyn is yours, then?' she asked him. 'The Duke of Bewcastle has sold it to you?'

'Yes,' he told her, 'though I have not lived there yet. We will move in together.'

As he held her glance, he knew that she was remembering what had happened at Tŷ Gwyn. It was there that today had become inevitable.

'We will not be in Bath long enough to hire a dressmaker,' he said. 'I hope we will be able to find sufficient ready-made clothes for you in the shops this afternoon.'

'Clothes?' She flushed again. 'I do not need to buy any clothes.'

This day and their new relationship were as unreal

for her as they were for him, he realized as he saw in her eyes the dawning understanding that now he had every right – and obligation – to clothe her in a manner suited to his wife. But causing her embarrassment or even distress was the farthest thing from his intentions.

'A new wardrobe will be my wedding gift to you, Anne,' he said. 'I have looked forward to it.'

'A wedding gift,' she said as the carriage turned onto Milsom Street and proceeded in the direction of the Royal York. 'But I have none for you.'

'It is quite unnecessary,' he said.

'No, it is not,' she said firmly. 'I shall buy something for you too this afternoon. We will all have gifts.'

They looked at each other. She was the first to smile.

She *did* need new clothes – quite desperately. It had been perfectly obvious to him during the summer that she had very few, and today she had worn an old evening gown for her wedding. The winter was coming on, and so were the advanced stages of her pregnancy. She needed clothes, and he was going to purchase them for her.

And after the shopping expedition, he thought, they would dine together in their private suite of rooms, the three of them, before David went to bed. And then there would be the wedding night.

He hoped he could do better than he had at Tŷ Gwyn. He hoped she would grow accustomed to him and find it possible to derive some pleasure from their marriage bed. He *hoped* so.

He remembered her as he had first seen her on the cliffs above the beach at Glandwr – like beauty personified stepping out of the dusk and into his dreams. And here she was three months later . . .

She was Anne Butler.

Mrs Sydnam Butler.

David was ready for bed soon after the evening meal had been eaten. It had been an emotional day for him, though not without some pleasurable excitement. After they had all arrived back at the hotel from several hours of shopping, he had spread all his new painting supplies over one of the narrow beds in the room assigned to him and touched and examined them all one at a time with reverence and awe. He was going to be very impatient, Anne knew, to reach Tŷ Gwyn and meet the new art instructor Sydnam had promised to find for him.

But she had been hardly less excited about her own gifts and had spread them over the other bed in the room so that she could admire all the day dresses, the three evening gowns – one of which she was now wearing – the shoes and bonnets and reticules and other garments and accessories that Sydnam had insisted she needed. She had realized anew during the day how wealthy he must be. He had even insisted upon taking her to a jeweler's, where he had bought her the diamond earrings and gold chain with a diamond pendant that she was also wearing this evening.

She had bought him a new fob for his watch at the same jeweler's, recklessly spending almost all the money she possessed. He had stood in the doorway of the bedchamber, fingering it as he watched her and David admire their own far more lavish gifts.

Anne had been very aware all evening of the other bedchamber – the one with the large canopied bed – at the other side of the private sitting and dining room, where she would presumably spend her wedding night with her new husband.

Although David had been with them the whole time, something in Sydnam's manner all afternoon and during dinner had assured her that though this had been a forced marriage, he nevertheless desired her and had no intention of making this a mere marriage of convenience.

She did not want a marriage of convenience either. She wanted to be a normal woman. She wanted to have a normal marriage.

And perhaps, she thought, now that she had been with him once, her body would believe what her mind had told her. Perhaps it would be a magical wedding night.

All day she had been partly terrified, partly excited at the prospect.

She felt the tension again now as she sat on the side of David's bed telling him a story, as she still did each evening before he settled for sleep.

As usual she picked up the narrative from where she had left it the night before, continued it for ten minutes or so, making it up as she went along, and then broke off at a particularly suspenseful moment. As usual she laughed at David's sleepy protest and bent to kiss him.

'How are we expected to live until tomorrow night before finding out what happens to poor Jim?' Sydnam asked from the doorway, where she knew he had been standing though she had been sitting with her back to him.

'You have no choice,' she said, getting to her feet. 'Until tomorrow night I will not know myself what is to be Jim's fate.'

She turned back to smooth David's hair away from his brow and saw resentment in his eyes for a moment before he closed them.

Oh, David, she told him silently, *give him a chance. Please give him a chance.*

'Good night, David,' Sydnam said, not advancing farther into the room.

'Good night, sir,' David said – and then, after a brief pause, 'Thank you again for my paints.'

Anne followed Sydnam back into the private sitting room a few moments later, closing the door of the bedchamber behind her.

'He will be wanting to get to Tŷ Gwyn as quickly as the carriage wheels can turn,' she said, 'so that he may use his new paints. You could not possibly have given him a more welcome gift.'

'I think we will not go there immediately,' he

said. 'We are relatively close to Alvesley. I would like to have my parents meet my new wife. I believe we will go there for a few days.'

Anne froze as she sat again at the cleared dining table and Sydnam sat opposite and picked up his wineglass. It was strange that in all the time she had waited for him to come to marry her, it had not once occurred to her that she would also be marrying into the family of the Earl of Redfield. Whatever would they think of her? The answer did not bear contemplating.

'Do they know about me?' she asked.

'No,' he said.

And for the first time she realized what an awkward position she had put him in with his family. Though she must not begin to think that way. He was as much to blame for what had happened as she was – if *blame* was the right word.

'We must indeed go to Alvesley, then,' she said.

There was a twinkle in his eye suddenly and he smiled his lopsided grin.

'You sound as if you are agreeing to attend your own execution,' he said. 'You will like them, Anne, and they will love you.'

She doubted that very much indeed. Even though she might continue to reassure herself with the knowledge that they were equally responsible for having conceived a child and thus having been precipitated into an unplanned marriage, she did not doubt that his family would see matters quite otherwise.

'Will we tell them . . . everything?' she asked.

He set down his glass, though his fingers played with the stem.

'I want them to know,' he said, smiling again, 'that I am to be a father. But for your sake we will say nothing at present. I will let them know in a letter after we have gone home to Tŷ Gwyn, and they may draw whatever conclusions they wish when the child is born sooner than expected.'

His gaze slipped downward to her abdomen, and Anne resisted the urge to spread her hand there. It seemed strangely unreal that they had created life together in her womb. She felt an unexpected but very welcome surge of desire between her thighs and in the passage within.

'Kit and Lauren have three children,' he said. 'They are all considerably younger than David, but even so he may enjoy having some cousins to meet.'

'He loves playing with young children,' she said. 'I think it is a natural reaction to having spent the last few years with older girls. Young children make him feel important.'

'We will leave for Alvesley in the morning, then,' he said.

They fell into a short silence that might have been comfortable if it had not been so charged with sexual tension. But the discomfort, Anne thought, feeling her breath quicken and her nipples harden, was very pleasurable. They were man and wife, and tonight and for the rest of their lives they would share a marital bed, and they would make love whenever they wished.

Dread receded to be replaced by hope. She remembered the desire, the need, the pleasure with which she had approached their lovemaking last time. It had all been perfectly wonderful until the moment when he came inside her. But the memory of him there had surely replaced the other memory. All would be well. They had not married under the best of circumstances, it was true – she knew that he had not really wanted her as his wife – but she knew equally that he would make the best of those circumstances just as she would.

'Anne,' he said, 'after going to Alvesley we ought to go into Gloucestershire so that I may meet your family.'

'No!' she exclaimed.

'It would be a fitting time to do it,' he said. 'Any embarrassment they may have felt over your unmarried state while you had a child will be soothed by the knowledge of your recent marriage. And we will be able to assure them that I look upon David as my son just as if he had been born of my seed. It is time—'

'It is *not* time,' she cried, getting to her feet and crossing to the fireplace, where she stood with her back to him, looking into the glowing coals, 'and never will be. I have no family.'

'You do,' he said with quiet persistence. 'You have a husband and son. You have in-laws and nephews and a niece at Alvesley. And you have

298

parents and siblings in Gloucestershire – *my* in-laws and David's grandparents and aunts and uncles. Perhaps cousins too. You have never given me full details.'

'Deliberately so,' she told him, 'because I do not know the details myself. My family was not there to comfort and support me when I needed comfort and support, and so I managed without them and discovered that in fact I did not need them at all and would never need them again.'

'We always need family,' he said. 'Some poor souls literally have none, and they are much to be pitied. Other people turn away from the family they do have and are perhaps more to be pitied. But at least they always have the chance to turn back again.'

'I was not the one who turned away,' she told him, angry and upset that he should bring up this topic now when she had told him her feelings on it while they were in Wales. 'I have no turning back to do.'

'I disagree with you, Anne,' he said. 'I know you are not a happy person. I do not believe you ever will be happy until you have at least tried to reconcile with your family and to make your son – and your husband – known to them.'

'And I suppose,' she said, turning on him, 'my new child too, who will be very legitimate indeed and very respectable – the grandson or grand-daughter of the Earl of Redfield no less. And then there will be David Jewell, still illegitimate, still a bastard.'

She had never seen him angry before. The left side of his face looked pale and chiseled and more handsome than ever. The right side of his face looked more immobile in contrast, the black eye patch almost sinister.

'That is an ugly word,' he said, 'and unworthy of you, Anne. David is my stepson. I intend to take measures to adopt him fully. I will even give him my name if he can be persuaded to take it.'

'David is *my son.*' She glared back at him, her hands balled into fists at her sides. 'He is not yours or anyone else's. He is *David Jewell.* And he does not need anyone but me.'

They stared tensely at each other for several moments until he looked away and pushed his empty wineglass farther to the center of the table.

'I am sorry,' he said. 'I wanted to avoid being the autocrat, the domineering partner in our marriage, the sort of husband who either demands obedience of his wife or expects it as his right. I thought to inform you of my wish to take you to Alvesley to introduce you to my family and then give you the equal chance to take me to your own family. But I have only succeeded in hurting and angering you. I am sorry.'

The anger drained out of her, leaving her shaken. She was not often given to anger. And she had liked Sydnam – she still did, she hoped. But here they were on their wedding day, quarreling quite bitterly. He had all but called her a coward. He had called her unhappy, implying that she was not whole, that she was incapable of wholeness and healing unless she turned back to people who had turned from *her* and from her son, who was guilty of nothing except being born of the ugliness of rape. He had scolded her for calling David by a name she knew some people used to describe him.

And he had claimed not to wish to be an autocrat, yet he had spoken of adopting David and giving him his name just as if all the care she had given her son in almost ten years and the Jewell name were nothing. Just as if both she and David needed to be saved from something, lifted up to respectability.

She knew she was being unfair to him – and that fact did not help restore her mood to tranquillity.

'I am sorry too,' she said. 'I did not mean to quarrel with you today of all days – or any day for that matter. I suppose I am just tired. The last few weeks have been rather stressful.'

'Perhaps,' he suggested, 'you would like to sleep in the other bed in David's room tonight.'

The suggestion was so unexpected that all she could do was stare at him, trying not to show the dismay she felt. It was not what she would like at all – she had wanted to take a determined step toward normality tonight. And she did not believe it was what he wanted either – she could not be the only one who had felt the sexual tension all afternoon and evening. But something had been ruined and she found herself answering in kind when she wanted – and perhaps he wanted it too – to deny his suggestion.

'Yes,' she said. 'Thank you. Perhaps that would be a good idea. And if David wakes up in a strange place, he will be reassured to find me close by.'

Oh, stupid, stupid, she thought.

'Yes, of course.' He got to his feet and came toward her, reaching out a hand formally for hers and carrying it to his lips. It was her left hand. She could see her new wedding ring gleaming in the candlelight and willed him to lift his head and kiss her on the lips and end this madness so that the night could proceed as they must both have expected it to.

Instead he smiled kindly at her.

'Good night, Anne. I hope you both sleep well. Shall we plan to make an early start in the morning?'

'Yes,' she said, sliding her hand from his and smiling back. 'Good night, Sydnam.'

Ten minutes later she was lying in the narrow bed close to David, staring up at the canopy over her head and ignoring the hot tears that were trickling diagonally across her cheeks and dripping onto the pillow on either side of her head.

It did not help at all that she recognized the absurdity of the situation – and of both their behavior.

It was her wedding night and a whole private

sitting and dining room separated her bedchamber from that of her new husband.

And all because they had quarreled – *though they had apologized to each other.*

She had desperately hoped that their wedding night would set them on the path to a happy future, even if not a happily-ever-after.

Now she was afraid all might be ruined.

She thought of getting up and going to him after all. But she was the one who had initiated their love-making at Tŷ Gwyn – and then she had let him down. She did not have the courage to do it again, knowing that it was quite possible the same thing would happen.

CHAPTER 16

The carriage turned to pass between two great wrought-iron gates and made its way along a wide graveled driveway, woods on each side, a sure signal that it was traveling through the outer limits of a private park surrounding a great house. Although the scenery was different, Anne was powerfully reminded of her first approach to Glandwr – where all this had started.

She was feeling much as she had felt then.

She was sitting with David on the forward-facing seat while Sydnam sat with his back to the horses. It was impossible to tell if he was excited at the prospect of seeing his family soon or apprehensive at the nature of his return. He sat quietly looking out through the window.

None of them had talked a great deal since leaving Bath, and when they had spoken, it had been about inconsequentials.

What would happen between them tonight? she wondered.

But it struck her as she spotted water and lawns ahead that there was a great deal to be faced between now and tonight.

'Soon you will be able to see the inner park,' Sydnam said. 'It always takes my breath away even though I am familiar with it.'

Even as he spoke the carriage drew clear of the trees, and the interior was flooded with light. Anne could see that the water was a river. Beyond it were wide lawns dotted with ancient trees sloping up to a mansion, still some distance away. Off to the left-hand side there was a lake, partially surrounded by trees.

Her first sight of Alvesley and the inner park made Anne realize more fully the extent of what she had done. She had married a son of this grand and stately home. She was the daughter-in-law of an earl.

Her stomach performed an uncomfortable flip-flop that reminded her of the morning nausea that had worn off hours ago.

With every turn of the carriage wheels she felt a growing dread. David, apparently feeling a similar apprehension, moved closer to her side and pressed his arm against hers. She smiled reassuringly down at him as the wheels of the carriage rumbled onto a roofed stone Palladian bridge across the river, and then onto the driveway through the park.

'It is all quite magnificent,' she said. 'Is it not, David?'

There were people out on the lawn close to the house, she could see as they drew closer – two ladies, one young, the other older, and two children, a boy about four years old and a girl somewhat younger. Both ladies were looking toward the carriage, the older one shading her eyes with her hand.

'My mother,' Sydnam said, leaning closer to the window, 'and Lauren. And Andrew. The little girl must be Sophie. She was a baby when I last saw her, but there is another baby in the nursery now. I have not even seen him yet.'

His manner, Anne saw, was animated. He was happy to be home. She felt a surging of tenderness for him – and a stabbing of loneliness for herself.

And then, as the carriage made a great swing onto the terrace before the marble steps and pillared portico that sheltered the double front doors of the house, Anne could see two gentlemen in riding clothes stepping out of the stable block.

'My father,' Sydnam said, 'and Kit. It seems that we are arriving at a provident moment. Everyone is here – except the baby.'

Anne leaned back in her seat as if by doing so she could hide forever from the ordeal to come. Sydnam turned his attention to her.

'Your bonnet and your spencer are the exact color of your eyes,' he said. 'You look lovely, Anne.'

She was wearing one of her new outfits. Her dress was a shade paler than the spencer. She remembered the pleasure of their shopping expedition in Bath and smiled at him.

The carriage drew to a halt, and as soon as the steps were put down Sydnam descended. But he was given no chance to turn to hand Anne down. His brother must have seen him through the window and had already stridden across the terrace to catch him up in his arms.

'Syd, you old devil!' he exclaimed, laughing. 'What *is* this?'

He was not as tall as Sydnam, and his hair was fairer. He was not quite as handsome either, in Anne's opinion, though he looked fit and lithe and had a good-humored face.

But before Sydnam could answer, his mother came hurrying up and took him from his brother's arms into her own.

'Sydnam,' she said, her voice bright and glad. 'Sydnam, Sydnam.'

'Mama.' He patted her back with his one hand.

David hid his face against Anne's arm.

Sydnam's father stood in the background, beaming genially, and his sister-in-law came into view, the curly-haired little girl astride her hip, the young boy holding her hand, the wide brim of her straw hat flapping in the breeze – a beautiful dark-haired violet-eyed lady.

'Sydnam,' she cried, 'what an absolutely wonderful surprise!'

Ah, yes, indeed, they were a close and happy family.

None of them seemed aware of her presence or David's inside the carriage. But Sydnam soon extricated himself from his mother's embrace and turned to smile up at Anne.

'There are two people here I want you all to meet,' he said, reaching out his hand to help her down.

It closed warmly about hers, and everyone turned to look at her with surprise and curiosity. 'May I present Anne, my wife, and David Jewell, her son? Anne, David, I wish you to meet the Earl and Countess of Redfield, my father and mother, and Kit and Lauren, Viscount and Lady Ravensberg, my brother and sister-in-law. And Andrew and Sophia Butler, their children, I assume.'

Anne curtsied. David, who had scrambled down the carriage steps on his own, bobbed his head in a jerky bow and moved closer to her until the side of his body was pressed to hers.

'Your *wife*?'

'You *devil*, you, Syd.'

'You are *married*, Sydnam?'

'Oh, Sydnam, how *wonderful*!'

They all spoke at once. But surprised, even shocked, as they undoubtedly were, they did not look horrified. Not yet.

The little boy stared at Sydnam and then patted his father's leg insistently until Viscount Ravensberg swung him up into his arms. The little girl hid her face on the viscountess's shoulder.

The countess, regal and handsome, turned her full attention on her new daughter-in-law and smiled.

'Anne, my dear,' she said, taking both of Anne's hands in her own and squeezing them tightly, 'my son has married you and did not even inform us? How *could* he have been so remiss? We would have arranged a grand wedding for you. Oh, how provoking of you, Sydnam.'

'Ramshackle doings, Syd, old chap,' the viscount said. 'Anne – may we call you that? I am delighted to make your acquaintance.' He smiled at her too so that his eyes crinkled attractively in the corners, and held out his free hand to shake hers.

'And I yours,' Anne said, taking it.

'Do you not remember Uncle Syd, Andrew?' he said, looking down at his son.

'The army surgeon chopped your arm off with a big knife,' the boy said, peeping at Sydnam and making a slashing motion with the side of one hand. 'Papa told me.'

'And I am delighted too,' the viscountess said warmly, stepping forward to hug Anne and set one cheek against hers while she still held Sophia. 'More than delighted. And how do we know, Mother, that Anne and Sydnam did not have a grand wedding? Or an equally beautiful *small* wedding? Either way I am sorry in my heart that we missed it. And David.' She turned her full attention on him and stooped slightly to hug him too. 'How lovely to have a new nephew and an older cousin for Andrew and Sophie and Geoffrey, who is missing all the excitement while he enjoys his afternoon nap in the nursery.'

'You are very welcome indeed to this family, Anne,' the earl said, stepping forward and offering her a large hand. 'But Sydnam has some explaining to do to his mother. Why have we known nothing at all of you until this moment?'

'We were married quietly in Bath yesterday by special license, my lord,' she said.

'By special license?' The earl frowned at Sydnam. 'But why the great hurry, son? And why Bath of all places?'

'I was teaching at a girls' school there until two days ago,' Anne explained, relaxing just a little. It looked as if after all his family was prepared to take her to its bosom. 'Sydnam did not want to delay the wedding.'

'I did not,' he agreed, laughing. 'I am s—'

'My mother is going to have a baby,' David said quite distinctly in his treble voice, drawing everyone's shocked attention his way.

There was a very brief silence, during which Anne closed her eyes and then opened them again to find David looking uncertainly up at her. She tried to smile at him.

'In a little more than six months' time,' Sydnam told his family. 'We are enormously happy about it, are we not, Anne? I am going to be a *father*.'

The atmosphere had undergone a distinct change in less than a minute. The chill of autumn seemed to have sliced through the unseasonable warmth of the day.

'And Mr Jewell passed away how long ago?' the countess asked, her manner suddenly stiff and formal.

Ah. All hope of a gradual introduction to Sydnam's family was dashed.

'I have not been married before yesterday, ma'am,' Anne said.

'David Jewell!' the viscountess exclaimed suddenly.

'But of course! *Miss* Jewell. You were at the Duke of Bewcastle's Welsh estate this summer, Anne. Christine has spoken of you. She said that you were a friend of Sydnam's.'

There was a short, awkward silence, during which they must all have realized that the two of them had been more than just friends during the summer.

'Well,' the viscount said with false heartiness, 'if we stand out here on the terrace much longer, darkness will be falling. I am for my tea, and I am sure Anne and Syd must be after the long journey from Bath. Shall we go inside? David, my boy, would you like to come with Andrew and me and we will find you a room close to his? How old are you?'

'Nine, sir,' David said. 'Going on ten.'

'Nine going on ten! An elder cousin indeed,' Kit said. 'And I had better be *Uncle Kit* to you since that is what I am. What are you clever at? Mathematics? Cricket? Standing on your head?'

He set Andrew down and took Sophia from his wife's arms. David laughed and detached himself from Anne, leaving disaster behind him, and went off with them, a new spring in his step. Andrew was gazing worshipfully up at him.

The viscountess linked an arm through Anne's and led her up the steps into the house. Sydnam followed, between his mother and father.

There was a horrible, heavy silence to succeed the loud delight with which they had all greeted Sydnam's return home just a few minutes ago and his announcement that he was married.

311

'Children!' the viscountess said softly and with apparent sympathy. 'They would hang one every time, would they not? Even when they are nine years old. Or perhaps especially when they are nine years old.'

The rest of the day did not get any easier for Anne.

It continued with her second quarrel with Sydnam – one day into her marriage.

'If only I could have been swallowed up in a black hole out there on the terrace and never been heard from again,' she said after they had been taken up to his old suite of rooms and left alone there to freshen up before going to the drawing room for tea, 'I would have been happy.'

'Don't be angry with David,' he said. 'He merely wished to assert himself as a member of our group. Anyway, Anne, do you not think that on the whole it was for the best that the truth came out right at the start as it did?'

'What must they *think* of me?' she asked him, pulling off her bonnet and dropping it onto the bed. 'First they were introduced to me and *my son*, then they were told that we married in haste without even informing them, then they were told that I am with child, and then they learned that I have never been married before.' She slapped the points off on her fingers. 'But perhaps what they think is no more than the truth. I had no business marrying the son—'

'Anne!' he said sharply. 'Please don't. Whatever

they think of you over this pregnancy they must think of me too. It took both of us to make the child.'

'Oh, no,' she said, 'you really do not understand, do you? It is always the woman who is to blame – even when she has been raped.'

'Are you trying to say that I took you by force at Tŷ Gwyn?' he asked her, his hand clutching the bedpost, color flooding into the left side of his face.

'No, of course not,' she said. 'Your family will see it quite otherwise, in fact. I will be the one who seduced *you*.'

'Nonsense!' he said. 'They are going to love you as soon as they get to know you and as soon as they see how much you mean to me.'

He did not understand at all. He was at home with his family, secure in their love and the familiarity of his surroundings and their presence. He could not see her through their eyes – or the situation through hers.

'Show me where I can straighten my hair and wash my hands,' she said. 'They will be expecting us.'

'The trouble with you, Anne,' he said when they were ready to leave the room, 'is that you do not trust anyone else but yourself and your own small circle of friends.'

'The trouble with *me*,' she said tartly, 'is that I did not believe disaster could strike me twice. I am a slow learner, it would seem.'

'Is our child a disaster, then?' he asked softly,

though she could hear anger trembling in his voice. 'Is David a disaster?'

'And the trouble with *you*,' she said, almost suffocated with anger herself, 'is that you do not fight fair, Sydnam Butler. That is *not* what I meant. You *know* it is not what I meant.'

'You do not need to yell,' he said. 'You do not need to signal to the whole house that we are having a disagreement. What *did* you mean?'

She was normally an even-tempered woman. As a teacher she had been renowned for it. She was usually sensible and reasonable too. She really did not know quite what had got into her. She did not even recognize the note of bitterness in her voice. The unaccustomed anger drained from her now, as it had the night before.

'I do not know what I meant,' she said. 'I just want to go home.'

Except that she did not know where home was. It had not been the house in Gloucestershire for a long, long time. She no longer belonged at the school in Bath. She had been to Tŷ Gwyn on just one memorable occasion. There was no home – no *safe* home – to go to.

Sydnam was right, perhaps. She did not trust, she did not belong. But this time her predicament was entirely her own fault.

'I'll take you there soon,' he said, his manner softening too. 'But since we have come here, we might as well stay for a few days, would you not agree?'

'Yes,' she said. 'Yes, of course.'

She opened the door and preceded him from the room. He offered his arm as they descended the stairs and she took it. But the shadow of an unresolved quarrel and a marriage shakily begun lay dark between them. It was not helped by her awareness that she had been petulant and self-pitying. She did not *know* what his family thought of her, did she?

Everyone was remarkably polite during tea and again later at dinner. Conversation did not flag. But the warm delight with which Sydnam and she too had been greeted on their arrival was definitely gone. No one ignored Anne. Indeed, she was drawn firmly into the conversation.

The earl questioned her and discovered that her father was a gentleman, that she had a younger sister and an elder brother, that the expense of sending her brother first to Eton and then to Oxford had put such a severe strain on her father's purse that she had offered to seek a governess's position for a few years before marrying.

The countess questioned her and discovered that she had indeed been a governess before David was born and teacher to a few pupils in a Cornish village for a few years afterward until she had been fortunate enough to be recommended to the position of mathematics and geography teacher at Miss Martin's School for Girls in Bath.

'Miss Martin?' Kit said, grinning – he had asked Anne to call him by his given name, as had his wife.

'The famous Miss Martin who left her position at Lindsey Hall after trying to teach Freyja and refusing a letter of recommendation from Bewcastle?'

'Yes,' Anne said. 'That Miss Martin.'

Kit asked more questions and discovered that she had been invited to Glandwr because the Marquess of Hallmere had befriended her in Cornwall and Lady Hallmere was the one who had recommended her to the school.

'It is to be hoped,' he said, chuckling, 'that Miss Martin does not know that particular juicy fact.'

'She does,' Anne said. 'But she did not when she hired me.'

The earl with a single question discovered that she had been estranged from her family for ten years. No one asked why. The reason, Anne supposed, was self-evident.

At dinner Lauren learned that Anne's ivory lace-over-silk gown, which she had admired, was a wedding gift from Sydnam and that it was part of a whole wardrobe of ready-made clothes he had bought for her in Bath yesterday. And when the countess remarked upon her gold and diamond chain and earrings, she learned that they were a wedding gift too.

'Would you not agree that I have excellent taste, Mama?' Sydnam asked, smiling at Anne. 'Not that my wife's beauty needs embellishment.'

Anne wished that she had worn her old green silk and no jewelry at all.

For of course as the evening progressed she could

see herself with stark clarity as she must appear through their eyes – as a fortune hunter. It was clear that she was no longer a very young woman – she had a son who was almost ten years old. She had never been wealthy. She had been forced to work for a living because her father was short of funds. Her son was illegitimate. Her future prospects were not bright – she could expect to live out her days as a spinster school-teacher. Her only asset was her beauty. And so she had used that beauty this past summer when opportunity had presented itself to snare for herself a husband of rank and fortune whose own future prospects were equally bleak, though for a different reason – a man who was so badly maimed that he could expect only solitude and loneliness for the rest of his life. Her plan had succeeded extremely well. By the end of the summer she had been with child – by a gentleman to whom honor obviously meant more than life. His maimed body proved that.

That was how they must see her.

How could they not? The facts appeared to speak for themselves.

It was a very damning portrait.

They were polite to her because she was a guest in their home and she was Sydnam's wife – and it was perfectly obvious to her that all of them adored him.

But how they must despise her!

By the time she retired for the night she was exhausted. She was thankful that Sydnam remained in the drawing room for a while to finish a conversation with his brother – they were talking about land and crops and livestock.

Although the suite of rooms included a sitting room and a large dressing room, there was only the one bedroom – and the one bed.

Anne undressed and washed, pulled on a nightgown, and brushed out her hair as quickly as she could, climbed into the big bed, moved over as far to the edge of it as she was able, pulled the covers up over her ears, and closed her eyes.

And then it struck her that this was probably the very bed where Sydnam had lain for long months recuperating from his experiences at the hands of torturers. She could have wept then but did not because she no longer had the privacy of a room of her own.

Last night – her wedding night – had been a terrible mistake. She had hoped that perhaps they could make amends tonight. But tonight she was too weary to want anything except to weep for the man Sydnam must have been before the torture.

The man she would never have met.

When he let himself quietly into the room perhaps fifteen minutes after she had lain down, she pretended to be asleep.

CHAPTER 17

The nightmares almost always followed the same pattern.

They were never of the physical torture itself.

They were of the intervals between – the waiting for the next session, the never knowing exactly when it would be, the always knowing *what* it would be. They had always told him that in graphic detail in advance. And the temptation – the terrible, almost overwhelming temptation to give them what they wanted, to sell Kit out, to betray his country and her allies so that he would be granted the blessed release of death.

'No.' He was not speaking to them. He was speaking to *it* – the temptation. 'No. No! *No!*' He did not want to scream. He tried desperately not to. He never screamed during the sessions. He would not give them the satisfaction. But even in the times between they would hear, and so he tried not to scream. But sometimes . . .

'*No-o-o-o-o-o!*'

As always he woke himself up with the screaming. He sat bolt upright on the bed, bathed in sweat, threw off the covers, stumbled over them anyway as he got out because he had thrown them with his *right* hand, and gasped for air like a drowning man.

He was almost instantly aware of Anne, sitting up on her side of the bed, reaching for him though he was too far away from her. He was still more than half in the nightmare and would be for some time, he knew from long experience. His body and his mind were too heavily drugged with the past to deal with the present for a while or even to display the common courtesies.

'Get out!' he told her. 'Get out of here.'

'Sydnam—'

'Get out!'

'Sydnam—'

She was out of bed too and rounding the foot of it to come to him. He would have lashed out at her then if he had had a right arm to do it with.

Someone knocked on the door – hammered on it actually.

'Syd?' It was Kit's voice. 'Syd? Anne? May I come in?'

Anne changed direction and headed for the door, which opened just before she reached it.

'Syd?' Kit said again. 'You are still having the nightmares? Let me help you. Anne—'

'Go away! Get out of here!'

He was still almost screaming. Soon the shaking would begin. He hated that weakness more than anything else. He hated for anyone to see it.

'Anne,' Kit said again, sounding like the military officer Sydnam had briefly known him as. 'Go with Lauren. Mother is here too. Go with them. I'll see to this.'

'Get out! All of you.'

'He has had a nightmare,' Anne said, her voice soft but quite firm. 'I will see to him, Kit, thank you.'

'But—'

'He is my husband,' she said. 'He wishes to be alone. Go back to bed. Everything will be all right. I will see to him.'

And when she closed the door, she remained on Sydnam's side of it.

He began to shake – every cell in his body shook, or so it seemed. All he could do was grasp a bedpost, cling tightly, and clamp his teeth together while the breath rasped in and out of his lungs.

'Sit down,' she said softly an indeterminate length of time later, one hand touching his arm, the other curling about his waist from behind.

When he sat, he found a chair behind him. A cover from the bed came over him then and was tucked warmly about him and beneath his chin and about his neck and shoulders so that he felt cocooned by its soft warmth. She must have gone down onto her knees before him. She set her head on his lap, turned it to one side, and wrapped her arms about his waist.

She did not move again or say another word while he shook and sweated and finally felt the comfort of the warm cover and the weight of her head on his knees and her arms clasped about him.

His mother, his father, Jerome, his various nurses, his valet before they went to Wales – they had all in their turn tried to talk him out of the aftermath of nightmare, but had only succeeded in pushing it deeper.

He appreciated her silence more than he could say. And he appreciated her presence more than he could possibly have expected.

'I am so sorry,' he said at last.

His hand was under the covers. He would have laid it on her head if it had been free. But she lifted her head and looked up at him, and in the faint moonlight that beamed through the window it seemed to him that she had never looked more beautiful.

'I am too,' she said. 'Oh, Sydnam, my dear, I am so sorry. Do you need to talk about it?'

'Good God, no!' he exclaimed. 'I beg your pardon, Anne, but no, thank you. It is my personal demon that will be with me forever, I daresay. One cannot go through something like that and expect only the body to be scarred. Just as my body will never be whole again, neither will my mind. I have accepted that. The nightmares are no longer as frequent as they used to be, and when I do have them, I seem to be able to break free of them more quickly most of the time. But I am sorry for the distress this one has caused you and that other ones will in future.'

'Sydnam,' she said, and he realized that her arms were stretched along his outer thighs, 'I married *you*. All of you. I know I cannot share this pain with you, but you must not feel obliged to shield me from it or try to minimize it. I will be saddened if you do. We have been friends almost since we met, have we not? But we are more than friends now despite a rather shaky start to our marriage. We are husband and wife. We are . . . lovers.'

Once they had been lovers. But that once had produced life in her womb and had bound them forever. He could not feel sorry it had happened even though he had seen her distress last evening and today and had felt a certain guilt yesterday about taking her from the people and the environment she had grown to love. He should have been offering her nothing but comfort for the past two days, not quarreling with her and now burdening her with this.

He lowered the blanket and stroked his fingers over her arm.

'I suppose I am vain and conceited,' he said. 'I hate having you witness my weakness.'

'I think,' she said, 'you are probably the least weak person I know, Sydnam Butler.'

He smiled at her.

'Did Andrew have the story right?' she asked him. 'Was it an army surgeon who amputated your arm?'

'A British surgeon, yes,' he said, 'after Kit and a group of Spanish partisans had rescued me. It was impossible to save it.'

'Sydnam,' she said, 'I want to see you.'

It was impossible to misunderstand her meaning.

He had worn his shirt and breeches to bed even though she had been asleep by the time he came upstairs.

He shook his head.

'I *need* to,' she said.

It was, he supposed, inevitable unless they were to live a separate, celibate existence for the rest of their lives, something he would find immeasurably less tolerable than remaining single. Sooner or later she would have to see him.

He just wished it could be later rather than sooner. He was so very tired . . .

But she was not waiting for his permission. She had got to her feet and lit a single candle on the small table on the near side of the bed. And then she came to kneel in front of him again and drew his shirt free of the waistband of his breeches after taking the blanket away. It would have been churlish of him not to raise his arm when she drew the shirt upward so that she could lift it off over his head.

He did not close his eye. He watched her.

The surgeon had amputated his arm a few inches below the shoulder. Because there had been no recent battle and consequently the surgeon had not been pressed for time while other wounded soldiers awaited their turn to go under his knife, he had done a good, neat job. The stump of the arm was not unsightly – as amputations went.

'I still have my arm, you know,' he said with a somewhat twisted smile, 'and my hand. In my mind they are still there and very real. I can *feel* them. Sometimes they itch. I can almost *use* my hand. But they are both gone, as you can see.'

It was not just the stump of his arm she could see, though. The whole right side of his body was purple from the burns, the crisscrossing scars of the old cuts livid in contrast. They extended all the way down his side and leg to the knee.

She set her hand against the naked flesh of his side, just above the band of his breeches.

'Is there still pain?' she asked.

He hesitated.

'Yes,' he admitted. 'Particularly about my eye, about the stump of my arm, and in my knee, which was not actually destroyed. But not always and not unbearable. It is worst in damp weather. It is something I am accustomed to, something that is quite within my control. One can learn to live with a great deal of discomfort and even pain, Anne. For about six months of my life, I wished fervently to die, but I am glad I did not. Life is very sweet despite all the losses I have sustained. I am not generally, I think, a complainer.'

'You are not,' she agreed.

She reached up her hand then and cupped it

about the right side of his face. He closed his eye and leaned into her hand. So few people except physicians had touched his right side since he came home from the Peninsula. It was as if his torturers had laid everlasting claim to it. He had not even realized just how much he had craved someone's touch – a gentle touch after all the violence. It felt almost as if healing flowed through her hand, as if after she had lifted it away his flesh would be whole again.

He swallowed against a gurgle in his throat.

And then he felt her thumb move beneath the black ribbon of his eye patch and realized her intent. He grabbed for her wrist and opened his left eye, but it was too late. She set the eye patch down on the floor beside his chair.

He gazed at her in horror and misery.

'It is all right,' she told him softly. 'Sydnam, you are my husband. It is all right.'

But it was *not* all right. His right eye was gone. His closed eyelid lay flat against where it had been and there was some heavy scarring. To say it was not a pretty sight would be a gross understatement.

He would not close his eye. He clamped his teeth hard together and watched her as she gazed at him. And then she got to her feet, leaned over him, her hands on his shoulders, and set her lips softly against the outer corner of his eyelid.

He fought the tears that ached in his throat.

She was looking down at him then, a smile on her face.

'You look less like a pirate without the patch,' she said.

'Is that good or bad?' he asked.

'I think some women,' she said, 'find pirates quite irresistible.'

'Perhaps, then,' he said, 'I should put it back on.'

'You had better not tempt me,' she said. 'I am a married lady.'

'Ah,' he said, 'that is sad.'

'Not for me,' she told him. 'I do not need a pirate, you see. I find my husband irresistible.'

He smiled and so did she.

But the air fairly crackled between them, and he was amazed to realize that his weariness had fled, to be replaced by an intense desire for her. And surely this time she was blatantly seducing him.

'I think,' he said, getting to his feet, 'I had better find out if that is true.'

'I think,' she said, 'you had better.'

She moved against him, and her fingers slipped beneath the waistband of his breeches while she opened the buttons and undressed him until he was naked before her. Her eyes took in the wounds all the way down to his knee.

'Anne,' he said, 'perhaps your condition—'

'We are married, Sydnam,' she said. 'We married yesterday. We did it because of my condition, of course. We had said good-bye. We would not have seen each other again. But we *are* married. I want to be married to you in every sense of the word, and I believe you want it too. You do, don't you?'

It was not exactly a declaration of love, only a practical acceptance of the relationship in which they found themselves – because of her condition. But for now it was enough. She was looking at his naked, damaged body, and yet she still wanted a consummation of their marriage. For tonight, for now, that was gift enough.

'And the baby?'

'I asked the physician Claudia insisted I see,' she said, 'since I fully expected that you would come and wed me. He told me there should be no discomfort and no danger – except in the final month or so.'

In the shivering light of the candle he watched a blush spread over the exposed part of her bosom and up her neck into her face. She had actually asked the physician? He smiled slowly.

'Well, then,' he said, 'why are we still standing here?'

'Because we have not yet lain down,' she said. And she crossed her arms and drew her night-gown up and off over her head in one fluid motion.

He explored and caressed her naked, shapely body with his hand, his fingers, and his fingertips after they had lain down. It was only as he did so that he realized they had left the candle burning. But he let it be. He would not hide himself from her any longer. If they were to enter deeply into all the many intimacies of marriage, he must give her the whole of himself as he was and trust her to accept his deficiencies.

He explored her and aroused her with his lips, his teeth, his tongue, his hand.

He spread his mouth over one slightly swollen nipple, licking it with his tongue, sucking on it, pulsing his teeth about it while caressing her in the hot, moist secret place between her legs. She moaned and threaded her fingers in his hair. And then, when he lifted his head to feather kisses over her face, to suckle one of her earlobes, her hands found his naked erection. One hand caressed him while one finger of the other hand circled him and the pad of her thumb stroked feather-light over the tip.

He closed his eye and inhaled slowly. He let the breath out on an audible sigh.

He moved onto her then, regretting fleetingly that he did not have two arms so that he could lift some of his weight off her. But she received him eagerly, spreading her legs, twining them about his, wrapping her arms about him, moving her hips until he was pressed to her opening.

He plunged deep inside and again had to inhale slowly in order to prevent himself from spilling into her too soon, before she had had time to share the pleasure.

This was their real wedding night, he thought suddenly, and he was making love with his wife. With Anne. The wonder of it caught at his heart, and he held deep in her, savoring the knowledge that he was not just a man having sex or sharing a sexual experience with a desirable, willing woman.

He was *making* love with his *wife*, with the woman whom he had married yesterday and with whom he would share the rest of his life.

He withdrew slowly and pressed inward again, withdrew and entered, setting up a slow rhythm, feeling all the exquisite pain of holding back his desire so that it could be a shared experience of pleasure.

Except that he realized suddenly that she was lying quietly beneath him, her body slightly tense – though not with the tension of sexual desire. It was all pretense, he realized – or all a valiant attempt to be a good wife to him, to treat him as if he were a normal man.

And he had left the candle burning!

Desire almost died in him.

But if it did, she would know that he knew – and how would they be able to carry on together? She was doing this for him, because she cared. She *did* care, he knew.

He quickened the rhythm. He shut his mind to all else but his own sexual need, and finally he held deep in her and felt the blessed release of completion. He almost despised the pure physical pleasure of the moment.

He moved off her almost immediately and tucked the blankets up over her shoulders. She was looking at him, he saw in the flickering light of the candle. He wished she had kept her eyes closed and pretended to sleep. He smiled at her. Perhaps she did not know he knew. She had been so very kind to him tonight.

'Thank you,' he said softly.

But he was alarmed to see her eyes fill with tears. Were they not going to be allowed to pretend to each other, then?

'Sydnam,' she said. She was almost whispering. 'It is not you. Please, *please* believe me that it is not you. It is me.'

And the truth of what she had said crashed in on him like a tidal wave. But, of course, of course! He suffered from dreadful nightmares because of the unspeakable atrocities that had been done to his body.

Anne had suffered an atrocity at least equally unspeakable.

Did she suffer from nightmares too?

Or was it physical intimacy that was her nightmare – a physical intimacy that had happened twice since the atrocity, once at Tŷ Gwyn, and once tonight.

He gazed back at her, appalled. Had she known with her mind on both occasions that it was he but had felt with her body that it was Moore?

'It is me,' she said again. 'Please believe that it is not you. You are beautiful, Sydnam, and you are sweet and gentle.'

'Anne.' He touched his lips to hers. 'Anne, I understand. I do. Like a block, I did not even really consider it before now. But I do understand. What can I do? Shall I— Would you like me to go sleep in the sitting room?'

'No!' She clung to him, pressed herself to him.

'Please, please, no. Not unless you cannot bear – Sydnam, I am so sorry.'

'Shh,' he said against her hair. 'Hush, love. Let me just hold you as you held me earlier. Shh.'

He kissed her temple and made sure the blanket was tucked all about her. He warmed her body with his own.

And incredibly, blessedly, he felt her warm and relax within minutes and realized soon after that she slept.

He ought not to have slept too. It had been a night of turmoil.

It had also been totally exhausting.

He fell asleep only a few minutes after.

Anne woke up when something tickled her nose and a few sleepy swipes with one hand did not dislodge whatever it was that was doing it. She realized before she opened her eyes that it was a human knuckle – Sydnam's, to be precise.

She opened her eyes.

'Good morning, Mrs Butler,' he said. 'Are you planning to get up sometime today?'

He was lying on the bed beside her, but on top of the bedcovers, fully clothed, and now that she was awake, she could hear his valet bumping around behind the closed door of the dressing room. It was unlike her to sleep late.

'You have even shaved,' she said, reaching out a hand to touch the smooth skin of his jaw on the left side.

'Are not pirates usually clean-shaven?' he asked her.

'Blue*beard*?' She raised her eyebrows. 'Black*beard*?'

He grinned at her.

Not for a moment had she forgotten last night – not any of it. And it was impossible that he had forgotten any of it either. But he had chosen not to begin the day with tragedy. And why should she? They both had demons to fight. Why fight each other too?

She smiled back.

'Before I came upstairs last night, I agreed to go out riding with Kit and my father this morning,' he said, 'to see the farms. I was actually my father's steward here for a few years after my recovery. Did I ever tell you that? Will you mind if I go with them?'

She minded very much. She would be left alone with his mother and Lauren and the children. But what had she expected? That she could cower in his shadow for as long as he chose to remain here? This was the family she had married into, and now she must do all within her power to fit in, to show them that she was not the unprincipled fortune hunter they must think her.

And since when had she needed anyone to cling to in abject dependence?

'Of course I will not mind,' she said. 'Enjoy yourself.'

He rolled off the bed and got to his feet.

'Lauren will take care of you,' he said.

'Of course she will,' she said. The viscountess was very beautiful, very elegant, very proper. She had also been kind – even after David's disastrous announcement.

'When Kit first brought her here as his betrothed,' Sydnam told her, 'he and I were bitterly estranged. I'll explain it all to you one day. Lauren singled me out one day, determined to have a talk with me, and it was clear I was not her favorite person in the world. But she listened to me – *really* listened. She was the first person during all those years of turmoil to do that and to understand my point of view. She forced a confrontation between Kit and me. Both of us were reluctant, awkward, and sheepish. But it worked. Lauren is one of *my* favorite people. She even kissed me here once.' He tapped his forefinger against his right cheek.

'Did she?' Anne said.

'Jealous?'

'Mortally.'

They smiled at each other, and Anne knew that one thing at least had not died last night. He was still her friend. It was not much to cling to, perhaps, when they were a married couple, but it was definitely something. And she was quite determined to begin this new day with optimism.

'If you get dressed immediately or sooner,' he said, 'we can go down to breakfast together.'

It was only as they were descending the stairs ten minutes later that Anne realized there had

334

been no nausea yet this morning. She had been too preoccupied to give it a chance, she supposed.

The rest of the day proceeded far more smoothly than Anne had feared it might. The men left the breakfast table early, and the countess addressed Anne as soon as they were out of earshot.

'We were worried for you as well as Sydnam last night, Anne,' she said. 'Oh, and a little annoyed with you too for shutting the door in our faces when I daresay you have had no experience of dealing with my son after he has had one of his nightmares. But we did not hear another sound, and this morning he is as cheerful and full of energy as I have ever seen him. He is usually tired and listless the day after. How did you do it?'

'I merely wrapped him up warmly and held him until he had stopped shaking,' Anne said, feeling herself flush.

Her mother-in-law looked steadily at her without smiling.

'He was foolish,' she said, 'so very foolish to go to war – just to prove that he was as brave as Kit.'

'Which he did indeed prove, you must admit, Mother,' Lauren said.

'But at such a tragic cost,' the countess said. 'He was very talented, Anne. Did you know that?'

'As a painter?' Anne said. 'Yes, I did.'

'Not just talented,' the countess said, 'but consumed by the dream of being a great painter. Why on earth he put that dream at risk by going to the Peninsula I will never understand.'

'Sometimes,' Anne said, 'men who are quiet and artistic feel the need to prove their masculinity, especially when they are very young, as Sydnam was. What better way to prove it than by going to war?'

All three women shook their heads at the foolishness of the male of the species, and it struck Anne suddenly that her decision to stay with Sydnam last night when Kit had been prepared to deal with him had actually endeared her to his family. Perhaps after all they would come to accept her and understand that she had not schemed to marry a wealthy, well-connected man.

'Do any of his paintings still exist?' she asked.

Lady Redfield sighed.

'They used to hang all over the house,' she said. 'But after he was brought back here and long before he was able to leave his own rooms he commanded us to destroy every one of them. Yes, our gentle son *commanded* us. They are stacked up in the attic with his old easels and painting supplies. I have sometimes thought of hanging one or two of them again now that he has gone from Alvesley, but I cannot bring myself to do what I believe would still be against his wishes. And I am not sure I would be able to bear to see any of them after so long.'

'But Sydnam is not a tragic figure,' Lauren said, smiling at Anne. 'You must have discovered that for yourself, Anne. He has made a meaningful new life for himself, difficult as it has been with his disabilities. And now he has a wife and family for his personal happiness.'

Her smile seemed to possess genuine warmth.

'You will come visiting with Lauren and me this afternoon, Anne,' the countess said in a tone that brooked no contradiction. 'You must be presented to our neighbors, and the hasty, secret nature of your marriage must be somehow explained. We will *not* take your son with us.'

Lauren laughed softly and got to her feet.

'David is delightful,' she said. 'He was playing with Andrew and Sophie when I went up to the nursery to feed Geoffrey last evening and even settled a quarrel between them before I could intervene. Shall we go up there now, Anne?'

They spent the rest of the morning there, though there was no need to amuse the children. Andrew was clearly delighted to have an older cousin willing and able to build an impressive castle with him out of painted wooden bricks, and Sophia was content with gazing at her new cousin and edging closer to him until she was able to reach out and touch his hair. David turned and smiled at her, and she was permitted to hand him the bricks, though Andrew forbade her to touch the castle.

David was simply happy.

Geoffrey, plump and contented, lay in Anne's arms after he had been fed, his eyelids fighting a losing battle with sleep. He had his mother's startlingly violet eyes, she noticed.

'I think,' Lauren said after a while, 'it is going to be remarkably pleasant to have another sister. And for my children to have another aunt and more cousins.'

'You have sisters of your own, then?' Anne asked.

'Cousins by marriage, with whom I grew up,' Lauren told her. 'I still think of Gwen as a sister and of her brother Neville as my brother. I almost married him at one time. Indeed, I had arrived at the church for our wedding.'

Anne stared at her. 'What happened?' she asked.

Lauren told her about the death of her father, Viscount Whitleaf, when she was an infant and her mother's remarriage within the year to a younger brother of the Earl of Kilbourne. She told of her mother's leaving on a wedding trip overseas and never returning, though they were now back in communication with each other. Lauren had grown up in the Earl of Kilbourne's home with the earl's son and daughter and the expectation that she and Neville would wed when they were grown up. Neville went to war and told her not to wait for him, but she waited anyway, and eventually he came home and courted her and their wedding day dawned. But just as she arrived at the church, another woman – a woman who looked like a beggar – arrived there too, claiming that Neville was her husband, that he had married her in the Peninsula.

'And the ghastly thing was,' Lauren said, running one hand softly over the almost-bald head of her sleeping baby as he lay in Anne's arms, 'that she was telling the truth.'

'Oh,' Anne said. 'Oh, poor Lauren.'

'I thought the world had come to an end,' Lauren admitted. 'As I was growing up my adoptive family could not have been kinder to me if I had been a daughter of the house, but I was always aware that I was not. I spent my growing years trying to be worthy, trying to be lovable – though I already was loved. And all I ever wanted of life was to marry Neville.'

The refined and perfect Lauren had known unbearable pain too, then, Anne thought. Everyone had, she supposed, at some time in life. It was always a mistake to believe that one had been singled out for unusual suffering.

'And then a year later,' Lauren said, 'I met Kit. We did not by any means have a smooth courtship, but it did not take me very long to understand why Lily had had to come back into Neville's life and why I had had to be cut adrift. Fate was saving me for Kit. I do believe in fate, Anne – not a blind fate that gives one no freedom of choice, but a fate that sets down a pattern for each of our lives and gives us choices, *numerous* choices, by which to find that pattern and be happy.'

'Oh,' Anne said, 'I believe that too. I really do.'

'Fate led you to meet Sydnam and he you, I daresay,' Lauren said. 'Despite appearances – forgive me! – I can see quite clearly that you are fond of each other.'

They smiled at each other, and soon the conversation moved into other channels, but Anne felt enormously comforted, as if some blessing had been bestowed. She felt that she and her sister-in-law would be friends – perhaps even *sisters*.

And her mother-in-law had looked on her with approval for staying with Sydnam last night and was to take her visiting this afternoon.

Perhaps families did not always reject. Perhaps at least sometimes they opened their arms in welcome. Perhaps sometimes love was to be trusted.

CHAPTER 18

S ydnam's day started well enough.

It started with hope. Anne had smiled this morning and even joked with him. She had not repeated her wish to go home without further delay, and she had not objected to being left alone with Lauren and his mother. He and she were, he thought, still friends. And for a while he was content – he *must be content – with friendship and with a mutual compassion for the dark places in each other's life.*

The morning proceeded well as he rode about the home farm with his father and Kit, meeting farmworkers and their wives whom he had not seen in years, since he had been steward here, in fact. It was all very enjoyable.

But the afternoon brought home to him a reality that depressed him and might, he feared, put yet another strain on his marriage. Anne had been taken visiting by his mother and Lauren. He went up to the nursery while she was gone to suggest taking David – and the other children too, if they wished – for a walk about the lake. But Kit was there before him to take Andrew out for a riding lesson.

'You must come too, David,' he said.

'But I cannot ride,' the boy protested.

'You have never ridden?' Kit said, setting a hand on his shoulder. 'We are going to have to set that right without any further delay.'

'Will you teach me, Uncle Kit?' David asked, his face lighting up with eagerness.

'What are uncles for?' Kit said, grinning down at him. 'You will come too, Syd?'

A few minutes later they were all on their way out to the stables, David and Andrew dashing ahead, Sophia riding on Kit's arm.

A groom mounted Andrew on his little pony in the paddock behind the stables while Kit chose a quiet mare for David and then taught him some of the rudiments of riding before mounting him and leading him about the paddock and finally allowing him to take a slow turn on his own while walking beside him, calling up instructions and encouragement.

David was as animated and excited as Sydnam had seen him once or twice at Glandwr with the Bedwyn men and Hallmere. And he laughed and chattered, quite at his ease with Kit, calling him *Uncle Kit* as though the two of them had been the best of friends for years.

If David had already had even some small experience at riding, Sydnam thought, he himself might have ridden with the boy and taught him some of the finer points of horsemanship as they went. The shared activity would have offered a chance for them to forge some sort of familial bond. But under the circumstances it had seemed more practical to leave the teaching to his brother, though Kit *had* looked inquiringly at him before proceeding with the lesson.

Instead Sydnam made friends with Sophia, who had been plucking daisy heads from the grass beyond the paddock and now patted Sydnam on the leg and handed him the bouquet. He stooped down on his haunches to thank her, but though she looked warily at his eye patch, she did not run away. Instead, she suddenly reached out one small finger to touch it and then chuckled.

'Funny, is it?' he said. 'Is Uncle Syd funny?'

She chuckled again, a happy infant sound.

They spent the next half hour picking daisies and buttercups together.

When it came time for them all to return to the house and Kit would have picked her up, Sophia shook her soft curls quite firmly and lifted her arms to Sydnam. He gave her their flowers to hold and scooped her up on his arm, and Andrew trotted along beside them asking Sydnam what it had felt like to have his arm chopped off.

But David walked with Kit, still animated and chattering after his first riding lesson. And when they arrived back at the nursery and found Anne waiting for them there, looking flushed and lovely in one of her smartest new dresses, the boy rushed to her to tell her of his accomplishments, the name *Uncle Kit* prominent on his lips.

It was small consolation to Sydnam that Sophia patted his leg again in order to show him one of her dolls.

He had missed an opportunity to be the sort of father his stepson craved. Yet he could have done it. He could have taught David to mount without having to lift him bodily onto the horse's back. But he had allowed himself to feel inferior to Kit and so had held back. He mentally kicked himself now that it was too late.

He could only urge patience on himself. Perhaps next time he would not miss such a chance.

His resolve was put to the test later that very day – and for a while it wavered again.

Anne had gone upstairs after dinner to tell David a story, as she always did at bedtime, and to tuck him into bed for the night. Sydnam hesitated for a while, having been aware on the evening of his wedding in Bath that the boy had resented his intrusion into the ritual, but then followed her up. His father was reading in the drawing room and his mother was engrossed in her embroidery. Lauren was also up in the nursery feeding Geoffrey, and Kit had gone with her.

Sydnam let himself quietly into David's room after tapping on the open door and sat in a chair somewhat removed from the bed while Anne told her story. He smiled when she broke off, as she had done in Bath, at a particularly suspenseful point in the narrative. He did not say anything this time, though.

'Mama!' the boy protested, as he had then.

'More tomorrow night,' she said, getting to her feet and bending over him to kiss him. 'As always.'

Sydnam noticed that Kit had come to stand in the doorway.

'Mothers can be the cruelest of creatures, David,' he said with a wink. 'They should be made to finish a story once they have started it. There ought to be a law. Are you going to come riding again tomorrow? Maybe beyond the paddock this time?'

'Yes, please, Uncle Kit,' David said. 'But most of all I want to paint. *He* ... my ... Mr Butler bought me oil paints and lots of other things in Bath, but I cannot use them because there is no one to show me how. Can *you* show me? Can Aunt Lauren? *Please?*'

He had sat up in bed and was gazing pleadingly at Kit.

Kit glanced at Sydnam – rather as he had done in the paddock earlier.

'I was never a painter, David,' he said. 'Neither is Aunt Lauren – not in oils anyway. I cannot think of anyone close by who is. Except ...' He glanced at Sydnam again and raised his eyebrows.

Sydnam gripped the arm of his chair with his left hand. He felt suddenly dizzy.

And then he could see that David, still sitting up in bed, had turned his attention to him too and was gazing imploringly at him.

'*You* can show me how, sir,' he said. '*Will* you? *Please?*'

'David—' Anne said rather sharply.

Sydnam had a sudden, sickening memory of an almost-identical moment in his own life. His parents had given him paints for Christmas when he was nine or ten, and he had wanted desperately to use them. But there was a houseful of relatives staying at Alvesley, and parties and other activities, all planned for the amusement of the children, had filled every moment of every day. He had been told to put away the paints until after everyone had left and their tutor had returned from his vacation. It had been the longest, dreariest Christmas of his childhood.

'Please, sir?' David said again. 'It has been two whole days. And it is going to be forever until we get to Wales and my teacher.'

Sydnam licked dry lips.

It was ridiculous really. Ridiculous! He had dabbled in painting during his growing years and had enjoyed it. He had even had some skill at it. He had since lost his right arm and could no longer paint. It was no big thing. There were plenty of other things he *could* do. He could be a father to his stepson for one. But—

'David,' he said, 'I was right-handed. I can no longer paint. I—'

'But you can tell me how,' the boy said. 'You do not have to *do* it for me. Just *tell* me.'

But that was not the point at all. It was simply not the point.

'David,' Anne said firmly. 'Can you not see—'

'I suppose I can do that,' Sydnam heard himself

say as if his voice were coming from far away. 'I can tell you how. You are good enough to pick up the skills without my having to hold your hand.'

'Sydnam—'

'You *will*, sir?' David leaned across the bed, all eager excitement. 'Tomorrow? We will get out all my new things and I will *paint*?'

'Tomorrow morning after breakfast.' Sydnam smiled at him and got to his feet. 'Lie down and go to sleep now or we will both incur the wrath of your mother.'

David plopped himself back on the pillow, both his cheeks suddenly flushed.

'Tomorrow,' he said, 'is going to be the *best* day. I can hardly wait!'

Sydnam slipped out of the room ahead of Anne. Kit had already disappeared.

It would not hurt him to give his stepson some pointers. This aversion he felt to painting – even to other people painting – was something he just had to get over. It was amounting to something like a sickness. He had felt actual nausea when he had smelled Morgan's paints back at Glandwr – and when he had been buying David's in Bath.

Anyway, he had committed himself now. He was going to do something with his stepson – because his marriage and his commitment to the boy were more important than his own particular sickness.

But for a moment he had to pause on the stairs. He felt dizzy.

★   ★   ★

347

Anne was sitting on a low chair in a large, light-filled, almost completely unfurnished room on the nursery floor that she guessed was the schoolroom whenever there were children in the house old enough to need one.

In the middle of the room David's very new easel was set up. A small canvas rested on it, and David stood before it, his new palette in his left hand, a new brush in his right. On a table beside him was propped an oil painting of the sea, which Sydnam was using for instruction – he was standing behind David's right shoulder.

The air was heavy with the strong smell of the oils.

Anne watched Sydnam more than she did David or his painting. He was abnormally pale. Last night he had been uncommunicative. He had not touched her after they went to bed, but had turned onto his side away from her and pretended to fall asleep fast. But he had not slept for a long time, just as she had not, though she had pretended just as diligently as he.

Did he believe what she had told him the night before – though he had not asked for and she had not offered details? Or did he still think himself ugly and untouchable?

She guessed that he had felt a failure during the afternoon because it was Kit who had given David his first riding lesson. And she knew that he had agreed to the painting lesson in order to redeem himself and be the father he was determined to be. She knew too that painting was something he did not even like to think about, let alone involve himself in.

But this was a challenge he had chosen to face – for the sake of *her* son. She fell a little deeper in love with him as she watched. How many men, even if they had married her, would have been prepared to do more than tolerate her illegitimate son?

'No, no,' she heard him say now. 'You are still gliding the brush as if you were using watercolors. Try using your wrist more to produce the texture of those waves. *Flick* the brush.'

'I just cannot *do* it,' David said in exasperation after trying again. 'Show me.'

Something happened then – or did not happen – that made Anne turn cold. How she knew she never afterward understood – but she *did* know that Sydnam had lifted his right hand to take the brush, only to discover that it was no longer there.

She covered her face with her hands and drew a few slow, silent breaths before looking again.

Sydnam had the brush in his *left* hand and was bending closer to the canvas. But the hand shook, and it was obvious that he could not perform the demonstration he had intended. He made a low, inarticulate sound of distress and then bent forward to take the end of the brush in his mouth while adjusting his hold on the brush so that he held it grasped in his fist. He made a few bold brush-strokes on the canvas and drew back.

'Ah!' David cried. '*Now* I understand. *Now* I can see. Those are waves and they are not flat. Let *me* try.'

He took the brush from Sydnam's hand and made his own strokes on the canvas before looking up with triumph into Sydnam's face.

'Yes,' Sydnam said, laying his hand on his shoulder. 'Yes, David. Now you have it. Just look at the difference.'

'But it is all one color,' David said after returning his attention to the canvas. 'Water is not all one color.'

'Exactly,' Sydnam said. 'And you can do much more mixing and blending of colors and shades with oils than with watercolors, as you will soon discover. Let me show you.'

Anne watched them, her two men, their heads bent together, utterly absorbed in what they did, quite oblivious to her presence.

Was there to be some healing after all?

Was healing possible when grave damage had been done?

Was wholeness possible when one had been horribly maimed?

She spread a hand over her abdomen, where she sheltered the unborn member of their family.

The food on Sydnam's plate tasted like straw.

He could not get the smell of the oils out of his nose or out of his head.

'Are Kit and Lauren going to accompany you and

350

Anne to Lindsey Hall this afternoon, Sydnam?' his mother asked.

They ought to have called there yesterday. He had written to Bewcastle, of course, to inform him that he was taking a short leave of absence – to which the terms of his employment entitled him. But he had not explained the reason. Common good manners dictated that he call at Lindsey Hall with his new bride before Bewcastle heard from someone else that he was at Alvesley. They certainly ought to go today.

'Perhaps you would like to take my place in the carriage, Mama,' he said. 'I feel a little indisposed. I will stay here.'

Anne looked at him sharply across the table.

'So will I,' she said. 'We can go to Lindsey Hall some other time.'

It was impossible to argue with her when they were not alone together. But all he wanted was to be left literally alone.

'We will take the children riding, then, Lauren, will we?' Kit suggested. 'I daresay David will come too, with your permission, Anne.'

'Oh, certainly,' she said. 'He is looking forward to it.'

Not long afterward Sydnam and Anne were upstairs in their rooms together.

'I need some air,' he said, 'and some solitude. I am going outside to walk. Will you stay here or do something with my mother?'

'I want to come with you,' she said.

'I will not be good company,' he told her. 'I feel indisposed.'

'I know,' she said.

And the trouble was that he thought she probably did.

It struck him suddenly that loneliness was not perhaps the least desirable state in the world. Was marriage going to feel too crowded? It was an alarming and unwelcome thought. He had always longed for a wife, for a life's companion. But foolishly he had thought of marriage as a happily-ever-after, as a destination rather than a new fork in the path through life.

'Don't shut me out of your life, Sydnam,' she said as if she knew very well what he was thinking. 'We must try to make our marriage work if we possibly can. We were friends in Wales, were we not? Let's continue to be friends now. I want to come with you.'

'Come, then,' he said grudgingly, finding his hat and waiting for her to pull on her warm new pelisse and tie the ribbons of her bonnet beneath her chin.

They walked without talking or touching down the driveway and across the Palladian bridge before he turned onto a path that led among the trees until it arrived at the marble temple folly that stood on the southern shore of the lake and made a picturesque prospect from the opposite shore.

It was a chilly, cloudy day and blustery too. The

352

ground was carpeted with leaves, though there were still plenty left on the trees. Anne went to sit inside the shelter of the temple while he stood outside gazing across the choppy water.

He was not often depressed. He did not allow himself to be. Whenever his spirits threatened to droop, he always found more work to do. Work was an amazing antidote to depression. And he did not often give in to self-pity. It was tedious and cowardly and pointless. He preferred to count his blessings, which were many. He was alive. Even that was a miracle.

But just occasionally depression or self-pity or both assaulted him no matter how determinedly he tried to keep them at bay. He dreaded such times. Sometimes neither work nor positive thinking would help.

This was one of those times.

The smell of the oils was still in his head.

He still remembered the moment when he had lifted his hand to take the brush from David.

His *right* hand.

And he still remembered lifting his left hand to the canvas.

'Sydnam—'

He had almost forgotten Anne's presence. She was his wife, his bride. She was bearing their child. And she had shown him enormous kindness even in the midst of her own pain.

'Sydnam,' she said again, 'is there no way you can paint again?'

Ah. Already she understood him too well.

He stared bleakly into the folly.

'My right hand is no longer there,' he said. 'My left will not do my bidding. You must have seen that this morning.'

'You used your mouth,' she said, 'and changed your grip on the brush. And then you made brush-strokes that caused David to understand what you had been telling him.'

'I cannot produce *art* with my left fist and my mouth,' he said. 'Forgive me, but you do not understand, Anne. There is the vision, but it flows down my right arm, which is not there. Am I to produce phantom paintings?'

'Perhaps,' she said, 'you have allowed the vision to master you instead of bending it to your will.'

She was sitting very upright on the stone bench at the back of the folly, her feet together, her hands cradled in each other, palm-up, in her lap. She looked very much like the rather prim teacher she had been until a few days ago – and ever and always dazzlingly beautiful. He turned his head away.

'The vision is not like a muscle to be exercised,' he said softly. 'I have lost an eye as well as an arm, Anne. I do not see properly. Everything is changed. Everything has narrowed and flattened and lost perspective. How could I even *see* accurately to paint?'

'*Properly*,' she said, picking up on the one word he had spoken. 'How do we know what is *proper* or *accurate* vision?'

'That which involves two eyes?' he said rather bitterly.

'But *whose* two eyes?' she asked. 'Have you ever watched a bird of prey hovering so high in the sky that it is almost indiscernible to the human eye and then diving to catch a mouse on the ground? Can you even begin to imagine the vision that bird has, Sydnam? Can you imagine seeing the world through its eyes? And have you seen a cat at night, able to see what is invisible to us in the darkness? What must it be like to see as a cat does? How do we know what is *proper* vision? Is there any such thing? Because you have only one eye, you see differently from me or from yourself when you had two. But is it therefore *improper* vision? Perhaps your artistic vision is great enough to see new meaning in things and to find a different way of expressing itself without in any way diminishing itself in the process. Perhaps it has needed the changes so that it may challenge you to do great things you never even imagined before.'

He stood looking out over the lake as she spoke, its surface gray and rough in the wind but nevertheless reflecting some of the myriad colors of autumn that the trees were sporting.

He felt a painful surge of love for her. She wanted so badly to help him, just as she had the night before last after he had woken from his nightmare. And yet there seemed no way he could help her.

'Anne,' he said, 'I cannot paint again. I *cannot*. Yet I cannot live without painting.'

Those final words were wrenched unwillingly from him and horrified him. He had never dared even *think* such thoughts before. He dared not believe in the truth of them now. For if they *were* true, there was no real hope left in life.

Suddenly, without warning, he hit the very bottom of despair.

And then he was horrified anew as he sobbed aloud and, when he tried to strangle the sound, sobbed once more.

After that he could not stop the sobs that tore at his chest and embarrassed him horribly. He turned to stumble away, but two arms came about him and held him tightly even when he would have broken away from them.

'No,' Anne said, 'it is all right. It is all right, my love. It is all right.'

Not once before now had he wept. He had screamed when he had been unable to stop himself, he had groaned and moaned and later raged and suffered in silence and endured. But he had never wept.

Now he could not stop weeping as Anne held him and crooned to him as if he were a child who had hurt himself. And like a child that had hurt itself, he drew comfort from her arms and her warmth and her murmurings. And finally the sobs turned to a few shuddering hiccups and stopped entirely.

'My God, Anne,' he said, pulling back from her and fumbling in his pocket for a handkerchief.

'I am so sorry. What kind of a man will you take me for?'

'One who has conquered every aspect of his pain except the deepest,' she said.

He sighed and realized suddenly that it had started to rain.

'Come and shelter inside,' he said, taking her hand and drawing her back under the roof of the temple. 'I am so sorry, Anne. This morning seriously discomposed me. But I am glad I did it. David was happy. And he is going to be good with oils.'

She had laced her fingers with his.

'You must face the final, deepest pain,' she said. 'No, more than that. You have, in fact, just faced it. But you have looked at it with despair. There must be hope, Sydnam. There is your artistic vision and your talent, and there is you. They have to be enough to propel you onward even without your right arm and your right eye.'

He raised their hands and kissed the back of hers before releasing it. He tried to smile at her.

'I will teach David,' he said. 'I will be a father to him in every way I can. I will ride with him. I will—'

'You must paint with him,' she said. 'You must *paint*.'

But though he had calmed down considerably, there was still a coldness and a rawness at the core of his being, where he had not dared tread during all the years since he returned from the Peninsula.

357

'And you,' he said, realizing something suddenly with blinding clarity when he had not even been thinking about it, 'need to go home, Anne.'

There was a brief, tense silence between them while the faint rushing sound of rain beyond the shelter mingled with the lapping sounds of the lake water.

'To Tŷ Gwyn?' she asked.

'To Gloucestershire,' he said.

'No.'

'Sometimes,' he said, 'it is necessary to go back before we can move forward. At least I think that must be so, unwelcome as the thought is. I suppose we both need to go back, Anne. Perhaps if we do it, both of us, there will be hope. I cannot see it in my own case, but I must try.'

When he looked at her, he found her staring back, her face pale, her look inscrutable.

'It is what you want me to do,' he said.

'But . . .' She paused for a long moment. 'I cannot and will not go home, Sydnam. It would change and solve nothing. You are wrong.'

'So be it, then,' he said, taking her hand in his again.

They sat in silence, watching the rain.

CHAPTER 19

Anne eyed the horses apprehensively. They looked so very large and full of energy, and the stable yard seemed to be filled with them. It was some time since she had ridden. But she would do so this morning in a good cause. She glanced over to where Sydnam and Kit were supervising David as he mounted. Having accomplished the task successfully, her son gazed down, triumphant and happy, at *both* men – and then across the stable yard at her.

'Look at me, Mama,' he called.

'I am looking,' she assured him.

Kit had turned his attention to Lauren, helping her mount her sidesaddle, and lifting Sophia up to sit with her.

Sydnam came striding toward Anne.

'Riding is not something you forget,' he assured her, correctly interpreting the look on her face. He grinned at her in his attractive, lopsided way. 'And Kit has chosen a good horse for you.'

'Meaning she is ancient and lame in all four legs?' she asked hopefully.

He laughed.

'Set your boot on my hand and you will be in the saddle in no time,' he said.

'Let me do that, Syd,' Kit suggested, coming toward them.

'I thought I broke you of that habit years ago,' Sydnam said, still grinning.

'Of underestimating you?' Kit said. 'Go ahead, then, and show off for your bride. Impress all of us.' He was chuckling too.

Anne set her booted foot in Sydnam's hand and found it as solid as a mounting block. A few moments later she sat in her sidesaddle, smiling down at him as she arranged her skirts about her. Kit had slapped a hand on his shoulder. They were both laughing.

'You have made your point,' Kit said. 'No one needs two arms. The second one is superfluous.'

Just yesterday afternoon Anne had been in the depths of gloom, sitting in the temple folly by the lake while it rained, convinced that she had made a terrible mistake in marrying Sydnam, convinced that what she had said to him – quite unplanned – had hurt him beyond measure, and convinced that he was terribly wrong in saying that they – *she* – must go back before they could go forward. The only chance anyone had in life was to move constantly onward.

But then, after the rain had stopped, they had picked their way through the wet woods and walked side by side up the long driveway, and David had met them in the hall with his excited tale of riding on his own, first with a leading rope and then with none, beyond the paddock and to the limits of the park before turning around and being rained upon before they arrived safely back at the stables.

'You should have seen me, Mama,' he had cried. 'You should have seen me, sir. Uncle Kit says I have a good seat.'

'I could see that yesterday.' Sydnam had reached out a hand to ruffle his hair, and David had beamed happily up at him.

And suddenly a great deal of the gloom had dispersed.

And suddenly and for no real reason it had seemed that after all there was hope.

This morning they were going to ride over to Lindsey Hall to call upon the Duke and Duchess of Bewcastle. When they had mentioned their plans in the nursery after breakfast, David had begged to go too and had renewed his pleas even after Anne had explained to him that all the children with whom he had played at Glandwr were now at their separate homes.

'But James will be there,' he had reminded her. 'Let me come, Mama. Please, sir?'

And then, of course, Andrew had wanted to go too. And Sophia had wormed her way into the group and tugged at the tassel on Sydnam's Hessian boot to gain his attention.

Yes, this morning, despite a night spent at opposite sides of their bed and no real resolution to any of their problems, Anne was filled with hope. The sun was even shining again from a cloudless sky, and there was warmth in the air.

Andrew, mounted on his pony, was attached to Kit's horse by a leading rope, the understanding being that he would ride as far as he was able and then be taken up before his father.

The two men mounted last.

Anne watched Sydnam, appreciating anew the power of his leg muscles, his sense of balance, his control over a horse that was not even his own. He sat squarely in the saddle and gathered the reins in his hand.

'Ho!' David said admiringly. 'How did you do that, sir?'

'There is very little a person cannot do if he has the will to do it,' Sydnam said, smiling at the boy and glancing at Anne. 'A horse is not ridden with the hands, after all, but with the thighs. I heard Uncle Kit telling you that the day before yesterday.'

'I did not know then that you could ride,' David said, 'or *you* could have taught me.'

'I would not be able to do my work at Glandwr if I could not ride, would I?' Sydnam said. 'But now that *you* can ride, you will be able to come with me whenever you wish.'

'Will I?' David sounded interested.

'Of course,' Sydnam said. 'You are my boy, are you not?'

They rode off side by side, following after Kit and Lauren and Andrew, and Anne drew her horse in alongside them. Sydnam smiled at her across David's horse, and she smiled back. There was genuine warmth in the wordless communication, she thought. They were a family.

They rode at a very sedate pace all the way to Lindsey Hall, much to Anne's relief, though she thought that the men might find the speed irksome. Lauren looked back when they were almost there and called out to Anne.

'I am always thankful to have Andrew with us when we go riding,' she said. 'Kit is less likely to challenge me to a race.'

They both laughed.

'A *race*?' Kit said. 'Heaven help us, a *race* with Lauren involves taking our horses into a fairly moderate trot. It is enough to make one weep, Syd, I swear.'

But Anne's attention was soon taken by the approach to Lindsey Hall along a straight, tree-lined driveway – the very driveway down which Claudia must have stridden on the day she resigned from her post as Lady Hallmere's governess. The house itself, huge and sprawling, was a mixture of architectural designs, testament to its great age and to the attempts of former dukes to enlarge and improve it. It was impressive and surprisingly beautiful. Before it was a large circular flower garden, still colorful though it was late in the year. At its center was a massive stone fountain, though the waterworks must have been turned off for the approaching winter.

After dismounting at the stables and turning the horses over to the care of grooms, they were shown into the house, and Anne's breath was fairly taken away by the medieval splendor of it, with its intricately carved minstrel gallery, its huge stone fireplace and whitewashed walls covered with shields and banners, and the enormous oak banqueting table that stretched along its length.

But they were not left long to contemplate it. The duchess came hurrying into the hall only a minute or two after the butler had disappeared to announce their arrival. Both her arms were stretched out ahead of her.

'Lauren, Kit,' she said. 'And Andrew and Sophie. What a delight! And Miss Jewell – it *is* you. And *David*. And Mr Butler.' She laughed. 'Oh, what *is* this? Do tell me.'

'Not Miss Jewell, your grace,' Sydnam said, 'but Mrs Butler.'

The duchess clasped her hands to her bosom and beamed from one to the other of them. But before she could say any more, the Duke of Bewcastle himself strolled into the hall, his eyebrows raised, his quizzing glass in his hand and halfway to his eye.

'Oh, Wulfric,' the duchess said, hurrying to his side and taking his arm with both hands, 'here are Lauren and Kit and the children, and Mr Butler has married Miss Jewell after all. We were right, you see, and you were wrong.'

'I beg your pardon, my love,' his grace said,

364

making a slight bow that encompassed them all, 'but I must protest in my own defense. I do not believe I ever said that either you or my brothers and sisters and their spouses were *wrong*. What I did say, if you will remember, is that matchmaking was an undignified and unnecessary activity when the two people concerned were quite capable of conducting their own courtship. It would seem, then, that *I* was right. And so you have taken leave of absence from your post in order to *marry*, have you, Sydnam? My felicitations. Ma'am?' He bowed again to Anne.

'And we are going to have a new baby,' David blurted happily.

The duchess's hands flew to her mouth, though her eyes danced with merriment above them. Kit and Lauren were very quiet. The duke raised his quizzing glass all the way to his silver eye and directed it at David.

'Are you, indeed?' he said frostily. 'But I would wager, my boy, that that was your mama's secret to tell – or not tell. I doubt you would be delighted if she divulged one of *your* secrets.'

The duchess lowered her hands and stepped closer to hug David.

'But it is the most splendid secret in the world,' she said, 'and belongs to your whole family, not just to your mama. But why are we standing here just as if there were no nursery for the children to play in and no morning room where there is a warm fire for the rest of us to take coffee? Mama and Eleanor are up there and will be delighted to welcome company.'

Anne felt somewhat as she had felt on her arrival at Alvesley. *Why* had she not thought of having a word with David before they came here? She glanced helplessly at Sydnam, who looked back, a twinkle in his eye. The wretch! He was actually enjoying this!

The duchess linked an arm through hers and led her in the direction of the staircase.

'I am so very happy for you, Mrs Butler,' she said. 'Is it not the most *glorious* feeling in the world to discover that one is with child? Both Wulfric and I believed when we married that we could not have children. James is our miracle, the little rascal. He kept his nurse up half of last night with his crying and then fell promptly asleep after his feed this morning when I wished to play with him.'

They had discussed a possible courtship between her and Sydnam, Anne was thinking – all the Bedwyns, that was, at Glandwr. They had tried to *matchmake*.

She had had no idea.

She would have died of embarrassment if she had.

She turned to catch Sydnam's eye and surprised herself by exchanging a smile with him.

Had he known?

Had he minded?

Had he *wanted* to court her? When he had asked

her to marry him at Tŷ Gwyn, had he meant it? Had he wanted her to say yes?

It would make all the difference in the world if he had.

But *if* he had, why had he asked in such a way? *If you wish, Anne, we will marry.*

But she would have said no anyway, she supposed. Just as she ought to have said no in Bath. But how could she have refused then?

They were indeed going to have a new baby in their family, and that child was of far more importance than either she or Sydnam.

They did not stay long at Lindsey Hall though they were well received there. Indeed, the duchess was beside herself with delight. And even Bewcastle stayed in the morning room to take coffee with them.

They were back home in time for luncheon, and Sydnam felt that at last he could put into effect what he had made up his mind to yesterday. When he had told Anne out at the temple folly that they both needed to go back before they could move forward, he had not known just how that could apply to himself. He had thought it would mean merely allowing himself to remember – to look back upon what had excited him about painting and to try to remember exactly what it was he had tried to capture and accomplish with his brush. It would have been painful – for many years he had not allowed himself to remember.

But there was more than memories.

When they had been walking home after the rain stopped, largely in silence, he had said one thing as he made his way ahead of her through the woods and held back a branch that would have deluged her face with water as she passed, as it had just done to his.

'I wish,' he had said, 'I could see just one of my old paintings. But they were all destroyed.'

'Oh, no, they were not,' she had said, taking the branch from his hand so that he could move ahead. 'They were put up in the attic. Your mother told me.'

He had turned away without a word, and he had not spoken a word on the subject since. He had convinced himself when they arrived back at the house that it was too late in the day to see them properly. And this morning he had felt it necessary to make the visit to Lindsey Hall.

But now the time had come – and he would have grasped at any excuse that offered itself not to do what he must do, he thought.

Anne was sitting at the other side of the luncheon table, listening to his mother's account of the duchess's first visit to Alvesley, before it had dawned on any of them that Bewcastle was courting her.

'We had so given up all expectation that Bewcastle would marry,' she said, 'and Christine was so very different from any bride we might have imagined him choosing that we did not

368

dream of what was about to happen. But though he is as dour as ever, I do believe he is content with her.'

'Oh, more than content, Mother,' Lauren said. 'He *adores* her.'

'I would have to agree,' Anne said. 'One night when I was at Glandwr, I saw them from the window of my bedchamber strolling together toward the cliff top above the sea. He had his arm about her shoulders and she had hers about his waist.'

She turned her head to smile at him.

'I am going upstairs,' he told her when the meal was over, and they left the dining room together.

'To rest?' she asked him.

'No,' he said. 'Not to our rooms.'

'To the nurs—' But there was sudden awareness in her eyes. 'No. Not there. You are going up to the attic, Sydnam?'

'Yes,' he said. 'I think I will.'

She looked searchingly at him as they stood alone together at the foot of the stairs.

'Would you rather go alone?' she asked him. 'Or may I go with you?'

He was not sure he had the courage to go alone, though that was what he had intended.

'Come with me?' he said. 'Please?'

She took his hand in hers and they went up together, their fingers laced.

One half of the attic floor was taken up with servants' rooms. The other half, in a quite separate wing from them, was used for storage. He had come up here frequently as a boy. They all had – he and Jerome and Kit. They had rummaged through old boxes and devised stories and games from what they had discovered. It was Jerome who had most frequently worn the old bag wig and skirted, brocaded coat and long, embroidered waistcoat of an ancestor from the past century, since he was the eldest. But it was Sydnam who had donned them one day after painting his face from the old pots of rouge and kohl and placing black patches in provocative places. He had minced about the attic floor in the high, red-heeled shoes they had found with the outfit, the tarnished small sword at his side. They had all agreed, after rolling about with laughter, that men in those days must have been very confident in their masculinity if they were prepared to dress with such apparent effeminacy.

But today he was going up there for a grimmer purpose.

He found what he was looking for in the third room he tried. It was, in fact, he discovered, a room devoted to him – and he wondered fleetingly if there were similar rooms for Jerome and Kit.

His military kit and his dress uniform were at one side of the small room, behind the door. The scarlet of the coat had faded somewhat to pink. But he did not pay them much attention. He could smell paint. All his old easels and supplies were arranged neatly. They were not even covered with dust, leading him to the conclusion that these rooms must be cleaned occasionally. They all looked shockingly familiar, as if he had walked into someone else's life and made the disorienting discovery that it was his own. It all seemed so very long ago.

Unconsciously he tightened his grip on Anne's hand and she winced almost imperceptibly. He looked down at her and released her.

'It is not easy,' he said, 'to look back into one's own past, especially when one believed that all traces had been obliterated.'

'No,' she said.

He looked at everything without touching anything. He breathed in slowly the smells of his former life.

He was terribly aware of the framed pictures and the canvases stacked against the far wall, face-in.

'Perhaps,' he said, 'it is as well to leave it all in the past.'

She closed the door behind her back and he noticed that the window too was clean and was letting in a great deal of light from the sunny day outside.

'But then,' he said, 'I will be haunted by it forever. I think perhaps I spoke the truth yesterday. And they are just paintings, when all is said and done.'

He walked forward, touched one of the picture frames, hesitated, drew in a breath, and lifted and turned it to set against the wall to one side.

It had been his mother's favorite – it had hung in her boudoir. It was of the small humpbacked bridge that spanned the stream at the foot of the formal gardens to the east of the house and depicted bridge and water and overhanging trees. He turned another and set it beside the first. It was of the old gamekeeper's hut in the woods south of the Palladian bridge, showing the weathered wood of the building, the worn path to its door, the shining, smooth old stone that formed its door sill, the trees surrounding it. He turned another.

By the time he had finished he had them all turned over, the heavier pictures in their frames at the back, the canvases propped in front of them in such a way that he could see all of them. There were the temple folly painted from across the water, one of the boats moored in the reeds, the rose arbor, and numerous other scenes, almost all of them within the park of Alvesley. There were watercolors and oils.

He had no idea how much time had passed since he began. But he became aware suddenly that Anne had not moved from her position against the door and that she had not spoken a word. He drew a deep breath and looked at her.

'They really were quite good,' he said.

'*Were?*' She gazed steadily at him.

'I could see,' he said, 'the essential oneness of all things. I could see that the bridge connected the cultivated park and the wilder wilderness walk

372

but that really they were all one. I could see that people had walked across the bridge, that water flowed beneath it, essential to all. I could see that the boat in this other picture had been rowed by people but that it was only a part of everything, not in any way making the people superior. That old hut was part of the woods and would return to them eventually when people were done with it. The roses were carefully cultivated, but their power was stronger than the hand that planted and pruned them – and yet that hand was a part of it all too, creating order and beauty out of wildness, which is what human nature impels us to do. Am I babbling? Am I making sense?'

'Yes,' she said. 'And I know that this was your vision, Sydnam. I can see it in the paintings. They throb with something greater than themselves.'

'They were really quite good,' he said with a sigh.

'You have said it again,' she said. 'They *were* quite good. Are they not good in the present tense? They amaze me. They smite me here.' She touched her hand to her heart.

'They are the work of a boy,' he said. 'What amazes me is that they are not nearly as good as I remember them.'

'Sydnam—' she said, but he held up his hand.

'People change,' he said. '*I* have changed. I am not this boy any longer. I had not realized that about artistic vision. I have thought it a static thing. What was it you said yesterday? Something about the vision adapting?'

373

Perhaps you have allowed the vision to master you instead of bending it to your will. He could remember her exact words.

'Yes,' she said. 'I thought perhaps it would if you gave it a chance.'

'You were talking about my physical condition,' he said. 'But it applies to age and time too. My age and experience would have exerted an influence over the vision.'

'How would you paint differently now?' she asked.

'This boy,' he said, indicating the paintings with one sweep of his arm, 'was a romantic. He thought that it was beauty that bound everything together. And for him it was true. Life had been beautiful for him. He was very young. He knew very little of life. He saw beauty but he did not feel any true passion. How could he? He did not *know*. He had not really encountered the force of beauty's opposite.'

'Are you more cynical now, then?' she asked him.

'Cynical?' He frowned. 'No, not that. I know that there is an ugly side of life – and not just human life. I know that everything is not simply beautiful. I am not a romantic as this boy was. But I am not a cynic either. There is something enduring in all of life, Anne, something tough. *Something.* Something terribly weak yet incredibly powerful. God, perhaps, though I hesitate to use that word to describe what it is that holds all together since the mind immediately creates a picture of a superhuman being. That is not what I mean.'

'Love?' she suggested.

'Love?' He frowned in thought.

'I remember something Lady Rosthorn said that day she and David were out painting on the cliffs when you came by,' she said. 'It struck me powerfully at the time and I committed it to memory. Let me see.' She closed her eyes and thought for a moment. 'Yes, this is it. *The real meaning of things lies deep down and the real meaning of things is always beautiful because it is simply love.*'

'Simply love,' he said. 'Morgan said that? I'll have to think about it. Perhaps she is right. Love. It *is* terribly tough, is it not? I could not have lived through all those days in the Peninsula had it not been for love. Hatred would not do it. I came very close to crumbling when I concentrated upon my hatred for my captors. I thought of Kit instead and the rest of my family. And in the end I thought of the mothers and wives and children of the men who did those things to me. We are in the habit, I think, of believing that love is one of the weakest of human emotions. But it is not weak at all. Perhaps it *is* the force that runs through everything and binds everything. *Simply love.* I like it.'

'And what will you do about it?' she asked Sydnam now.

He turned his head to look at her.

'I certainly am not satisfied with these paintings,'

he said. 'I cannot leave them as my sole artistic legacy. I am going to have to paint, I suppose.'

'How?' she asked.

Terror gripped him for a moment and a terrible frustration. With his left fist and his mouth?

Perhaps you have allowed the vision to master you instead of bending it to your will.

'With a great deal of willpower,' he replied, and moved to stand against her. He leaned forward so that all his weight was against her. 'I do not know how. *Somehow.* What fate brought you into my life, Anne?'

'I don't know,' she said, and he could see that there were tears in her eyes.

'You were there and waiting,' he said, 'even before all this happened to me, your own experiences preparing you to come to my rescue. And even before all this happened to me I was being prepared to come to yours. Tell me I am right. Tell me we can help each other.' He set his mouth lightly to hers.

'You are right,' she said. 'All the experiences of our lives have brought us to this moment. How strange! Lauren said something very similar just yesterday.'

He pressed his mouth hard against hers.

But the greatest miracle, he knew, was not that he was going to paint again – mad and insane as the idea sounded – but that he had met this woman, whose own experiences had equipped her to understand his pain and give him the courage to face it instead of suppressing it as he had not really realized he had done in all the years since the Peninsula. And his own experiences had equipped him to understand her pain. Ah, let him find some way of helping her to healing. Let him find some way.

'Let's go down and walk outside, shall we?' he suggested. 'It is such a lovely day despite the chill.'

He opened the door and stepped out of the room with her, lacing their fingers together again after he had closed the door. He left his paintings and his former self and vision behind him, still spread out against the walls, where dust motes danced against them in the light of the sun streaming through the window.

Strangely, now that he had decided to paint again, he understood that painting could never be the single-minded, all-consuming passion of his life that it had once been. There were so many more important things.

There was his wife. There was his stepson. There was the unborn child.

His family.

Simply love.

Trust Morgan to think of a phrase like that.

CHAPTER 20

There was still an autumn chill in the air the next day, but Anne could feel some heat from the sun. She lifted her face to it and gave up all pretense of reading. She had brought a book outside with her only so that neither David nor Sydnam would feel self-conscious about her being there. But neither of them even knew she existed. She set the book down on the blanket she had spread on the grass to absorb any lingering dampness from the night dew and clasped her arms about her knees beneath the warm cloak she wore.

David and Sydnam were painting – both of them.

Painting with oils outdoors was not the most convenient of activities, since so many supplies were needed. But David had wanted to come outside – and so had Sydnam.

Anne had also buried her nose in her book earlier, she admitted now, because she was almost afraid to look at Sydnam. His easel was set up on the northern bank of the lake, but far distant from the house. She recognized the place from one of the paintings she had seen yesterday. There were reeds in the water. An old rowing boat was moored to a short wooden jetty. There was a small island in the middle of the lake, not far away.

The sun was shining on the water, as it had been in that old painting. But there was also a breeze blowing today, and it ruffled the surface of the lake into little waves. It had been glassy calm in the painting she had seen.

David had asked for help several times, and each time Sydnam had offered it without complaint at the interruption to his own work. But for most of the time – all of an hour – he had been laboring at his own easel, his brush clenched in his left fist like a dagger, its end steadied in his mouth as he painted.

Anne could not see the results from where she sat. But whereas at first she had half expected signs and sounds of frustration and even worse, she was now able to entertain the hope that she had not made a terrible mistake in urging him to try what might well be impossible.

She tried to relax, afraid that any tension or doubt she felt might convey itself to Sydnam. But she knew he was unaware of her existence.

She wondered what was happening right now at school. Was Lila Walton doing well enough with the geography and mathematics classes to be permanently promoted to senior teacher? But she was still so young! Had Agnes Ryde settled into life at school and realized that she belonged there without having to fight for acceptance? Who was going to produce the Christmas play this year? Was Susanna missing her? Was Claudia?

She was missing them. For a few moments she rested her forehead against her knees and felt a wave of homesickness for the familiar surroundings and smells and atmosphere of the school. Did all new wives, no matter how basically happy, feel somewhat bereft at first from having been snatched from their families?

Susanna and Claudia were her family.

And you need to go home, Anne.

To Gloucestershire.

Sydnam had dared to hope, to dream again. He was painting.

But there was no similarity between their situations.

When she could see that he was cleaning his brush in his characteristic awkward yet efficient one-handed way, she got to her feet and approached him rather warily. But he saw her come and stood wordlessly aside so that she could see his canvas.

It was extraordinary, quite different from any painting she had seen before, including his own canvases at the house. The paint had been boldly slapped on. There was also a certain clumsiness to it – each brush-stroke was thick and distinct from all the others. But Anne did not notice the defects – if they *were* defects. What she *did* notice was that the lake and the reeds were alive with light and energy and motion and had a fierce beauty that threatened to overwhelm and destroy both boat and jetty. And yet they possessed something that was almost dignified, something resilient that held them there as though by right. Humankind had not imposed mastery over nature. Rather, the water had allowed humankind to be a part of it, to borrow its power and share its buoyancy.

Simply love.

Or perhaps she was reading too much into what was undoubtedly an awkwardly rendered scene. Perhaps she simply wanted to see signs of greatness.

Except that the signs were *there*. Even her untutored eye could see them.

It was a painting that was suffused with vision and passion.

She looked up into his eye and was very aware of the black patch over his absent right eye. His vision had changed – both the inner and outer vision. And *he* had changed from the boy whose work she had viewed yesterday. He had seen ugliness as well as beauty since then, but he had not been broken. And he had accepted defeat with grace and then risen above it to turn it into triumph.

'Sydnam.' She smiled slowly at him and blinked her eyes to clear them of the tears that had gathered there.

'It is quite dreadful,' he said, but his eye was bright and his voice strong. 'And the process is like beating my way through dense forest after years of ambling along a well-worn path. But I *will* forge a new path. The next canvas will be better, and the next will be better still. And so begins again the elusive quest for perfection.'

That, at least, she could identify with.

'Every year I taught,' she said, 'I would change something about the content and method of my classes, convinced that *this* time I would have a perfect year.'

'Anne,' he said, and some of the fierce light went from his eye so that he was regarding her with soft awareness. 'Anne, my dearest, you have already given me so much. And yet I have taken you from everything you held dear except your son. How may I make amends?'

But David called to them before she could protest, and they made their way to him.

'The boat is still too brown, sir,' he said, virtually ignoring Anne, 'and the water too blue. But I like the way it is no longer flat.'

'Hmm,' Sydnam said. 'I see what you mean. But the great thing about oils is that you can keep adding to what is already there. The boat looks almost new, does it not? How can you age it the way you see it there on the lake? Ah, but I can see that the wood is flaking away in places – you have captured that with your brushstrokes. Well done.'

'Should I try blending some of this color in, sir?'

Anne strolled back to the blanket while they

talked, and opened the small picnic basket her mother-in-law had suggested they bring out with them. There were bread buns filled with cheese and new carrots from the kitchen garden, a shiny apple each, one bottle of cider and another of lemonade.

They ate and drank everything after all the painting things had been cleaned and put away and the wet canvases left to dry on the easels. It felt like a blessed day to Anne, who felt more hope than ever that once they were home in Tŷ Gwyn they would be able to function as a family and could even expect some happiness with one another. And there was the new baby to look forward to. There had been so much apprehension, even fear, involved in her discovery that she was with child that it was only now she could turn her mind to the great pleasure of knowing that she was to be a mother again. She *hoped* it would be a girl this time, though it would be just as lovely to have another boy. What she really hoped was that it would be a live, healthy baby.

Of course, there was still the major problem of a marriage that was threatening to be a celibate one . . .

And then, quite without warning, when she least expected it, when all her defenses were down, she found herself confronted with the crisis she had known must happen one day soon now but for which she was still unprepared. David began to ask questions.

'You are my stepfather, sir,' he said, kneeling on one edge of the blanket and looking intently at Sydnam. 'Aren't you?'

'I am,' Sydnam said, pausing before taking another bite out of his apple. 'I am married to your mother and so you are my stepson.'

'But you are not my real father,' David said. 'He is dead. He drowned.'

'I am not your real father,' Sydnam admitted.

David turned his gaze on Anne.

'What was his name?' he asked.

She drew a slow breath.

'He was Albert Moore,' she said, unable any longer to convince herself that he was too young to be given truthful answers.

'Why am I not David Moore, then?' he asked.

'I was never married to your father,' Anne explained. 'And so you were given my name.'

'But he would have married you if he had not died.' David frowned.

She could not quite speak the lie, and yet he was still too young for the bare truth.

'But he did die,' she said. 'I am so sorry, sweetheart.'

Though she was not.

'Cousin Joshua is Joshua *Moore*,' he said. 'He *is* my cousin, then?'

'He was Albert's cousin,' Anne explained to him. 'So he is a sort of cousin to you too.' First cousin once removed, in fact.

'Daniel and Emily are my cousins too,' he said.

'Second cousins, yes,' she agreed.

'Mama.' He looked at her with wounded eyes. 'Who else do I have? Mr Butler has Uncle Kit and Aunt Lauren and Andrew and Sophie and Geoffrey and Grandmama and Grandpapa, but for me they are only *step*-people because he is only my stepfather. Who else do I have of my very own?'

Sydnam's hand touched hers on the blanket and she realized it was not accidental even though the touch did not linger. He got to his feet and strolled closer to the bank of the lake, though he remained within hearing distance.

'You know Lady Prudence from Cornwall,' Anne said, pulling David right onto the blanket to sit beside her. 'She is married to Ben Turner, the fisherman. And Lady Constance, married to Mr Saunders, the steward at Penhallow. And perhaps you remember Lady Chastity, who used to live at Penhallow when we were at Lydmere, though she is now Lady Meecham and lives with her husband. They were all your father's sisters. They are your aunts.'

David's eyes were wider and even more wounded.

'They never *said* so,' he said. 'And you never said so.'

'I was never married to their brother, David,' she explained. 'And when you are older, you will understand that that makes a difference. I did not wish to impose on them. But Joshua has told me that they all wish to acknowledge the relationship and welcome you as their nephew.'

It was not, of course, that she had not wanted to

impose on them. It was that she had not even wanted to admit to herself that David had had a father and that he had been Albert Moore. But she had come to realize that what she wanted for herself was not necessarily what was good for David.

Ghastly as the thought was, Albert Moore had been his *father*.

'Do I have anyone else?' he asked.

She would not mention the dowager Marchioness of Hallmere, David's grandmother, who no longer lived in Cornwall and who hated Anne and therefore David with a passion. She looked up almost unwillingly to find Sydnam looking over his shoulder at her, his gaze steady.

She drew in a deep breath again and released it slowly.

'You have a grandmother and grandfather in Gloucestershire,' she said. '*Real* grandparents – my mother and father. And an Aunt Sarah and an Uncle Matthew, my sister and brother.'

He was up on his knees again then and gazing at her with saucer eyes.

'And cousins?' he asked.

'I do not know, David,' she said. 'I have not seen or heard in years.' But there was, of course, another uncle. And she *had* heard, though her mother's twice-yearly letters were always brief and about matters that did not relate to the family.

'*Why?*' he demanded to know.

'I suppose,' she said, smiling at him, 'I have always been too busy. Or they have.'

He continued to gaze at her, and she somehow knew what he would say next even before he opened his mouth to say it.

'But you are not too busy now,' he said. 'We can go to see them now, Mama. We can. My stepfather will take us. We can go. Can't we?'

Anne licked dry lips. She would not look at Sydnam again, though she was half aware that he had turned back to face the lake again.

She ought to have lied.

But no, it was time. He had a right to the truth.

'Perhaps we can go sometime,' she said.

'When?'

'After we have finished visiting here, perhaps,' she said. 'But perhaps—'

'Famous!' he cried, jumping to his feet. 'Did you hear that, sir? I have a real grandmama and grandpapa, and we are going to see them. I am going to tell Uncle Kit and Aunt Lauren. I am going to tell them *now.*'

'You had better take your painting things with you,' Anne said, and he bounded over to them, picked them all up, careful not to smudge the surface of his canvas, and trotted off in the direction of the house without waiting for either Anne or Sydnam.

She hugged her knees tightly and bent her head to rest her forehead against her knees.

He wondered if she would have told David about

her family and even agreed to take him there if he had not said what he had at the temple folly two afternoons ago.

They had rejected her. No, they had *forgiven* her, which had apparently been worse. And they had never asked about David or expressed any wish to see him.

He could only imagine what she was feeling now. But her decision, he knew, was irrevocable. David was excited about going.

'Have you ever rowed a boat?' he asked.

'What?' She looked up at him with blank, uncomprehending eyes.

'I have,' he said, 'but not for years. I could do it now, I suppose, but the exercise would be mildly self-defeating. It strikes me that a one-armed rower would move in a perpetual circle and never get anywhere. Which is something like life, I suppose, if one cares to take a pessimistic view of it.'

He grinned at her. Making fun of his disabilities was something he rather enjoyed being able to do.

'I have rowed a boat, yes,' she said, looking warily beyond him to the boat both he and David had painted a little while ago. 'I lived in Cornwall right by the sea for a few years. But I have not done it for a long time. And I was never very good at it. I always used to dig the oars too deep and try to push the sea past the boat instead of moving the boat through the sea.'

'Sounds exhausting,' he said.

'And impossible,' she agreed.

'I have not been to the island for years,' he said. 'Do you fancy going there today?'

'With me rowing?' She shaded her eyes, presumably to judge the distance. 'If you have an hour or three to spare.'

'But I am far too gallant to expect you to do all the rowing alone,' he said. 'I was thinking of us as a team – you on the right hand oar, me on the left.'

'It sounds like a recipe for disaster,' she said.

'Can you swim?' he asked.

'Yes,' she said.

'And I can bob around and somehow keep my head above water,' he said. 'We would survive a ducking, which I do not expect. I trust your rowing prowess and my own. Of course, if you do not have the nerve . . .'

She smiled and then chuckled and then laughed aloud.

'You are mad,' she said.

'Guilty as charged.' He grinned back at her. 'But the question is – did I marry a mad wife?'

'How deep is that water?' She shaded her eyes again and looked dubious.

'About up to your eyebrows at its deepest point,' he said.

'My *raised* eyebrows?'

'You *are* a coward,' he said. 'Let's go back to the house, then.'

'We will never fit side by side on that seat,' she said, turning her attention on the boat again.

'Yes, we will,' he said, 'provided you do not mind some intimacy. I do not have a right arm to take up room, remember. And you are not very large – yet.'

Her eyes flew to his and she blushed.

'You *are* insane,' she said again. 'Let's do it.'

It *was* a mad suggestion – he did not mind admitting it to himself. He had long ago decided what was difficult but possible – riding a horse, for example – and what was absolutely impossible. Rowing a boat fit into the latter category. But then so did painting. Indeed, that had always been at the top of the list. But he had painted this morning. And now he felt capable of anything. He felt like a veritable Hercules.

The jetty was not as steady as he remembered it. But he walked carefully out onto it and held the boat while she stepped into it – *very* gingerly and without the aid of his hand since the only one he possessed was holding the boat. She turned and sat on the seat and laughed and looked terrified as she pushed her cloak out of the way of her arms. He climbed in after her, and she edged along the seat to give him room, causing the boat to tip and rock alarmingly. She shrieked and they both laughed.

She had been almost right. They were very tightly packed on the seat.

'I hope,' she said, picking up one of the oars and fitting it into its lock, 'I remembered to say my prayers last night.'

'I did if you did not,' he said, grappling with the other oar. 'They cover both of us.'

He unwound the mooring rope and pushed them away from the jetty.

She shrieked and laughed again.

It took them all of half an hour to row across to the island. But as he informed her when they finally pulled onto the beach there and jumped out to drag the boat together up onto dry land, they might have crossed the English Channel and back if only they had proceeded in a straight line instead of meandering around in rough circles for the first twenty minutes while they both tried to recapture the knack of rowing and – once that was more or less accomplished – tried to row in harmony with each other.

They were both laughing so hard that she could scarcely get any words out.

'How on earth are we going to get ba-a-a-ack?' she asked.

'Not on earth,' he said, 'unless you want to try running over the lake bottom, Anne. You had better keep your eyebrows raised if you do, though, or you will get them wet. I intend rowing back.'

He took her hand in his, noticed that her palm was red and ridged from the oar, and held it to his lips.

'If you end up with blisters,' he said, 'I will never forgive myself.'

'A few blisters would be a small price to pay,' she

said, 'for the fun of doing this. When did you last have *fun*, Sydnam? Silly, mad fun like this, I mean?'

He tried to remember and could not.

'It was forever ago,' he said.

'And at least that long ago for me,' she said.

'This *has* been fun,' he agreed. 'But perhaps we had better wait until we have our feet safely back on the other shore before we pass a final judgment. Come and see the other beach.'

It was a tiny man-made island. But the adjacent side of it had always been a favorite spot, since it offered excellent swimming and faced away from the house, which was well out of sight anyway. The grassy bank sloped gradually into the water and was covered with wildflowers in the summer. Even now some hardy varieties survived. He and his brothers had often swum nude here, but they had never been caught.

'It is really quite blissful here,' Anne said, sitting down and gazing into the water.

'We ought to have brought the blanket,' he said.

'The grass is dry.' She rubbed it with one hand. 'And it is sheltered from the breeze here. It feels almost warm.'

He sat beside her and lay back to gaze up at the sky.

'Sydnam,' she said several minutes later, bending over him to look into his face, 'you will take us?'

'To Gloucestershire?' he said. 'Yes, of course. You know I will.'

She gazed down at him.

'I suppose,' she said, 'I ought to tell you what happened.'

'Yes,' he said, 'I think you ought.'

He lifted his hand and touched the backs of his fingers to her cheek.

'Come down here,' he said, and spread his arm across the grass so that she could rest her head on it. When she had done so after tossing aside her bonnet, he wrapped his arm about her and drew her head onto his shoulder.

'I think you ought to tell me,' he said again.

'I was going to marry Henry Arnold,' she said. 'But we were both very young – too young to marry – and my father was having financial difficulties and I offered to take employment as a governess for a couple of years. I went to Cornwall and thought for a while that my heart would break – I had known Henry all my life and missed him more than I missed any of my family. We were not officially betrothed, but everyone knew we had an understanding. Everyone was happy about it – both his family and mine.'

And he had abandoned her. Sydnam waited for the most painful part of her story.

'And then,' she said, 'soon after I had made a visit home and we had celebrated Henry's twentieth birthday, I was forced to write home to tell . . . what had happened to me. I wrote to Henry too.'

And the blackguard had rejected her.

'My mother wrote back,' she said. 'She told me that they forgave me and that I could come home

393

afterward if I wished – I assumed she meant after the baby was born – but that perhaps it would be better if I did not.'

Sydnam closed his eye, and his hand played with her hair. How could any mother not have rushed to her side at such a time? How could any father not have rushed to call to account the rogue who had ruined her?

'Henry did not write,' she said.

No, he would not have done.

'And then, just three weeks after her first letter,' she said, 'my mother wrote again to announce that Sarah, my younger sister, had just been married – to Henry Arnold. One month after my letter must have arrived. Just time for the banns to be called. She added again that perhaps it would be best if I did not come home – and I assumed she meant ever.'

Sydnam's hand lay still in her hair.

'I did not know how many more blows I could take,' she said, her voice more high-pitched. 'First, Albert. And then the discovery that I was with child. Then my dismissal by the Marchioness of Hallmere – Albert's mother. And then rejection by my own mother and father. And finally the betrayal. You cannot know how dreadful that was, Sydnam. I had *loved* Henry with all my young heart. And Sarah was my beloved sister. We had confided all our youthful hopes and dreams in each other. She *knew* how I felt about him.'

She buried her face against his shoulder.

He turned his face to kiss the top of her head and realized that she was weeping. He held her close, as she had held him just two days ago. He did not attempt to speak to her. What was there to say?

She was still at last and quiet.

'Do you wonder,' she asked him, 'that I have never gone home?'

'No,' he said.

'My mother writes at Christmas and my birthday,' she told him. 'She never says a great deal of any significance, and she has never once mentioned David, though whenever I write back I tell her all about him.'

'But she *does* write,' he said.

'Yes.'

'I tell you what I would do,' he said, kissing the top of her head again, 'if Albert Moore were still alive. I would find him, and I would take him limb from limb even with my one hand.'

She half choked on a laugh.

'Would you?' she said. 'Would you really? I would almost pity him. *Almost.*'

They fell silent for a few moments.

'What I have never been able to contemplate with any calmness,' she said, 'is the fact that David is his son. He even looks like him. I try so very hard not to see that. I did not even know I was about to admit it aloud now until the words came out of my mouth. He *looks* like him.'

'But David is not Albert,' Sydnam said. 'I am

not my father, Anne, and you are not your mother. We are separate persons even if heredity does cause some physical resemblance at times. David is David. He is not even you.'

She sighed.

'How did Albert Moore die?' he asked. 'Apart from the fact that he drowned, I mean?'

'Oh.' He could hear that the breath she drew was ragged. 'I was already with child and living in the village. Lady Chastity Moore came one evening and told me that Albert and Joshua were out in a fishing boat. Joshua was apparently confronting him over what had happened. But Lady Chastity, Albert's sister, was going down to the harbor to await their return. She had discovered the truth – from Prudence, I suppose. She had a gun. I went with her.'

'He was *shot*?' Sydnam asked.

'No,' she said. 'When the boat came back, Joshua was rowing it and Albert was swimming alongside. Apparently he had jumped out when Joshua threatened him. Joshua turned without seeing us and rowed away as soon as he saw that Albert could wade safely to shore, but Lady Chastity raised the gun and would not let Albert come to land until he had promised to confess to his father and to leave home forever. He laughed at her and swam away. It was a rather stormy night. He never did come back. His body was discovered later.'

'Ah,' Sydnam said.

Sometimes, it seemed, justice was done.

They lay there in silence for a while.

'I *will* take Henry Arnold limb from limb if you wish,' he said at last. 'Do you?'

'Oh, no.' She laughed softly and touched his face – the damaged side – with one hand. 'No, Sydnam. I stopped hating him a long time ago.'

'And did you also stop loving him?' he asked softly.

She drew back her head and looked at him. She was flushed and red-eyed and lovely.

'Oh, yes,' she said. 'Yes, I did. And I am glad now that he did not have the courage to stand by me. If he had, there would not be you.'

'And that would be bad?' he asked.

'Yes.' She stroked her fingers lightly over his cheek. 'Yes, it would.'

And she turned farther onto her side in order to kiss him on the lips. He felt himself stir into an unwelcome arousal.

'It is hard to understand,' she said, 'how if all the bad things had not happened in both our lives, we would not have met. We would not be here now. But it is true, is it not?'

'It is true,' he said.

'Has it been worth it?' she asked. 'Going through all we have been through in order that we may be together now like this?'

He could no longer imagine his life without Anne in it.

'It has been worth it,' he said.

'Yes,' she said, 'it has.'

She gazed steadily at him.

'Make love to me,' she said.

He gazed back at her, and she licked her lips.

'It is bright and sunny here,' she said. 'It feels . . . clean here. I want to feel clean again. I don't believe I have felt quite clean in ten years. How foolish a thing is that? I feel so . . . *soiled.*'

'Shh, Anne.' He turned onto his side and set his mouth to hers. 'Don't upset yourself again.'

'Make love to me,' she said. 'Make me clean again. Please make me clean.'

'Anne,' he said. 'Ah, my dearest.'

'But perhaps,' she said, 'you do not want to. I have not been—'

He kissed her into silence.

She had not even known that about herself – that she felt unclean. The hurt, the ugliness, the injustice, the pain had all been pushed ruthlessly inside her, beneath the necessity of living on, of maintaining dignity and integrity, of earning a living, of raising a son.

She had never talked it all out before now. She had never even allowed herself to *think* it all through. She had denied her own suffering. She had never wept – until now, today.

But the weeping had eased the pain, had enabled her to put it all in the past – Albert Moore, Henry Arnold, Sarah, her parents. *All* of it.

And now what was left was the Anne who had

survived it all and found solace with another lonely soul, whose life had been as turned inside out as hers had been by circumstances beyond his control. He was here with her now – Sydnam Butler, her husband, her lover.

They were here in this lovely place, just the two of them, surrounded by natural beauty and solitude.

All was perfect – except this feeling of being unclean, spoiled.

Yet cleanliness, peace, joy were surely within her reach at last. They were contained in the power, the energy of love. She had reached out to Sydnam with a love that went far beyond the merely romantic, and now she knew that she could also receive love, that at last – oh, surely – she was worthy of being loved.

Even if he could not give her the sort of love that any woman dreamed of having from her mate . . .

It did not matter.

He was Sydnam, and he could . . .

'Make me clean,' she murmured again against his mouth.

He remained on his side facing her as he raised her skirts and unbuttoned his breeches and stroked her stomach and her hip and her inner thighs with his lovely warm, long-fingered left hand. She gazed into his face, so beautiful despite the burns and scars – no, beautiful *because* of them, because of the person they had made him into.

Behind his head and all about them the sky was blue and sun-filled.

He touched the moist heat between her thighs.

'You are ready, Anne?' he asked her.

'Yes.'

He lifted her leg over his hip, adjusted his position, and pressed slowly into her. He kept his head back the whole time and held her gaze with his own.

It was exquisite. And it was Sydnam who was inside her. She closed her muscles about him, holding him deep, and smiled.

'Yes,' she murmured.

Perhaps, she thought over the next few minutes, he would not have chosen her as the companion of his life if he had been given a free choice, but he was nevertheless a man filled with love, with tenderness, with compassion. He loved her slowly, deeply, rhythmically, very deliberately, his eye on hers. She bit her lower lip as swirls of pleasure and of wonder radiated up through her womb to fill her whole being with warmth and light until finally there was no room left for ugliness or hatred or bitterness.

Only love.

Simply love.

He kissed her as he released into her and something in her flowed to meet him.

It was surely the most glorious moment of her whole life. She could smell grass and water and sunlight and sex.

'Anne,' he whispered to her. 'You are so beautiful. So very beautiful.'

'And clean,' she said, smiling sleepily at him as he withdrew from inside her. 'Clean again. And whole again. Thank you.'

His lips rested warm against hers again as she sank into sleep.

CHAPTER 21

'They have *gone*? Already?'
The Duchess of Bewcastle sank into a chair in the drawing room at Alvesley and held her hands out to warm them at the fire.

'They left this morning,' Lauren said. 'How disappointing that you missed seeing them.'

'You will be thinking me very rag-mannered,' the duchess said, smiling at the countess and Lauren, 'as if I came here only to see Mr and Mrs Butler when in reality I came just as much to see you. But it *is* a disappointment to find them gone, I must confess, Lauren. It has been bothering me that they did not have much of a wedding.'

'We were upset about that too, Christine,' the countess said. 'But they were in a hurry to marry, you know, because . . . Well, because they were in love, I suppose.'

The duchess dimpled.

'Yes,' she said, 'David told us all about that. The poor child even had to endure the full force of Wulfric's quizzing glass as a consequence.'

All three ladies dissolved into laughter.

'Sydnam is painting again,' Lauren said, leaning

forward in her chair, 'with his left hand and his mouth. And the one painting he showed us was wonderful, was it not, Mother, though he declared that it was perfectly dreadful. He said it with a smile, though, and it was clear he was pleased with himself and determined to try again. Father had to leave the room in a hurry, but we could all hear him blowing his nose very loudly outside the door.'

'Oh,' the duchess said, her hands clasped to her bosom, 'Wulfric *will* be pleased – about Mr Butler painting again, that is. And so will Morgan. I must write to her.'

'And it appears that it is all Anne's doing,' the countess said. 'We must thank you, Christine, for inviting her to Glandwr during the summer and giving Sydnam a chance to meet her.'

'But it was Freyja who invited her,' the duchess said. 'Joshua and David's father were cousins, you know, and Joshua is very fond of the boy. But I will take credit if you insist. If I had not decided to go to Wales with Wulfric after James's christening, after all, then no one else would have gone there, would they? And Anne would not have been invited.'

'We have grown exceedingly fond of her,' Lauren said.

'We all tried very hard to bring them together during the summer,' the duchess told them. 'All except Wulfric and Aidan, who have the peculiar and very *male* notion that true love never needs a helping hand.'

They all laughed again.

'I *do* wish they had stayed here a little longer,' she added.

'They are on their way to Gloucestershire,' the countess explained, 'to visit Anne's family.'

'Indeed?' The duchess looked interested. 'Joshua told us she was estranged from them. I *do* think it is sad to be estranged from one's family. I know from experience, though it was in-laws in my case – in-laws from my first marriage.'

'We have guessed,' Lauren said, 'that it is Sydnam who has persuaded Anne to go home.'

'Ah.' The duchess sighed and sat back in her chair, her hands warm again, 'it really is turning into a *good* marriage, is it not? But they did not have much of a wedding for all that. When I broached the matter with Wulfric last evening, he insisted that Mr Butler would probably hate any fuss, but he did finally relent and agree to allow me to organize a grand wedding reception for them. I came to consult you about it. But I am too late – they are gone. How very provoking!'

'Oh,' Lauren said, 'how wonderful that would have been. I wish I had thought of it myself.'

The duchess sighed. 'Wulfric will look smug when I go home and tell him they are gone,' she said.

'It was a very good thought, Christine,' the countess told her.

'Well,' she said, looking from one to the other of them, 'there can be no wedding reception at Lindsey Hall within the next few days after all.

But I am not discouraged. How many people could be assembled there at such short notice, after all? Perhaps it was not the best of plans.'

'You have another?' Lauren asked.

The duchess chuckled. 'I *always* have another plan,' she said. 'Shall we put our heads together?'

Mr Jewell lived with his wife in a modest square manor just beyond the village of Wyckel in Gloucestershire, a picturesque part of the country.

It occurred to Sydnam as the carriage drove through the village and then turned between two stone gateposts and covered the short distance across a paved courtyard to the front door that they must be no more than twenty-five or thirty miles from Bath.

Anne had been that close to her family for several years.

She was looking very smart in a russet brown pelisse and matching bonnet with burnt-orange ribbons. She was also looking rather pale. Her gloved hand lay in his – today he was sitting beside her while David rode with his back to the horses. At the moment his nose was pressed against the glass and excitement was fairly bursting out of him.

Sydnam smiled at Anne and lifted her hand to his lips. She smiled back, but he could see that even her lips were pale.

'I am glad I wrote to say I was coming,' she said.

'At least,' he said, 'the gate was open.'

He wondered how she would feel – and how

David would feel – if they were refused admittance. But he still believed this was the right thing to do. Anne had faced most of the darkness in her life on the little island at Alvesley four days ago, and it seemed that the sunshine had got inside her since then. They had made love each night, and it had been clear to him that doing so had given her as much pleasure as it had given him.

But today, of course, the sun was not shining – either beyond the confines of the carriage or through her.

'*This* is where my grandmama and grandpapa live?' David asked rather redundantly.

'It is indeed,' Anne said as the coachman opened the door and set down the steps. 'This is where I grew up.'

Her voice was low and pleasant. Her face looked like parchment.

The house door opened before anyone had knocked on it, and a servant, presumably the housekeeper, stepped outside and bobbed a small curtsy to Sydnam, who had already descended to the courtyard, his good side to her.

'Good day, sir,' she said. 'Ma'am.'

She looked up at Anne, who was descending, one hand on his.

But even as Sydnam opened his mouth to reply, the servant stepped to one side and a lady and gentleman of middle years appeared in the doorway and came through it. Two other, younger, couples followed them out, and behind them a group of children clustered in the doorway and peered curiously out.

Ah, Sydnam thought, they had gathered in droves to greet the lost sheep, had they? Perhaps on the assumption that there was safety in numbers?

Anne's hand tightened in his.

'Anne,' the older lady said, stepping ahead of the gentleman Sydnam assumed was Mr Jewell. She was plump and pleasant-looking, neatly dressed and with a lacy cap covering her graying hair. 'Oh, Anne, it *is* you!'

She took a couple more steps forward, both hands stretched out before her.

Anne did not move. She kept one of her hands in Sydnam's and reached up to David with the other. He came scrambling down the steps and stood beside her, his eyes wide with excitement.

'Yes, it is I,' Anne said, her voice cool – and her mother stopped in her tracks and dropped her arms to her sides.

'You have come home,' Mrs Jewell said. 'And here we all are to greet you.'

Anne's eyes went beyond her mother to survey her father and the two younger couples. She looked toward the doorway and the children fairly bursting out through it.

'We have called here *on our way home*,' she said with slight emphasis on the last words. 'I have brought David to meet you. My son. And Sydnam Butler, my husband.'

Mrs Jewell's eyes had been fairly devouring David, but she looked politely at Sydnam, who had turned fully to face them all. She recoiled quite noticeably. There was a sort of collective stiffening of manner among the others too. Some of the children disappeared inside the house. A few bolder ones openly gawked.

Just a few months ago Sydnam might have been upset – especially about the children. He had spent years basically hidden away in a place where he was known and accepted and very few strangers ever came. But it did not matter to him any longer. Anne had accepted him as he was. More important, perhaps, he had finally accepted himself for what he was, with all his limitations and all the exhilarating challenges they offered him.

Besides, this moment was not about him. It was all about Anne.

'Mr Butler.' Mrs Jewell curtsied as he bowed and turned to introduce the others – Mr Jewell; their son, Mr Matthew Jewell, and Susan, his wife; Sarah Arnold, their daughter, and Mr Henry Arnold, her husband.

Sydnam's eye alighted on that last gentleman and saw a man of medium height and pleasant looks and balding fair hair – neither a hero nor a villain as far as looks went. He exchanged a brief but measured look with the man and had the satisfaction of seeing that Arnold knew that *he* knew.

There were bows and curtsies and murmured greetings – and a great deal of awkwardness as

Anne inclined her head to them all as if they were strangers.

But Mrs Jewell had returned her attention to David.

'David.' She ate him up with her eyes again, though she did not move from where she stood.

'Are you my grandmama?' David asked, his voice and eyes still eager. He seemed unaware of the awkward, tense atmosphere that was affecting all the adults. His eyes moved to Mr Jewell, a tall, lean gentleman with gray hair and stern demeanor. 'Are you my grandpapa?'

Mr Jewell clasped his hands behind him.

'I am,' he said.

'My *real* grandmama and grandpapa,' David said, stepping away from Anne and looking from one to the other of them. 'I have new grandparents at Alvesley, and I like them very well indeed. But they are my stepfather's mama and papa and so they are really my step-grandmama and my *step*-grandpapa. But you are real.'

'David.' Mrs Jewell had set one hand over her mouth and seemed to be half laughing and half crying. 'Oh, yes, we are real. Indeed we are. And these are your uncles and aunts, and those children, who were told that on no condition were they to step outside, are your cousins. Come inside and meet them. And you must be hungry.'

'Cousins?' David looked eagerly to the doorway.

Mrs Jewell reached out her hand to him and he took it.

'What a big boy you are already,' she said. 'And nine years old.'

'Going on ten,' David said.

Anne stood where she was as if she were made of marble. Her hand was stiff and motionless in Sydnam's.

'Well, Anne, Butler,' Mr Jewell said abruptly, 'you must come inside and warm yourselves by the fire.'

'It is teatime, Anne,' her brother, Matthew, said. 'We have been waiting, hoping you would arrive soon.'

'I am very pleased to meet you at last, Anne,' his wife said. 'And your husband.'

'Anne,' her sister, Sarah, said quietly before taking her husband's arm to return to the house, but it was doubtful Anne even heard, as she was not looking their way.

It was not a joyful homecoming, Sydnam thought as he led Anne in the direction of the open door. But neither was it an unwelcoming one. All her family members had taken on the challenge of meeting her again too – presumably they did not all live here. They had come, however unwillingly, because Anne was expected.

Surely there was hope in that fact.

He held Anne's hand in a firm grip.

The house was disorientingly familiar – it was where Anne had grown up and been happy. And yet she sat with rigidly straight back on her chair in the front parlor, like a stranger.

Her father looked older. His hair was now entirely gray, and the lines running from his nose to the outer corners of his mouth were more pronounced and made him look more austere than ever.

He looked achingly familiar, yet he was a stranger.

Her mother had put on weight. Her hair had grayed too. She looked anxious and bright-eyed. She was the woman who had been a rock of security through Anne's growing years. Now she was a stranger.

Matthew had lost his boyish look, though he was still lean and still had all his hair. Five years ago he had been appointed vicar of a church five miles away – he had just said so. His wife, Susan, was pretty and fair-haired and was doing her very best to converse as if this were any ordinary social occasion. They had two children – Amanda, aged seven, and Michael, aged five.

Strangers.

Sarah had grown plump, and Henry had grown bald. They had four children – Charles, aged nine, Jeremy, aged seven, Louisa, aged four, and Penelope, aged two.

Charles, aged nine.

David was with the children, his cousins, somewhere else in the house. He was probably reveling in their company and in their relationship to him. He never seemed to be able to get enough of other children, particularly cousins. Yet his life until a

411

very short while ago had been quite devoid of the latter.

Anne sipped her tea without tasting it and was content to leave all the talking to her mother, Sydnam, Matthew, and Susan.

She had not expected this sort of reception. She had expected her mother and father to be alone. She had imagined that Matthew, as a clergyman, might disdain to receive her. She had expected Sarah and Henry to stay well out of her sight until she was long gone. She had not decided if she would try to force them to confront her.

But they had come here, knowing she was expected.

Neither of them had spoken a word.

But then neither had she since coming inside the house except to murmur thanks every time someone offered her food or tea.

The last time she had been in this house was when she had come from Cornwall to spend a short vacation. They had celebrated Henry's twentieth birthday and planned that the *next* year they would celebrate his coming of age by announcing their betrothal. But by his twenty-first birthday she was with child and Henry was married to Sarah.

Sydnam was telling them all about Alvesley and his family. He was telling them about Glandwr, where he was the Duke of Bewcastle's steward, and about Tŷ Gwyn, which he had recently purchased and to which he was eager to take his bride and stepson. He told them that he had been

412

a military officer in the Peninsula, where he had sustained his injuries.

'But I survived.' He smiled at all of them. 'Many thousands did not.'

It struck Anne suddenly that at Glandwr Sydnam had always been quiet, that he had always taken up a position in a quiet corner of the drawing room, that while he was never morose or unsociable, he never put himself forward either. Yet here he was, taking upon himself the brunt of the conversation, knowing himself to be the very center of attention.

She felt a wave of gratitude and love.

Her mother got to her feet.

'Matthew and Susan live five miles away,' she said, 'and Sarah and Henry scarcely less. It is quite a distance with young children. They are all to stay here tonight since no one wanted to rush away before dinner. You must be tired after your journey, Anne. And Mr Butler too. Come upstairs to your room and have a rest. We can all talk again later.'

Yes, she had come here to talk, Anne thought. She had come here to face them, to confront them, to make some sort of peace with them if it was possible. But perhaps it was best left until later. Her mother was right – she *was* tired.

But she did not get up. She stared at her hands spread in her lap instead.

'Why?' she asked. 'It is what I want to know from all of you, what I came to ask. Why?'

She was appalled at her own words. It *was* why she had come. But there was surely a better time. When, though? When would be a better time? She had already waited ten years.

Everyone else was appalled too. She could tell that by the quality of the silence that filled the room. But they must have known she would ask the question. Or hadn't they? Had they thought she would come now that she was married and respectable again to be taken back to the bosom of the family, content that nothing be said about the past?

Her mother sat down again. Anne looked up at her.

'What did you mean,' she asked, 'when you said that you forgave me. *We* was the word you used. Who was *we*? And what had I done to need forgiveness?'

Matthew cleared his throat, but it was their father who replied.

'He was a wealthy man, Anne,' he said, 'and heir to a marquess's title. I daresay you thought he would marry you, and so he ought to have done. But you should have known that such as he would not marry such as you – especially after you had already given him what he wanted.'

Anne's mother made an inarticulate sound of distress, Sydnam got to his feet and crossed to the window, where he stood looking out, and Anne clasped her hands very tightly in her lap.

'You thought I was trying to snare Albert Moore as a husband?' she asked.

'Maybe not quite in the way it turned out,' her father said. 'But I daresay you teased him and he lost control. It is what happens. And the man always gets blamed.'

Blamed.

The man always gets blamed.

'I was to marry Henry,' Anne said, ignoring the almost palpable discomfort of Henry himself – and of Sarah. 'You knew that. I had known him and loved him all my life. I did not look higher. It never even occurred to me to be ambitious. I lived for the day when I could come back home to marry.'

'Anne,' Sarah said, but she did not continue, and everyone ignored her anyway.

'But you must have been able to stop him if you had really wanted to do so, Anne,' her father said. 'Surely you could have.'

'He was stronger than I,' she said. 'Much stronger.'

He winced almost noticeably and then frowned. Her mother's face was hidden in her handkerchief.

'Your mother wanted to go to you,' her father said. 'I was going to write to the marquess to ask what his son's intentions to you were. But what would have been the point? You were a governess there. I would merely have made myself look foolish. And then Sarah told us that she was going to marry Arnold, and he came on the heels of her announcement to offer for her and when I refused my consent they both threatened to elope. Matthew was about to take up his first curacy where he is now and there was all the question of what the scandals would do to his career. I refused to allow your mother to go to you – there was a wedding to arrange, anyway. But I did instruct her to write to you and tell you we forgave you. I did not believe you had been deliberately depraved.'

It was, Anne supposed, little different from what she had imagined. She gazed at her father, at the pillar of strength she had loved and admired and obeyed as a girl. But there came a time in everyone's life, she supposed, when one's parent became a person in one's eyes. And persons, unlike parents, were never perfect. Sometimes they were far from perfection.

Her mother lowered her hands.

'And your father – and *we*,' she said, 'thought it best that you not come back here, Anne – at least for a while. It would have been upsetting, and there would have been scandal in the neighborhood. It would have been dreadful for you.'

And for her and Papa and Sarah and Henry and Matthew, Anne thought with a half-smile.

'But I have missed you dreadfully,' her mother cried. 'I have pined for you, Anne. And for David.'

But not enough ever to come and visit her? Anne thought. But then her mother had always been a dutiful wife. She had never done anything without Papa's full approval and consent. It had always seemed to be a virtue . . .

'He is such a handsome child, Anne,' her mother said. 'And he looks just like you.'

'David looks,' Anne said, 'like Albert Moore, his

father. He was a handsome man. David also has some of my characteristics. But more than anything else, he is himself. He has most in common with his new father. Sydnam is a painter and so is David. They paint together.'

It astounded her that she could admit aloud that David looked like his father without cringing from the very fact that Albert Moore *was* his father. She glanced at Sydnam, who still stood with his back to the room, and felt a knee-weakening love for him.

'Anne,' Sarah said, 'please forgive me. *Please* do. It was a terrible thing I did, but I was *so* in love. That was no excuse, though. I have not known a day's happiness since. I am so very sorry. But I cannot expect you to forgive me.'

Anne looked at her fully for the first time. She *had* grown plumper. She looked very much like their mother. But she was still the sister who had been Anne's closest friend and confidante throughout their growing years.

'Anne,' Henry said, 'I would have married you if you had come home as planned without— Well . . . You must know I would have. But you were there and Sarah was here.'

Anne bent her gaze on him. She would have liked to see him as ugly and unappealing. She would like to wonder what she had ever seen in him. He certainly had weaknesses of character that were unattractive. But he was Henry, and they had been close friends for years before planning a closer relationship.

'All things happen for a purpose,' she said, 'though sometimes they take their time. If I had married you, Henry, there would not be David, and he has been the most precious person in my life for many years. And if I had married you, I would not have been able to marry Sydnam. And so I would have lost my chance for a lifetime of happiness.'

Matthew cleared his throat again.

'You have done well for yourself, Anne,' he said. 'First you had a home and some pupils in that village in Cornwall, and then you got that teaching post in Bath. And now you have married a son of the Earl of Redfield.'

'It is strange,' Anne said, 'that you know all these things about me. I have known nothing about your lives. I did not even know of the existence of any of my nephews and nieces.'

'I thought it best, Anne,' her mother said. 'I thought you would pine.'

'I need to ask you all,' Anne said, 'if the fact that I have come through these years rather well makes you feel better about turning your backs on me.'

'Oh, Anne.' Sarah's voice was high with distress.

But it was her father who gave a lengthier reply.

'No,' he said abruptly. 'No better at all. It was easier to believe that you had brought your suffering on yourself and then to feel relieved that you were coping on your own. It was easier to believe that you were better off where you were, away from the gossiping tongues of our neighbors.

You did suffer and you did cope, and perhaps it really was good that you avoided the gossip. But no, I for one do not feel better about my treatment of you. I never have felt good about it. And now today, now that I have to look you in the eye, I feel worse – as I deserve to do. Don't blame your mother. She would have come to you at the start, but I would not countenance it.'

'I ought at least to have written to you, Anne,' Matthew said. 'If it had not been for my extravagances at Oxford, you would not even have had to take a position as governess.'

'Sarah has always been miserable about the whole thing,' Henry said quietly. 'So have I.'

'Well,' Anne said, getting to her feet, 'if I was not tired before I am exhausted now. I will avail myself of the suggestion that I withdraw until dinnertime. I am sure Sydnam is weary too. Ancient history is a dreadful thing when it is one's own, is it not? It cannot be changed. None of us can go back and do things differently. We can only go forward and hope that the past has at least taught us some wisdom to take with us. I have stayed away in more recent years because I bore a grudge, because I hoped you were all suffering, because I could feed my bitterness, which somehow seemed my right. But here I am. And though I will doubtless weep when I get upstairs, I am glad I came. For what it is worth, I forgive you all – and hope you will forgive me for what I have contributed to your unhappiness.'

They were all on their feet and all hovering. The scene could degenerate into high sentimental drama at any moment, Anne thought. But no one moved to hug her, and she did not move to hug anyone.

It was too soon yet.

But the time would come, she believed. They were all very much in need of pardon and peace. And, when all was said and done, they were family. And they had come today.

Sydnam was at her side and offering her his arm. She linked her own arm through it, half smiled about at the room's occupants, and followed her mother from the parlor and up the broad wooden stairs, past her old room, and on to the room that had always been kept for such special guests that in effect it had almost never been used.

They had been deemed very special guests, then, had they?

After she had stepped inside the room, Anne turned to look at her mother, who was hovering in the doorway, looking anxious.

'I am glad you have come home, Anne,' she said. 'I am glad you have brought David. And I am glad you have married Mr Butler.'

'Sydnam, if you please, ma'am,' he said.

'Sydnam.' She smiled nervously at him.

Anne stepped forward without a word and wrapped her arms about her mother's stout form. Her mother hugged her back tightly and wordlessly.

'Rest now,' she said when Anne stepped back.

'Yes.' Anne nodded. 'Mama.'

And then the door closed and she was alone with Sydnam.

'Excuse me,' she said, 'but I think I am going to weep.'

'Anne,' he said, and he was laughing softly as his arm came about her and his hand drew her head down to rest on his shoulder. 'Of course you are.'

'Was painting again this difficult for you?' she asked.

'Yes,' he said with conviction, kissing the top of her head. 'And there is much anguish to come. I have only just begun, and the first effort really was quite abysmal. But I am not going to stop. I have begun and I will continue – to failure or to success. But failure does not matter because it will only spur me on to try harder as it always used to do. And even if I never succeed, at least I will know that I tried, that I did not hide from life.'

'At last,' she said, 'I have stopped hiding too.'

'Yes,' he said, laughing softly again. 'You surely have.'

The tears came at last.

CHAPTER 22

Both the younger Jewells and the Arnolds remained at the manor for longer than the one night they had planned.

David was in heaven. Though he dragged Sydnam off one morning to paint, taking Amanda with them, he was content to spend almost all the rest of his time with his cousins, particularly Charles Arnold, who was only a few months younger than he.

Sydnam went out riding a few times with the men after they discovered – through David – that he *could* ride. He found them all very willing to make his acquaintance. He had been prepared to dislike them – the elder Mr Jewell no less than Henry Arnold, but though he had seethed with rage while listening to what they had to say to Anne on the first day, he discovered on closer acquaintance that they were just ordinary, basically amiable gentlemen with whose views on life and justice he could occasionally disagree.

Anne spent most of her days with her mother and sister and sister-in-law, and her evenings with everyone. They all appeared to be making a concerted effort to be a family together again.

It would take time, Sydnam guessed, remembering how it had taken a while for him and Kit to feel thoroughly comfortable with each other again after their lengthy estrangement following his return from the Peninsula. But it seemed to him that Anne and her family had been restored to one another and that the last of the dark shadows had been lifted from her life.

She seemed happy.

And he? Well, he could not forget one thing Anne had said to Arnold in the parlor that first afternoon – *If I had married you, I would not have been able to marry Sydnam. And so I would have lost my chance for a lifetime of happiness.*

How much of that was the truth and how much had been spoken entirely for the benefit of the man who had rejected her and promptly married her sister, Sydnam was not sure. But he *thought* he knew.

Yes, he was happy too.

They had intended to stay for a few days if they were made welcome, less if they were not. But Anne seemed in no hurry to leave now that she had found her family again, and Sydnam was content to give her time. They stayed even after Matthew and his family returned to the vicarage where they lived and Henry Arnold took his family home – bearing David with them for a couple of days.

Mrs Jewell, who was clearly beside herself with delight to have her elder daughter at home, planned a whole series of visits to neighbors and teas and dinners for various guests. And the younger Jewells and the Arnolds were eager to entertain them in their own homes.

And so the planned few days stretched into a week.

And then on the eighth day a letter arrived for Anne. Mr Jewell brought it to the breakfast table one morning and set it down beside her plate.

'It is from Bath,' she said, picking it up to examine it. 'But it is not Claudia's handwriting or Susanna's. I have seen it before, though. I should know it.'

'There is one way of finding out,' her father said dryly.

She laughed and broke the seal with her thumb.

'Lady Potford,' she said, looking first to the signature. 'Yes, of course, I have seen her hand before.'

'Lady Potford?' Sydnam asked.

'Joshua's grandmother,' she explained. 'She lives in Bath. I have visited her several times.'

She read the letter while her mother plied Sydnam with more toast and then watched as he chased it around his plate with the butter knife.

'Oh, Sydnam,' Anne said, looking up, 'Lady Potford is quite hurt over the fact that I did not inform her of our nuptials. She would have come, she writes here, and she would have arranged a wedding breakfast for us. Is that not kind?'

'It is very obliging of her,' her mother agreed. 'She must be fond of you, Anne.'

424

But there was more in the letter than just regrets.

'Oh,' Anne said, her eyes moving over the rest of its contents. 'Joshua is expected in Bath next week. Lady Potford is quite convinced that he will be upset at missing our wedding and not even seeing us afterward. She wants us to return to Bath before going on into Wales so that she can arrange a small reception for us.'

She looked up.

It was not a great distance to Bath. However, going there would take them in the wrong direction. And really, Sydnam thought, he *was* longing to be home. He wanted to establish his new family at Tŷ Gwyn. And Anne was increasing. She ought not to be traveling more than was necessary.

But Bath had been Anne's home for a number of years. Her friends were there. Hallmere was a relative – of David's anyway – and had been remarkably kind to her. Without the Hallmeres he, Sydnam, would never have met her.

Her teeth sank into her lower lip.

'Do you wish to go?' he asked.

'It would be foolish,' she said. 'All that way in order to have tea or perhaps dinner with Joshua and Lady Potford.'

'But do you want to go?' he asked again.

He knew the answer, though. He could see it in her eyes.

'He invited David and me to Penhallow for Christmas this year,' she said. 'We will not be able to go, of course. David will probably not see him

425

for a long time. But . . .' She bit her lip again. 'But he *is* David's cousin. I . . .'

He laughed. 'Anne, do you wish to go?'

'Perhaps we ought,' she said. 'Will you mind terribly?'

Tŷ Gwyn, he thought, would have to wait.

'Next week?' he said. He turned to Mrs Jewell. 'May we impose upon your hospitality for a few days longer than expected, then, ma'am?'

'A *month* longer if you wish, Sydnam,' that lady said, and clasped her hands to her bosom.

Mr Jewell smirked slightly at some private thought – or as if he knew a secret no one else even suspected – and left the breakfast parlor, presumably to return to his study.

And so in the middle of the following week, well after they had originally expected to be home in Wales, Anne and Sydnam were on their way back to Bath, David sitting with his back to the horses, partly tearful at having just taken his leave of his grandparents, partly excited at the prospect of seeing Joshua again – and Miss Martin and Miss Osbourne and Mr Keeble, the school porter who apparently used to slip him sweets from the depths of his pocket whenever no one was looking.

Anne had been a little tearful at the parting too, but her father had assured her after kissing her on both cheeks that they would all doubtless see one another again before they knew it, and her mother had hugged her and agreed with her husband.

Now Anne sat with her hand in Sydnam's, her shoulder resting companionably against his.

Marriage was beginning to feel like a very pleasant state indeed.

They had been invited to stay at Lady Potford's in Bath. When their carriage drew up outside the tall house on Great Pulteney Street, the door opened almost immediately and her ladyship's butler peered out. But David's whoop of joy as Anne descended to the pavement, her hand in Sydnam's, alerted her to the fact that Joshua was already here. And sure enough, David dashed out and past her and up the steps to be scooped up and swung about in a circle.

'You have not grown one ounce the lighter since the summer, lad,' Joshua said. 'And so your mama has got herself married, has she?'

'Yes,' David cried as if he were addressing someone half a mile away. 'To my stepfather. He can ride. He can even jump hedges, though I haven't seen him do it and Uncle Kit says that he will tie him to the nearest post and leave him there if *he* ever sees him try it. And he is teaching me to paint with oils. He was going to get me a teacher when we go home to Tŷ Gwyn, but he decided to teach me himself. He is the *best* teacher – much better than Mr Upton,' he added disloyally. 'I have *lots* of cousins where my mama used to live. Charles is nine too, but he is younger than I am and only comes up to here.' He smote

427

himself just above the right ear. 'Are Daniel and Emily here?'

'They are,' Joshua said, chuckling. 'You had better put Daniel out of his misery and dash up to the nursery without pausing for another breath, if you will, lad.'

And he turned to grin at Sydnam and to catch Anne up in a bear hug that was quite undignified considering the fact that the front door was still wide open.

Lady Hallmere and the children had come to Bath too, then, Anne realized. Lady Potford's letter had not mentioned that fact.

'Freyja and all the other Bedwyns and assorted spouses had decided that their matchmaking skills must have eluded them this past summer,' Joshua said. 'But it would seem they were wrong. One can only imagine on what poor unwed mortal their collective eye will alight next. Marriage must agree with you both. I do not see a single gray hair between the two of you.'

Anne laughed. The Bedwyns really had noticed her relationship with Sydnam during the summer, then, and had even tried to promote it? How mortified she would have been if she had realized that at the time.

'It agrees,' Sydnam said. 'Very well indeed, in fact.'

'Come up and report to Freyja and my grandmother,' Joshua said. 'Neither one of them was best pleased to learn that you had slunk off and got wed with great secrecy. They would have liked nothing better than to have given you a royal send-off.'

Anne felt a little wistful despite herself. Most people, she supposed, dreamed of a large wedding surrounded by family and friends – and she was no different from the norm. But she must not complain. She had had Claudia and Susanna with her, as well as David, and her marriage since that day had brought her far more happiness than she had expected when she sent off her letter to summon Sydnam.

Of course *he* had had no one of his own at their wedding.

It was only as she proceeded up the stairs on Joshua's arm, Sydnam coming up behind them, that it occurred to her to wonder how Lady Potford had learned of their marriage – and, even more puzzling, how she had known to send her letter to Gloucestershire.

But it was something she did not feel she could ask.

If Lady Potford had intended to host her small reception at home, it appeared that she had changed her mind. Indeed, there was no further mention of an actual reception. Instead, she announced that she had booked a table at the Upper Assembly Rooms for tea the following afternoon. It would be a nice treat for all of them, she said, now that the weather had turned wintry and prevented much outdoor exercise. They must all get dressed up in their finest attire as if they were attending a wedding.

The children must come too, she added – she would arrange for Daniel and Emily's nurse to look after them there.

'I hope you do not mind this too terribly much,' Anne said to Sydnam the next day, meeting his eye in the mirror of the dressing table after the maid Lady Potford had insisted upon sending up to her had left and he had come out of the adjoining dressing room, all ready to go. 'Oh.' She swiveled about on the stool. 'You look exceedingly handsome.'

He was wearing a black-tailed coat with ivory silk breeches and embroidered waistcoat and very white linen.

He looked nothing short of gorgeous, in fact.

'And you,' he said, 'are looking quite exquisite.'

She was wearing her rose pink muslin dress, the prettiest of all her new ones, with its flounced, scalloped hem and soft folds falling from the high waistline, its short, puffed sleeves and modestly scooped neck. Lady Potford's maid had done something very elaborate but very becoming with her hair. She was wearing her diamond pendant and earrings.

'Thank you, sir,' she said, smiling and getting to her feet. 'But we are merely going to the Upper Assembly Rooms for *tea*, Sydnam. Whatever will the other people there think of us? We look far too grand for afternoon.'

Of course, she had always dreamed of taking tea and even dancing at the Upper Rooms and could remember how envious she had been more than two years ago when Frances had been invited to an assembly there.

'Well,' he said, 'they will probably take one look at me and scream and run long before they can notice how grand we look.'

'Oh, Sydnam!' she exclaimed, but he was grinning at her in his lopsided way, and she ended up laughing with him.

'There is just this afternoon to live through,' she said as they were leaving the room together, 'and a brief visit to the school tomorrow if you do not mind – I did send off a note to Claudia this morning to tell her we were here – and then we may go home. You will be so glad.'

'And you?' he said, offering his arm.

'Oh, yes,' she said, taking his arm and squeezing it. 'I can hardly wait.'

But first there was to be tea in the Upper Rooms, and Anne looked forward to it. She and Sydnam traveled in Lady Potford's carriage while Joshua and Lady Hallmere came behind and the children came behind *them* in a carriage with the nurse.

'You look very lovely, my dear,' Lady Potford said to Anne as they descended to the small court-yard outside the Upper Rooms. 'You also look half frightened to death. Let me set your mind at rest. I have reserved the whole of the tearoom for our use and so you will not be confronted by curious

431

strangers. I have reserved the ballroom too. I thought a little music might be pleasant while we eat, and the extra space will give the children somewhere to run about without disturbing us.'

What? Anne exchanged a startled look with Sydnam. They were to have the whole of the tearoom to themselves, just the five of them plus the three children and the nurse? And the ballroom too? And there was to be music?

'I perceive, ma'am,' Sydnam said, 'that you have arranged a small reception for us after all – small in number but large in space. We are delighted, are we not, Anne?'

'And overwhelmed.' Anne laughed and looked at Joshua, who had just handed Lady Hallmere down from their carriage. 'Did *you* know about this, Joshua?'

'About what?' He raised his eyebrows, all innocence.

'About this reception for five adults and three children and the whole of the tearoom and ballroom in which to celebrate,' she said.

'Oh, that?' he said. 'Yes. My grandmother is something of an eccentric. Had you not realized?'

They entered the building and made their way down a long, wide hallway. It was indeed devoid of people and noise. But Sydnam had been quite right – this *was* delightful.

Joshua paused when they arrived outside the door that must lead into the tearoom. A smartly clad servant stood waiting to open it.

'Grandmama? Freyja?' Joshua said, offering an arm to each of them. 'We will lead the way in. Sydnam, you may bring Anne in after us.'

Anne turned her head to exchange a smile of amusement with Sydnam. She could hear the children coming along the hallway behind them.

The door opened.

For the first bewildered moment Anne felt embarrassed for Lady Potford. Obviously something must have gone terribly wrong with her plans – a mistaken day, perhaps. The tearoom, large and high-ceilinged and lovely, was actually filled with people. And they were all getting to their feet and looking toward the door and—

And then she and Sydnam were being rained upon by – by *rose* petals of all things in November.

And then there was noise to replace the unnatural quiet that had preceded it – voices and laughter and the scraping of chairs on the polished wood floor.

And finally, only moments after the doors had opened, she realized that wherever she looked the faces of the people were familiar.

'What the devil?' Sydnam said, clamping her hand harder to his side. And then he began to laugh.

'Sitting ducks,' Lord Alleyne Bedwyn said from close beside him. 'You will be sorry you wore black, Syd.'

'But the petals look good in Anne's hair,' the Earl of Rosthorn said.

433

'Oh,' Anne said. 'Oh.'

She had spotted her mother and father across the room, her father looking austere and pleased with himself, her mother beaming but holding a handkerchief close to her face too. Sarah and Susan were on one side of them, Matthew and Henry on the other.

And then she saw Frances and the Earl of Edgecombe, and then Miss Thompson – and beside her the Duchess of Bewcastle and Lady Alleyne, and then *Sydnam's* parents with Kit and Lauren, and then Susanna and Claudia and Lord Aidan Bedwyn with the Duke of Bewcastle.

But it was all a flashing impression. There was too much to see and too much to comprehend all at once. There were numerous other people present.

The Duchess of Bewcastle clapped her hands, and a silence of sorts descended on the gathering. Anne and Sydnam were still standing just inside the doorway in a pool of deep red rose petals.

'Well, Mr and Mrs Butler,' she said, bright and animated and smiling warmly, 'you may have thought yourselves very clever indeed when you married in great secrecy a few weeks ago. But your relatives and friends have caught up with you after all. Welcome to your wedding breakfast.'

Looking back afterward on what turned out to be one of the happiest days of her life, Anne found it hard to remember the exact sequence of events after that first moment. She certainly had no recollection of eating anything, though she supposed she must have done so since she certainly was not hungry for the rest of the day.

But she did remember the noise and the laughter and the wonderful, heady sensation of being the focus of loving attention with Sydnam. She remembered being hugged and kissed and exclaimed over again and again. She even had a few clear memories.

She remembered Joshua bringing forward a pretty, guilelessly smiling young lady, whose free hand was flapping with excitement at her side and realizing that she was Prue Moore – now Prue Turner. She remembered Prue hugging her as if to break every bone in her body.

'Miss Jewell, Miss Jewell,' she cried in her sweet, childish voice, 'I love you. I do love you. And now you are Mrs Butler. I like Mr Butler even if he *does* have to wear a black patch on his eye. And I am David's aunt. Joshua says so and Constance says so, and I am glad about it. Are you?'

And then she turned to hug Sydnam with just as much enthusiasm.

Anne remembered being hugged by Constance too – the former Lady Constance Moore – and realizing that they must have come all the way from Cornwall just for this occasion.

She remembered Frances shedding tears over her.

She remembered Lauren's happy smile and the young man she introduced – Viscount Whitleaf, her cousin, a young man who had her lovely violet eyes. He had come to Alvesley to visit the week after Anne and Sydnam left.

She remembered what Claudia said to her when they hugged.

'Anne,' she said severely, 'I hope you realize just how much I love you. I have actually consented for your sake to be in the same room with *that woman* and *that man*. I feel as sorry for the Duchess of Bewcastle as I feel for the Marquess of Hallmere. She is remarkably sweet – but one wonders for how long under *his* influence.'

Anne remembered that Claudia and Miss Thompson sat together talking through much of the afternoon.

She remembered her father laughing and telling her what a splendid joke it had been to keep secret the fact that he had received a letter from Lady Potford on the same morning that Anne's had arrived.

She remembered her mother's happy tears – and Sarah's.

She remembered the cousins of Sydnam's who had been located in time and brought to Bath and were introduced to Anne – though he had to remind her of all their names the next day.

She remembered that for the first chaotic minutes children dashed noisily about getting under everyone's feet until someone arranged to have them all shooed into the ballroom. Anne suspected it might have been the Duke of Bewcastle – he had probably raised an eyebrow or perhaps even his quizzing glass in the right direction.

And she remembered Sydnam's bright and happy look, his laughter – and of course the impromptu speech of thanks he gave from both of them for such an unexpected gathering.

'You may all expect,' he said to much laughter, 'that Anne and I will put our heads together over the winter when there is nothing else to do and devise a suitable revenge.'

But there was one part of the reception that was not at all jumbled in with all the other memories.

Music had been wafting from the ballroom all through the tea – or the *breakfast*, if one wished to humor the duchess. No one seemed to have been paying it much attention. But Joshua, seated close by, must have noticed.

'It was just here that we waltzed for the first time, Freyja,' he said. 'Do you remember?'

'How could I forget?' she said. 'It was while we waltzed that you begged me to enter into a fake betrothal with you, and before we knew it we were in a marriage together – but not a fake one at all.'

They both laughed.

'And it was here we danced together, Frances,' the Earl of Edgecombe said, 'though it was not quite the first time, if you recall.'

'The first time,' Frances said, 'was in a cold, dark, empty ballroom with no music.'

'It was heavenly,' the earl said with a grin.

'It would be a shame,' Kit said, 'to have an

437

orchestra and the use of one of the most famous ballrooms in the country and not dance. I shall instruct the orchestra to play a waltz. But we must remember that this is a wedding celebration. The bride must dance first. Will you waltz with me, Anne?'

But he was looking, Anne noticed, at Sydnam.

Sydnam stood up.

'Thank you, Kit,' he said firmly, 'but if it is not the custom for the bridegroom to be first to dance with his bride, then it ought to be. Anne, will you waltz with me?'

For the merest moment she felt alarm. Everyone had hushed and was listening. They all would doubtless come and watch. She had not done a great deal of dancing herself, except at school, but Sydnam—

But Sydnam could do anything in the world he set his mind to – except perhaps clap his hands.

She smiled at him.

'Yes, I will,' she said.

She did not think it was her imagination that the guests gathered around them let out a sort of collective sigh.

She set her hand on Sydnam's offered sleeve and he led her into the ballroom. Almost everyone, it seemed to her, followed them and arranged them-selves about the perimeter of the room while Kit spoke to the orchestra leader. The children were drawn back too, though most of them ran off into the tearoom to play.

And they waltzed together, Anne and Sydnam, three weeks after their wedding while their wedding guests looked on.

He took her right hand in his left, and she set her left hand on his shoulder. When the music began, they moved rather slowly and rather awkwardly until he smiled at her, drew her hand to rest against his heart, and so invited her to slide her other hand up behind his neck and thus stand closer to him.

After that they moved as one and twirled about to the music until other couples gradually joined them on the floor – Joshua with Lady Hallmere, Kit with Lauren, Frances with Lord Edgecombe, the duchess with the Duke of Bewcastle, the other Bedwyns with their spouses, Sarah with Henry, Susanna with Viscount Whitleaf, and Susan with Matthew.

'Happy?' Sydnam asked against Anne's ear.

'Oh, yes,' she said. 'Yes, I am. Yes, I *am*. Are you?'

'More than I can say,' he said.

And they smiled at each other, their faces only inches apart.

No, Anne had no difficulty at all in remembering that part of their wedding reception.

She would remember it for the rest of her life.

CHAPTER 23

Anne and Sydnam arrived home at Tŷ Gwyn with David on *a* crisp afternoon in November. But, cold as it was, the sun was shining and Sydnam let the window down impulsively when his coachman stopped to open the gate into the park and informed him that he could continue on alone to the stable and coach house.

'We will walk the rest of the way,' he said.

And so they stood, the three of them, a few minutes later, watching the carriage drive down into the slight bowl of the park before climbing up the other side.

'Well, David,' Sydnam said, setting his hand on the boy's shoulder, 'this is Tŷ Gwyn. This is home. What do you think?'

'Do those sheep belong here?' David asked. 'May I go closer to them?'

'You may indeed,' Sydnam said. 'You may even try to catch one if you wish. But I warn you that they are quite elusive.'

The boy ran off into the meadow with whoops

440

of delight after hours of being cooped up inside the carriage. The sheep, forewarned, moved out of his path.

Sydnam turned to smile at his wife.

'Well, Anne,' he said.

'Well.' She was staring off at the house in the distance. But then she turned her eyes on him. 'I am going to have to go over the stile, you know. I have to redeem myself. I was horribly clumsy the last time.'

'I did have the bottom step seen to,' he said.

He watched as she climbed then sat on the top bar and swung her legs over to the other side, warmly clad in her russet pelisse, her cheeks already rosy from the cold, a few strands of honey-colored hair pulled loose from her neatly pinned hair and wafting in the breeze, her eyes bright and laughing. His beautiful Anne.

He strode toward her.

'Allow me, ma'am,' he said, offering his hand.

'Thank you, sir.' She set her hand in his and descended to the ground. 'You see? Like a queen.'

They stood face-to-face, their hands still joined, and gazed deeply at each other for several moments while her smile faded.

'Sydnam,' she said, 'I know you did not want any of this—'

'Do you?' he said.

'You were contented as you were,' she said, 'and I was not the sort of woman you would have chosen to marry.'

441

'Were you not?' he said. 'And was I the sort of man *you* would have chosen to marry?'

'We were lonely,' she said, 'and we came here on a lovely day and—'

'It *was* a lovely day,' he said.

She tipped her head to one side and frowned slightly.

'Why will you not let me finish anything I am trying to say?' she asked.

'Because,' he said, 'you are still not sure I do not regret our marriage deep down, are you? And I suppose I am still not sure *you* do not. I suppose I ought to have told you something long ago. But at first I did not want you to pity me or feel obligated to me, and after that I convinced myself that the words were not necessary. Men do tend to do that, you know, Anne. We do not find it easy to spill our feelings in words. But I *do* love you. I always have, I think. And I *know* I always will.'

'Sydnam.' Tears sprang to her eyes. The tip of her nose was growing rosy, he noticed. 'Oh, Sydnam, I *do* love you. I love you so very, very much.'

He leaned forward, rubbed his nose against hers, and kissed her. She wound her arms about his neck and kissed him back.

'You always have?' She tipped back her head and laughed at him. 'Right from the start?'

'I thought,' he said, 'that you had stepped out of the night into my dreams. But then you turned and fled.'

'Oh, Sydnam.' She tightened her grip about his neck again. 'Oh, my love.'

'And I have in my pocket something that always lives on my person,' he said, 'and may convince you that I have always loved you. If you even remember it, that is – or them, since there are more than one.'

She stepped back and watched curiously as he drew a handkerchief out of the inner pocket of his greatcoat and flicked open the folds with his thumb to reveal a little cluster of seashells within. He would, he thought, feel foolish if she did not remember.

She touched one forefinger to them.

'You kept them,' she said. 'Oh, Sydnam, you have kept them all this time.'

'Foolish, was it not?' He smiled at her.

But a shout distracted them as he flicked the corners of the handkerchief in place and put it back into his pocket.

'Mama, look!' David called from the middle of the meadow. 'Look, Papa, I have caught one.'

But even as they looked the indignant sheep pulled free and ambled away to resume the serious business of cropping grass and clover. David, laughing gleefully, went chasing after it.

Sydnam wrapped his arm about Anne's waist and drew her back against him. He spread his hand over her abdomen and hid his face against the side of her neck as she tipped back her head onto his shoulder. He felt almost dizzy.

'He called you Papa,' she said softly.

'Yes.'

He raised his head and looked around him at his home. All of it – the house and stables, the garden, the meadow, the circling trees, the boy chasing sheep, the woman in his arms. And he felt the future beneath his fingers in the slight rounding of his wife's womb.

'Are we mad,' he asked her, 'standing out here in the cold like this when a warm house awaits us?'

'Utterly mad.' She turned her head to smile at him and kiss his lips. 'Take me home, Sydnam.'

'We *are* home, love,' he said, releasing her in order to take her hand in his. 'We are always home. But I'll take you to the house. I want to see if the morning room looks like sunshine.'

'And if the hall looks more cheerful without the browns,' she said.

They half ran down the slight slope in the direction of the house. They were also laughing. Their fingers were laced together.